One Tiny Miracle

STELLA BAGWELL

JENNIFER GREENE

AMI WEAVER

First Published in Great Britain 2017
By Mills & Boon, an imprint of HarperCollins*Publishers*
1 London Bridge Street, London, SE1 9GF

ONE TINY MIRACLE © 2017 Harlequin Books S. A.

Branded With His Baby, *The Baby Bump* and *An Accidental Family* were first published in Great Britain by Harlequin (UK) Limited.

Branded With His Baby © 2010 Stella Bagwell
The Baby Bump © 2013 by Alison Hart
An Accidental Family © 2013 Ami Weaver

ISBN: 978-0-263-92975-1

05-0817

BRANDED WITH HIS BABY

BY
STELLA BAGWELL

Stella Bagwell has written more than seventy novels. She credits her loyal readers and hopes her stories have brightened their lives in some small way. A cowgirl through and through, she loves to watch old westerns, and has recently learned how to rope a steer. Her days begin and end helping her husband care for a beloved herd of horses on their little ranch located on the south Texas coast. When she's not ropin' and ridin', you'll find her at her desk, creating her next tale of love. The couple have a son, who is a maths teacher and athletic coach.

To my sissy, Thelma Foster.
To have a sister like you is to be truly blessed.
I love you.

Chapter One

The moment Quint Cantrell walked through the door of his grandfather's ranch house, he got the eerie feeling that something was wrong.

At this time of the early evening Abe was usually watching the news on the small television situated in a corner of the cozy living room. Instead, the old man's leather recliner was empty and the TV screen was black.

Uneasy, Quint started to call out, but stopped as he caught the sound of a radio coming from the direction of the kitchen. As he quickly strode toward the back of the house, he realized with another start that the singer was Billie Holiday.

What the heck was going on around this place? His grandfather liked music, but certainly not that kind! And the house held the peculiar scent of roses instead of pipe tobacco and old boots.

Rounding the open doorway to the kitchen, he practically skidded to a halt as he spotted a woman standing at the cabinet counter. Yesterday, while he'd been eating lunch at the Blue Mesa, a family acquaintance had stopped by his table and mentioned that a rumor was going around about a woman staying out at Apache Wells. Quint had laughingly dismissed the idea as nothing more than a wild rumor. Since his grandmother had passed away fifteen years ago, the only females who ever stepped foot in this house were Quint's mother or sister. Hell freezing over would be more likely to happen than a woman living in Abe's house. Or so Quint had believed.

Stunned by this turn of events, Quint stared.

Tall and slender with hair the color of a black cherry hanging nearly to her waist, she was dressed casually in blue jeans and a green Western shirt with darker green flowers dotting the yokes and cuffs. If her face looked anything like her backside, Quint decided, she was definitely a pretty woman.

"Uh—excuse me, ma'am."

Obviously surprised by the sound of his voice, the woman whirled around to stare at him. Her dark eyes were wide, and her lips parted as she took a halting step in his direction.

"Oh! I didn't realize anyone had come in," she said in a breathy voice. "You gave me a fright."

He stepped forward and even though his gaze was focused solely on her, he knew his grandfather wasn't in the room. He also realized his initial guess had been correct. The woman was pretty—though quietly so. Like a violet hidden beneath a clump of sagebrush, it might take a second look to find the beauty, but it was there.

"I could say the same about you," he replied, his eyes sliding over her face. She appeared vaguely familiar. "It's not every day I walk into my grandfather's house and find a woman. Who are you, anyway?"

Her lips, which were full and dusky pink, twisted ever so slightly. "I'm sorry. I urged Abe to warn you about me, but you know that he pretty much does things his own way. He wanted me to be a surprise," she said with a mixture of amusement and regret. "As to who I am, I thought you might recognize me. But I suppose I've been away from Lincoln County too long for you to remember."

So his earlier assumption had been right. He had met the woman before. But where? he wondered, as his gaze scanned her dark green eyes, high cheekbones and heart-shaped face. She was definitely easy to look at, he realized, and then his memory kicked in like a startled mule. Hellfire, she was one of the Donovan bunch! A rich, rough and rowdy family that owned a notable horse farm down in the Hondo Valley.

"I remember now," he said. "You're one of the Donovan brood. A nurse. You were at the hospital when my sister had her baby."

She inclined her head forward. "That's right. I'm Maura—second oldest of six siblings. You've probably seen us around from time to time."

Shrugging, he wondered why her suggestion made him feel like a recluse. "I don't do much socializing anymore. But I know your brothers and sisters. Bridget is my mother's doctor."

She nodded. "Bridget is very good at her job. And very busy."

Folding his arms against his chest, Quint glanced beyond her shoulder to where a pot of something was simmering on the stove. It was filling the whole room with the scent of chicken and spices. Where was Jim, the old bunkhouse cook who usually prepared his grandfather's meals? And why in the world would a Donovan be here at his grandfather's ranch?

"Yesterday, when someone in town told me that a woman was staying on the ranch, I practically called him a liar." Quint shook his head as he tried to assemble the questions running rampant in it. "I don't mean to sound meddlesome, but why are you here? And where is Gramps?"

Her breasts rose and fell as she drew in a deep breath, then blew it out. His questions appeared to make her uncomfortable, which only roused his curiosity even more.

"Abe is down at the ranch yard visiting with the hands," she answered. "And I'm here because I live here now. With your grandfather, as his nurse."

If she'd whacked Quint's shins with an ax handle, the shock couldn't have been any greater. He sputtered. "His nurse!"

"That's right," she said smoothly, then quickly added, "Excuse me, would you? I need to tend to the soup."

Dazed by her revelation, Quint watched her turn to the cookstove, where she stirred a bubbling pot with a wooden spoon. Her movements seemed so casual, that he got the feeling she'd been here long enough to feel at home.

Two weeks had passed since he'd taken the time to drive to Apache Wells, but he'd talked on the phone to his grandfather several times and nothing had been mentioned about a nurse, or any need for one. She'd said that Abe had wanted to surprise him. Well, the old man had done that and more, Quint thought.

Walking farther into the room, Quint lifted the gray Stetson from his head and raked a hand through his curly hair. He'd had a day that would try a saint, and he wasn't in the mood for beating around the bush.

"Okay, is this one of my grandfather's outlandish jokes? Abe doesn't need a nurse. He's as healthy as a horse."

"Is that what you think?" she asked politely.

"Hell, yes!" he blurted out, then stabbed his fingers through his hair again and added in a calmer tone, "I mean of course, I do. Gramps went for a checkup about three weeks ago. The man pronounced Abe as fit as a fiddle. Or is there something I need to know?"

"I doubt that. Abe says you're aware of his vertigo problem."

Putting down the spoon, she turned to face him and Quint was knocked for a loop all over again. Of the three Donovan sisters, he was least familiar with this one. If his calculations were right, she'd finished high school a few years ahead of him. Which would make her midthirties— though she sure didn't look five or six years older than his twenty-nine. He recalled hearing, a long time ago, that she'd moved away and married some man from Albuquerque. But from the look of her empty ring finger— Quint told himself he didn't know why he had looked there first—her marital status had changed along with her residence.

"I'm aware that he has dizzy spells," Quint replied. "But the way I understand it, the condition isn't life-threatening and it only hits him occasionally."

"If a spell of vertigo caused him to suffer a bad fall, it could be life-threatening."

"Sorry, Ms. Donovan, but I could suffer a fall walking across the backyard. Any of us could."

"The likelihood of that happening skyrockets when a person's head is spinning."

Quint couldn't argue that point. He'd been with his grandfather when one of these spells hit him and the old man had been unable to walk without someone to assist him.

"So? I'd rather see him die than to chain him to a chair. And you can't go around holding onto his arm all day. In fact, I doubt you could keep up with him," Quint added.

She sighed. "Abe isn't a young man anymore, you know."

Quint bristled. He didn't want anyone insinuating that Abe was getting old and decrepit. He wasn't. And Quint refused to let anyone make him believe otherwise.

"Eighty-four may sound old to you," Quint said to her, "but trust me, Gramps has the mind and the body of a man twenty years younger."

"I agree with that."

His expression turned incredulous. "If you know that, then what the hell are you doing here?"

She walked forward and leaned a hip against the edge of a chrome-and-Formica dining table. Quint couldn't help but notice the sensual curve of her breasts and waist, the way her dark red hair waved against her pale cheek. He didn't recall Maura Donovan as being so sexy. But back before she'd left the area, he'd only had eyes for Holly. Lovely, fickle Holly.

"Are you angry because I'm living here?" she asked.

Was he? The question jarred him almost as much as the sight of her. No. He wasn't angry. He was confused, shaken and a bit hurt that Abe hadn't seen fit to consult him about hiring Maura Donovan. But then, his grandfather had always been a maverick. The only person he'd ever answered to was his late wife, Jenna. There was no reason for Quint to think Abe needed or wanted his grandson's opinion.

"I'm not angry. I'm confused. Abe isn't sick. And there's no way you can protect him from a dizzy spell. So why did he hire you?"

A faint smile tilted the corners of her lips and it suddenly dawned on Quint that it was the first semblance of warmth he'd seen on her face since he'd walked into the room. The subtle expression softened her features and he found himself looking at things about her that had nothing to do with anything. Like her skin that was all smooth and pink and pearly.

Hell, what had she done to Abe? he wondered. Batted her long lashes at him and smiled? He could see how a young man would succumb to this woman's charms. Quint was feeling the effects of her presence himself. But Abe? Sure, his grandfather was still a man, but he'd always been so crazy in love with his late wife that he'd never looked twice at another woman. But maybe she did something to change that, Quint thought.

"Your grandfather suffers from benign paroxysmal positional vertigo. When it happens I can help him with the exercises and head maneuvers he needs to do in order to get over it. And see that he takes his medication, whenever it's needed. Having a nurse close by makes him feel safe and cared for. Surely you wouldn't want to deny the man that much?"

Shaking his head with resignation, Quint pulled out one of the dining chairs and flopped down on the seat. He'd been building fences all day. Sweat and dirt stained his shirt and jeans and he was tired enough to sleep for a week. He wasn't in any shape to argue with Maura Donovan. And maybe he shouldn't be arguing, he thought wearily. Maybe he should just thank his lucky stars that Abe was being looked after on a daily basis.

"I didn't realize nurses also cooked for their patients," he said, his gaze straying to the simmering pot on the stove, then back to her.

He watched faint color warm her cheeks and then his gaze dropped to her lips. She didn't appear to wear lipstick. But then, she didn't need to. Her lips were already dark and moist and the idea of biting into them, kissing them, flashed through his mind, shocking him with the totally erotic thought.

"I understand that before I came Jim did all the cooking around here, but I offered to take over because—" Pausing, she wrinkled her nose. "Well, neither man was eating a healthy diet. Red meat and potatoes was about all I could find around here."

"That's what Gramps likes," Quint said automatically while he pushed his mind to more pertinent issues. How long was she planning on staying here and was she thinking to get more out of his grandfather than just nurse's wages? The Donovans were wealthy people. If Maura never worked a day in her life, she could still live in luxury. So why would she want to hide herself away here on Apache Wells? Abe's ranch was remote, with the nearest neighbor—an old woman everyone called Crazy Gertie—fifteen miles away. Gertie was someone who'd been known to take potshots at anyone who decided to come near the shack she lived in. As for his grandfather, Abe could be charming whenever he chose to be, but for the most part he was set in his ways and didn't hesitate to speak his mind. A young, beautiful woman like Maura wouldn't deliberately choose to spend her days like this unless there was something in it for her, would she?

The questions were really none of Quint's business and probably totally out of line. But damn it, Abe was his grandfather! Someone had to look out for the old man's security. Two years ago his sister had married a Texas Ranger and moved to his ranch near San Antonio. A month ago, Alexa had given birth to daughter Jessica. Add her to the couple's toddler son, J.D., and his sister's life was consumed with caring for her own family. That left only Quint and his mother, Frankie, to keep an eye on their aging relative.

"What we like and what's good for us aren't always the same, Mr. Cantrell."

Amen to that, he thought drily. "My grandfather never was one to follow rules—good or bad."

And Maura figured the man sitting at the small dining table wasn't much of a rule follower, either. He'd said he wasn't angry about her being here, yet she could see doubts and questions unfolding like a picture show across his rough-hewn face.

Well, she couldn't blame the man. She'd had her own doubts about taking this job. But Abe had been persistent. He'd also come along with the proposition at just the right time. She'd loved her job at Sierra General Hospital. Helping ailing patients get back on their feet was something she'd always wanted and needed to do since she'd become a nurse nearly fourteen years ago. But recently Dr. Weston's uninvited pursuit of her had turned the job she'd once cherished into a walking nightmare. On the whole he was a nice man and an excellent doctor, but he'd refused to believe she didn't want to see him romantically. His attention hadn't quite crossed over to harassment, but it was making her a bit uncomfortable. So she'd spent the past two months running around the hospital trying to dodge the man.

Turning back to the cabinet counter, she began to gather makings for a fresh pot of coffee while she attempted to convince herself that Quint Cantrell wasn't making her heart beat fast, her mouth go dry. She'd not expected him to look so raw and sexy, so much a man. Even with her back to him, she could easily visualize the rusty-brown color of his hair, the sky-blue of his eyes and the strong, stubborn square of his jaw.

Taking a deep breath, she said, "When Abe approached me a few weeks ago, he was going through tests to find the cause of his vertigo. He told me then that he was afraid of falling and breaking a bone."

Quint snorted. "What a bunch of bull. Gramps has never been afraid of falling. Why, only a few weeks ago, he rode a green broke horse on roundup. The thing reared up and fell over backward with him. Do you think that scared him? Hell, no. He climbed back on and rode the animal that day and the rest of the week."

Pausing in the middle of her task, Maura glanced over her shoulder at him and as her eyes settled on his face, some subtle thing fluttered in the pit of her stomach. She'd never been properly introduced to Quint Cantrell, but their families had often traveled in the same circles and she recalled seeing him a few times oh so many years ago. He'd been a handsome young guy then, one that as a teenager, her younger sister Bridget had swooned over. But according to Bridget, he'd never given her the time of day. Instead he'd steadily dated Holly Johnson and everyone in Lincoln and Ortero Counties had believed the two would eventually get married. Maura had never heard what happened with the couple, but she'd heard nasty rumors. But then, Maura knew all too well that most breakups were ugly.

"I'm hardly saying your grandfather is scared," she said quietly. "I think—well, I think you should ask him yourself why he believes he needs a nurse. As for me, I'm very happy to be here. Abe is—" She broke off with a fond smile. "He's quite a character, and I'll be honest, I've already fallen a little in love with him."

His lips pressed into a thin line of disapproval, but Maura told herself she didn't care what this man was thinking. Let him think what he wanted. Her relationship with Abe was between the old man and her.

"I didn't think nurses were supposed to become emotionally involved with their patients," he said.

Turning back to the cabinet counter, she poured water into the coffeemaker, then shoved the carafe in place. "That's right. But I have a heart in my chest, not a rock. And it has a mind of its own."

He didn't make any sort of reply and after a few moments, the air in the kitchen felt so tense that she had to turn and face him. Yet the sardonic expression she expected to see wasn't there. Instead, she was jolted by his sober blue gaze honing in on her like a microscope.

"Abe tells me that you've been developing more of your family land," she said as casually as she could.

"Gramps purchased the property over near Capitan more than twenty years ago and since then has done little with it. For some reason, he thinks I can make something out of the place."

He didn't go on to tell her that the property was the only Cantrell land that belonged solely to Quint. Along with that, it possessed some of the finest grazing land in southern New Mexico. Unlike the other two family ranches, the Golden Spur, named after the old gold mine on the property, was being built with Quint's own two hands and from his own ideas and dreams. And that made it all very special to him.

"I heard about your father dying—what was it—two years ago?"

His gaze turned uncomfortably away from her. "Over two years now."

"I was very sorry to hear about Lewis's passing. I met him a couple of times. He was a warm, perfect gentleman."

She saw him swallow and realized that the hurt of losing his father was still a raw wound in him. The vulnerable side of the man touched Maura in a way she'd not expected. She would have liked to place a comforting hand on his shoulder, but to do such a thing would only rouse his suspicions of her. And he did have suspicions, she thought wryly. She'd spotted them in his eyes the moment she'd told him she was living with Abe.

"Yeah. Everyone liked Dad."

Clearing her throat, she replied, "So who's managing the Chaparral now? Obviously, not you."

"Laramie Jones. But I still keep a hand in things there. That's where Mom still makes her home." Eventually, the Chaparral would go to his sister Alexa, and Apache Wells would be split equally between the two siblings. As of now, it was Quint's job to keep an eye on both properties. Not an easy task for Quint, especially since he had his own place to deal with, too. But ranching was his life and he considered the extra work a labor of love.

"I see."

Behind her the coffeemaker gurgled its last drop. Maura walked to the end of the cabinet where the cups were located. "Would you like coffee?" she asked.

"Sure. Thanks."

She gathered up two cups and proceeded to fill both of them. After she'd carried them over to the table and took a seat across from him, she reached for a small pitcher of cream.

As he stirred sugar into his own cup, he said, "This may sound insensitive, but I thought you were married."

Maura tried not to cringe. Being divorced wasn't like she'd committed some sort of shameful crime, but for some reason it bothered her to think this man might be viewing her as a failure. Especially at being a wife, a woman, a lover.

"I was married for five years," she replied. "But it ended more than a year ago. That's when I moved back to Lincoln County."

"Oh."

She pushed a hand through her hair and the thought suddenly struck her that her face was bare of makeup, her hair mussed. But her appearance hardly mattered. This man was at least six years younger. He'd never look at her in a romantic way. Which was more than okay with her. She wasn't ready to tangle herself up in any sort of emotional commitment again. And if she did ever get ready, she would hardly take her chances on a young man who was still in his twenties and apparently not looking to settle down.

"No children?" he asked.

Gripping her cup, she tried to push away the empty ache that always seemed to be lingering near her heart. "No. My ex-husband's job required him to travel all the time. I kept waiting for that to change. It didn't."

She could feel his blue eyes upon her, but she didn't have the courage to lift her gaze to his. "What about you, Mr. Cantrell? You've not married yet?"

He took his time sipping his coffee and as tense moments begin to tick away, Maura decided he was going to ignore her question entirely. Which was embarrassing. Especially since she'd talked about her personal life.

"No," he said finally. "I haven't been looking for a wife. Can't see that I need one."

And why would he? she asked herself. The man had everything. Cattle, horses, thousands of acres of prime ranch land at his disposal, anything that money could buy. And that probably included women; the sort that he could take or leave at his convenience. A young hunk like him probably didn't want to be saddled with a wife.

"And I wish you wouldn't call me Mr. Cantrell," he went on. "That was my father's name. I'm just Quint to everyone."

Calling him Mr. Cantrell helped keep him at an emotional distance. But it looked as though he meant to tear down even that flimsy barrier. Feeling even tenser, she drained her cup and rose to her feet. "Okay, Quint. Will you be staying for supper? There'll be plenty."

He got to his feet and Maura unconsciously stepped backward to put plenty of space between them. He was a big man. In size and presence. Strength and masculinity were stamped all over his rough features, broad shoulders and long, hard legs. Just being near him left her feeling cornered.

"I don't know yet. Right now I'm going to go find my grandfather." He placed his cup in the sink, then went out the back door, the screen banging behind him.

Maura stared after him and wondered why meeting Quint Cantrell had felt like going through an earthquake. Even her hands were still shaking.

Because Jenna Cantrell had wanted the dust and commotion of a ranch yard well away from her home, Abe had built the working part of Apache Wells two miles west of the house. Normally, he and Quint drove the distance, but there were times they chose to walk to the bunkhouse and work pens.

Down through the years, the outbuildings and barns had been built with no particular style or planning in mind, except durability and practical use. Some were made of wood, some corrugated iron, but one thing the buildings did have in common was their whitewashed walls and red tin roofs.

To one side of the network of buildings and connecting holding pens was a long arena where the hands gathered to train their horses to follow and cut cattle, and in quieter times, swap stories around a small campfire.

This late summer evening just happened to be cool enough to appreciate the warmth of a fire and, after Quint parked his truck, he found his grandfather with several of his hired hands squatting around the ring of rocks. The moment Abe spotted his approach, he left the circle of men and walked over to his grandson.

The older man was the same height as Quint and bony thin. He never went outdoors without his black hat and he always wore the legs of his jeans stuffed deep into his knee-high cowboy boots. This particular pair had lime-green tops with fancy yellow stitching and the leather was as scarred and worn as his grandfather's face. Tonight he was wearing a brown quilted vest to ward away the chill and the puffy garment camouflaged his wiry torso.

Stroking his thick white mustache, he said to Quint, "So I see you finally managed to come check on your grandfather."

Not allowing the old man any slack, Quint said, "I had to work at it. But I'm here."

Folding his arms across his chest, Abe rocked back on his high heels. "Well, it's about time." He jerked his head toward the men behind him. "Jim's makin' some camp coffee. Come have a cup with us."

"I just had coffee—with your nurse," Quint added pointedly.

Abe grinned that goofy sort of grin that men got on their faces when they talked about women. "So you met the little filly, did ya? What'd you think about her?"

If Quint hadn't been so shocked at his grandfather's ribald questions, he would have rolled his eyes and cursed a blue streak.

"Forget about that," he muttered. "What the hell are you doing, Gramps? You're not sick! You're using that vertigo problem of yours as an excuse to have her here. Aren't you?"

"S-s-shh! Don't be raising your voice so, damn it! She might hear you."

"*She's* in the house—two miles from here," Quint reasoned.

His head tilting one way and then the other, Abe chuckled. "Well, she thinks I'm needy—and I am. At times. You know, Quint, I always had it in my mind that nurses were hard-hearted women. They sure seem like it when a man is sick. But Maura ain't. She's as sweet as a summer peach."

"Since when did you need a summer peach?" Quint countered.

Abe shrugged. "Well—since I got dizzy."

Quint snorted. "Looks to me like you've gotten more than dizzy."

"That's right," Abe retorted. "I got the notion that I was tired of living alone."

Shaking his head, Quint looked out at the ranch yard. The dipping sun was lengthening the shadows of the buildings. A pen of horses munched on alfalfa while around their feet several dominickers pecked at the morsels of oats and corn that had fallen from the feed troughs. Apache Wells had always felt more like home to Quint than any of the other Cantrell properties in Lincoln County.

As a young child he'd spent many days and nights here with his grandparents and those memories were more than special to him. His time here had influenced his life. The endless days he'd spent with his grandfather working in and out of the saddle had set Quint's goals and visions for the future.

Yes, Apache Wells had always been special to him and he didn't want a woman coming along and changing anything about it.

"Living alone! Gramps, you have men all around you. That's hardly being alone."

"Is that what you tell yourself?" Abe countered with a question.

Quint frowned, then heaved out a heavy breath. "Look, Gramps, I'm not the one complaining about being lonely. You are. My life is one big whirlwind right now. I don't have time to be lonely. And frankly, neither do you. So spare me."

Abe scowled at him. "Spare you? I'd like to kick your ass."

Seeing he was getting nowhere, Quint took a different direction. "So how long do you plan on keeping this nurse?"

Abe gave him a palms-up gesture. "'Til I don't need her, I suppose. 'Course if I get over this dizzy problem, I'm hardly likely to run her off."

Quint suddenly decided he'd been all wrong about the old man. Abe was sick. With dementia or something like it. Had Maura already recognized Abe's problem and saw it as a way to get her foot in the door? He hated to think the woman might be that calculating. She didn't seem the sort, at all. But then, he'd spent four years believing that Holly Johnson was a true-blue innocent and look what that had gotten him. She'd run off with a rich real-estate mogul and Quint had become the laughingstock of Lincoln County.

"Gramps, I want you to have a complete checkup. You need blood work, scans, the whole nine yards. You're not yourself and we both know it."

Abe laughed gleefully. "I'm not acting like myself, am I? Just because I'm enjoying a little female company? I think any doc would say you're the one who's messed up."

"What about Granny?" Quint challenged him. "Doesn't she matter anymore?"

Abe's expression suddenly softened and he patted Quint on the shoulder. "She ain't here anymore, Quint. All I have is memories and photos. A man needs more and you ought to understand that."

Lord, did his grandfather have romantic intentions toward the nurse? "Gramps, did you hire her to be your nurse or something more personal?" Quint asked point-blank.

Abe turned a completely innocent look on him. "Why, to be my nurse, of course. But if she so happens to stumble around and fall in love with me—well, I sure as heck ain't gonna push her away. If you know what I mean."

Unfortunately, Quint knew all too well what his grandfather meant. He also knew that if he didn't do something about this situation and soon, Abe was going to be hurt. In more ways than one.

Gazing thoughtfully in the direction of the ranch house, Quint rubbed a hand against his jaw. "I think I'll stay for supper," he suddenly announced.

Clearly skeptical, Abe asked, "Why? You thinkin'

you're gonna hang around and horn in on your grandfather's business?"

Quint looked at him. "No. I'm thinking that soup she was making smelled mighty good."

He was also thinking that the moment he'd first walked into the kitchen, Maura Donovan had set off some sort of spark in him, a flash of heat that had taken Quint totally by surprise. Now he wanted to get closer to the woman, he decided. So close that he could see right into her pretty head. He could take a second look into her green eyes and found out for himself if that spark he'd felt had been real or imagined.

Though he wasn't too sure which direction he wanted the decision to land…

Chapter Two

Two days later, on the dirt drive that led to the Apache Wells ranch house, Maura was finishing the last of a two-mile jog. The early afternoon sun was hot. Sweat sheened her body and dampened her red tank top. The thought of languishing over a tall glass of iced tea pushed her forward, until the musical ring of her cell phone sounded in the pocket of her shorts.

Pausing in the middle of the narrow road, she fished out the small instrument and was immediately surprised to see the caller was her mother. Now that the Donovan children were all grown and capable of running the Diamond D horse ranch without them, her parents, Fiona and Doyle Donovan, had become regular globe-trotters. Only two days ago they'd been in Ireland visiting relatives on both sides of their extensive families.

"Hello, Mother!"

"You're out of breath," Fiona observed. "What did you do, run to the phone?"

"No. I'm out jogging," Maura explained.

"Oh. I can call back later."

Having five siblings meant that getting any exclusive, one-on-one attention from their mother was rare and precious. Just having her mother call so quickly after her return home made Maura feel special.

"Nonsense. I can walk and talk for a while," she assured the other woman. "It's so good to hear your voice. When did you get home?"

"Late last night. Your father and I are so jet-lagged we're just getting around to having breakfast. Dallas was the only one still up when we arrived last night and this afternoon everyone seems to be out of pocket."

"Just because you and Dad live the life of luxury doesn't mean your children can loll around in bed until midafternoon," Maura teased as she started to the house.

"Hmm. It's good to hear that we've taught you children good work ethics. And speaking of work, Dallas tells me you're still with Mr. Cantrell."

Before her parents had left for Ireland more than a month ago, Abe had not yet approached Maura about the job here at Apache Wells. But once she'd decided to take the old man's offer, she'd called her parents in Ireland and told them about her decision. Neither had understood her choice to abruptly change jobs, but they'd hardly tried to deter her. At thirty-six, it had been years since her parents had tried to tell her what to do. And even if they did try, Maura was too stubborn and strong-minded not to take the path she chose for herself. Even if it might be the wrong path, she thought drily.

"That's right."

"So what are your duties? Does he keep you busy fetching and complaining?"

Maura smiled to herself. "Not in the least. Right now Abe is out riding range with the rest of the ranch hands. I don't expect him in until later this afternoon."

"Riding—" Fiona gasped. "I thought—if I remember correctly, Abe Cantrell is older than your father! And I thought he was ill and needed a nurse!"

The smile on Maura's full lips deepened even more. "Abe is eighty-four. And he's as healthy as a horse. Except for when he gets vertigo. And thankfully that's only happened once since I've been here."

There was a long pause and then Fiona said in a slow, pointed voice, "Maura, I may be butting in, but I'd like to know why you gave up a wonderful, good-paying job at the hospital for a man who only needs you occasionally?"

"Abe needs me more than occasionally, Mother."

"You just assured me he was healthy and—"

"He needs me in other, emotional ways. Having me here makes him feel secure. Besides that, he's lonely and starved for affection."

"Maura!" Fiona said in a scolding tone. "You hardly know this man. His emotional needs aren't your responsibility."

Maura had told herself exactly that same thing. More than once. Yet for some reason she couldn't explain to anyone, a part of her had connected to the old man the minute she'd first met him striding down a hallway at Sierra General. He'd been trying to find his way through the maze of corridors to the closest exit and Maura had offered her help. The two of them had hit it off instantly and before Abe had left the building, he'd offered her the private nursing job.

"Mother, I'm a nurse and Abe needs mental and physical nourishing. That's what my job is all about," Maura responded. "The degree of his need has nothing to do with things."

On the other end of the line, she could hear her mother sighing softly. "You've gotten attached to this man. I can hear it in your voice," Fiona said flatly.

"I suppose I have."

"And what about Frankie, his daughter-in-law? And his grandson—what is his name?"

"Quint."

"Yes, Quint. What about them, aren't they around to see to Abe's needs?"

Maura talked to Frankie on a frequent basis and the woman had made it clear that even though she checked in on Abe from time to time, Quint was the one relative the old man wanted and needed in his life. Frankie had also assured her that she was going to keep mum about Maura and let Abe be the one to tell his grandson about having a nurse. Obviously Frankie had kept her word. Two days ago, when he'd appeared unannounced in the kitchen, he'd been shocked to find Maura there and she'd been totally tilted off-kilter by his presence. Since then it had been impossible to forget the strong physical reaction she'd felt toward the man. Just thinking about him made her feel utterly foolish.

"The Cantrells are busy people. Just like you and Dad. They have lives of their own to deal with."

In fact, the night Quint had sat down to eat supper with her and Abe, he'd received some sort of important call and hadn't even taken the time to gulp more than three bites before he'd quickly departed the ranch. Abe had clearly been disappointed when his grandson had rushed off. As for Maura, she'd felt deflated as she'd watched the man dash out the door. A part of her had wanted more of his company while the other part had been leery of the strange feelings he'd elicited in her.

"I'm sorry if I sounded fussy, darling," Fiona said after a pause. "If you like the job, that's all that matters. But I can't see why you'd want to isolate yourself out there on Apache Wells, though. It's miles and miles from anything."

Because the isolation was soothing to her fractured nerves, Maura thought. Because after going through a humiliating, heartbreaking divorce, not to mention the unwanted chase by Dr. Weston, Maura needed the calm quiet of Abe's home to restore herself.

"My truck is in good working order and I can drive into town whenever I want. I promise to see you and Dad soon."

"I'm holding you to that promise and—"

Fiona broke off as Maura caught the sound of her father's voice booming in the background for his wife to hang up the phone and come to breakfast.

"You'd better put the phone down, Mother. Dad never did like waiting on his meals."

Laughing, Fiona said goodbye and quickly closed the connection between them. Maura put her own phone back in her pocket and trotted on to the house.

She was nearing the porch when the screen door pushed open and Abe stepped onto the small alcove.

"There you are!" he exclaimed. "I've been huntin' all over for you."

"I've been out getting a little exercise," Maura said with a smile. "Did everything go okay on your ride? Any dizziness?"

He grinned at her and Maura thought that it must be true that the older a man got the more he resembled the boy he'd once been. Abe was one of the most mischievous, prank-playing men she'd ever been around and that included her three rowdy brothers.

"Not even one little spin. Everything went as fine as spring rain. Got the cattle moved and the old pump off the broken windmill. We'll have it fixed in a few days."

Maura gestured toward one of the two lawn chairs grouped together on the small porch. "Sit down and I'll get you coffee or something," she suggested.

"Don't have time. We got some green colts penned and some of the boys are gonna try to halter 'em. I'd better be there. These young'ns try to hurry things along. I have a hell of a time tryin' to teach them that when you're dealin' with horses, the slow way is the fastest way."

Maura smiled. How many times had she heard her own father say the same thing, she wondered fondly. Like Abe, Doyle Donovan was a horseman and would be until he died.

Turning toward the house, Abe motioned for her to follow. "Come along inside," Abe said to her. "I've got a chore for ya. That is, if you don't mind doin' it."

Curious, Maura followed the old man into the house, where he immediately walked over to a rolltop desk that was situated in one corner of the small living room. Inside the desk, he pulled a large white envelope from one of the storage slots, then waved it in Maura's face.

"This came in the mail yesterday. Quint needs to look it over. Pronto. I called him last night, but he says he can't get back over here for a few days. I'd like for you to take these papers over to the Golden Spur."

Go to Quint Cantrell's ranch? The thought of seeing the

man again sent a thrill of excitement zinging through Maura. Yet at the same time, she was wary of meeting him on her own without Abe's presence to act as a buffer. The other evening, during his short visit, Quint had been polite enough to her, yet she'd sensed he wasn't all that pleased about Abe's having a nurse. If he decided to really jump her out about the issue, she didn't know how she would handle him.

Lord, Maura, you wouldn't know how to handle Quint Cantrell under any circumstance. He's way too much man for a woman like you. And don't you forget it.

"I—well, if it's important to you, I'd be glad to," she finally said. After all, the man was paying her an extravagant wage for being his private nurse. And it was her job to see that he didn't fret unduly over things. "Is the ranch hard to find?"

"No trouble at all," he said with a dismissive wave of his hand. "I'll make you a little map while you go fix yourself up or whatever it is you women do before you leave the house."

Maura wasn't about to fix herself up for Quint Cantrell, but she couldn't say that to Abe. Instead she went to her room and hurriedly showered, then changed into a cool white shirt over a pair of Levi's. After swiping a brush through her hair and a bit of peach color across her lips, she returned to the living room and found Abe waiting with the map and papers in hand.

As he watched her approach, a wide grin spread across his face. "Here you go, honey. The map is easy to follow. Just take your time and don't get in no hurry to get back here. I feel good. Not nary a vertigo spell. Maybe I'm plumb over 'em."

Abe's way of putting things made Maura want to laugh

out loud. Instead, she said with a straight face, "If you're plumb over them, Abe, then you probably don't need me to keep hanging around here."

Frowning now, he reached out a bony hand to grip one of her shoulders. "Maura, now I was just tryin' to be positive. We both know that those damned spells could hit me right out of the blue. And I ain't lyin' when I say that they're scary things. Makes me feel like I'm dyin'. What would I do if you weren't around to get my head straight and all those little marbles back in place?"

He had ten men working here on this end of the ranch, not to mention several more on the western half of Apache Wells property. Except for the nights, the man was never alone. True, none of the ranch hands had any medical training, but then Abe wasn't looking for them or her to keep him physically safe, she realized. It was becoming obvious to her that he wanted her here for other, emotional reasons, and for now Maura was content to leave things at that.

"They're not marbles that make you dizzy, they're pieces of calcium that float around," she pointed out to him. "But don't worry, Abe. I'm not leaving. I just want to make sure that you're still okay with me being here."

The worried frown on his face eased into a genuine smile. "I'm better than okay. Havin' you around is almost like havin' Jenna back."

Maura patted his arm. Since she'd moved onto the ranch, Abe had talked to her a lot about his late wife. He was clearly still in love with the woman and missed her greatly. She empathized with the old man's loss. Especially now that she was on her own and her bed was as empty as her heart.

"I'm glad," she said softly, then clearing her throat, she promised, "I'll be back later this evening."

An hour later, on Highway 380, Maura very nearly missed the small sign on the left side of the road. *Golden Spur* were the only words written on the piece of tin nailed to a cedar fence post, but that was enough to tell Maura it was Cantrell property. The simple sign also told her that there was nothing showy about Quint Cantrell.

Turning into the entrance, she drove her Ford over the wooden cattle guard, then pulled to one side of the dusty road to study the map Abe had sketched for her.

From this point she would travel north for ten miles, then take the left fork in the road and drive due west for five more miles. The ranch house, Abe had told her, sat at the foot of a bald mountain.

Before she could take note of the butterflies in her stomach, Maura lifted her chin and stepped down on the gas. There wasn't any need for her nerves to jump around like a swarm of grasshoppers, she assured herself. It wasn't like she was going to see the man for personal reasons. All she was doing was making a delivery.

Normally, Quint was rarely in the house during the daytime. He couldn't waste the daylight. But today the wire stretchers had malfunctioned and barbed wire had popped loose, lashing backward to catch Quint's forearm. The long barbs had ripped the denim fabric of his shirt like a piece of fragile paper and torn a deep gash into his flesh.

The bleeding had forced him to come to the house and make an effort to patch up the wound. Now as he stood at the bathroom sink, pouring alcohol into the angry lesion and gritting his teeth against the sting, he heard a faint knock at the front door.

Figuring it was the man he'd been working with, he

yelled out, "Come on in, Jake. Get yourself a beer from the fridge, while I try to wrap up this thing."

"Um—this isn't Jake," a female voice called back.

Stunned by the sound, Quint wrapped a small towel around the wounded arm and hurried out of the bathroom and down a short hallway to the living room. The moment he spotted Maura standing just inside the door, he halted in his tracks.

"What are you doing here?" he asked without preamble.

She answered his question by holding up a long white envelope. "The papers your grandfather wanted you to have. He sent me to deliver them."

Papers? Quint couldn't remember talking to his grandfather about papers, but then his days and nights were filled with so many tasks that after a while everything began to run together. Besides, he could hardly think. Just seeing Maura Donovan standing inside the walls of his house was enough to jar his senses. Dressed in a pair of clinging jeans and a close-fitting shirt, she was just as sexy and attractive as he remembered and for a few seconds he forgot about the pain slicing through his arm.

"Oh. Well, just lay them anywhere, would you? Right now I'm—" Grimacing he glanced ruefully down at his arm. "I'm in a bit of a mess. If you'll excuse me, I'll—"

Her eyes followed his gaze down to the bloody towel wrapped around his arm. Quickly stepping forward, she exclaimed, "You've hurt yourself! Let me help."

Quint unconsciously took a step backward. "It's not that bad. Just give me a minute and I'll slap a bandage on it."

Concern marking her brow, Maura placed the envelope on the nearest end table, then closed the distance between them. "Don't be silly, Quint. I'm a nurse." Not waiting for his permission, she wrapped her hand firmly around his upper arm. "It's my job to deal with wounds."

Since Quint could hardly argue that point, especially now that she had a grip on him, he said, "Okay. I have some things set out in the bathroom. Let's go in there."

Dropping her hold on his arm, she followed him down a short hallway and into the small room. A vanity surrounded a white lavatory and after he'd removed the towel and his shirt, she quickly positioned his injured limb over the clean basin.

"How did this happen?" she asked.

"A piece of barbed wire came loose from the stretcher and whacked me."

She was taller than he'd first thought, he realized. If her head hadn't been bent over his arm, the top of it would have measured to a spot just beneath chin.

"It looks to me as though this could use a stitch or two," she told him. "Have you had a tetanus shot lately?"

The close proximity of her body was rattling him, while the sweet, flowery scent of her skin and hair seemed foreign to a man that mostly kept his distance from women.

"No," he answered gruffly. "Just clean the thing out and I'll take my chances."

Turning her head, she gave him an impatient glance. "That's not very smart of you."

"I've never been accused of being smart. Besides, you medical people go overboard with precautionary measures. Gramps would consider this a scratch."

A soft sigh escaped her. "Have you always tried to fashion yourself after your grandfather?"

"Not always." Quint certainly wouldn't have a nurse living with him, he thought ruefully. Especially if he didn't need one.

Thankfully, she turned her attention back to his arm and Quint gritted his teeth as she used a nail brush to scrub the lesion with water and antibacterial soap.

"What the hell are you doing?" he demanded. "Trying to rip open my arm even more?"

"Sorry. I know it hurts, but it's important to make sure no debris is left behind. Was the wire rusty?"

"No. It was new—galvanized." To his surprise the scrubbing hadn't made the bleeding worse. In fact, it was on the verge of stopping completely.

"That's good," she said. "At least we don't have that problem to worry about."

We? It was his arm. As far as he could see, she didn't have anything to worry about. But he kept the thought to himself. If she was kind enough to offer her services, he could at least show his gratitude.

Once she had the cut clean and dried, she applied antiseptic, then ointment. Quint couldn't help but notice how her hands had gentled during the process and now her fingers felt warm and soothing against his flesh as she slowly wrapped gauze around his forearm.

"Is this all the gauze you have?" she asked.

"Afraid so. I might have some horse bandage down at the barn," he suggested.

She glanced up at him and Quint felt something inside him jerk as he met her earthy-green gaze. There was something very womanly about Maura Donovan, something he couldn't ignore, but was desperately trying to.

"No thanks," she replied. "I'll make do."

Her focus returned to his arm and Quint found himself taking in her dark hair. It was smooth and shiny and threaded with lighter and darker shades that all blended to make an auburn shade so deep it verged on being black.

The length of it nearly reached her waist and Quint wondered how it would look draped against her naked back.

"There. That should keep it protected for a while," she announced as she rose to her full height. "But I wouldn't advise getting the bandage wet and you'll have to change it tomorrow or the next day."

To Quint's dismay, he realized he'd only caught a portion of her words because his mind had been too busy conjuring erotic images of her. What was the matter with him? Since Holly had dumped him for another man, he'd found it damned easy to ignore the sexual pull of a woman. The humiliation she'd put him through had killed his libido deader than a dose of potassium nitrate.

But now, with this sultry nurse standing far too close for his comfort, he was feeling things again. Things that could only lead to trouble.

"I'll be sure to take good care of it."

She slowly released her hold on him, then turned to fetch his shirt from the end of the vanity. When she pivoted back, she was holding the shirt out for him to stick his arms through.

"Let me have it," he said. "I don't need help getting dressed."

"Don't try to act like such a he-man," she said softly. "I won't tell anybody I helped you."

Knowing it wasn't wise to linger in such close quarters with her, he decided not to argue and was glad that he hadn't as he struggled to push the bundled arm through the shirtsleeve.

"Don't be surprised if your arm is already starting to feel stiff," she said. "You're going to have one hell of a sore muscle for a while."

"I'm finding that out," Quint muttered.

Once his arms were in the sleeves, she smoothed the fabric over his shoulders, then stepped back to allow him to button the garment himself. Quint found it safer to look at the buttons rather than her.

"A couple of over-the-counter pain relievers will help."

"I have some in the kitchen," he told her, then motioned for her to precede him out the door. "Would you like something cool to drink? It's the least I can do for bandaging me. I was having a heck of a time trying to manage with one hand."

He began to move down a short hallway and Maura followed him into a large kitchen. A row of paned windows ran along the west wall of the room and without any curtains or shades to cover them, the afternoon sun streamed golden shafts across the old printed linoleum covering the floor.

The house was very livable, yet it was far from fancy. In fact, Maura was totally surprised to see how modest Quint's living quarters actually were. Anyone who'd lived for any length of time in Lincoln County and beyond was aware that the Cantrell family was rich. Abe owned thousands and thousands of acres and his cattle ranch, Apache Wells, had long been one of the most profitable in the state. On another section of land, just north of Alto, Quint's father, Lewis, had also built a cattle empire called the Chaparral. Maura had never visited that particular ranch, but her parents and older brother Conall had attended a party there. From what they'd said, the Chaparral house was a showy hacienda with luxury and space to spare. So why was the younger Cantrell living like this? she wondered. Because he wanted to emulate his grandfather?

While he headed to the refrigerator, he gestured toward

a small, round dining table. "Have a seat," he invited. "I have beer, soda or fruit juice. Take your pick."

"Soda is fine," she told him as she eased onto one of the wooden chairs.

He carried two chilled cans of cola over to the table and pushed one her way, but didn't immediately take a seat. Instead, he walked over to a row of cabinets, fished out a bottle of acetaminophen and shook two out in the palm of his hand.

"I'm glad to see you're going to take my advice," she said as she popped the lid on her drink.

He tossed the pills into his mouth and washed them down with a long drink of the soda before he walked over to the table and took a seat across from her.

"I still have a stretch of fence to finish before it gets dark," he explained. "I don't want my arm to get too stiff to work."

There was no way he needed to be straining his arm using post-hole diggers or wire stretchers, but she wasn't going to bother pointing that out to him. He was a grown man and his well-being was not her responsibility. Besides, being a nurse had taught her that there wasn't a man alive who wanted a woman to hamper him with limitations.

"So this is where you've been doing all this work that Abe talks about," she commented. "As I drove up I noticed the new barn. It looks nice."

"Thanks. The barn is taking a lot more work and twice as much money as I'd first anticipated. But I think it's turning out okay."

He must have removed his hat when he'd come into the house to attend his cut, she thought. It was only the second time she'd seen him without the battered felt atop his head.

The other being when he'd sat down at Abe's dinner table. But that occasion hadn't lasted long enough for him to get the chair warm. Now, as quiet moments ticked by, she couldn't help but notice the thick, rusty wave dipped across one corner of his forehead, the unruly strands curling around his ears.

His face and arms were tanned as dark as a coffee bean, but the glimpses she'd had of his bare chest told her he wasn't into lounging around in the sun without his shirt. She doubted he was into lounging around anywhere. From the looks of his lean, hard muscles, the man worked tirelessly.

Her carnal thoughts brought her up short. The two of them were entirely alone and with the letter delivered and his arm bandaged, she no longer had any good reason to remain in Quint Cantrell's house.

Quickly rising to her feet, she said nervously, "Well, I'm glad that I didn't interrupt your work—though I guess the injury to your arm had already done that. But I won't keep you any longer. I promised Abe I'd be back to Apache Wells before it got too late."

Quint rose to his feet also. "You haven't finished your soda."

"I've had enough. Thank you."

She started out of the kitchen and as she did, she could feel Quint's presence following close behind her. The idea made her heart thump at a rapid pace and she drew in a deep breath in an attempt to calm it.

"I'm not in that big of a hurry to get back to work, Maura. Why don't you let me show you around before you leave?"

His suggestion caught her by surprise and she dared to glance over her shoulder at him. "Do you really want to?"

He suddenly chuckled and Maura was amazed at how different he looked with humor softening his features.

"I don't make offers unless I want to."

Something about the husky tone of his voice, the warmth in his eyes, sent prickles of excitement racing through her. She could feel her cheeks growing warm and pink and she suddenly felt like a foolish teenager instead of a thirty-six-year-old woman who'd been married and divorced.

But just for this once, she wasn't going to think about the dangers this man represented to her peace of mind. Tomorrow she would remind herself that she was behaving like an idiot. Today she was going to let herself enjoy the pleasure of being in the presence of a very sexy man.

"In that case," she said, "I'd love to have a look around."

Moving forward, he touched a hand to her back and Maura felt her senses splintering in all directions.

"Good," he murmured. "Just let me get my hat and we'll be on our way," he told her.

Chapter Three

Once they stepped onto the porch, Quint dropped his hand from her back and Maura was finally able to draw in a normal breath. But as they moved into the yard, he immediately wrapped a hold around her upper arm.

"Let's go to the barn first," he suggested. "I need to let Jake, my ranch hand, know I'm okay."

Nodding, she looked away from him and tried not to dwell on his warm, rough fingers pressing into her flesh.

The afternoon was all bright sunshine, while a soft west wind carried the scent of sagebrush and juniper. A lone aspen shaded one corner of the house, but that was the only bona fide tree that she could see for miles around. The rest of the vegetation growing beyond the ranch yard amounted to a few spindly pinyon pines, some twisted snags of juniper and a sea of jumping choya cactus and sagebrush. It was a stark, yet beautiful sight and Maura instinctively

knew it would be even more so in the late evening when
the sun fell from the sky and twilight purpled the nearby
mountains.

"How many men do you have working for you?" she
asked.

Now that they were walking abreast, he dropped his
hold on her arm and Maura didn't know whether to be disappointed or relieved. Either way, just being this near him
left her shaky and nothing like the practical, no-nonsense
nurse that had dealt calmly with all sorts of men. She kept
remembering the way he'd looked without his shirt and
how the warmth and scent of his body had filled up the
little bathroom and stifled her breath.

"The contractor working on the barn and storage sheds
has several men working with him. But as far as the ranch
goes, I only have two hands. Once I start putting livestock
on the place, I'll hire more. Though my grandfather deeded
over the land a few years ago, I only started full-time here
about two years ago."

She kept her gaze on the rocky ground in front of her.
"Do you have plenty of land here to support cattle?"

"Ten thousand acres. Not that much, but enough to do
what I want to do."

Glancing over at him, she asked curiously, "And what
is that?"

He shrugged and not for the first time, Maura couldn't
help thinking how serious and driven he was for a man his
age. Abe had commented one day that his grandson wasn't
yet thirty so that meant he was either twenty-eight or
twenty-nine. He certainly didn't look any older than that,
Maura thought. Yet he seemed older, as though the years
he'd been on this earth had pushed his soul to manhood
long before his body had caught up.

"My plans aren't anything grand. Just raise a few pure-bred cattle and a few horses."

"What about the old gold mine—the Golden Spur—that your ranch is named after?"

She'd not meant to ask that question. It had just slipped out on its own. The same way her heart seemed to jump into a crazy jig each time she looked at his face.

Frowning, he glanced her way. "What about it?" he asked curtly.

Knowing she'd touched on a tender spot, she shrugged in an effort to appear casual. "Nothing really. Except that I couldn't help noticing the letter Abe asked me to deliver to you. The return address was Red Bluff Mining Company. And your grandfather doesn't make any secret about wanting to reopen the old thing."

His footsteps paused on the barren ground and Maura came to a stop with him. As he looked at her, she could see frustration edging his features.

"Gramps thinks the mine could be profitable again. But I don't want anything to do with it. Having a bunch of trucks and men and equipment going across the ranch is the last thing I need."

"If it turned out to be profitable, the extra money might come in handy," she suggested. "Especially when you start buying stock for this place."

"I don't need the money," he said flatly. "Nor do I want it. I'm a rancher, not a miner."

He picked up his stride again, only this time it was much longer and purposeful as he covered the last few yards to the barn. Maura quickened her steps to stay up with him.

"So if money isn't the issue, why does your grandfather want to reopen the mine?" she said, darting a quick glance at his sober face.

"For the adventure, Maura. He's always wanted to turn over a rock just to see what was beneath it. That's how he got rich in the first place—on the plains of Texas, drilling for oil. He hit it big and brought his fortune out here to New Mexico to buy land and cattle. To him, the mine takes him back to those days when he was drilling for black gold. Guess it makes him feel young all over again. He didn't care about the mine for years when he owned it, but now that I have the land, it's all he seems to care about."

"Sometimes feeling young or having a dream is very important. Sometimes it even keeps a person from dying."

The muscles around his hard mouth tightened with impatience. "Don't try to make me believe that Gramps is dying. That he needs you or the mine to keep him healthy."

"I wouldn't attempt such a thing," she said defensively. "Abe isn't ill. He has a perfectly good mind. And the way I see it, he has the right to dream his own dreams. Just like you."

By now they had reached the massive barn. Instead of opening the huge double doors at the south end of the building, Quint led her to a smaller entrance at the side.

With his hand pausing on the door latch, he turned a searching look on her. "And what about you, Maura? What are your dreams?"

A few years ago his questions would have been easy to answer. Her dreams were waiting for the day her roving husband would settle down to a life exclusively with her. She'd been dreaming of the time they could start having children and Gilbert would be home so that they could parent them together. She'd waited because he kept promising he'd be ready the next year, and she wanted to raise her children with her husband home every night. But none of those dreams had come true. Instead, she'd discovered he'd changed women as often as he'd changed the cities his job had taken him to. And she'd had to accept the fact of his infidelity and that he'd never intended to change his job and settle down to family life. That had only been one of his false promises.

Maura had spent the past year trying to restore her broken self-confidence and move on from her shattered marriage. For months after her divorce, she'd struggled to simply put one foot in front of the other, and looking back, she realized her responsibilities as a nurse had been the only thing keeping her going. She was good at her job and no man could take that fact away from her. As for her dreams, she wasn't sure what they were now.

"I don't know, Quint," she said honestly. "Sometimes dreams get lost along the way."

Nobody had to tell him that, he thought grimly. His romantic dreams had been busted years ago. Now his goals were concrete and didn't depend on another person—particularly a woman.

"Yeah," he murmured. "And when that happens, it's damned hard to find new ones."

While the two of them had been talking, her face had taken on a sad hue and Quint realized he didn't like seeing her in such a mood. Maybe because it reminded him of his own lonely existence. Or maybe because he simply didn't like to think of this woman suffering over anyone or anything.

The unwanted notions disturbed him so much that he quickly turned away from her and shoved open the door.

"Let's go in," he urged. "I think Jake is probably at the back of the building where the men are working."

Since livestock hadn't yet been moved onto the ranch, the barn was missing the smells of animals and hay and leather. Instead, the scents of sawdust and fresh paint filled the air. On the opposite side of the building, a table saw buzzed and hammers rang out as men erected a frame of lumber that Quint explained would eventually become a large feed room.

"The contractor hasn't yet finished the horse stalls or the tack room. They'll get to that next," Quint continued as they slowly made their way through the building.

She was looking around her with real interest, a fact that surprised Quint. Even though she came from a ranching background, she didn't seem the sort that would be personally interested in such things. After all, she'd chosen a profession outside the Diamond D, her family's famous thoroughbred ranch. Add to that, she had a soft, feminine air about her that was totally opposite of an outdoor girl.

"This is going to be very nice," she said. "And I like the way you've laid out everything. When you open the big doors, the horses will be able to look outside. They like that, you know. When they can see what's going on, they're more content."

Bemused by her observation, Quint paused to look at her. Now that they were indoors, her features were muted by shadows, yet the dimness couldn't diminish the pearly sheen of her skin and for a brief moment he wondered what it would feel like to press his cheek against hers, to experience such softness next to him.

"You know about horses, do you?" he asked.

A smile tilted her lips and at that moment he decided he'd never seen anything so fetching or genuine.

"Why wouldn't I? My family raises thoroughbreds."

He folded his arms against his chest. "But you don't work with them. The horses, I mean."

Her smile turned whimsical. "No. Not since I went

into nursing. But I spent a lot of time at the barns when I was young."

"I know that Bridget is a doctor, but if I remember correctly, you have another sister. What does she do?"

She glanced away from him. "Dallas operates Angel Wing Stables, a therapy riding clinic for handicapped children. It's completely nonprofit and something she feels deeply about."

So all three of the Donovan sisters were dedicated to helping needy people. That should have reassured Quint and allowed him to quit worrying about Abe hiring Maura as his nurse. But it didn't. The more he got to know this woman, the more concerned he was. And not because he believed she was out to snag any sort of money from the old man. No, he'd written that idea off fairly quickly. The more he'd thought about it, the more he'd concluded she wasn't the gold-digger sort. Furthermore, the Donovans had just as much money or more than the Cantrells. She didn't need it.

No, Quint was far more concerned about his grandfather's emotional state than his bank account. It was obvious the old man had already grown extremely fond of Maura. And just because Abe was in his eighties, didn't mean he was immune to a female's charms. His grandfather might even fall in love with her. Stranger things had happened. And Maura had just now talked about the importance of a man's dreams. When she left Apache Wells, and she would, what would happen to his grandfather's dreams? They'd be broken.

Forcing his thoughts back to the moment, he touched a hand to her shoulder and urged her forward. "I see Jake. Let's go catch up with him."

At the end of the building, a young man wearing a black cowboy hat and ranch gear was applying neat's-foot oil to a fancy tooled saddle. The moment he saw their approach, he laid the oily rag to one side and stepped up to meet them.

"I was about to come to the house to make sure you weren't bleeding to death," he said to Quint, while his gaze strayed curiously over to Maura.

"I'm fine," Quint replied. "It just so happens that Maura is a nurse. She was kind enough to bandage me up."

A wry grin crossed the man's face. "Now isn't that something? A beautiful woman comes to your house and she's a nurse—just when you need one. You always were a lucky dog, Quint."

Quint couldn't see where slicing his arm open was lucky, but apparently Jake considered having Maura as a nurse more than fortunate. The idea grated on Quint to no end. Which was a ridiculous reaction. She wasn't anything to him. If Jake, or any man, wanted to make a play for her, then that was their business, not his.

"Maura, this is my good friend and ranch hand, Jake Rollins. Jake, this is Maura Donovan. She's my grandfather's personal nurse."

Ignoring the last tidbit, the dark-haired man reached to take Maura's hand. "Are you by any chance related to Liam Donovan?" he asked.

She smiled at Jake and Quint had to fight the urge to jerk her away from the other man and usher her back outside where the two of them would be alone, where her smiles would be directed only at him.

What the hell was coming over him? Quint wondered with self-disgust. Instead of worrying about his grandfather, he needed to be concerned about his own reaction to this woman. He was behaving like a moony bull turned loose in a herd of cows.

"He's my brother," Maura said.

"I know him from working the barns at Ruidoso Downs," Jake informed her. "Nice guy. Heck of a trainer, too. No one told me that he had a beautiful sister."

Quint made a loud display of clearing his throat. "You'd better finish that saddle, Jake. In a few minutes, we've got to get back on that wire stretcher."

The other man cast him a look of faint surprise, then reluctantly dropped Maura's hand. "Maybe you'd better keep Maura around. Just in case one of us gets hurt again," he joked. "Next time it might be me who needs her touch."

"Keep it up, Jake, and I'll make sure you get tangled up in barbed wire," Quint muttered, then carefully steered Maura away from the ranch hand and out a back door.

Once they were well away from the barn, Maura asked, "Have you two known each other long?"

Quint grimaced. "Since kindergarten. We grew up together. He's like a brother. That's why I put up with his big mouth."

Smiling, Maura shrugged. "I didn't pay him any mind. He was only joking."

"Don't bet on it. Jake loves women. Always has."

They were walking toward a long corral built of rough cedar boards. Attached to one end were several smaller pens with separate gates leading to the outside. Like the barn, the riding arena would have taken lots of time and effort to build. And as Maura looked around her, she could plainly see that Quint was far from the idle sort. He obviously worked hard for everything he had and she admired him greatly for that. Especially when she knew he loved what he was doing.

Gilbert, her ex-husband, had been a pharmaceutical representative and his job was to sell medical products to doctors in private practices, health clinics and hospitals. There was nothing physical about the job. He'd used his mouth and a pen. Two things he was good at. Especially the mouth, she thought grimly. He could sweet-talk a rabid dog into lying down and wagging his tail.

Thanks to his glib tongue, everyone had liked Gil and for several years running, he'd been top salesperson for his company. And that same gift of gab had made him very attractive to women, including Maura. In the beginning of their marriage his sweet talk had sustained and convinced her of his love. Then later, when things between them had grown difficult and doubts of his sincerity had haunted her, that same sweet, persuasive talk had kept her clinging to a man who was incapable of changing.

Yes, she knew all about flirts and all about trying to keep a man at her side. The first had fooled her into thinking she could succeed at the second. And in the end, her five-year marriage had crumbled along with her self-worth.

Shaking away the humiliating thoughts, Maura leaned a shoulder against the board fence and gazed back at the simple stucco house. What would it be like, she wondered, to live in such a simple place? With Quint Cantrell? He wasn't a wanderer. Apparently he was a homebody, choosing to make his livelihood, his future, with the land. But it didn't appear that he was a family man. Or maybe he was and just keeping those plans hidden, she silently mused.

"You're going to have a fine place to raise a family here someday, Quint."

His features stiffened. "It'll raise cattle and horses. As for a family—I'm not looking for a woman or family right now," he said flatly. "And I'm sure not holding my breath until that day."

Seeing that her comment had rubbed him the wrong way, she pushed away from the fence. "Well, thanks for the tour, Quint. I enjoyed it. But I'd better be heading back. It's not exactly a short drive back to Apache Wells."

She started walking back in the direction of the house and her parked truck. Quint followed alongside her.

"Gramps rarely leaves Apache Wells. Maybe you can talk him into coming over here and taking a look at all the work we've finished. If that doesn't interest him, then maybe visiting the old mine might budge him."

Just from his words, Maura could see that having his grandfather's admiration meant a lot to him. But what else really mattered to this man? If there was no special woman, no children to be had in his dreams, then what was the Golden Spur going to mean to him? Other than just a place to hang his hat?

At least the man has a future planned for himself, Maura. You have nothing on your agenda, except taking care of an old cantankerous man who could buy a dozen nurses like yourself.

Shoving away the mocking voice in her head, she said to Quint, "I'll see what I can do about getting him to come for a visit. But I'm sure I don't have to tell you that your grandfather does what he wants. Not what others would like for him to do."

"No. You don't have to tell me that."

As they walked the remaining distance to the house, Quint realized he couldn't keep his eyes off the woman. Her white shirt was sheer enough for him to see the imprint of her bra, the pattern of feminine lace covering her breasts.

She was not a small woman and he could tell by the silhouette of her curves that one breast would be more than enough to fill his hand, his mouth. The idea caused desire to flicker in some part of him that he'd long ago crossed off as dead. And he could only wonder what it was about her that had suddenly stirred him like this.

Since Holly had removed herself from his life, and he'd gotten burned by some superficial gold diggers, sex had become casual, something to forget afterward. And down through the years he'd pushed so hard and so long that he'd felt positive he'd never want another woman in his lifetime.

So why had Maura Donovan come along and reminded him that he was still a man? Lord, he didn't know the answer. But now that she had, he was going to have to deal with her and himself in a smart and practical way.

At the truck, Quint opened the driver's door and helped her up into the cab. She smiled down at him and he felt his practicality fly off with the dusty wind.

"Thank you for taking care of my cut," he said.

"You're welcome. Although, I wish you would consider going to a doctor. With a stitch or two, you would heal even quicker. And depending on how long it's been since you've had one, you might need a tetanus shot."

His lips took on a wry slant. "If I ran into town and got a tetanus shot every time I cut or punctured myself, I'd need a new set of tires every few weeks. Not to mention my body would look like a pincushion," he said, then added in a more serious tone, "But I promise I had a booster a little while ago."

Her smile turned to one of patient resignation. "Okay, I guess I trust you to take care of yourself." She turned her attention to starting the engine, then glanced back at him. "Goodbye, Quint."

He lifted a hand in farewell and she quickly backed

away from him, then headed the nose of her truck down the rocky drive.

The urge to watch her drive away clawed at Quint, but he forced himself to turn in the direction of the barn. Her unexpected visit was over, he told himself. More than likely she wouldn't return to the Golden Spur. And that was for the best.

The Diamond D thoroughbred ranch was located in a stretch of valley known as the Hondo Valley, a rich, fertile area where ranchers raised cattle and horses, and farmers tended acres of fruit orchards. To the north and south of the Donovan ranch house, desert mountains jutted starkly toward the sky, while in-between, irrigated meadows grew seas of knee-deep grass. The three-mile graveled track leading to the house split through one of those lush meadows and Maura drove slowly as she watched a herd of mares frolic with their colts behind a white board fence. Closer to the road, tall Lombardy poplars edged the long drive and towered like green spires into a sky as blue as Quint Cantrell's eyes.

A rueful grimace touched Maura's mouth as she steered her truck to a stop in front of the huge house built of native rock trimmed with rough cedar. She'd driven to the Diamond D this afternoon for a quick hello to her parents, whom she'd not seen in several weeks. This was hardly the time to be thinking about the young rancher with sky-blue eyes. In fact, no time was a good time to let her mind dwell on the man, Maura told herself. But for the past three days, since she'd visited his ranch, daydreaming about Abe's grandson was all that she seemed to be doing.

After letting herself in, Maura passed through a long foyer and was entering a formal great room, when Regina, a tall, middle-aged woman with short, brown hair, appeared through an open doorway.

The woman spotted her immediately and gave her a little wave. "Well, look who's here! Are you lost or something?"

Chuckling, Maura hurried across the room to kiss the woman's cheek. For the past twenty years Regina had worked as a maid for the family. To the Donovans she was as much a part of the family as the six children were.

"I had a few chores to do in town," Maura explained. "So I thought I'd drive out and let everyone know I'm still alive. Are my parents home? And Grandmother?"

Reggie snagged a hold on Maura's shoulder and turned her toward the rear section of the house. "Fiona's here. But Doyle drove your grandmother to Ruidoso for a visit with the dentist."

"Oh, shoot," Maura practically wailed, then sighed with resignation. "I should have called beforehand."

Reggie said, "Well, the dentist visit was unexpected. Kate bit down on a piece of hard candy and chipped a tooth. Doyle practically twisted his mother's arm to make her go have it examined."

At age eighty-three, Kate Donovan was still in great health and just independent enough to think she didn't need anyone taking care of her. Maura had always admired her grandmother's spunk, especially after Arthur, her husband and Maura's grandfather, died eight years ago. Since then Kate hadn't waned or whined. She'd continued to have an input into the ranch her husband had founded more than forty years ago.

By now Maura and the maid had reached a point in the hallway where a wide opening led into a huge family room. With a flick of her hand, Reggie gestured toward the opening.

"Fiona is still in there, I think. Would you like me to bring in some fresh coffee, Maura? And I think Opal did some baking."

Maura smiled gratefully at the woman. "You're wonderful, Reggie. That would be great."

Moments later, as Maura stepped into the long room, she spotted her mother sitting at a small desk. Even from several feet away, Fiona's beauty radiated like a full bloomed rose. Her hair, threaded with silver, was still mostly black and wrapped in an elegant chignon at the back of her neck. A pair of dark slacks and pale pink blouse enhanced her slender figure.

Maura couldn't imagine looking so wonderful at fifty-nine years of age, especially after giving birth to six children and raising them to adulthood. But then Maura couldn't imagine herself with even one child. To have a family, she first needed a man. And after being so careful and turning down dates in her twenties, she'd done a miserable job when she'd chosen Gil.

Fiona must have heard her footsteps on the tile because she suddenly looked up from her work.

"Maura! Darling!"

The other woman put the ledger aside and rose to her feet. Maura hurried toward her mother's outstretched arms. After a brief hug, Fiona stepped back and gave her daughter a thorough glance. "My gracious! You look so rested and pretty! And that dress—I've never seen you wear anything like it."

For the first time in ages, Maura had felt a bit daring this morning. Instead of her usual jeans and blouse, she'd pulled a halter-styled sundress from her closet. The flowery fabric exposed Maura's back and arms and revealed a hint of cleavage. No doubt her mother was wondering about this new flirtatious image. Especially since Maura was considered the most reserved of the Donovan sisters and usually dressed the part.

"It's very warm out today," she said in a dismissive way, then took her mother by the hand and drew her down on a long couch upholstered in red suede.

"Your father and grandmother are at the dentist's office," Fiona explained. "They should be back well before dinner. Do you plan to stay?"

Having dinner with her big, boisterous family was probably just the thing Maura needed to get Quint Cantrell from her mind. But Abe would be looking for her to return soon and though he didn't demand her company every minute of the night and day, she wanted to get back to Apache Wells before a late hour.

"Not tonight, Mother. Abe will be expecting me."

Fiona grimaced. "You told me the man wasn't that ill. Surely you could be away for one evening," she argued. "Aren't there other people on the ranch who could watch out for him?"

Maura bit back a sigh. She wasn't in the mood to defend her job to her mother. She didn't want to have to explain to Fiona that her fondness for Abe was only part of the reason she'd chosen to live and work on Apache Wells. The problems she'd endured at the hospital with Dr. Weston were something she'd only shared with her sister Bridget. And she'd only discussed the matter with her because Bridget was a doctor and understood the nuances of medical life.

Before Maura had taken the job with Abe, Bridget had advised her to tell Dr. Weston to take his tacky flirting and go jump in the lake. And Maura had attempted to do that. Only in a nicer way. He'd not gotten the message and as

Maura had contemplated Abe's offer, she'd decided that even if Dr. Weston had gotten the message and quit pursuing her, the awkwardness of being around him would remain.

Face it, Maura, you jumped at Abe's offer because you're afraid to deal with men. Because you're too much of a chicken to think about the dating game or confronting a man that might want you in a romantic way. You knew that you could hide on Apache Wells. Hide from men and your own failure as a woman.

The mocking voice inside her caused Maura to instinctively stiffen her spine. Maybe taking the job with Abe had been an escape for her. But since then she'd developed deep feelings for Abe and he'd become an important part of her life. To Maura, that alone was enough to justify her job.

"Tonight isn't a good time, Mother. But I'll make a point to come out for supper soon. I promise."

Thankfully, Fiona didn't press the issue and after Reggie arrived with coffee and homemade pralines, their conversation turned to Maura's siblings and other happenings within the Donovan family.

A little more than an hour later, Maura bade her mother goodbye and was walking through the foyer to leave the house when her younger sister suddenly popped through the door.

"Maura!"

"Bridget!"

Both women laughed as their names came out in unison.

"Okay, you first, big sister," Bridget said. "What are you doing here?"

Maura gave her younger sister a brief hug. "I could ask the same of you. Aren't you working today?"

Bridget, who was somewhat shorter than Maura and had flaming copper hair, grinned in naughty fashion. "S-s-shh. I'm supposed to be back at the clinic by now. But I made a house call not far from here and I thought I'd stop by for a few minutes and see what I can swipe from the kitchen."

"Opal just made pralines," Maura told her.

"Sugar. That's not what I need," she said while patting a hand on her waist, then her green eyes sparkled as she took a closer look at Maura.

"My, my. You're looking sexy today. What's the occasion? Trying to give old Mr. Cantrell a heart attack or something?"

"Bridget! You're awful! You shouldn't be allowed to practice medicine!" Maura scolded.

Bridget laughed and Maura wondered how it would feel to be able to really laugh, to look at life with the same fun and excitement she'd once had. Perhaps if she'd been smart enough to avoid men entirely, the way her little sister had, she'd still be a happy woman.

"I've had a few patients tell me that very thing," she confessed with another chuckle.

Maura started to scold her again, but the cell phone in her purse suddenly rang. Quickly, she fished out the small instrument and was faintly surprised to see the caller was Abe.

"Excuse me for a moment, Bridget. I'd better take this."

Bridget lingered in the foyer while Maura exchanged a few brief words with the man. Once she'd ended the call, Bridget looked at her with concern.

"What's the matter? Who was that? You've gone pale."

As her sister shot questions at her, Maura slowly put the phone back in her handbag.

"It was Abe. He wanted to let me know that we're going to have company tonight."

"Is that all? From the look on your face I thought a tornado was about to hit. Who is this company anyway? Someone interesting?"

Maura did her best to wipe all expression from her face. "You might think so. It's Quint Cantrell. Abe's grandson."

"Mmm. I saw him not too long ago in Ruidoso," Bridget said thoughtfully. "I was pulling into a parking space on the street and he was coming out of the Blue Mesa. I have to admit he looks sexier now than he did when we were in high school."

Like a jolt of loud, unexpected thunder, jealousy shook Maura. "Then maybe you should join us for dinner," she quipped. "I'm sure you'd be more than welcome."

Unaware of her sister's reaction, Bridget playfully wrinkled her nose. "No thanks, sis. Quint obviously isn't into redheads with freckles. Actually," she added in a more serious tone, "I don't think he's into women. Period. Not after the wringer Holly put him through."

For the past few days that was exactly what Maura had been telling herself. The man didn't want a woman in his life. Yet during that short time she'd spent with him on the Golden Spur, he'd touched her, looked at her as though he'd actually wanted to be close to her. Or had that only been the twisted imaginings of a lonely divorcée?

One way or the other, Maura supposed she would find out tonight. And she wasn't ready for the answer.

"Maura? Are you all right?"

As Bridget touched her arm, Maura's thoughts jerked back to the present and she turned a strained look on her sister.

"Sure. Why wouldn't I be?"

Her gaze shrewdly studying Maura's face, Bridget shrugged. "I don't know. You tell me. Is something going on with Quint that you haven't told me about?"

Setting her jaw, Maura quickly turned and started toward the door. "Don't worry, little sister. If I see that Quint Cantrell is back into women you'll be the first to know."

Chapter Four

An hour later, when Maura arrived back at Apache Wells, she was surprised to find Quint's pickup already parked next to Abe's old Ford. But once she entered the small ranch house, neither he nor Abe was anywhere to be found.

But before she could get to her room to change out of her revealing dress she heard voices on the porch, then footsteps entering the house.

"Maura! Where are you, girl?"

Abe's yells had her groaning as she turned from her room. Quint would just have to see her like this and she'd have to appear as though she was comfortable with exposing plenty of skin to his sharp gaze.

"Here I am," she announced as she stepped into the cozy living room.

Abe, who'd been reclining in his favorite leather chair, plopped his boots on the floor and let out a low whistle.

Across from him, sitting at one end of a long couch, Quint stared at her. Maura found it much easier to focus her gaze on the elder Cantrell.

"Ooooeee! Don't you look pretty!" The old man glanced over at Quint. "Look at her, boy. Have you ever seen anything so pretty around here?"

Quint's shocked stare couldn't decide if it wanted to settle on Maura or his grandfather. "Grandma wasn't exactly ugly," he reminded a grinning Abe.

Abe's grin turned into an impatient frown for his grandson. "Been many a long year since your grandma was with us. It's high time we had another pretty woman in the house."

Across the room, Maura cleared her throat and like a magnet Quint felt his gaze drawn to her slender image outlined by the open doorway. The flowered dress she was wearing made her look all woman and then some. His male ego wanted to think she'd worn the sexy garment for his benefit, but he knew otherwise.

"You should have warned me earlier that Quint would be here for supper," Maura said to Abe. "I would've gotten back sooner. It will take me a while to prepare something and—"

"Forget about cookin', honey!" Abe interrupted. "I didn't hire you as kitchen help! Jim has already fixed things. All we have to do is heat it up."

She looked surprised and Quint got the feeling that his grandfather probably manipulated his nurse as much as he tried to maneuver him. He could only wonder how long Maura would be willing to put up with the old man and what it would do to him when she flew the coop.

Maura said, "Oh. Well, I usually prepare our meals. You—"

"Tonight you're gettin' a rest," Abe interrupted again. "So don't worry about it."

A smile fluttered around her lips. "All right."

Abe motioned for Quint to get to his feet. "Go find us some of that blackberry wine and pour us all a drink, Quint. I feel like celebrating tonight."

Quint rose from the couch and ambled toward the door-way where Maura still stood. "What do you have to be celebrating?" he asked his grandfather.

"Bein' alive. Ain't that enough?"

Quint exchanged a pointed look with Maura and this time when she smiled the expression was genuine.

"I'll help you find some glasses," she told him.

He followed her down a short hallway and into the small kitchen. Along the way, he caught the rosy scent of her perfume as his eyes watched the folds of her dress move to the sway of her shapely hips.

Lord, it was no wonder Abe was behaving in such a goofy manner, Quint thought. Just looking at this woman was enough to send a man's temperature skyrocketing.

"I think the wine is over there," she said while pointing to a white metal cabinet situated at the far end of the room. "If you'll look for it, I'll find the wineglasses."

Drawing in a deep breath, Quint tore his eyes off her backside and headed to the cabinet. "Gramps hardly ever drinks spirits. I don't know what's come over him—he's acting strangely happy," he mumbled as he pushed aside cans and jars on the jammed pantry shelf. "Is it okay for him to drink this stuff, anyway?"

He pulled out the bottle of blackberry wine and walked over to the cabinet where she was placing goblets on a silver tray.

"A small amount won't hurt," she said, then slanted a

glance at him. "And why do you call Abe being happy strange? I'd think him being happy is a good thing."

It would be a good thing, Quint thought, if his grandfather's joy didn't depend on a woman. He'd learned through the years that they were fickle creatures and more often than not slanted the truth to their own advantage. Before their breakup, he'd caught Holly in several lies, yet she'd insisted she'd kept the truth from him because she'd loved him. He'd heard the same excuse from his own mother when he'd discovered she'd been dishonest about her past. Women never separated right and wrong with a clear line. They always wanted to soften and blur the edges with emotions and reasons. As though that would keep a man from feeling hurt and betrayed.

"I just don't want his bubble burst."

After twisting off the cap, he offered the wine bottle to her. She took it and carefully began to fill each glass with a small amount of the dark liquid. Quint's gaze fell to the shiny crown of her head and the dark red strands of hair lying on her bare shoulders.

"You think I'm going to do something to hurt your grandfather?" she asked.

He wasn't expecting such a direct question from her, but then he probably should have. She had a blunt way of getting things out in the open.

"Not necessarily. Sometimes Gramps just expects too much out of people. And when they fall short he gets disappointed."

She leveled her green gaze on him and Quint felt his heart pause, then jerk into a rapid thud.

"Have you ever disappointed anyone, Quint?"

What was the matter with him? Why did just watching

her speak feel like an erotic adventure? Sexual starvation, he thought. And that was a fixable problem.

"Hell, yeah," he answered. "Haven't you?"

Something flickered in the depths of her eyes before they dropped away from his.

"Oh, yes. More than I'd like to think."

She drew in a deep breath, then looked up at him one more time. "Whatever you're thinking, Quint, I'm here to help your grandfather. Not hurt him. As long as you understand that, I think you and I can be friends."

He wanted to be more than Maura's friend. When he'd come to that realization, he wasn't sure. Maybe just a few seconds ago when he'd looked at her moist lips. Or had it been minutes ago when he'd first looked up and saw her standing in the doorway, that dress hugging her breasts like the hands of a lover? Yes, he wanted to be more than Maura Donovan's friend and the idea was shaking the fire right out of him. She wasn't a casual sort of woman. But his body didn't seem to care one whit about that fact.

"I believe you're here to help Gramps. So let's not rehash the issue, okay?"

A slow smile spread across her face and Quint stifled a groan. If he could just kiss those luscious lips once, maybe twice, then he could hopefully put these crazy urges behind him.

"I'm perfectly agreeable to that," she said, then picked up the tray and offered it to him. "We'd better get back to Abe before he thinks we've deserted him."

Smiling to himself, Quint took the tray and followed her out of the room.

Much later, as the three of them finished coffee around the dinner table, Maura quietly listened while Quint and his grandfather discussed the pros and cons of allowing Red Bluff Mining Company to reopen the Golden Spur. Maura's knowledge about mining or taking gold from raw ore was practically nil, but from listening to their debate she could see that each man had good, solid reasons to back up his stand on the subject.

Throughout the meal, Maura had been a bit surprised to see that Quint wasn't a yes-man to Abe on any subject, even though the elder Cantrell was the patriarch of the family and held the strings to a fortune in land and money. Clearly Quint respected his grandfather, but he wasn't shy about speaking up when he didn't agree with the old man.

Maura admired Quint's spunk, but she was touched even more by the closeness and love she felt flowing between the two men. Gilbert had never shown much respect for his parents or tried to be a part of her family. She'd often voiced her disapproval about his lack of family connection and tried to make him see the joys he was missing, but her pleas had gone unheeded. One thing she knew for certain about Quint, he'd always be around for anyone he cared about.

"All right, Gramps, I'll call them. Maybe not in the next few days. But soon. And I'll get a rough estimate as to the initial cost to start things up. But that's all I'm going to promise. I'm not interested in gold," Quint was saying to Abe.

Maura smiled to herself as she saw Abe's eyes begin to twinkle. Clearly he believed he was the winner tonight.

"Maybe not. But the gold will make it easier for you to be a rancher. And it sure as heck might be nice to leave to your young'ns."

The muscles around Quint's mouth tightened, but he didn't make any sort of reply to his grandfather's suggestion. Maura wasn't surprised. When she'd brought up the idea of him raising children, he'd turned as cool as a frosty morning. Which could only mean he wasn't interested in acquiring a wife, much less kids.

Putting down his coffee cup, Abe stretched his arms over his head, then pushed back his chair. "Well, I'm gonna go watch a little news," he said. "Quint, why don't you take Maura down to the stables and show her the new stud. She's not seen him yet."

Fully expecting Quint to come up with an excuse to leave, Maura got to her feet and began gathering the dirty dishes. "That's all right, Abe," she said, not bothering to glance Quint's way. "I can walk down to the stables another time. It's almost dark anyway."

"It's at least another half hour until dark," Quint spoke up. "We have plenty of time."

Maura's gaze jerked to the end of the table just in time to see him rising from his seat. Instead of a look of boredom, she was surprised to see a smile on his face.

"Are you game?" he asked.

"Uh—sure." She glanced down at the plates she was holding. "Just let me put these away."

"I'll help you clear the table."

Flustered by this turn of events, Maura hardly noticed Abe quietly leaving the kitchen.

"There's no need," she told him. "I'll gather everything up later. We'd better not waste daylight."

She put the plates in the sink, then turned to see he was waiting for her by the door. As she joined him, her heart began to pitter-patter like a rain shower threatening to turn into an all-out storm.

"The evening might get cool before we get back," he suggested, his eyes sliding slowly over her bare shoulders. "Do you think you might need something to cover your arms?"

"You're probably right. Hold on," she told him, then hurried out of the room. By the time she fetched a shawl from her bedroom closet, she was breathless and silently berating herself for behaving like some besotted teenager. Quint Cantrell was merely being polite and friendly, she told herself. This was only a walk. Not a date.

Once the two of them were off the back porch and walking down the middle of the dirt road that led to the ranch yard, Maura breathed deeply and tried to relax.

"I really didn't expect you to go through with this," she said honestly. "I mean—Abe can be so obvious sometimes. And he doesn't stop to think that you might have more important things to do than show me a horse."

Except for the crunch of gravel beneath their feet, the night was quiet. When Quint chuckled softly, the sound wrapped around her like the warm night air.

"I think showing you a horse is far more important than talking about that damned old mine. I was glad for an excuse to get away."

Smiling, she glanced at him. "Well, I understand you're not keen on inviting that sort of mining hubbub onto your ranch, but I think you're wonderful for listening to your grandfather's dreams and taking them seriously."

He shrugged as though he didn't warrant her compliment. "He's always listened to mine. And in spite of him being so cantankerous, he's a very wise man. I'd be a fool not to listen to him."

Too bad Gilbert had been so full of himself that he'd not looked to his family or anyone for advice, Maura thought. He'd believed himself to be smarter, slicker and savvier than anyone around him. And to a point, he had been, she thought grimly. He'd certainly fooled her for years. Was that what love did to a woman? Blinded her ability to see the truth, twisted her judgment? Until her love for him had begun to crumble, she'd not seen the real man.

"So how is your arm doing?" she asked after a moment. "I don't suppose you went to the doctor and got stitches."

"No. But it's healing."

It seemed the farther they walked, the closer he was drawing to her side. Maura tried not to notice, but that was fairly impossible to do when her heart was hammering in her chest.

"One of the best things I like about working for your grandfather is having time to be outdoors," she said. "Before, putting in long hours at the hospital didn't leave me much time or energy for walks outside."

"Did you do hospital work before you moved back to Hondo Valley?" he asked.

Before her divorce, she thought ruefully. Clearing her throat, she gazed ahead at a stand of tall pines and the long, dark shadows slipping across the road. Beyond the distant mountains, the sinking sun painted a bank of clouds pink and gold and as she admired the beauty, she realized she was just now coming awake after a long, long sleep.

"No. I worked at a large health clinic. Which was hectic, but rewarding."

"Forgive me if this sounds tacky, Maura, but we both know that you don't have to work at anything. I mean— your family has made millions and you're obviously wealthy. You could travel the world and be a lady of leisure."

She looked at him, then burst out laughing. "Oh, Quint. That's so funny. Me, a lady of leisure? I'd be bored out of my mind. And everyone has a reason for being, don't you think? I like to be doing—to make a difference for others. Don't you?"

He smiled and then his expression turned sober. "I guess I've never thought about it that much. I suppose from the time I was a boy I've been on a mission to keep the ranches going. As for making a difference for others—I must be selfish. I do what I do, because in the end, it pleases me."

Her eyes softened as she studied his face. "That's not entirely true, Quint. I don't know you all that well, but I can see that you want to make a difference for your grandfather, your mother. That's not a self-centered man."

One corner of his lips tilted to a wicked little grin. "You're wrong, Maura. I am selfish." One hand reached out and wrapped itself around her shoulder. "Because right now all I'm thinking about is what I want."

She shivered as heat rushed from the spot where he was touching her and shot to every particle of her body.

"And what is that?" she asked in a strained voice.

"To kiss you."

He watched her lips part with shock, but he didn't give her the chance to utter a word or move away. Placing a finger beneath her chin, he bent his head and settled his lips firmly over hers.

Soft. Incredibly soft. And oh, so sweet. Those thoughts tumbled through Quint's brain as his lips began to move against hers, to search for even more of her honeyed goodness. Mindlessly, his arms slipped around her waist and drew her ever closer.

Between them, he felt her hands flatten against his chest, then reach upward to his shoulders. The warmth of her spread through him like a white-hot sun baking his skin, heat seeping right down to his bones.

How long had it been since he'd kissed a woman? Since he'd wanted to kiss a woman? He couldn't remember.

Couldn't think. While his mind turned to mush, the rest of his body burst to life, buzzed as though her lips were liquid spirit, intoxicating, luring, begging him to surrender to the moment. To her.

Fired by a hunger that threatened to consume him, his hands pressed into her back and crushed her body up against his. Beneath his lips, hers opened like an exotic flower, tempting him to taste the center. When his tongue delved inside, she moaned low in her throat.

The feral sound matched the urgency inside him and it was all he could do to keep his hands anchored at her back instead of allowing them to cup her breasts, the swell of her bottom, to drag her hips forward and grind them against his aching arousal.

He wasn't sure how much time had ticked by when she finally pulled her mouth from beneath his and stepped back. For all he knew, it could have been long minutes or even hours since he'd first tugged her into his arms.

No matter, he thought, as he sucked in a harsh breath and tried to collect his senses. However long their kiss had lasted, it hadn't gone on long enough to suit him. Even though she was looking at him with stunned dismay, everything inside him was screeching for him to hang on to her, to capture her lips all over again.

So much for kissing Maura and getting her out of your system, Quint.

"I...think we'd better forget about walking on to the stables," she said in a breathless rush. Then before he could say anything, she turned on her heel and took off in long strides toward the house.

Before she could take three steps, Quint caught her by the shoulder and spun her back to him.

"Wait, Maura! We can't go back to the house now!"

Her breasts moved up and down as she struggled to regain her breath and Quint was amazed to find himself just as winded and shaken as she. As he watched her lips form a perfect O, he had to fight the urge to sear them back together with another kiss.

"We can't?" she murmured. "Why?"

"Because—" Heaving out another heavy breath, he shook his head. "After what just happened we—"

"Need to come to our senses and get back to safety," she finished for him.

His hands wrapped around her upper arms and held them tightly as though he wanted to make sure she couldn't escape.

"Safety? You think I... That we—our attraction is something to run from?"

She needed to run from herself more than him. But she couldn't admit such a thing. It would be like telling him she wasn't capable of controlling herself or her sexual urges whenever she was near him. Oh, God, how embarrassing.

"I think—" Twisting her head aside, she closed her eyes and tried not to think about the heavenly way he'd made her feel. So alive. So sexy. So wanted. "Things were about to get carried away, Quint. And I—I'm not ready for something like that."

There was a long pause, and while she waited for his reply, she tried to calm her racing heart, tried to tell herself that the kiss was no big deal. Even though it was the biggest thing she could ever remember happening to her.

"I never meant for the kiss to go so far, Maura," he said lowly. "That just seemed to happen."

Turning her face back to his, she opened her eyes and felt a jolt to her senses as she gazed into his blue ones. He was probably the most sexual, sensual man she'd ever met and to say that his kiss had been potent would be an understatement. Her knees were still quivering.

Mortified, she said, "I was in on it, too, Quint. It's just as much as my fault for letting it go on." And on and on, she mentally added.

"Why should it be anyone's fault? Why are you so bothered about this? It's not like we committed a crime—or hurt anyone."

She looked down at the ground while inside her emotions were tumbling, falling, rolling away at a speed too fast to allow her to catch up.

"That's true."

"And you did like it. As much as I liked it," he pointed out.

"I can't deny that," she admitted.

"So? Why are you trying to race back to the house? To end our walk?"

He called this a walk? She shivered to think what a deliberate rendezvous would be.

Her gaze dropped to the toes of his brown boots. "I shouldn't have to explain. But it looks as though I must." Her eyes fluttered back up to his. "I'm not the type to—well, just be a diversion for a man. And we both know that's all you want. A kiss, maybe two. Maybe you even want to have sex with me."

"The thought did occur to me."

Her nostrils flared at his flippant reply. "Well, it isn't going to happen."

Amusement dimpled his cheek long before a chuckle passed his lips. "That's what you think."

A mixture of annoyance and excitement rushed through her, pushing her heartbeat to an even higher rate. "And why? Why would you want a woman like me?"

Before he could answer, she twisted away from his grasp and began walking. By now it was growing dark and she could only think how easy it would be to fall into Quint's arms, to let him show her, remind her that she was still a woman. A woman who'd not been made love to in a long, long time.

He snaked an arm around her waist and once again forced her to stop in her tracks and face him.

"What does that mean? A woman like you?"

He brought his palms up to her face and Maura felt her knees threaten to buckle as he rubbed his thumbs against her cheeks. She was getting glimpses of what he would be like as a lover and those indications were far too tempting for a wounded woman like her.

"Oh, Quint," she said in a strained voice, "surely you can see what I'm talking about. For starters I'm six years older than you."

He frowned. "What does that have to do with anything?"

Maura rolled her eyes. "There's a gap between us."

"We can fix that," he drawled, then jerked her forward until the front of her body was brushing his. "See? No gap at all. In fact, I can tighten it even more."

He was being a hopeless flirt. Almost playful. Something she didn't think him capable of. Before this evening, the only Quint Cantrell she'd seen was a serious, work-driven man. She couldn't imagine what had brought about this change in him. Surely not her.

"There are other kinds of gaps, Quint. You're young and single." She didn't bother to add "rich, attractive and considered one of the biggest catches in Lincoln County."

"You are, too."

"I'm divorced," she said thickly.

"That doesn't make you contaminated."

She couldn't do anything but laugh and when a smile suddenly spread across his face, it made her feel good, better than she'd felt in a long, long while.

"See," he said, "you were taking one little kiss way too seriously."

The embrace that had gone on between them had been more than one little kiss. But he was right. The best thing she could do for both of them was to treat this whole thing in a casual way. The last thing he needed to know was that he'd shaken the very earth beneath her feet.

"You're right. I suppose I have been making too much of it."

The grin on his face deepened. "We still have a little twilight left. Let's walk on to the stables," he urged. "You don't want to have to tell Gramps you couldn't make it that far."

That wouldn't be nearly as embarrassing as returning to the house with red cheeks and swollen lips, she thought wryly. "All right. Let's go on. But—"

When she broke off with uncertainty, he quickly finished, "Don't worry, you've made it clear you've had enough kissing for tonight."

He slipped his arm across the back of her waist and as he urged her on toward the ranch yard, Maura could only think she might have Quint completely fooled, but not herself. She'd not had nearly enough of his kisses. Or his company. And with each step she took by his side, she wondered if she was headed toward a very special place or the hell of another heartache.

Chapter Five

A few days later, as the weekend approached, Maura was considering driving over to the Diamond D on Saturday. Her mother was still hounding her about having supper with her family and Maura knew that Fiona wouldn't let up with her nagging until her eldest daughter showed up.

But on Friday evening Abe came in early from the ranch yard and spent the last waning hours of sunlight in his easy chair. The behavior was out of character and, though he insisted he felt fine, Maura suspected the man was dizzy but just didn't want to admit it to her.

Deciding she needed to stay close, Maura crossed the family meal off her plans and promised herself to go another time, when Abe wasn't behaving so peculiarly. But by Saturday afternoon, he appeared to be back to his normal self and raring to get back with the ranch hands.

Late that evening, sometime after dark, Abe was still out when she answered the phone and was vaguely surprised to hear Quint's voice. Since Abe carried his own cell phone, his relatives usually called him directly on it rather than over the landline.

"Hi," he said. "I was about to think you weren't in the house."

Just the sound of his voice caused her heart to trip over itself and she realized no man had ever made her feel so giddy and young.

"I was in the laundry room," she explained. "Abe is still down at the ranch yard. Did you try his cell?"

"I'm not calling to talk to Gramps," he answered. "I wanted to speak with you."

A warm flush swept up her torso and over her face. Since the night of their little kissing spree, she'd not seen or heard from him and she'd tried to write the whole thing off as a frivolous impulse on his part. There'd not been any other way to explain his behavior.

"Oh. Well, if you've been concerned about Abe, don't be. He appears to be back to normal."

"Concerned? I didn't realize anything had been amiss with Gramps. I talked to him this morning. He sounded fine. Has anything been wrong?"

"Not exactly. Yesterday he stayed indoors more than usual. That's all. But that appears to be over with now."

"Good. Then you wouldn't feel anxious about leaving the ranch for a few hours?"

Maura's mind raced ahead. What could he be getting at? "No. I wouldn't worry. Why?"

There was a long pause and then he spoke in a low voice that skittered lazily down Maura's backbone.

"Because I wanted to see if you'd like to come over to

the Golden Spur tomorrow. I've finally gotten a few of my good horses moved over here and I thought the two of us might take a ride. Maybe have a little picnic."

It was a good thing Maura had sat on the edge of the armchair when she'd picked up the phone, otherwise she would probably be collapsing with shock.

"You're inviting me on an outing?" she asked bluntly.

He chuckled. "Why not? I can't think of anybody else I'd rather ask."

What about asking no one and going on the ride alone, she silently asked. What about the guy who was so swamped with work he didn't socialize? The guy who wasn't that interested in women?

Her hands began to tremble ever so slightly and she gripped them tightly around each end of the telephone receiver in order to steady them.

"I don't know, Quint. It's been ages since I've been on a horse."

"More reason for you to accept my invitation. So you can get back in the saddle."

The heat in her cheeks grew hotter and she was very relieved he couldn't see her. "I thought you had lots of work to do," she countered. "That's what Abe is always telling me."

"He's right. My kind of work never gets caught up. But tomorrow is Sunday. After church, I don't work."

She'd not expected him to be a man who kept the Sabbath. But then she didn't really know everything there was to know about Abe's grandson. Other than he was as sexy as all get-out and the perfect picture of walking, talking danger.

Releasing a long breath, she passed the tip of her tongue over her lips. The other night, after they'd walked on to the horse stables, he'd remained a perfect gentleman. She couldn't believe the man was going to this much trouble just for a chance to kiss her again. Maybe he actually wanted her company? Liked her company? The idea thrilled her even more than the memory of their torrid kiss.

"Oh. Well, you make it sound like I shouldn't refuse."

"I'm not going to let you. Can you be here by twelve?"

If she went on this outing with Quint, what would Abe think? What would her own family think?

You're a grown woman, Maura. This is nobody's business but yours. And it's high time you started acting like a woman instead of a fraidy cat.

Bolstered by that idea, she blurted, "Sure. I can be there by noon. What do I need to bring?"

"Nothing, except yourself. Just be sure to wear heavy jeans and cowboy boots. Just in case you get too close to a jumping cactus."

She assured him that she'd be there at twelve and wearing appropriate riding gear, then they exchanged goodbyes. As Maura slipped the receiver back on its hook, she stared dazedly around the small kitchen, while a part of her wanted to dance and shout, laugh and run about the room like a wild thing that had just been let loose from a cage.

But she stopped herself short of expressing such exuberance. This wasn't the first date she'd been asked on since her divorce with Gilbert, she grimly reminded herself. One of the main reasons she was here on Apache Wells was because Dr. Weston had made a daily habit of asking her to go out with him. So why had she continually turned him down and jumped at the first chance she'd gotten to be with Quint?

Because when Dr. Weston had looked at her, talked to her, the only thing Maura had felt was annoyance. There'd been no sudden pounding of her heart or normally even breaths dissolving into soft little gasps. No heat firing her blood, urging her to touch, to move closer and even closer still.

Had she gone crazy? She'd run from Dr. Weston as though he was the devil incarnate and straight to Quint Cantrell. A man that made the good doctor seem as hazardous as downing a bowl of vanilla pudding.

The next morning, Quint slapped pieces of meat between slices of white bread sopped with mayonnaise, then covered them in plastic wrap and shoved them in a worn saddlebag. For dessert, he smeared peanut butter and jelly on wheat bread, wrapped the lot up and added them to the meat sandwiches. In the opposite saddlebag, he packed cans of beer and soda, then felt enormously proud of himself for remembering to add napkins.

He supposed he should have driven into town and purchased something special for the picnic meal. Like fried chicken and chocolate cake. But he was miles from town. And anyway, he didn't want to buy Maura's friendship. He wanted her to like him just for himself. Not because he was rich. Or young. Or good-looking. The last of which he'd never thought of himself, until she'd said such a thing to him the other night.

The other night.

Even now, days later, he could easily recall the way she'd felt wrapped in his arms, the way her lips had tasted against his. For a moment he closed his eyes as images and sensations assaulted his senses, filled him with hunger.

Maybe spending more time with Maura was asking for trouble. For the past four days, he'd been asking himself what he was doing by allowing himself to get so caught up in the woman. He'd not set out to get this involved. He'd only meant to kiss her, to prove to himself that she wasn't some sort of walking goddess.

But that kiss had done something to him and by the time it had ended he'd felt as though he'd been spun around in a violent whirlwind, then dropped into another world. Everything around him had suddenly seemed different, felt different.

Later, he'd realized he had to find out why she'd affected him so. Why one little red-haired nurse had put a spark in him like no woman he'd ever met.

With the saddlebags packed, Quint carried them down to the barn, where he began saddling two of his most dependable horses. He was tightening the back cinch on the last mount when a male voice sounded behind him.

"Hey, what's with the horses? You're not going to ride fence today, are you?"

Groaning inwardly, Quint turned around to see Jake standing a few feet behind him. He wished the other man hadn't shown up right now. Maura would be here soon and he'd just as soon not discuss his personal life with his old friend.

"No. I have something else planned," he told the other man.

"Oh. Well, I came by to see if you'd like to drive over to Bonito Lake and do a little trout fishing."

Resting his arm on the mare's rump, Quint stared at the other man. "Fishing? Since when have you taken up a rod?"

Shrugging, Jake turned his gaze toward the open doorway of the barn. "I used to like it. When I was young and Dad was still around."

"You've never told me that."

"No."

"So what made you want to go fishing today?" Quint persisted.

"Mom has been wanting some fresh trout. And she hasn't been feeling well." With a self-deprecating grin, he glanced at Quint. "I don't always just think of myself."

Quint figured most people thought of Jake as a rounder, a guy who was only out to have fun, but he knew there was another side to his old friend, one that he kept fairly hidden.

Quint smoothed his hand over the mare's rump. "Well, I would have liked to go with you," he said. "But I'm going on a picnic."

Jake chuckled. "Picnic, hell."

"Okay, let me rephrase this so you'll understand. I'm going riding and taking food with me."

"Man, you'd better get that redheaded nurse back over here to check your temperature. 'Cause you're definitely sick."

Turning back to the mare's side, Quint began to unnecessarily adjust the latigo. "You don't need to worry about my health, Jake. The redheaded nurse is going with me."

Quint could hear the other man's footsteps drawing closer.

"Maura Donovan? You're going riding with her?"

"That's right."

There was a very long pause and then Jake said, "A man only takes a woman he *really* likes riding."

Quint supposed Jake was right. The few women he'd tried to get interested in since Holly, he'd taken on traditional dates like dinner and a movie. During those outings, he been bored and wondering why he'd bothered in the first place.

"If you're asking if I like Maura, I do."

"Hmm. You gettin' serious about her?"

Faint unease stabbed Quint as he combed his fingers through the mare's black mane. "Me? Get serious about a woman? You know me better than that, ol' buddy."

"Yeah. How could I forget that you're a warped man? You don't have a decent thing to offer a woman."

Turning from the horse, Quint glared at the other man. "Don't you think you'd better head on to the lake? You can't catch a fish in the middle of the day."

Jake chuckled. "Aren't you lucky that term doesn't apply to a woman?"

Before Quint could make a retort, the other man turned and headed toward the open doorway.

"See you in the morning," he called out.

As Jake disappeared from view, Quint wondered if catching Maura was what he really wanted. If he did catch her, what would he do, besides the obvious? He didn't want a wife. At least, he didn't think he did. To be a good husband, a man had to invest a hell of a lot of himself.

At one time, when he'd been engaged to Holly, he'd thought that way of life was the way he wanted to go. His father, Lewis, had been a great husband and father. He'd been a happy man and he'd loved his wife until the last second of his life. Quint had wanted to follow his example. He'd wanted that same deep connection with a woman that his father had shared with his mother. But Quint had failed at a real love. Why the heck would he want to risk going through all that pain and humiliation over again?

Because your house is empty. Your bed is empty. Your heart is empty.

"Quint? Are you in here?"

Maura's voice jerked him back to the present and he

looked around to see she'd entered the cavernous barn. The sight of her was like a sudden ray of sunshine and at that moment he decided that today he wasn't going to analyze or fret over his motives toward Maura. A man didn't have to have a good reason to simply enjoy himself.

"Over here," he called to her.

Spotting him, she walked to the middle of the wide alleyway and stood while he led the horses over to her.

As he drew near, she asked, "Have you been waiting on me?"

The smile on her face was bright and lovely and made Quint feel so unexpectedly happy that he could have waited on her for hours and not complained.

"Not really. I've just now finished saddling the horses. And Jake came by for a few minutes."

"As I was driving in, I met a truck on the road," she commented. "I thought you might have had company this morning.".

He grinned. "Jake isn't company. He's family."

"Yes. We Donovans have family like that, too," she said, then peered around his shoulder at the two horses. "Beautiful horses. Which one is mine?"

"The roan mare, Pearl. She's very smart and very mannerly. So I think you'll like her."

"I'm sure I will."

As she'd promised, she was dressed ruggedly in boots and blue jeans and a white shirt with the sleeves rolled back against her forearms. Her long hair was tied back from her face with a pale pink scarf and earrings made from polished cedar beads hung from her earlobes. Short of his mother, she was the only woman he knew that looked strong, yet utterly feminine at the same time, and in spite of himself he was totally drawn to her.

Using his head, he motioned toward the open doorway. "Shall we go? Do you have everything you'll need with you?"

"I brought saddlebags packed with a few things. They're just outside the barn door," she told him.

Once they were outside, Quint tied Maura's saddle-bags onto the back of Pearl's saddle.

"I thought we'd ride over to Chillicothe. That's about five miles from here. Think you can go that far before we eat?"

She chuckled. "Shouldn't you be asking if I can make it that far? Period?"

He turned to face her and Maura was completely taken with the easy smile on his face, the fetching dimple in his cheek.

"Sorry. I wasn't thinking that you might not be hardened to riding. Can you make it that far?" he asked.

"I think so. If not, just tie me to the saddle and swat Pearl on the rump. The two of us will end up some-where," she joked.

"I wouldn't think of putting Pearl through that sort of torture," he teased back, then added in a serious tone, "Don't worry. We'll take a break or two before we get there."

He handed her the mare's reins and she took a few moments to let the horse get accustomed to her smell.

"So where or what is Chillicothe?"

"A ghost town. It was built back in the mid-eighteen hundreds, when the Golden Spur was thriving. The old mine is just a short distance away from the town. I thought you might enjoy looking it all over."

"I'm sure I'll love it."

She led Pearl up a few steps, then lifted the reins over

her head. As she put her foot in the stirrup, she felt Quint's hands wrap around the sides of her waist. She wasn't expecting him to help her into the saddle and she glanced around with surprise.

"Pearl isn't that tall. I can manage," she assured him.

"My father always helped a lady into the saddle. So just in case he's watching I don't want to disappoint him."

With her toe still in the stirrup and her weight balanced on one boot, she paused long enough to allow her gaze to slide warmly over his face. "I'm very glad you invited me out today, Quint," she said softly.

"I'm very glad you're here," he replied, his gaze locking onto hers.

Feeling suddenly quite breathless, she cleared her throat and turned back to the horse. Taking her cue, he helped her into the saddle. Once he was confident that she was in control, he moved away and mounted his horse, a big brown gelding with a stripe down his nose.

"Chillicothe is to the northwest. This way," he said, motioning slightly to their left. "Not far from here, we'll hit the old road that led to the town. It's just a dim path now, but it makes for easy riding."

"Sounds great."

As they moved away from the barn, Maura swung Pearl alongside the big brown and the horses set out in an easy trot toward a pasture full of jumping choya. It was the time of summer for the plants to be in full bloom and the pink and yellow blossoms made for a pretty sight as they maneuvered their way through the prickly cacti.

"All of this area needs to be cleared away for pasture," Quint told her. "That's one of the things I'll be doing now that most of the barn and outbuildings are nearly finished."

"Oh, what a shame. The flowers are so beautiful."

"Yes, but there would be triple the amount of grass without them."

Maura cast him an impish look. "You're a practical man, aren't you? And not very much like Abe."

"Oh, I can loosen up—when I need to," he added.

She laughed. "Well, if you put a third less cattle on this particular range, then you could keep the flowers," she suggested.

Normally, Quint would have been quick to shoot down such a suggestion, calling it ridiculous and wasteful. But something about the pleasure she was gleaning from the cactus roses made him happy, made him reconsider even the smallest things around him.

"I'll think about that," he said.

Halfway through the ride to Chillicothe, they stopped near a deep arroyo. A shallow amount of water covered the rocky bottom while desert willows and twisted juniper grew at precarious angles from its loamy banks.

They rode down into the mini canyon, then dismounted and led the horses to the water's edge. The day had grown exceptionally warm and while the horses drank deeply, Quint shared his canteen with Maura.

Once the animals had their fill of water, they led them over to the bank and tethered the reins loosely around a willow limb.

After they were certain the horses were secured, Quint said, "I see a nice flat rock over there. Let's sit a few minutes before we head on to Chillicothe."

"Sounds good to me," she agreed. "Right now my legs feel like two pieces of rubber."

He offered his arm to her. "Here. You'd better hang on to me. Just in case you stumble."

"Thanks." She wrapped a hand around his forearm, then

quickly moved her clutch higher toward his elbow. "This is your cut arm," she explained. "I don't want to injure it again."

She could have torn the cut wide open again and Quint probably wouldn't have noticed. Just having her touching him again, walking close by his side, her body brushing against his was enough to send his libido into overdrive.

"Was my grandfather okay with you being gone from Apache Wells today?" Quint asked as he helped her get seated on the big boulder.

Smiling contentedly, she stretched her legs out in front of her. "He was more than okay. He was very happy."

He eased down beside her on the rock. "Hmmph. That's not surprising," he admitted. "Abe thinks I should show more interest in women. And he gets very disgusted with me when I don't."

Sighing, she looked up toward the sky. What had started out as nothing but bright blue sky this morning was now filled with fluffy white clouds.

"I know the feeling. Since my divorce, my mother thinks I should be out searching daily for another man." She shook her head. "She's been married to my father for nearly forty years. She has no idea how scary it would be without him."

Quint cast a curious glance her way. "Is it scary for you to be without your ex-husband?"

Her brows arched with faint surprise, she looked at him. "No. I know how to take care of myself. I just meant that it's scary to think about dating again. I guess—after Gilbert I don't trust men," she said, then swiftly shook her head. "That didn't exactly come out the way it should have. What I was trying to say is that I don't trust myself to pick the right man."

Oh, Lord, there had been so many times he'd felt that very same way, he thought. Choosing Holly had been one of the worst mistakes he'd ever made. And though Holly had done the cheating and the leaving, he still considered the whole affair as his mistake.

It had taken Quint quite a while to finally understand and admit to himself that he'd been blind and young where Holly had been concerned. He'd not been mature or wise enough to see that she'd been wrong for him in the first place.

Picking up a few pieces of gravel, he began to toss the tiny pebbles toward the pool of water. "You probably wouldn't want to tell me what happened to your marriage, would you?"

Even though he could only see her profile, it was enough to tell him that her expression had become shuttered.

"I wouldn't mind," she said, then glancing at him, her lips twisted sourly. "Gilbert married me for my money. I didn't know that at first. In fact, I didn't know it with certainty until the very end of our marriage. You see, he was a great actor."

"What do you mean by that?"

"Maybe I should start from the first to explain," she told him. "I'd been working at a clinic in Alamogordo when I first met Gil. We dated for about four months before I finally decided to accept his marriage proposal. Which was impulsive for me. Up until I met Gil I was very cautious about my relationships with men. But he'd come along at a time when I wanted to get on with my life and he'd been so attentive, so considerate of my needs and wants. He kept reassuring me that he wasn't interested in my money and I foolishly believed him. After all, he earned a good salary of his own and he never asked me for anything that was connected to finances."

"You're a rich woman, Maura. You never had suspicions about his motives?" His brows pulled together. "Damn, you must have been a trusting soul."

She groaned with regret. "That's what I meant about being a good actor. Gil was the sort that could make a person believe the sun was shining in the middle of a rainstorm. Even Mother believed he was sincere. But Daddy totally disapproved of him. He described Gil as slicker than an oil pit. At that time I thought Daddy was just being overly protective with his daughter. But unfortunately, it turned out that Daddy was right and I was the naive one. I believed Gil truly loved me."

He caught the sound of self-deprecation in her voice and was amazed at how much that sound depicted his own feelings.

"So how did you learn he'd married you for your money? Weren't there signs on the wall that you could have read?"

Maura answered ruefully, "There was nothing about Gil that appeared out of line. Until after we were married. And even then I didn't think it suspicious when he wanted to use our money—or technically you could call it my money—to buy luxury items like vehicles and boats and exotic vacations. He always reasoned the purchases away by insisting he wanted me to have the best of things. Because he loved me. Because I worked so hard as a nurse that I deserved them." Full of shame, she looked at him. "I couldn't see through him, Quint. I wanted to believe that he loved me so much he merely wanted to spoil me with gifts. I didn't want to consider, even for a moment, that he was in the marriage for ulterior reasons. But as time went on I couldn't ignore his lavish spending. Then finally I started asking myself if he was really buying these things for himself and using me as an excuse."

"How did you discover the truth?" he asked gently.

She let out a long sigh. "It all happened over the course of two or three years," she told him. "But the turning point began when I wanted to get pregnant and have a child."

Struck by that, he turned toward her. "He didn't want children?"

Shaking her head, she said, "Gil's job had him traveling at least three or four days out of the week, sometimes more. We both agreed that wasn't conducive to raising a family. So I promised to wait and he promised to put in for a desk job that would allow him to stay home. But year after year began to pass and everything stayed the same. He always came up with excuses as to why he couldn't change jobs within the company."

His expression stern, he said, "Maybe he resented the fact that you were working at a career you liked while you expected him to change jobs? What did he think about you working?"

"He did resent me asking him to change—but I didn't find out about that until—" She paused, then went on bitterly, "Well, until later. But as for me working, he was all for it. My job kept me occupied and out of his way. So that he'd be free to do his own thing."

"I think I see," he said thoughtfully. "So what did you do?"

She turned her palm upward in a helpless gesture. "I began to question him and he promptly accused me of nagging." Bending her head, she said in a strained voice, "Most women want to bear a child, Quint. That's all I wanted. But he couldn't even give me that much."

The pain in her voice stabbed him right in the middle of his chest. What kind of man would want to hurt this woman, lose this woman? he wondered.

"That's why you divorced him?"

She grimaced. "That was only a part of it, Quint. I found out…at the clinic where I worked, I accidentally overheard a couple of nurses discussing us. They were saying how sorry they felt for me because he'd had so many women during his travels and I didn't seem to know."

"What they were saying could have been unfounded gossip," he reasoned.

"That's what I wanted to think. But I confronted Gilbert about it and he confessed. He'd never intended to take a desk job or have a family. He liked things as they were. In short, he wanted his fun and a rich wife on the side."

"Sounds like a real nice bastard."

Her expression was stark as she turned her head and looked at him. "See. A man like that—I should have known all along. From the very first my father tried to warn me about Gilbert. But I was so blinded I wouldn't listen to him. I let love lead me around by the nose. And now—well, I'm not going to let that happen again."

Her firm vow sounded like so many he'd made to himself. And yet he had the strangest urge to tell her she shouldn't be bitter or wary. She was a gentle and lovely woman and some man would eventually come along and love her. Really love her. So why wasn't he thinking that about himself? he wondered wryly. He was a good and honest man. Why didn't he believe a good, sincere woman would come along and love him?

Quint couldn't answer that question. He didn't even try. Instead, all he could say was, "I understand where you're coming from, Maura."

Twisting her body toward his, she reached over and clasped his hand between hers. The unexpected touch warmed him, excited him in ways he'd couldn't explain.

"Do you, Quint? You and Holly—"

"Weren't compatible," he finished for her. "Mainly she wanted a different lifestyle than me. A rancher's day-to-day grind wasn't glamorous enough for her."

Maura frowned. "Everyone around here knew you would always be a rancher. Surely she didn't think you would change that for her."

Grimacing, he shook his head. "No. We'd been dating since high school, but when we got engaged we were both in our senior year of college and I was earning a degree in agriculture business. She had hopes that I would put that to use in other ways than a hands-on rancher. She saw me becoming an executive for some cattle-buying firm or working my up to a prestigious position in the equine business. Or even just sitting back and managing the ranch from an office."

A faint smile curved her lips. "I can't see you doing any of that. You're an outdoor man."

He grunted cynically. "Holly never understood that about me. She also believed we'd make our home at the Chaparral. I explained that I considered that my parents' home and I wanted something of my own. And when I made it clear that I wanted something far more modest than the Chaparral, she didn't hide her disappointment in me. In her opinion, I gave her plenty of reasons to look elsewhere. And maybe I did. But a man can't compromise his basic roots."

"Well, if I remember right the Johnsons were well-off," Maura reasoned. "I guess Holly's parents had always given her whatever she wanted. That's never a good thing."

Quint grimaced. "I thought her family being well-off meant that she couldn't be interested in my money. Not when she already had her own. I was a fool for not realizing that people like Holly always want more. I suppose when she met that rich real estate guy up in Denver she saw her chance to get everything she wanted. It didn't matter that he was nearly twice her age." Sarcasm twisted his features. "She would consider my little house on the Golden Spur a shack. But you know what, it's me and I like it. I wouldn't change it for her. For anyone."

"You shouldn't have to," she said softly.

Her fingers moved gently over the top of his hand as though she wanted to console him in some way. But Quint could have told her that he didn't need that sort of comforting from her. He wanted her lips fastened to his, her body crushed beneath him. The thought of making love to this woman was beginning to consume him and make everything else seem very unimportant. That couldn't be healthy. But he'd already gone past the point of stopping it.

He sighed. "Since Holly, I've met a few women who thought they could change me. In a way, I guess I've had the same sort of problem that you had with your ex. Most of the women I've dated seemed to equate Cantrell money with easy living. But that's not what I'm about, Maura."

"No," she said gently. "I can see you're not that sort of man."

He believed her and that in itself was scary. He wasn't expecting this woman to be able to read him, empathize with him. He'd looked for her to be cut from the same cloth as the rest that had come and gone in his life. The fact that she was so different knocked him totally off guard.

Clearing his throat, he tugged on her hand. "Well, time is getting on, we'd better mount up," he told her.

With his hand beneath her elbow, he helped her across the rocky ground and over to where the horses stood tethered in the shade. After a few minutes of untying reins and tightening girths, they were ready to mount up and Quint automatically moved behind Maura to assist her into the saddle.

He was about to reach for a hold on her waist when she suddenly turned to face him. And as he found his face close to hers, he felt his heart thudding hard and fast. She was looking at him with eyes as soft as a summer night.

"I just wanted to thank you, Quint. For listening to my troubles. I used to be terribly embarrassed for anyone to know that Gilbert chased after other women." Her long lashes fluttered demurely downward to hide her green eyes. "For a long time I thought—well, that I must be lacking as a woman. Now I'm beginning to believe that he was the one who was lacking something. Not me."

Quint couldn't stop himself from groaning as his hands settled on her shoulders. "Oh, Maura, you're lovely and sexy and I want to kiss you. Very much."

Maura didn't stop to think or even speak. She simply closed her eyes and leaned into him. And when his lips came hungrily down on hers, something inside her melted like a sand castle beneath a wash of tide. He swept her away, made her forget, made her long for all the things she'd been trying to forget.

Expecting the kiss to turn as torrid as it had the other night when he'd visited Apache Wells, Maura was surprised when he soon lifted his head and gave her a crooked grin.

"We'd better mount up this time," he said huskily. "Before I forget where we are."

Unable to do much more than nod, Maura turned to Pearl and, with Quint's help, climbed into the saddle. But as the two of them rode out of the quiet arroyo, all she could think about was being in his arms.

Chapter Six

Chillicothe consisted of five buildings grouped together in one small area and split by a dimly rutted road that, back in the town's heyday, had probably been considered the main street. These days, tall sage and prickly pear had taken over most of the roadway.

As Quint and Maura rode through the ghostly village, she looked around with keen interest.

"This is very neat—having an old mining settlement on your property," she said.

He shrugged. "It can also be a nuisance. Gramps and I are often approached about opening the place up to tourists. Some even suggest rebuilding it into a wild west town and charging admission. Can you imagine what a circus that would cause around here?"

"I wouldn't like it," she admitted. "What does Abe think?"

"Thank God he agrees with me on that issue. This little town is just like a grave site. It shouldn't be trampled on by a bunch of strangers."

Shaded by several tall cottonwood trees, the largest building of the lot had once been a company store and directly across from it, the swinging doors of an old saloon had long ago fallen from their hinges and landed on the planked porch. Down the street three more buildings were partially standing, one of which appeared to have been a blacksmith shop. Part of a forge was visible in the open doorway.

"We'll come back in a few minutes for a closer look and have lunch," he told her. "Right now let's ride on to the mine. It's just a short distance from here."

"Fine," she agreed.

After leaving the remnants of Chillicothe, they rode northwest for another quarter of a mile. Here the landscape changed to low mountains covered with short grass, a sprinkling of orange and purple wildflowers and a few pines.

When they reached a small creek trickling with crystal clear water, Quint said, "Back in the eighteen hundreds the miners first found gold panning this little creek. But it was a long time afterward before they began to dig for it."

Bemused, Maura looked down at the stream. "I wonder if any nuggets are still around?"

"You're welcome to pan," he teased.

Laughing, she looked over at him. "No thanks. I might get the fever and then I'd have to set up camp out here."

The grin slowly faded from his face. "That might not be a bad thing. Then I wouldn't have to make excuses to see you."

Since their stop at the arroyo, something had changed

between them, Maura thought. She didn't know exactly what it was or what had brought it about. But with every beat of her heart she could feel herself drawing closer and closer to this man. With every breath she took, the protective wall she'd built around her was crumbling away into useless rubble.

"You mean showing me Chillicothe and the mine was just an excuse to see me?" she asked.

His low chuckle was both sensual and suggestive and Maura's cheeks burned with self-conscious heat. In her younger days, she'd never had trouble attracting the opposite sex and even since her divorce from Gilbert, she'd been asked on dates by a few men. But she could safely say none of them had been half as masculine or sexy as Quint. And just the idea that a man like this young rancher wanted her company rattled her senses.

"No. I honestly wanted you to see them," he admitted with a grin. "Having your company is a nice addition." He motioned for her to follow him across the creek. "Come on. The mine is just around this next hill."

Maura was surprised when the entrance to the Golden Spur finally came into view. From all the talk that Abe had been doing about the mine, she'd expected something far more grand than a small hole in the side of the mountain.

Like the buildings in the nearby ghost town, the lumber used to frame the entrance had now weathered to little more than gray pieces of wood. In some places the nails had rusted completely away and the boards looked as though a strong puff of wind would cause them to collapse. But above the dark entrance, a large piece of tin with the name of the mine was still erect and dark enough to read.

After they dismounted and tethered their horses on an old broken wheel that someone had discarded, they walked near enough to the entrance to peer inside.

"So this is what has Abe all stirred up," Maura said with amazement. "It doesn't look like much from here."

"It probably isn't. As far as I know no one has been inside to do any type of work since back in the 1950s. At that time the miners weren't pulling enough gold out to warrant keeping the thing open. But for some reason Gramps believes there are more veins of gold ore to be found here. Why, I don't know," Quint said wryly. "He just gets these hunches."

"Well, from what he's told me about his oil-drilling days, he's had some good hunches." Bracing her hand against one of the sturdier boards, Maura stuck her head inside and tried to peer into the dark cavern. "Can we go inside?"

"You mean you'd want to?" he asked with a bit of amazement.

"Sure. I'm not a scaredy cat." As long as losing her heart to a man wasn't involved, she thought. Though, she had to admit that the longer she hung around Quint, the more she was feeling the danger.

"Well, want to or not, it wouldn't be safe. A few months ago, I went a short distance inside and from what I could see the timbers appeared to still be intact, but I'm sure the years have compromised their sturdiness. Since no one knew I was out here, I decided it would be foolish to explore any deeper."

"Do you have any idea how far the mine goes back into the mountain? I'll bet you could probably find old maps through county archives."

"Gramps has a copy of one of the most recent maps

made. There's a network of shafts in there, but I don't remember how deep they go. A fair distance, I think."

She turned away from the dark cave to find Quint standing a few inches behind her and she wondered if he realized how tempting he was, how much she wanted to reach out and connect to him, even in the most simple ways.

Drawing in a breath, she asked, "Have you decided anything about bringing in the mining company to reopen the Golden Spur?"

His gaze narrowed keenly on her face. "I haven't. Not yet. Why?"

She smiled gently. "Just curious. And if you're thinking I'm going to take Abe's side of things, you're wrong. I'm not going to take yours or his. This old mine is between the two of you. The only thing I will say is that I can see pros and cons either way."

He chuckled. "Very diplomatic, Maura. Maybe you should have been a politician instead of a nurse."

She laughed along with him. "Well, my dad set me on a fence long before he put me on a horse. So I learned to straddle it first."

His hand wrapped around her shoulder and she felt her breath catch in her throat as his fingers gently kneaded her flesh.

"Thank you, Maura. It feels good to be able to laugh and not take the mine issue so seriously."

As she looked into his eyes, nerves fluttered in her stomach and unconsciously the tip of her tongue came out to moisten her lips. If he kissed her again, as he had in the arroyo, she didn't know if she could hide the desire that was subtly simmering deep within her. "It feels good to me to be here and forget about a lot of things."

Suddenly clearing his throat, he urged her away from

the cave door. "Let's go have our lunch. I don't know about you, but I'm starving."

Yes, she was starving all right, Maura thought. And she'd not realized just how much until Quint had stepped into her lonely life.

By the time they rode back to Chillicothe, the clouds overhead were pulling together to form a gray, menacing sky. After leaving their horses in the shelter of the old blacksmith shop, they carried their saddlebags down to the mercantile building.

Maura was totally surprised when Quint opened the door and she stepped inside to see an old table and chairs in the middle of the large wooden floor.

"I know this hasn't been here since the town was deserted," she declared.

"No. Jake and I hauled it out here. This building is in the best condition of all of them, so we chose it to fix up for a line shack. You never know when an electrical storm or a blizzard might blow up and it's good to have a place to shelter or even spend the night, if need be. We have candles, kerosene lanterns, firewood and some canned goods and bedding all stored in the back."

"This is neat," she said as she gazed around her at the rows of dusty shelves lining the walls and a long counter running across the back. "We can leave the door open for light and it will almost be like we're eating outside."

Quint slanted her a rueful glance. "Unfortunately we only have an outhouse for a bathroom. It's behind this building just in case you need it. But there's piped water from a nearby spring for washing. You'll find it at the side of the building near a wooden water trough."

"Thanks," she told him. "I'll be right back."

When she returned he had sandwiches laid out on the tabletop, along with four cans of beverages. In the middle of the table, a fat candle held by a shallow jar lid was now lit and the glow of the flame helped chase away the gloom of the threatening rain clouds. She'd been present at a few candlelight dinners before, but none had been quite like this. And Maura realized the quaintness of their surroundings had only a small part to play in the specialness of the meal. It was Quint who was making it all so unique. Quint who was making her very aware of their isolated setting.

He helped her into one of the chairs and as she thanked him, he said, "I'd better warn you that the food is sorta sloppy. I'm not too good with kitchen duties."

"I can eat most anything," she told him. "And I brought a few things, too. Potato chips, candy bars and brownies."

"That sort of bad stuff? From a nurse?" He chuckled as he took the chair across from her. "Where did you pick up such nasty habits?"

Laughing along with him, she said, "S-s-shh. Don't tell anyone, but we nurses don't always follow doctor's orders."

"I'm glad to hear that. Now I won't feel guilty about stuffing myself."

Quint passed the sandwiches and drinks between them and they began to eat.

After Maura had downed a few bites in silence, his expression turned rueful.

"What are you thinking?" he asked. "That the sandwiches are soggy?"

"I couldn't have made better," she assured him with a smile, then added thoughtfully, "I was just trying to picture the people who used to live in this little town. I wonder if there were whole families who made their home here? Babies born here?"

He shrugged as he reached for one of the beer cans. "Probably. I think there was a population of about three hundred at one time. There's another area just to the south of these buildings where you can find old foundations and other signs of houses. Gramps says not long after he purchased the land a fire swept through here, so the home sites might have burned. Thankfully that was many years after this little community died."

She sighed wistfully. "Well, when the place was booming it must have been an exciting time for people. Each morning they probably climbed out of bed thinking today they'd discover the mother lode."

He leveled a suggestive grin at her. "Why, Maura, you sound like a gamble excites you."

He excited her. And he was definitely a gamble, she thought as her heart danced rapidly against her ribs.

"Funny you should say that. I'm considered the cautious little mouse of my family." Her gaze fluttered awkwardly down to the planked tabletop. "And I suppose I am. I've never been one to play the odds—at anything. Out at the mine I told you I wasn't a scaredy cat, but that was sort of an exaggeration. I'd like to be more adventurous, but I guess I'm just a sure-thing sort of person."

"You got married," he said softly. "I'd say you were adventurous."

A cynical grimace tightened her lips. "Marriage isn't supposed to be a risk. At least, I thought it wasn't. I figured I knew all the important things there were to know about Gil. But I guess a person sometimes takes chances when she doesn't even realize she's doing it."

The corners of his mouth tilted into a faint smile.

"That might be a good thing. Otherwise, we'd all be living in bubbles."

Normally, Maura didn't eat mayonnaise, but as she took another bite of the sandwich that Quint had made, she was surprised at how much she liked the taste. She was even more surprised at how much she was beginning to like him. Which was something completely separate from being swept away by his kiss.

"What about you, Quint? Are you a man who takes chances?"

"Only when I need to."

His answer was evasive, but Maura didn't prod him. Today was the most special day she'd had in a long, long time. There was no need for serious talk. This was a day to simply enjoy.

"That was a silly question from me," she said after a moment. "Ranchers take risks every day. Dad always says that raising horses is like raising children—the job is hard as hell and you never know if any of them will turn out to be worth a damn." She let out a short laugh. "But he loves us all—the horses and the kids—no matter if we aren't stars."

He looked at her quizzically. "Surely you don't think you're any less important than your siblings?"

One of her shoulders lifted and fell. "Did I say that?"

"Not in so many words. But there was something in your voice." He reached across the table and touched his fingers to hers. "I sometimes get the feeling, Maura, that you're down on yourself."

The touch of his fingers was like a branding iron, sizzling a fire right through her hand and straight up her arm. He couldn't possibly know how shaky and vulnerable he made her feel.

"My sisters are special. They're both very beautiful

and spunky. They go at life at full speed. I'm…just drifting."

He frowned at her. "That's plain wrong. You have a meaningful, admirable profession. You're young and intelligent and very lovely. And you're not drifting—unless you consider seeing after Gramps trivial."

Surprise parted her lips. "Oh, no! I didn't mean that at all. Abe is very important to me. I just meant that personally I'm drifting." She sighed with a bit of frustration, then tried her best to smile. "I'm not down on myself, Quint. Just a little disappointed in the mistakes I've made."

Unable to bear the burning touch of his fingers any longer, she pulled her hand away and reached for a plastic bag filled with brownies.

"Aren't we all?" he murmured.

Her eyes locked with his and suddenly her heart lifted and a soft smile curved her lips.

"Yes," she said huskily, then deciding it was time to change the subject completely, joked, "Is there a coffee house down the street? Coffee would be great with all these desserts we have."

"We don't have to go down the street, my lady. We can make coffee right here." His eyes twinkled as he popped the last of a sandwich into his mouth and rose to his feet. "Come here. I'll show you."

She followed him to where the long counter separated the front of the room from the back. Behind the L-shaped barrier she was surprised to see a cast-iron potbellied stove and a small metal cabinet filled with canned food and basic staples for cooking. On the opposite side of the space, jammed in an out-of-the-way corner, an army cot covered with a faded Navajo blanket served as a bunk.

Clearly, Quint had taken special efforts to make the place comfortable for him and the hired hands.

With his money, he could have gone overboard and rebuilt the whole structure. He could have supplied it with electricity, a bathroom and all the comforts of home. Instead, he'd chosen to keep the old building simple and full of character. He didn't need or want everything he had to be new or perfect. And she realized she liked that very much about him.

"This is all very neat," she told him. "Have you ever stayed here overnight?"

He chuckled as he shoved a few sticks of wood into the stove. "Once. About a year ago when Jake and I first started building the ranch. The two of us got caught out here in a blizzard and we ended up sleeping on the floor in our bedrolls and freezing our behinds. After that, we decided to fix this place up."

He stuck a match to the kindling and when tiny flames began to lick at the sticks of wood, he shut the door on the stove and turned the damper wide.

"You're very close to Jake, aren't you?"

"He's like a brother to me," he said as he fetched a sack of coffee from the metal cabinet.

"Is that why you have him working for you?" she asked.

A faint grin touched his mouth as he filled the granite pot with water from his canteen. "I have him working for me because he knows everything there is to know about horses and cattle and can do more than three men put together. He was making good money at the track, working as manager over the training barns. But I was fortunate enough to talk him into helping me."

"Hmm. From what I can see, you two are so different. How did you get to be such good friends?"

He poured a hefty amount of grounds into the water, then set the pot on the stove.

"In kindergarten and grade school we constantly whipped up on each other. He was always lipping off, daring me to do something I shouldn't do. And I was the quiet one who exploded when he pushed too far. After a while, we both realized that neither could beat the other one up and we earned each other's respect." He looked at her and chuckled. "Thankfully, we don't test each other anymore. Now that we're grown men, I'm not sure who'd win. But I do know we'd fight *for* each other."

She gravitated toward him and the heat that was now radiating from the stove. "I wish I could say I had a friend like that. But I don't. In school, I guess you could say I was a loner of sorts. I had friends, but I didn't build deep bonds with them. I saved all that for my sisters. The three of us are very close."

"There's nothing wrong with that. My sister is my buddy, too. Although I don't get to see her much now that she's moved to Texas. Abe is trying to lure her and Jonas back, but I don't think he'll get that done. You see, Jonas is a Texas Ranger."

"Abe tells me that you've driven him to San Antonio a couple of times to visit them," Maura said. "If I remember right, he said the two of you made the trip to see Alexa and Jonas's new daughter shortly before he started suffering from vertigo. That's a long drive to make."

Quint shrugged. "Gramps won't fly. He says he doesn't want to get any higher off the ground than a horse's back. And when he dies he wants it to be with his boots on. But

I don't want to think of him dying in any fashion. I want to think of him living to be a hundred."

Maura smiled gently. "And he's just ornery enough to do it."

His gaze met hers. "Yeah. He is."

Something in his eyes, the softness in his voice, drew her to him in a way that was somehow even deeper and stronger than his kiss.

It was a strange sensation and so unsettling that she finally had to turn away and draw in a calming breath.

Behind her, she heard him move away, then the scrape of cans being pushed around the metal shelf. Glancing over her shoulder, she saw that he was putting away the sack of coffee grounds. Nearer to her, in the corner of her eye, she could see part of the makeshift bed and though she tried to keep her mind off it, she couldn't stop herself from imagining how it might feel to lie with him here in the quietness, to feel his hands and lips moving over her body.

"Oh, hell! It's going to storm!"

Quint's exclamation had her spinning around just in time to see a huge gust of wind ripping through the doorway and snuffing out the candle on the table. Except for the light coming from outside, the space around them suddenly went dim and shadowy.

"I'll get the door!" he shouted as he rushed around the counter and hurried to fasten the door.

Maura raced after him and peered through the slatted boards covering the empty squares that used to hold glass windows.

A wall of blue-black clouds was descending upon them at a rapid rate. Cold wind was tearing down the street, ripping clumps of dry sagebrush from the soil to send them rolling in erratic trails toward the opposite end of town.

"Oh, my, Quint, this looks like it's going to be nasty!"

She'd hardly gotten the words past her mouth when a streak of lightning bolted across the sky and sent her leaping backward from the rickety window. Deafening thunder followed and she wrapped her arms protectively around herself as she waited for the sound to subside.

With the door latched as securely as he could manage, Quint walked over to her. Her face was pale with alarm and he instinctively reached out and circled his arm around her shoulders.

"We'll be fine," he tried to reassure her. "And the horses are safely sheltered away from the lightning. So we don't need to worry about them."

She looked up at him and tried to smile, but he could see her lips were quivering with the effort.

"I'm okay, Quint. I'm not normally afraid of storms. But in this flimsy old building, the force of it just feels closer."

He gave her an encouraging grin. "Just think of it this way, Maura. This old store has been here for more than a century. Why should it crumble around us now?"

"Why indeed?" she asked, then just as she was trying to laugh at their predicament another clap of thunder rattled the roof far above their heads. "Oh!"

Grabbing her hand, he urged, "Let's go to the back. The building is studier there. And the coffee is boiling over. I've got to get the pot off the stove."

By the time they rounded the counter, rain was driving against the old walls with a shuddering force. Behind them, water began to pour through the cracks in the roof and pelt the food they'd left lying on the table.

"You stay here by the stove," he ordered after he'd dealt with the coffeepot. "I'll gather up our food from the table."

"No!" she cried, clutching his arm. "Please. Stay here with me. We don't need the food!"

Seeing she was becoming really frightened, he wrapped his arms around her and pulled her tightly against his chest. "All right, Maura," he said close to her ear so that she could hear him above the deafening sounds of the storm. "I'll stay right here. Close your eyes, honey. Imagine you're somewhere nice and sunny. Like on a beach. In a bikini. With me rubbing oil on your back."

After a moment her shoulders began to shake and when he eased his head back and looked into her face, he could see she was trying to laugh through her fear.

"That's a wicked thought, Quint Cantrell."

He kneaded her back while the heat of her body snuggled up against his was a damn sight hotter than the crackling fire in the stove. Even hotter than the lightning crackling around the old building.

"Hmm. A very nice one, too."

Her head tilted back from his chest and as he looked down into her eyes, he felt something sweet and hot and protective sweep through him all at the same time.

"I— The lightning, Quint. A bolt of it hit too close to me once when I was out riding with my brother Brady. I was knocked from my horse and wasn't breathing. If he hadn't known CPR—"

She broke off with a shudder and he didn't ask her to finish. He didn't have to. He understood her fear and admired her for not falling completely apart.

"I'm not going to let anything hurt you. I promise."

Her arms slid around his waist and clung tightly, her face buried into his shirt. The fact that she trusted him, that she was seeking him for comfort and security, swelled his chest and touched his heart in a way that it had never been touched.

"I know," she said, her voice muffled. "Just hold me."

Quint gladly obliged her request and after a few minutes, the lightning began to subside, even though the rain continued to pour. With the thunder drawing farther and farther away, he could feel Maura began to relax in his arms.

And then everything suddenly began to change. Her hands started to move against his back, her head tilted backward, her lips parted. Something deep and hot and primitive began to beat inside him, and with a needy groan he dropped his head and covered her mouth with his.

Quint didn't know if the storm had charged the air around them, or if the desire between them was setting off sparks. Either way, the fire inside him had already ignited and he wasn't about to try to extinguish it.

The kiss he gave her was long and hungry and by the time their mouths finally parted, they were both breathing heavily and staring at each other in shocked wonder.

Finally, Maura lifted her hand to cup the side of his face. "Oh, Quint," she murmured. "Being with you—like this—is…special. So special."

Feeling raw and naked and unexpectedly emotional, Quint thrust his fingers into her hair and against her scalp. Then holding her head motionless, he lowered his lips back to hers.

This time he gentled his searching mouth and took his lazy time drinking in her sweet taste, while an ebb and flow of desire rushed through him like a high tide threatening to drown everything in its path.

When he finally broke the kiss and lifted his head, his

insides were shaking with a need like he'd never felt before. "I want to make love to you, Maura."

Apparently his kiss had already told her what he wanted, because there wasn't so much as a flicker of surprise to be found on her face. Instead, her green eyes were dark and smoldering, telling him that she needed him just as badly. The notion left him drunk with anticipation.

"I want that, too, Quint."

He didn't question her a second time. He didn't want to give her the chance to change her mind, to turn away from him and the consequences this might bring upon them tomorrow. Loving her. Being inside her was all he could think about. It was all that mattered.

Groaning with need, he swept her up into his arms and carried her the few steps over to the cot. After lying her gently atop the blanket, he immediately joined her on the narrow mattress, then reached for her.

With a sigh that was lost in the sound of the rain, she moved into his arms and their lips united over and over in a swarm of kisses that grew deeper and bolder with each passing minute.

Eventually their clothing became an annoying barrier and Quint reached for the buttons on Maura's shirt. Once it was out of the way, he quickly followed it with her jeans and boots, then stood to deal with his own clothing.

Peeled down to nothing but two lacy scraps of lingerie, Maura sat on the side of the cot and as she watched Quint fumble with the buttons on his shirt, there was only one thing on her mind. And that thought had nothing to do with the right or wrong about making love to this man. Instead, she was wondering what he was thinking as he looked at her.

No doubt he was accustomed to having far younger women than her in his bed. And even though her body was firm and curved in all the right places, she felt self-conscious as his blue eyes slid slowly over her.

She swallowed as his jeans dropped to the floor, then tried to speak as he shoved them and his boots out of the way. He was all long, lean muscle, a man in the prime of his young life.

"I—" Heat bloomed pink on her cheeks as she unwittingly touched a hand to her messed hair. "I must look horrible," she said huskily. "I'm sorry…"

Groaning, he knelt before her and drew her into his arms. "Oh, hell, Maura. You're the most sexy and gorgeous woman I've ever laid eyes on."

Her head twisted back and forth against his bare shoulder. "There's no need for you to go overboard."

A low chuckle rumbled from deep in his throat. "I went overboard that first night I kissed you. I haven't been able to think of anything else since. I've been wondering, imagining how it would be to make love to you. And now—"

Cupping her face with both his hands, he looked into her eyes and Maura felt her heart swell with a longing that had nothing to do with physical desire and everything to do with an emotional bond.

"I don't want to make love to an athletic body, Maura. I want a flesh-and-blood woman, who's all soft and lovely and feels just right in my arms. I want you."

By the time he uttered the last word, his lips were against hers and Maura's doubts had flown through the cracks in the wall.

Quint wanted her. Really wanted her. And that in itself was enough to send her senses spinning, to make her forget everything, including the storm outside.

With his lips fastened hungrily to hers, he eased her back onto the cot, then stretched out beside her. Tiny shivers of pleasure raced down her spine as their bared skin touched, the heat of their bodies melded together and his hard arousal burgeoned between them.

Whirling in a foggy haze, the kiss continued until she was completely starving for air. Yet when he did finally tear his lips from hers, she wanted to cry at the loss. But her disappointment was short-lived as he quickly began to nibble at the sensitive spot beneath her ear, then followed that with a trail of moist kisses down the side of her neck.

By the time he reached the valley between her breasts, her fingers clenched against her palms and her body arched toward his, toward the mindless magic his mouth was playing across her skin.

One by one, he slipped the straps of her bra down her shoulders, unfastened the hooks, then tossed the garment to the floor.

She sucked in ragged breaths, while beneath a veil of lashes, she watched his gaze settle hungrily on her breasts. The desire raging in the pit of her belly twisted into a fiery ache and with a low groan, she clutched his shoulders and urged him down to her. Amidst the sound of the storm, she heard the sharp intake of his breath and then his mouth was against one nipple as he took the tight bud between his teeth and laved it with his tongue.

Inside Maura, something snapped like a twig and all the pent-up hunger she'd been trying to contain flooded through her like the downpour outside. Suddenly she couldn't touch him enough, taste him enough. Her hands raced over his hot skin, exploring the hard muscles of his arms and back while her lips scattered broken kisses along his collarbone and up the side of his neck where her mouth tasted the wild beat of his heart.

She was barely aware of him removing her panties and

his shorts. A sea of sensation was washing over her, tugging, smothering, begging, wiping away all sense of perception. And when he positioned himself above her, she reached for him with a fierceness that frightened her.

"I hope you're protected," he mouthed against her ear, "because I have nothing with me."

Closing her eyes, she turned her lips into the side of his face. "I am," she whispered, then with a choked groan, added, "I want to feel you inside me, Quint. I want to feel us together. That way."

"Oh, Maura. My lovely, lovely, Maura."

The raw huskiness in his voice, the tenderness in his blue eyes, pierced her chest and sank straight to her heart. Suddenly her throat was burning and her eyes were stinging, and before he could guess at the emotions he'd evoked in her, she buried her face against his chest and wrapped her arms tightly around him.

And when he entered her, the pleasure careening through her body was so great, so all-consuming that she was totally unaware of the stream of tears marking her cheeks.

Chapter Seven

Much later, as Maura lay curled against Quint, her cheek pillowed by his chest, she listened to the even rhythm of his breathing, the slow beat of his heart, and knew they were sounds that would be with her for the rest of her life.

He'd taken her on a passionate trip the likes of which she'd never experienced. Even now, when she thought of how her whole body had exploded with pleasure, she was shocked and fascinated, dazed that he could have turned her into such a wild, uninhibited woman.

Oh, my, what had had happened? Making love to Quint had only shown her how much she'd done wrong. She'd not known that her ex-husband had been a selfish lover. Because Gil had been her first and only lover, she'd not had anyone to compare him to. But now, after Quint had touched her, lifted her to the sky and back, she realized she'd been missing so much, had wasted so many years on a one-sided relationship.

"I think the rain is letting up," Quint murmured against the top of her head. "But who cares? I could stay here all night. Just like this."

Moments ago, he'd pulled the Navajo blanket over them and now that the cooler air from the storm was filling the old storeroom, the warmth from the woven wool was welcome.

"Mmm. I'm thinking I could stay here forever," she said drowsily. "But something or someone would eventually show up to interrupt us."

She could feel his sigh ruffle her hair and then his hand was alongside her cheek, tilting her face up to his. When she looked into his blue eyes, her heart squeezed with bittersweet longing. Would he ever want to be with her again like this? Was she crazy to want to snatch what pleasure she could, whenever she could?

"Maura, before we leave here…I wanted you to know that this thing that's happened between us—I hadn't planned. Just in case you thought I'd calculated all this—"

He broke off as the upper part of her began to shake with soft chuckles.

"What's wrong?" he asked. "Am I funny or something?"

"Oh, Quint," she murmured, then scooting her whole body upward, she planted a kiss on his cheek. "For as long as I live, I would have never thought any such thing. You planning this with me? It's funny."

His expression sober, he arched one brow at her. "Really? What's so funny about it?"

Seeing he wasn't amused, she pressed her cheek against his. "I'm sorry if that didn't sound quite right. It's just that you—you can have any woman you want, Quint. The idea that you'd purposely pursue me is…well, ridiculous."

With his hands in her hair, he eased her face back from his. "Maura, I think I need to set your thinking straight about a few things. I'm not a playboy. I don't go after women."

"Of course not. You don't have to."

He groaned with frustration. "Okay, let me put it this way," he said. "Since the breakup with Holly, I've tried to date, to get interested in other women. And yes, I've had a few females deliberately try to catch my attention. But none of them sparked anything in me. Until now. Until you."

Could she believe him? Yes, she decided. Because he was talking about sexual desire, about that special spark of chemistry between a man and a woman. He wasn't talking about love. That was a whole other thing. A thing that he would never likely bring up. Nor would she.

Swallowing at the thickening in her throat, she said, "Then I'm very flattered, Quint, that you were attracted to me."

One corner of his rugged mouth turned upward. "And I'm very flattered that you wanted to get this close to me."

Her hand settled on the curve of his shoulder, then slipped down the hard, corded slope of his arm. Oh, yes, she thought, she wanted to be close to this man in a thousand, million ways.

"When you take a woman on a ride, you really take her on a ride," she teased softly.

He looked at her with faint disdain and then suddenly he was laughing, twisting her beneath him, and lowering his face down to hers. "You're good for me, Maura. You make me laugh. And that's not easy. Just ask Jake what I'm really like."

Her fingertip traced heart-shaped patterns upon his face. "I'd rather ask you."

He looked at her, his eyes gliding hungrily over her flushed cheeks and swollen lips, the tangled hair hiding one green eye.

"I'm not an easy man to like, Maura. I'm quiet and moody. And small talk mostly bores me. I'd rather be with my horses. I don't particularly like money and I hate crowds."

Her lips curved into a sexy little purse. "Mmm. You sound like a terrible sort of man. Anything else I should know?"

"Yeah. I don't know anything about being romantic and even if I did, I wouldn't bother."

"Why?"

"Because romance is looking at the world through rose-colored glasses. And when a woman looks at me, I want her to clearly see the flaws she'd be getting."

In order to keep her away? Maura decided the answer to that question didn't matter. She was looking at him and the future with clear eyes. Quint was a straightforward guy. She'd gone into his arms knowing not to pin any sort of hopes and dreams on the two of them being together permanently.

"Don't worry," she replied. "I won't be expecting flowers."

He stared at her for long moments and then his mouth crushed down on hers in a kiss that wiped everything from her mind and stirred the want in her all over again.

"Maybe we'd better stay here a little longer," he whispered huskily. "Until the rain stops."

Almost a week later, Quint found himself driving up the narrow dirt road that led to his grandfather's ranch house.

For the past few days, he'd fought the urge to return to Apache Wells. He didn't have the time or energy to make the forty-mile drive often. Hell, he didn't need to remind himself that he had a ranch of his own to run. With cattle to buy, fences to build, feeders to erect and horses to move from the Chaparral to the Golden Spur, he hardly had time to draw a good breath. But here he was anyway, he thought wryly. Because, in spite of his work and exhaustion, he desperately wanted to see Maura again.

Maura. With her wine-red hair and sea-green eyes. She'd bewitched him. That's what she'd done. He could scarcely close his eyes without thinking of her naked, her hips arching up to his, scattering his senses like bits of grass in the wind. He'd expected to enjoy making love to her. After all, she was pretty and sexy; a combination hard for any man to resist. But he'd also expected the incident to be a brief encounter to enjoy for the moment, then sweep entirely from his mind.

Face it, Quint. The woman turned you inside out. She shot you straight to heaven, then let you fall back to earth with the slow rocking motion of a drifting feather. You'd never felt anything like it. And now you're beginning to wonder if she's something special. The sex was special, you fool. Not her. Get over it.

The cynical voice that had followed Quint around for the last six years tormented him until he braked his truck to a halt in front of the house and climbed out. Yeah, it probably was pure sex that had pushed him to drive forty miles this evening when he should have been taking an early night at home, he thought. But what was wrong with that? He was a man after all. And a man had needs.

To his surprise, he found Abe in his recliner, the television off and a Bible lying open on his lap. Maura wasn't anywhere to be seen.

"Hey, Gramps," he greeted.

Looking up with surprise, Abe carefully folded the book together. "Well," he said mockingly, "the long-lost grandson has finally decided to honor me with a visit."

Quint grimaced. "Don't give me that bull. I was just over here last week. You expect me to come over here and hold your hand every day?"

Abe wiped a hand over his drooping white mustache. "No. After one or two days your smart lip would get mighty tryin'," he countered.

Quint took a seat on the end of the couch, while looking and listening for signs of Maura. The house seemed exceptionally quiet and he couldn't smell any sort of cooking coming from the kitchen.

"What are you doing in the house?" Quint asked him. "I thought you'd be down at the bunkhouse, playing cards with Jim and having coffee."

"If you thought that, what are you doing in the house?" Abe parried.

Quint was shocked to feel his face flushing with heat. There was no point for him to hide his interest in Maura. Abe was too crafty for that. "I wanted to talk to Maura."

"Well, you should have called first. She ain't here."

Quint had called three days ago. His conversation with Maura had been pleasant but brief, during which he'd told her he'd see her in a few days. The few days were up and here he was feeling like an idiot for presuming she'd be sitting around his grandfather's ranch, waiting for him to make an appearance.

"Where is she?"

Abe placed the Bible on the end table next to his chair. "She's at the hospital."

It was all Quint could do to keep from leaping to his

feet. "Hospital! Has something happened to her? And you didn't call me?"

Beneath his bushy brows, Abe leveled a disgusted look at him. "Hell, boy, if something was wrong with Maura you think I'd be sitting here?"

Relief pouring through him, Quint rubbed his palms down his thighs. "No," he conceded gruffly, "I guess not."

"Damn right I wouldn't," Abe stormed back at him. "I'd be right by her side. That's how a man shows his love."

Caught by those last words, Quint's brows arched with dismay. "You love Maura?"

Abe snorted as though Quint's question was absurd. "Of course I love her. I've loved her from the first moment I laid eyes on her."

Hell. That's exactly what Quint had feared all along. "I see."

"No, damn it, you don't see. You haven't seen much of anything about women since that silly little Johnson gal threw you over the fence for another man. You think they're all like her, that they've all got their claws out for you. Well, if you'd take the time to look, you'd see that Maura doesn't have any claws. That's one of the reasons I love her."

Dear God, Quint hadn't driven for nearly an hour to get this sort of preaching, to hear his grandfather admit that he loved the same woman that Quint had taken to his bed. This was insanity.

"Okay. You've made your point, Gramps," he said wearily. "You're in love with the woman and I should realize that she's an angel."

Abe's boots banged loudly against the footrest as he positioned the chair upright and got to his feet. "Quint, I didn't say I was 'in' love with Maura. I said I loved her.

There's a difference. Sometimes a man has to know his limitations and I can see that she's too young for me. So," he said with a shrug, "I just have to settle with havin' her company. Until she gets tangled up with a man who'll give her a family."

Quint let out a pent-up breath. "She's told you that she wants a family?"

"Not in so many words. But I can just tell when a woman is ripe for that sort of thing."

If that was the case, then Abe knew a hell of a lot more than Quint knew. From what Maura had implied to him, she wasn't ready to jump into a serious situation with any man. That was one of the reasons Quint had been drawn to her in the first place. He didn't have to worry about her getting all clingy and demanding.

"Tell me, Gramps, did Granny know that you were such an expert on women?"

"'Course she did. She taught me everything I know." He motioned for Quint to follow him to the kitchen. "C'mon. Let's find us something to eat. And maybe Maura will show up before long."

A few minutes later, when Maura arrived and spotted Quint's truck parked near the front gate, her heart leaped into a dizzying speed. Even though darkness had just now settled over the ranch, daylight savings time made the hour late. Had he made the long drive to see his grandfather? Or her?

After parking her car beneath a covered carport at the back, she entered the house through the kitchen door and discovered both men sitting at the table, eating leftovers from the day before.

As soon as Quint spotted her, he immediately rose to

his feet and Maura felt something melt inside as her gaze connected with his blue eyes.

"Come sit with us, Maura," he invited. "Gramps was just telling me that Brady was involved in some sort of scrape."

Brady was Maura's youngest brother had worked as the chief deputy to Lincoln County's sheriff, Ethan Hamilton. Earlier this afternoon, when Maura had gotten the call that he'd been wounded, she'd left the ranch at breakneck speed and with a litany of prayers passing her lips, sped to the hospital. The ordeal had drained her, but now, seeing Quint was refueling her with happy pleasure.

Shoving a hand through her hair, she pushed the disheveled strands away from her face. "Yes, unfortunately. Some of the men in the department had set up a drug sting and things went amiss when one of the dealers smelled a rat. He pulled out a gun and began shooting. Brady's arm was hit with a small caliber bullet, but thankfully it was a flesh wound and should heal in a short time."

She walked over to the table, where Quint already had a chair pulled out for her. As he helped her into it, his closeness shook her, reminded her that she'd spent the past several nights lying awake thinking about him and the way he'd made love to her in such a thorough, precious way.

"That's good to hear," Abe said. "Lord knows that brother of yours earns his money the hard way."

Maura smiled at the old man. "Being a deputy is what he loves to do. Like I love nursing you." She reached across the table and squeezed his hand. "Have you been feeling okay while I was gone?"

He grinned at her. "If I felt any better I'd have to go out

and jump a fence. And Quint here showed up to keep me company. That's somethin' that don't happen every day."

At the opposite end of the table, Quint cleared his throat. "We were just having a little supper, Maura. Would you like a plate? Something to drink?" he asked.

She wanted none of those things. She simply wanted to be in his arms, to feel herself all wrapped up against his hard body, his lips moving against hers. Oh my, oh my, what had this man done to her? She was sex-crazed, but only one certain man would do.

"No thanks. Before I left the hospital, I had something with Bridget and my grandmother."

"Kate was there?" Abe asked with surprise.

Maura smiled to herself. From time to time Abe had brought up the subject of Maura's grandmother, Kate. It was obvious he was interested in the woman, but she doubted he'd ever admit it, especially to Kate. If anything, Kate was even bolder spoken than Abe. Sparks would fly if the two of them ever got together.

"Dad couldn't keep her away. She's always been especially close to Brady. Maybe because he's the baby and much more like her than any of us. But everything is under control and when I left the hospital the rest of my family were heading for home."

"That's good," Abe said, then abruptly rose to his feet. "Well, that's about all I can eat right now. I'm gonna head down to the bunkhouse and see if Jim's up to a game of poker. Damn man skinned me for thirty dollars last night. I gotta win it back."

"It's dark outside," Quint warned him. "You'd better drive."

"I know how to get to my own bunkhouse," he muttered as he disappeared out the door.

Bemused by the old man's quick departure, Quint said, "What's wrong with him? He always wants coffee after he eats."

"From what he tells me, Jim always keeps a pot going on the stove," Maura reasoned.

"Well, the way he scooted out of here, you'd think he wanted to leave us alone," Quint said, then leveled a suggestive look at her. "What do you think?"

Heat swept through her body, making it feel like her cotton dress was actually a heavy woolen coat. Refraining from fanning herself, she rose to her feet and began to gather Abe's dirty dishes.

"Clearly," she said as she carried the things over to the sink.

Not bothering with his own dishes, Quint left the table and walked up behind her. As he slipped his arms around her waist and pressed his lips to the back of her neck, he said in a voice muffled by her skin, "I think the old man needs psychotherapy. He says he loves you."

She didn't so much as flinch. Instead, she asked, "Are you saying a man has to be mentally ill to love me?"

The coolness in her voice told him he'd gone at this all wrong. "No. But Gramps is eighty-four."

"So. You don't think you'll be capable of loving at eighty-four?"

Hell, he wasn't sure he was capable of loving a woman at twenty-nine, he thought. These past years since his break with Holly he'd tried to get close to other women, tried to recapture that blissful state of mind he'd had with his first sweetheart. But the most he'd experienced was a cold sweat, a sick repulsion at the idea of handing any woman the reins to his future.

Quint figured by the time he reached Abe's age, his

heart would more than likely be as hard as a piece of granite. Maybe it was now, he thought bitterly. Maybe Holly had turned him to stone and he'd never be able to love again.

Lifting his head, he answered, "Not a woman fifty years my junior!"

Twisting around, she slipped her arms around his midsection and linked her hands behind his back. "Oh, Quint," she said with a soft laugh, "Abe loves me as a daughter."

Her laughter was all he needed to lighten his thoughts and he smiled at her. "I suppose you're right. I just don't want his old heart broken."

As for his own heart, Quint wasn't worried about that. After all, a piece of rock wasn't capable of getting all soft and soppy and vulnerable.

"I was surprised to see you here tonight," she said huskily.

"Why? I told you on the phone that I'd see you soon."

The husky note in his voice sent a shiver of anticipation down Maura's spine. "That could mean anything. And you've been very busy."

"Jake and I have finally started stocking the ranch and for the past week, we've been moving cattle and horses from dawn 'til dusk. I've hardly taken time to eat." His hands gently framed her face. "But—oh, honey, you ought to know I've been going crazy to be with you again."

She sighed. "I've been wanting to see you again, too."

He bent his head and his lips wrapped desperately over hers. The force of his kiss rocked her head backward and she moaned as her hands reached for the anchor of his shoulders.

In spite of the overhead lighting, his kiss was tugging her down into a swirling darkness where there was nothing but his hands sizzling over her skin, his mouth demanding, yet at the same time giving.

When their lips finally broke apart and his forehead was resting against hers, she sucked in ragged breaths and attempted to calm her racing heart.

"This is crazy, Quint!"

"Yeah. But a good kind of crazy."

He pressed his lips across her forehead, then along one cheekbone, while goose bumps danced over Maura's skin.

"The way I want you is indecent," she whispered. "You shouldn't be making me feel like this."

Her head tilted sideways as his lips began a downward trail on the side of her neck, then paused against the throbbing vein at the juncture of her shoulder.

"I've got to make love to you, Maura."

"Yes…" The word floated out on a sigh.

His lips began working their way back up her throat and toward her lips. Aching with need, Maura's hips shamelessly arched into his.

"Not here—not in your grandfather's house," she uttered with dismay.

Groaning with frustration, he dipped his hand beneath the hem of her skirt, then glided his hand up her thigh until his fingers reached the silky fabric of her panties. While he teased the flesh of one buttock, he whispered, "Gramps will be gone for hours."

Knowing that she couldn't succumb to his seductive persuasions on this matter, she purposely pushed at his shoulders to wedge a few cooling inches between them. "Maybe. Maybe not. It doesn't matter. I wouldn't feel right."

Seeing she meant what she said, Quint grabbed her hand and began tugging her toward the door. "C'mon. I know somewhere we can go."

"Go? Now?" she asked dazedly. "Where?"

"You'll see. It's not far."

Unable to resist, Maura allowed him to lead her outside to the front of the house, where he quickly helped her into the cab of his truck. As he pulled away from the ranch house, a sense of reckless anticipation came over her and she looked at him as though they'd suddenly turned into sneaky partners in crime.

"What if Abe returns to the house and finds us gone? What are we going to tell him?"

Quint chuckled. "That I took you sightseeing."

Maura groaned with misgiving. "In the dark? The man isn't that ancient, Quint."

"Does it matter what he thinks?"

He reached across the seat for her hand and as his fingers closed around hers, she could feel her heart throbbing with excitement. What normal woman wouldn't thrill at the idea of her lover carrying her off in the dark to a secret hideaway?

"No," she whispered truthfully. "It can't matter."

About two miles from the house, he turned onto a dim dirt road that led north toward the mountains. During her morning jogs, Maura had noticed the road, but never explored it.

"Are we still on Apache Wells?" she asked after he'd driven for another five minutes.

By now the road had grown bumpy and a dense pine forest had narrowed the road down to the width of a single vehicle. As the truck climbed the rough terrain, Maura gripped the seat in order to steady herself.

"Honey, you have to drive ten miles back to the main highway before you're off of Apache Wells."

"I wasn't sure. We're going toward the mountains. And it doesn't look like anyone travels this road very often."

"Only me. And if any cattle go astray, the ranch hands might use it. But that's rare."

She was peering out the windshield, wondering how much farther the truck could handle the rough terrain when suddenly the road planed out, and straight ahead, in the beam of the headlights, stood a small log cabin embraced by a stand of tall pines.

Quint quickly stopped the truck, then helped her to ground. As they walked toward the entrance, their footsteps made silent by pine needles, Maura got the sense that the structure was old. Possibly even older than the ranch itself.

Using his shoulder, Quint shoved the door inward, then ordered her to stay put until he provided light.

Standing in the doorway, the cool night air to her back and the silence of the woods surrounding them, a brief moment of stark sanity raced through her mind.

What was she doing here? With a man younger than her and definitely far less committed? Had she lost her senses and thrown every scrap of self-respect to the wind?

Commitment. Self-respect. She'd had those things before. Or so she'd believed. They had brought her nothing but heartache. Being with Quint brought her joy. And no matter how short-lived that joy was she was going to take it, savor it and be glad for it.

After Quint lit a kerosene lantern and a fat candle, he motioned for Maura to enter the small, one-room cabin. As she stepped onto the bare, wooden floor and glanced around at the crude fixtures, he said, "It's a little dusty. But not bad. I'll open the windows and that should give us some fresh air."

At the front of the room, Quint unlatched two wooden squares that pushed outward to create window spaces.

After he'd securely propped them and the cool night air rushed in, he walked back to where she stood by a tiny table holding the burning lamp.

"Alone. At last," he said with a growl of satisfaction.

Maura's heart leaped to a reckless speed as his hands settled at the sides of her waist. "You've taken a lot of trouble to get me up here," she said huskily.

In the dim glow of the lamp, she watched his gaze travel straight to her swollen lips and her loins clenched with desire.

"And you're worth every minute of it."

He was not a man to hand her lines and as he pulled her into his arms, she wondered if he'd actually meant the words he'd whispered.

Don't go trying to figure the man now, Maura. Just remember this time with him isn't forever and you'll be okay.

Closing her eyes, she turned her lips up to his and as his kiss swept her into a vortex of pleasures she forgot about his motives and plans or the condition her heart might be in tomorrow. Tonight was all about him and her being together and nothing else.

Before long he was removing her clothing and carrying her to a built-in bunk spread with a down comforter. From the small bed, she watched him undress in the dim yellow glow of the lamplight and as the soft shadows slipped fingers across his hard body, her throat thickened with emotions she didn't understand or even want to analyze.

This amazing man wanted her. Needed her. That was enough for now.

At Chillicothe, she'd believed it impossible for Quint to thrill her more, to take her to even higher heights with his lovemaking, but somehow he did and it was a long time afterward before she could find the strength or composure to utter a word.

Lying in his arms, her body lax and replete, she rested her cheek upon his shoulder and savored the feel of his fingertips marking a gentle trail from her hip to her breast and back again.

"What is this place?" she asked drowsily.

"Our hideaway," he murmured.

By now the candle had burned out and the single flame of the lamp mottled the chinked walls with golden splashes of light. Beyond the open windows and above the tops of the pines, she could see a portion of the black sky riddled with stars and at that moment it was impossible to think of a more beautiful place to be.

Her lips tilted to a dreamy smile. "I mean before."

"The cabin was here before Gramps built the ranch and we figured pioneers must have lived here long ago. At one time Gramps used it as a hunting cabin. But now he'd rather feed the deer than shoot them. And so do I."

"Do you come here often?"

He shifted ever so slightly, and then she felt his lips brushing against the crown of her hair. It was such a sweet and loving contact that her throat suddenly stung with tears.

"No. The last time I was here was more than a year ago, when I learned that my mother had kept a secret life from me and my sister, Alexa."

"I heard bits and pieces about that even before I returned to Hondo Valley. Knowing your lovely mother, it's still hard for me to imagine her having another family that no one knew about."

He sighed and Maura could only imagine what the ordeal with Frankie Cantrell had done to him. It hurt to think of him going through such emotional turmoil. Like her, everything he'd believed in had been ripped asunder and she knew firsthand the deep wounds that deception left behind.

"No one knew about her first marriage but my father," he said lowly. "And he took the secret to his grave. Seems my parents decided that it would be too hard on Alexa and me to know that we had brothers in Texas, but couldn't associate with them. You see, Mom's first husband was abusive. She was forced to run from him and didn't stop running until she reached Ruidoso. He must have been a real bastard. On the other hand there must have been some good in the man because my two half brothers are great guys."

She smoothed her palm across his broad chest. "You get along with them?"

"Oh, sure. Why do you ask? Did you think I might resent them?"

"It would be only natural to feel resentment. Especially since Abe told me that your mother makes regular trips to Texas to see them."

His hand lifted from her hip and then his fingers pushed into her long hair to lift the strands away from her cheek and neck.

"I'd never be jealous of that. Mac and Ripp have families and she needs to be a part of their lives. She missed out on so much. And Alexa lives there now, too. So she has plenty of reasons to go there often."

"You ever get the itch to move closer to your siblings?" she asked thoughtfully.

"Move from New Mexico? Away from Gramps? Never. This land is a part of my soul. And Gramps is—well, ever since I've been big enough to walk, he's been my hero."

With a throaty groan, he rolled her onto her back and poised his lips over hers. "Besides, if I moved to Texas, you'd have to come up here to the cabin by yourself. And that wouldn't be any fun at all."

No. Life without Quint would be boring and lonely, Maura thought. It was something she refused to think about. At least, for tonight.

"How lucky for me that you're not a wanderer," she murmured, then latching her fingers around the back of his neck, she pulled his head down to hers and closed the last bit of space between their lips.

Chapter Eight

Two weeks later Maura stared numbly across the desk at her sister. It was past the clinic's normal working hours and the last of Bridget's patients had left the building. All except Maura.

"What did you say?" Maura asked in a slow, dazed voice.

Her hands folded in front of her, Bridget leaned forward and in her no-nonsense manner, repeated, "I said you're not suffering from an acid stomach. You're going to have a baby. I'd say in about eight months from now."

"A baby! How—how can…that be?"

Bridget smiled knowingly. "You meet a man, chemistry clicks and before you know it the two of you are too close for comfort."

With a loud wail, Maura's head shook back and forth. "That's not what I mean! I'm talking about birth control! How did it fail? All those years with Gil—"

"Yeah. Thank God it didn't fail with him," Bridget muttered, then smiled at Maura as though she couldn't be happier. "I suspect you unwittingly forgot a pill or two. Or it could be the dosage needs to be changed. In any case, do not take another one."

Dropping her head in her hand, Maura struggled to think past the shock of the moment to the past month or two, before she'd fallen into bed with Quint Cantrell. "Now that I think about it, I did get fouled up for a few days. That's when Dr. Weston was hounding me and I'd given the hospital notice to quit my job. I guess with all the stress I forgot to take a few pills. But I got back on schedule more than six weeks ago."

Bridget shook her head. "Apparently the interruption was enough to give your reproductive organs a window of opportunity. And they took it."

Oh, God. How was she going to explain this to Quint? How on earth was he going to react to the news that he was going to be a father?

Trembling now, she rose from the wooden chair and began to pace around the small space of Bridget's office.

"Oh, Brita, this is unbelievable! What am I going to do?"

Bridget's brows arched with faint surprise. "Why, Maura, there shouldn't be a question with you. You're going to have the baby."

Stopping in her tracks, Maura bit back a yell of frustration. "Of course there's no question about that! Every cell in my body loves and wants this baby. I was talking about the father! He—he is not going to be pleased. In fact, I figure he's going to be outraged."

Frowning with doubt, Bridget asked, "How do you know that? I've always thought of Quint as a sensible, responsible person. At least that's how I always saw him in high school. 'Course I can't say much for him hanging on to that gold-digging Holly like he did. But I forgive him because he was young and it takes a man longer to wise up about life. I'll bet after all this time he can see what a narrow escape he made with that witch."

Stunned, Maura stared at her. "How did you know the father was Quint? I haven't told you anything about seeing him and—"

A sly smile spread across Bridget's face. "I'm not blind. I'm your sister. And I've been seeing the change in you since you went to work for old Abe. Then that night at the hospital, when Brady was there with the gunshot wound, I overheard you telling Dr. Weston, in no uncertain terms, to get lost and stay lost. I knew then that you'd finally woken up and come out of your shell. And I figured Quint had to be reason. Abe is certainly too old to bring about that sort of change in you."

Groaning with embarrassment, Maura covered her face with her hands. "Oh, Lord, you must be thinking I've lost my mind. He's so young and—"

"A hunk to boot," Bridget finished for her, then let out a suggestive laugh. "I think for the first time ever, my sister has really blossomed into the woman she should be. And Maura, just think, you're going to have a child! Finally! Oh, how I envy you!"

Completely dismayed, Maura walked back over to Bridget's desk. "Envy me? Are you crazy? I'm divorced, single and pregnant. With a child whose father doesn't love me. I'm sure you'd jump at the chance to trade places with me."

Bridget shook her curly head. "How do you know Quint doesn't love you? Has he told you that?"

Maura's troubled gaze dropped to the floor. "No. But he doesn't have to. What we have—it's like you said a few moments ago. Just chemistry."

"So you don't love him, either? That's strange because I just can't imagine my big sister jumping into bed with a man she doesn't care about. Really care about."

Did she love Quint? For the past few weeks she'd been telling herself that her heart hadn't taken that big of leap for the man, but deep down she had to admit she'd only been fooling herself. She was wild about him. Crazy about him. She couldn't imagine life without him. If that meant she loved him, then she was definitely guilty.

"So maybe I do care about him," she muttered. "Maybe I do love him. That doesn't fix anything. He doesn't love me back. And he sure as heck doesn't want to get married."

Sighing, Bridget reached for a prescription pad and began to scribble instructions on it. "Maura, you need to remember you're not dealing with Gilbert anymore. Quint is a real man. Not a jerk."

Standing, she moved around the desk and handed the scrap of paper to her sister. "Here's a script for vitamins and something for your stomach. Take them all faithfully and try to eat right. Right now that little one's most important parts are developing. We want him to be healthy whenever he gets here. Or maybe it's a she," Bridget added with a happy grin. "I can't wait to see! Are you going to tell the family, or can I break the news?"

Maura's mouth fell open. She'd not yet thought about her parents' reaction to this news, or her other siblings. She'd always been the cautious, practical Donovan. Were they now going to see her as disgrace to the family?

"Don't say anything just yet. I need a few days to come to terms with all of this and gather my wits about me. I'm not sure I can face anyone with the news right now. Especially Quint. And he needs to hear this first."

A few minutes later as she left Bridget's office, Maura began to doubt the wisdom of holding her secret for a few more days. The longer she held this sort of news from Quint, the worse it would make things. Especially if Bridget accidentally let it slip to her family and the information got back to him before Maura had a chance to speak with him.

The thought of confronting Quint with this sort of life-changing news was twisting her nerves into knots and yet in spite of that, she was euphoric, thrilled to her very toes at the idea of a tiny life growing inside of her.

For years now she'd had to push aside her desire for a child. And after the humiliating divorce with Gilbert, she'd practically crossed out the idea that she'd ever be a mother. But now a baby was actually growing inside of her. Quint's baby! As far as she was concerned, it was a miraculous turn of events.

Nearly an hour later, when she parked in front of Abe's house, her mind was still spinning as she tried to decide how to approach Quint.

This past Sunday, she'd had a brief phone call from him, explaining that he and Jake were leaving for Clovis on Monday morning and weren't planning to be back until Wednesday, which was today. The trip was to purchase a special herd of cattle and haul them back to the Golden Spur. Calling him tonight wouldn't be the wise thing to do, she decided, as she let herself into the house.

No doubt he'd be tired and could possibly still be out on the range, moving the cattle to their new location. When she talked to him about the baby, she wanted his undivided attention. Early in the morning, before he became too deeply involved in work, she'd call and suggest they meet somewhere private. He'd probably get the idea that she was calling to make a date for them to make love. And he'd be partly right, she thought wryly.

"Maura, is that you, honey?"

Maura turned from putting her purse away to see Abe entering the living room. The look of concern on his face troubled her even more than she was already. She was here to see after Abe's health. Not the other way around. But several times this past week he'd caught her taking stomach medication instead of eating her breakfast and he'd pestered her until she'd promised to drive to town and visit the doctor.

Smoothing a hand over her hair, she wondered if she looked as unsettled as she felt. "I'm sorry I'm so late getting back, Abe. My sister was very busy and had to work me in as her last patient."

"Hmmph," he said with a snort. "You'd think being a relative you'd get special treatment."

"Bridget always plays fair," she said, then looked at him more closely. "Are you feeling okay?"

"Hell, yeah! Just worried about you." He took her by the arm and led through the small hallway toward the kitchen. "I've fixed you a nice little supper and I want you to sit and eat."

"Abe—"

"It's soup and crackers and iced tea. It'll soothe your stomach," he insisted.

Her heart melted. Abe wasn't a kitchen person. For him to take this much trouble for her was more than touching.

"Okay, I'll try to eat a little," she told him. "Let me go wash up and I'll be right back."

After a quick trip to the bathroom, Maura headed to the

kitchen and found Abe at the cookstove. As she sidled up to him, he winked at her and she suddenly realized that no matter what happened with Quint, she would always have this man's love. It was a comforting thought.

Stirring the broth and noodles, he explained, "Just giving the soup a little heat. Did that sister of yours give you something to fix your stomach?"

Maura let out a heavy breath. "Sort of."

Scowling, he practically shouted, "What the hell does that mean? Can't she fix an upset stomach? You need to eat. You're lookin' gaunt."

Emotions clogged her throat and stung her eyes. She tried to push it all away, but it was like fighting a tidal wave. Joy and fear were carrying on a giant war inside of her and she didn't know how to make the two emotions call a truce.

"I'll be fine," she said hoarsely. "It's just going to take a while for me to get over this."

Lying the spoon to one side, he thoughtfully ran his fingers down his drooping mustache, then cut his sharp gaze directly to her face.

"Why is that? You gonna have a baby?"

Maura gasped as warm color flooded her cheeks. "How did you guess?"

He grinned as though she'd just handed him a box of prized treasure. "My missus was pregnant twice. The first one she lost. The next one was Lewis. Both times she couldn't eat and she had that look about her. The same one you have now."

Maura's hands flew to her face. "Oh, Abe," she said with a tortured groan. "This is— I wasn't expecting this to happen to me. And I'm so happy. But I'm scared, too. I don't know what to think or what to do."

Horrified that she was going to cry in front of the old man, she bent her head and desperately tried to blink away the tears. As she tried to collect herself, she felt Abe's bony hands wrapping around her shoulders and pulling her into the circle of his arms.

"Maura, honey, this ain't anything to cry about. This is a wonderful thing. Really wonderful."

Resting her cheek against his shoulder, she sniffed. "You think so?"

Chuckles rumbled deep in his chest and the sound comforted Maura somewhat. If only Quint would react this way, she thought, then everything would be okay.

"God has blessed you. How can anything be bad about that?"

Lifting her head, she gave him a watery smile. "You're right. Babies are a gift," she agreed. "Even when they aren't planned."

"Now you're talkin' like my Maura girl." Patting her back, he leaned forward and pecked a kiss on her cheek. "Congratulations!"

Maura was giving the old man a grateful hug, when out of the blue Quint's voice sounded from across the room.

"Gramps? What—"

Turning away from Abe, she watched Quint saunter into the room. He looked tired and dusty and totally astounded as his squinted gaze vacillated between her and his grandfather.

Abe made a production of clearing his throat, then turned and switched off the fire beneath the copper saucepan.

"Looks like things are heated enough," he said in an overly loud voice. "You'd better take care of things now, Maura. I've got a date with the poker table."

The old man started out of the room, while a dumbfounded Quint stared after him. "Gramps! What are you doing? I—"

"Makin' myself scarce. That's what I'm doing," Abe interrupted. Then pausing at the door, he scowled at his grandson. "Make yourself at home, son. You always do."

Abe left the house, the screen door banging behind him. Quint immediately whirled on Maura for an explanation.

"What's the matter with him? And why was he kissing you? And why do you look so— What's happened around here?"

Closing her eyes, she breathed deeply and tried to compose herself. She wasn't ready for this. She needed more time to make a plan, to think of the best way to tell him he was going to be a daddy. But the moment Quint had walked into the room, all time had been snatched away from her.

"Abe's okay. He was trying to comfort me. Because… because—"

She couldn't finish and Quint crossed the room to where she stood, only to stop in his tracks when he spotted the damp trail of tears on her cheeks.

"You've been crying!" he exclaimed. "What's happened? Brady? He's not been wounded again, has he?"

Her stomach was fluttering, her heart racing madly. "No, my brother is fine. As far as I know everything with my family is okay. I've been a bit under the weather the past few days and—"

Uneasy now, he closed the last bit of space between them and wrapped his arms around her waist. "You didn't sound ill whenever I called you Sunday evening. You didn't mention anything to me then about being sick."

"No. I didn't know then what I know now."

A puzzled frown wrinkled his forehead. "You're not making sense."

Quint watched her wipe a shaky hand over her face and then she wrapped a hand around his arm and urged him toward the table. Like a lost lamb, he followed, his heart sinking with each step he took.

"I'm feeling a little shaky," she said. "While I explain, I need to sit. You need to sit."

Explain what? he wondered wildly. That she had some sort of terminal disease? That her days were numbered? The mere idea that he might lose her for any reason shook him right down to the heels of his boots. How, when had this woman come to mean so much to him? How had he let it happen?

"Maura, are you seriously ill? Tell me—"

At the head of the small dining table, she practically pushed him down in the chair, then sank limply in the one next to him.

Quint reached for her hand and squeezed it tightly. He needed to hold on to her. He needed to reassure himself that she was still the same vibrant woman he'd made love to in the hunting cabin.

"Please, Quint, this is nothing to worry about," she said quickly, trying to allay his fears. Then with a soft sigh she glanced to a spot across the room. "This is not the way I'd planned to do this. I wanted us to be in a nice, quiet place—somewhere special. I wanted you to be in a good mood and—"

"I am in a good mood. And Gramps's kitchen has always been a special place to me."

A faint smile touched her lips. "Maybe so. But you're frowning and nervous," she pointed out.

"Because you're making me that way with all this dallying around!" he said in a raised voice. "And you still haven't entirely explained why Gramps needed to comfort you with a kiss and a bear hug. Does he think that sort of stuff is going to heal you?"

Her nostrils flared and Quint could only think how beautiful she was when she was lying beneath him, her lips parted, her green eyes begging him to make love to her. He'd never had a woman who could weaken him with just a look. Until now.

"He wasn't trying to heal me," she said drolly. "He was congratulating me."

Seeing she was trying to make light of things, he teased, "For what? Keeping those dizzy rocks out of his ears?"

"No!" she wailed. Then she heaved out a heavy breath and turned her green eyes directly on his searching gaze. "Because I'm going to have a baby."

Quint didn't know how it happened, but suddenly his chair was teetering backward and he was in danger of hitting the hard tiled floor.

After scrambling to right himself, he stared at her in stunned fascination. "A—baby! How can that be? Are you sure?"

Nodding, she looked at him, her expression grim. "My sister ran a test. It's very accurate."

Momentarily paralyzed with shock, he tried to form the questions rushing at him like a hail of bullets. A baby! Him, a father! It was incredible! "But it's only been… It's not been that long since we… And you said you were on the pill!"

She closed her eyes and as he watched her bosom rapidly rise and fall, it suddenly dawned on him that she'd been crying because of the baby. Did that mean she didn't want it? That she'd told his grandfather about the pregnancy before she'd even bothered to tell him? Oh, God, what was going on in his lover's head? And why did everything in the room seem to be spinning around him as though he were drunk?

"Nowadays medical tests can tell when a woman is only a few days pregnant. Bridget estimates I'm three to four weeks along. So that means our trip to Chillicothe produced more than just a rainstorm," she said, then sucked in a deep breath and went on before Quint had time to digest half of her words. "As far as the birth control—that's a little harder to explain."

"Try."

Her lips pursed as she raked her eyes over his face and Quint realized he wasn't handling this in a sensitive enough way to suit her. But damn it, she'd shocked the hell out of him. And he wasn't a flowery man. She might as well get used to that and a whole lot more. Because it looked like their lives were about to drastically change.

Rising from the chair, she began to wander aimlessly around the small kitchen. Quint's gaze followed her slender figure while a wondrous sort of realization struck him. His baby was growing inside of her! A son. A daughter. And he wanted it as much as he wanted to draw his next breath.

She said, "A month before…uh…you and I…er…had sex, I got fouled up on my pill schedule. I didn't miss any, but they weren't taken in the proper succession. At the time I didn't think much about it. I mean since Gil I haven't been near a man. And when you…when we were together I'd long forgotten about getting out of sync with my pills."

Something inside of Quint suddenly wanted to shout out a joyous hallelujah. Yet at the same time icy shards of fear were splintering through him. How could he be so mixed up? How could he feel happy and terrified at the same time?

When he finally spoke, the tightness of his throat made his voice hoarse. "I see. So you told Abe about the baby before you bothered to even tell me."

Her pacing stopped and when she looked at him, her eyes flickered with uncertainty. What was she expecting him to do, throw a walleyed fit or something even more violent? The idea tore at him, made him realize that in spite of their lovemaking, she didn't know him as a man. Not as he wanted her to know him.

"I didn't run to Abe with the news, if that's what you're thinking," she answered. "Before I ever went to see Bridget, Abe was aware that I'd been feeling poorly and he guessed I was pregnant. I could hardly lie and deny it, Quint."

Rising to his feet, he went to her and gathered her hands in his. In spite of the connection, she continued to look up at him, her eyes searching, waiting, wanting. What was she expecting from him? And whatever it was, would he be able to give it to her?

"I should have known," he said gently. "The old man seems to have an inside line to God."

"Well—I can safely say your grandfather was happy about the news." Her troubled gaze dropped to the middle of his chest. "But I feel very badly, Quint. It's my fault that the birth control didn't work. And me being a nurse, I should have known—remembered about the pills and realized there could be a problem. But I— Well, that day at Chillicothe I wasn't thinking straight."

And that day his mind had stopped working completely, Quint realized. Even if she'd told him there was a chance she might get pregnant, he would have made love to her anyway. He'd wanted her that much.

His fingers tightened around hers. "No one is at fault, Maura. We did this together."

Her gaze lifted up to his and then a long breath eased out of her as though he'd just released a heavy yoke from around her neck. "Thank you, Quint," she said lowly. "I didn't want you to think… Well, I don't want you to feel obligated or—or cornered. I mean, I'll be happy for you to be all the father you want to be. But if you don't, I'll understand, too. After all, it's not like…we're madly in love or…engaged…or anything. And this all happened quite by accident."

As Maura spoke there were so many emotions erupting inside Quint that he couldn't describe any of them, much less understand why he was feeling them. The only thing he was able to disentangle from the messy turmoil was the sudden burst of anger shooting straight to the top of his head.

Dropping her hands, he repeated with cool amazement, "Cornered? Obligated? Do you realize how you sound? You're talking about my child. Mine! Everything inside of me is now obligated to him or her. And hell, yes, I'm going to be all the father I want to be! As far as I'm concerned, there's no questions or doubts as to what has to be done now. We're getting married."

Her mouth fell open and with a hand to her throat, she stumbled back from him. "M-m-married?" she stuttered.

He breathed deeply as he tried to gather himself together. "That's what I said."

Dazed, her head jerked back and forth. "You don't want to get married!"

Something stronger than himself was suddenly pushing at him, putting words on his tongue and pushing them past his lips before his mind could access any of them. "What you and I want has nothing to do with it. We have a child to think of now. And we're going to do our duty."

For a moment he feared she was going to burst into tears, but then a chilling look of disgust filled her eyes, shocking him with its intensity. What did she have to be disappointed about? He was stepping up to the plate, being a man about this whole thing.

"Duty? That's what you think this is all about?" She made a choking noise, then whirled away from him. "I'm sorry, Quint. This is all wrong. I can't marry you!"

"Maura!"

Quint didn't have the chance to say more. She raced past him and out of the room.

Dazed, Quint continued to stand in the middle of the room as he tried to figure out how one minute he'd gone from expecting to have a simple visit with his grandfather, to maybe kissing a woman he'd missed, to hearing he was going to become a father. It was more than a normal man could absorb in one night.

Tossing his hat on the table, he raked a hand through his hair, then stalked out of the room.

Down the hallway, to his right, he found the door to Maura's bedroom shut and locked. He rapped the back of his hand against the dark wood.

"Maura," he said firmly. "Let me in. We have to talk about this."

There was a long pause, then eventually, through the barrier of the door, she said in a choked voice, "We don't *have* to do anything. I've already given you my answer, Quint. No! I won't marry you."

"Why?"

After a moment, she sputtered back at him, "Because you're not husband material."

Closing his eyes, he pinched the bridge of his nose, while wondering where he'd gone wrong in all of this. And why was he making such an issue out of getting married? Truth be known, he'd never held much passion for the idea. Being married meant commitment, sacrifice, sharing his life on a daily basis. He couldn't imagine himself in that role. And yet something was driving him, telling him that nothing would ever be right unless Maura became his wife. It didn't make sense.

Dear God, was he losing his mind, or was that stone in his chest finally breaking apart, allowing him to want and feel and love? No. Not that last part, he thought. Love wasn't making him act like an idiot. It was the simple task of trying to deal with a woman that was tearing up his common sense.

"If that's what you thought, then why did you go to bed with me in the first place?" he wanted to know.

"For the same reason you climbed between the sheets with me!" she muttered back at him. "I like having sex!"

For one second, Quint considered kicking the door in, but stopped himself short. His grandfather would be furious with him and clearly Maura wasn't thinking too kindly of him at the moment. Losing his temper wasn't going to fix anything.

Right now he wasn't sure anything could be fixed.

"We'll talk about this later, Maura," he told her. "When you're thinking straight."

"An arrow couldn't be as straight as my thinking is right now," she countered flatly.

Instead of him rattling the door handle or shouting a reply, Maura heard his boots echoing down the hallway, then the slam of a door. Moments later, she heard his truck fire, and the beam of his headlights swept across the bedroom window before finally disappearing into the night.

His leaving relieved her and yet she felt so flat, so cold and full of pain that all she could do was fall across the bed and burst into racking sobs.

Obligation! Duty! He'd demanded she become his wife. He'd not even had the decency to propose to her, to gently give her a choice in the matter!

What did you expect, Maura? The man has never breathed the word love *to you in any shape, form or fashion. The only connection he has to you is the child growing in your belly. Get your head out of the clouds and get used to it.*

The voice inside her head stiffened her spine somewhat and she rose to a sitting position and carefully wiped her eyes with the back of her hand.

For a few minutes, the existence of the baby had marred her common sense, she realized. Momentarily, she'd let herself believe that Quint considered her more than a bed partner and she'd expected him to treat her as a man with his soul mate.

Oh, God, how could she have allowed herself to get so off course? Quint was viewing this whole thing from a practical point. And she—well, she'd behaved like a lovesick teenager who'd just realized her boyfriend was out for one thing and one thing only.

It was mortifying and she wasn't going to let it happen again. She'd already had one husband who hadn't loved her. She wasn't about to make the same mistake over again. The next time she talked to Quint, she would be cool, calm and collected. And she was going to tell him in a quiet, unwavering manner, that under no circumstances would she ever become his wife.

No matter what.

Chapter Nine

A little more than two weeks later, Maura sat with her mother on the couch in the Donovan family room. Once given the go-ahead, Bridget had wasted no time in spreading the news about Maura's pregnancy and for the past few days, each member of her family had, in their own way, offered her advice on the matter. Whether she'd asked for it or not.

In spite of Quint's continuing demands for her to marry him, Maura had persistently refused and all the Donovans believed she was making a mistake. Which only made her feel even more miserable about the whole predicament. As for Quint's family, Abe was clearly disappointed in her, but his mother, Frankie, had yet to say anything. Maura figured the woman felt as though she had no right to give advice on family matters. Not after she'd made some dicey choices of her own.

"Frankly, I don't understand you, Maura," Fiona said as she placed her teacup and saucer on the low table in front of them. "Quint is a respectable man. He's young and good-looking. And obviously you like him or you wouldn't be having his baby. Why don't you want to be his wife?"

The stubborn purse to Maura's lips broke as she let out a heavy sigh. "Mother, of all people, you shouldn't have to ask. You know what I went through with Gil. The humiliation, the dejection."

Her brows arched, the regal-looking woman leaned back against the couch. "What has Gil got to do with this? Surely you're not still carrying feelings for that hypocrite."

Rising from the couch, Maura walked over to the paned windows overlooking a view of the mountains. Compared to Quint's little house, the Donovan home was a lavish mansion and yet she'd felt completely comfortable there. Because he'd made the place special, she realized. He made everything special.

"Any feelings I had for Gil died a long time ago." Anguish twisted inside her chest and she closed her eyes as she prayed for the pain to go away. "I don't want to make another mistake, Mother. And Quint—he doesn't really want to be married. His desire to have us legally connected is all for the baby. Nothing else. I've had a marriage that wasn't based on a real love from both people and it didn't last. I don't want to be married to someone else who doesn't love me."

"And that bothers you."

With a muffled groan, Maura turned back to Fiona. "Of course it does!" she said, then swiping a helpless hand through her hair, she walked over to where she'd left her purse on the seat of a chair. "I'd better go, Mother. I told Bridget I'd meet her for lunch at the Blue Mesa. I'm going to have to hurry now to get there."

Quickly, Fiona rose from the couch and intercepted Maura before she could leave the room. "Darling," she said gently, "I understand what you want and need from Quint. But sometimes it's hard for a man to admit his feelings. Give him time."

The pain in Maura's chest dug deeper. "Quint doesn't love me. Time won't change that." Leaning forward, she pressed a kiss on her mother's cheek. "We'll talk about this later."

"Maura, please think about this carefully. If you care about Quint you should want to marry him. To try to make a life with him."

That was exactly why she didn't want to marry him, Maura thought. Because she loved him. Because deep down she considered his happiness far more important than hers. And he wouldn't be a happy man if he saddled himself to her out of obligation. And he'd never said anything about a life together—or even officially asked her out in public—before she found out she was pregnant.

"Goodbye, Mother. I'll call you soon."

On the drive leading off the Diamond D, she met Brady in his squad car, however when he waved at her and braked the vehicle to a stop, she just smiled at him and drove on. She'd already had one relative lecturing her this morning on the subject of Quint and no doubt over lunch Bridget would put her two cents in. Maura wasn't in the mood to deal with a third.

In Ruidoso, Maura was forced to park a block away from the Blue Mesa and walk back to the busy diner. Bridget was already there, sitting at one of the outside tables, which were all occupied by lunch-goers. She waved at Maura.

"I was lucky enough to get a table in the shade," she said as Maura pulled out a chair opposite her younger sister. "I hope you don't mind eating outside. The day is so lovely and I figured we could both use the fresh air."

"I'm just thrilled that I was able to smell food this morning without running to the bathroom and retching. But to be on the safe side, I only nibbled on dry toast for breakfast. So now I'm ravenous."

Chuckling, Bridget warned, "That will only get worse, dear sis."

Maura was shoving her handbag under the chair just as a waiter arrived at their table. After he'd taken their orders, Bridget asked, "Have you seen Quint lately?"

Even though she'd expected this from Bridget, she wasn't prepared for the bittersweet pain assaulting her senses. Not after she'd just gotten over the emotional exchange she'd had with her mother. Surely, she'd hurt enough for one day, she thought miserably.

"Two days ago. He came to Apache Wells. To see his grandfather, I assume."

Her pregnancy and refusal to marry him had thrown a cool wall between the two of them and Maura hated the distance between them. Every minute of the day she wished they could go back to being that man and woman making love at Chillicothe and the old hunting cabin. She missed being in his arms, missed the pleasure and joy of being close to him.

A frown puckered her sister's forehead. "Did you two talk?"

"Some. But nothing has changed, so don't bother asking," Maura said flatly.

Bridget simply retorted, "You're making a mistake, Maura."

Crossing her legs, Maura focused her gaze on the far distant peak of Sierra Blanca. The early autumn snows had yet to fall, but soon the white cap would appear. By then Maura's waist would be thick with Quint's child. The idea filled her with love, yet at the same time she felt totally lost. Where would her home be when the baby arrived? Would Quint still be interested in her and the child or would that end, too?

"I've made plenty of mistakes before," she said with wry sarcasm. "Why should I change now?"

"Maura! If a man like Quint wanted to marry me, do you know what I'd do? I'd jump at the chance!"

"Not if he didn't love you."

Bridget was clearly disgusted. "You clearly care for him. Doesn't that count? Doesn't that mean you want to be in his house, his bed?"

It did. But could Maura live with the idea that she was there only because of their child? Up until she'd met Quint, she'd always carefully weighed the decisions she'd made in her life. Even marrying Gil—though they'd only dated a few months—had been a thought-out process; at least, she'd believed she'd considered the serious step carefully, and by the time she'd walked down the aisle with him, she'd been twenty-nine years old. A mature woman. Not a teenager incapable of making important decisions. And yet with all her careful planning, she'd wound up getting her heart broken. Why in the world did her family expect her to jump into marriage now, without thinking, and to a man who didn't love her? A man who'd said he didn't believe in romance and never wanted to talk about feelings?

"Please, Bridget. I don't want to argue about this now.

That's all I've heard from Mother this morning and now you. I—"

Bridget threw up a both hands to ward off the rest of Maura's tirade. "Okay, sissy. I hear you loud and clear. We'll talk about something else."

Thankfully, Bridget kept her word and Maura managed to eat her lunch while the two of them discussed happenings at the hospital and the Donovan ranch.

Later, when the waiter questioned them about having dessert, Maura impulsively ordered a rich frosted brownie and decaffeinated coffee, then excused herself to find the bathroom.

As Maura rose to her feet, Bridget joked another warning, "That will get worse, too."

Maura arched a wry brow at her sister. "Is there anything that gets better with pregnancy?"

"Sure. Holding your little baby in your arms."

Maura smiled at her. "Thank you for reminding me, sis. And don't eat my brownie if it gets back to the table before I do."

Inside the restaurant, she made her way through the busy tables until she reached an annex where the ladies' room was located. Even that small space was filled to capacity, forcing her to wait in line until a stall was vacated.

Finally her turn came and she was still behind the locked cubicle, zipping her trousers, when she caught the sound of two women talking in hushed tones. Normally, Maura didn't take notice of that sort of thing. She didn't have the time or the appetite for gossip. But the words *pregnant* and *ranch* had caught her attention, causing her to purposely pause to catch more.

"—was the first time I saw her in ages. She looks gorgeous."

"Yeah. But divorced and pregnant. How would you like to have those problems on your plate?" the other woman responded.

Running water sounded, then the rip of paper towels. Above the noise, the first woman said, "I've been hearing lots of talk. You know she's been staying out at that old man's ranch."

"Yeah. Abe Cantrell," the second woman said, supplying the name. "Eccentric, I hear, but loaded to the gills with money. Guess he decided to buy himself some female attention."

"Well, I understand that some women are turned on by older men, but—" Woman One made a shuddering noise. "Having his baby. That's creepy."

Maura's fingers flew to her mouth. People were thinking she was pregnant with Abe's child? Oh, God, it couldn't be true! But it was! She was hearing it with her own ears.

"I'm just amazed that the old man is still that virile. He has to be in his eighties!" Woman Number Two exclaimed in a scandalous whisper, "And I sure can't figure the woman. She has plenty of her own money. Why would she be after his?"

"Who said she was?" Woman Number One giggled. "Maybe she's in it for the sex."

More laughter erupted before the two women finally shuffled out of the facility. By then Maura felt totally ill and though she wanted to race after the two women and confront them, she didn't. Other than humiliating herself, what good would it do? Assumptions about her and Abe had probably already spread over the county.

Stumbling to the lavatory, she splashed her face with cold water, then went out to rejoin Bridget.

As the two women finished their meal, Maura didn't mention the incident in the ladies' room. No doubt her family would hear the gossip soon enough and talking about it wouldn't ease Maura's guilt at marring the Donovan good name.

Later that afternoon, Quint was gritting his teeth, struggling to hold on to his temper, but Abe was pushing him to the breaking point.

He didn't know what in hell Abe was trying to do to him. Didn't he realize that his grandson had more serious things on his mind than reopening the Golden Spur? For the past week, his grandfather had continued to call and pester Quint about that damned old gold mine and, sick of arguing over the phone, Quint had decided to drive to Apache Wells and settle the matter once and for all. But as soon as he'd stepped through the door, Abe had dismissed the mine project and started pounding on him about Maura.

"Maura doesn't want to be my wife, Gramps! How many times do I have to tell you that?" Quint barked at his grandfather.

"She's gonna have your baby."

"Damn it all, don't you think I know that?" Quint muttered, then jumped up from the armchair he was in, left the living room and stalked to the kitchen.

Abe marched after him. "What are you gonna do about it?" the old man demanded. "Wait around until some other man grabs her? Some man that'll love her and make her happy?"

Quint jerked a beer from the bottom shelf, then turned to his grandfather as he twisted off the cap. "What am I supposed to do? Beg?"

Quint had never seen his grandfather look so furious. In fact, this was the first time he'd ever see the man truly angry with him. Sure, they often bantered in a sarcastic way, but they both understood it was done with underlying love. Abe's wasn't playing now and Quint was shaken by the change in him.

"Beg! That's not what Maura wants! And if you had half the sense I thought you had, you wouldn't have to be told what to do. You'd grab her—make her swoon, make her happy to be at your side!"

Quint was staring at his grandfather, wondering how he could possibly defend himself against that argument, when both men heard the bang of the screen door at the front of the house.

Momentarily stunned by the interruption, both turned to see Maura wearily entering the kitchen. She took one look at the two men, burst into tears and ran straight to Abe's arms.

"Here, here now, honey! What's all of this about?" he asked gently.

Hurt that she would run to Abe before coming to him, Quint stood to one side and wondered why he didn't have the right touch, the special words to bring her back to his arms. He'd never cared about that before, but somehow with Maura he hated that she'd gone to another man—even his grandfather—when she was troubled.

Pushing herself away from Abe's bony chest, she tried to dry her eyes. "Oh, Abe, people are talking! They think that you— That I'm having your baby!"

"Hellfire!" Quint barked with outrage.

A moment of silence passed before Abe finally slapped his knee and let out a loud whoop of laughter. "Well, I'll be damned. Me. Siring a baby. I didn't know I still had it in me!"

"Damn it, Gramps, this isn't funny!" Quint growled at him.

Folding his arms across his chest, Abe drew back his shoulders and grinned like a cat with a saucer of cream. "I sorta like it myself."

"Oh, Abe, it's terrible," Maura wailed. "They think I'm after your money or worse."

He swatted a dismissive hand through the air. "I know the truth. Who cares about a bunch of gossipin' tongues anyway."

"I do."

Maura and Quint spoke at the same time, causing Abe to level a long, measured look at the both of them.

"If that's the way you two feel then there's an easy way to put a stop to all the chin-waggin'. Get married."

Maura looked at Quint and felt something inside her snap with relief. She'd been resisting because she'd not wanted another one-sided marriage where she'd done all the loving. But to live with this man, under any circumstances, would be better than being alone, aching for the sound of his voice, the touch of his hand. And maybe someday he might actually grow to love her. She had to take that chance. She'd protect herself as best she could, holding back on admitting her feelings until she knew how he felt. Otherwise, she had no chance with him at all.

"Maura?" Quint gently questioned.

"I—" She licked her lips, then closed the last few steps between them. "Maybe it would be the best thing to do— for the baby."

A long breath eased from Quint and then he reached for

her. As he folded her into his arms, he said, "We'll be married as soon as possible."

Across the room, Abe smiled to himself and slipped out the door.

Fiona asked for a month to get the wedding organized, but instead Quint gave his future mother-in-law two weeks to prepare the church, ceremony and reception. The Donovan women worked overtime and when the day for the wedding finally rolled around, Our Lady of Guadalupe, the small church in Hondo Valley, was filled with flowers and music, flickering candlelight, family and well-wishers.

As the couple left the church beneath a rain of rice, the sky was sunny, the air crisp with the first nip of early fall. On the ride to the Donovan ranch, Quint could hardly take his eyes off Maura. He'd always heard the old saying that all brides were beautiful, but he couldn't imagine any woman looking more beautiful than Maura did today.

Her dress was creamy lace that framed her bosom with a heart-shaped V while the hem ended just below her knees. At the back of her head, her red hair was pinned in an elaborate twist and entwined with some sort of tiny, ivory-colored flowers that smelled sweet and alluring. Emeralds glistened in her ears and around her neck, yet the plain gold band on her left hand seemed far richer than any jewels Quint had ever seen. She was now Mrs. Quint Cantrell. A reality that was both heady and scary to Quint.

During the uncertain weeks after she'd told him about the pregnancy and up until today, they'd not made love. Not that Quint hadn't wanted to. Especially after she'd finally agreed to become his wife. These past days, every cell in him had been aching to be intimate with her again. But both of their schedules had been worse than hectic and the opportunity to be alone with her had never presented itself.

Now as he sat next to her in the back of the luxurious limousine that her family had provided, he could hardly keep his mind on anything else. And he wondered if, once they were on their honeymoon, she would be the same giving woman he'd made love to at the hunting cabin.

Her fight against this marriage had confused him and left him feeling very uncertain about their relationship, about her and even himself. Obviously she didn't love him. And he didn't expect that. Yet her reluctance to be his wife had stung him in a way he didn't want to think about. Especially not today, during this momentous time in their lives.

"I thought the ceremony was beautiful," he commented.

Smiling faintly, she glanced at him. "So did I. And I'm so glad your sister and brothers were able to fly in from Texas and attend. And that your brothers agreed to be your grooms."

Abe had been his best man and this morning as they'd prepared to head for the church, Quint had been shocked to see his grandfather all duded up in a dark Western suit, a bolo tie pushed tight against the collar of his starched white shirt. The old man had looked distinguished indeed and Quint couldn't help but wonder how Abe must have looked to his Grandmother Jenna all those years ago, when in the prime of their lives, they'd stood at the altar together.

Reaching for Maura's hand, he said gently, "I'm just very grateful that your family has accepted me like they have. With the baby and all—I wasn't sure what they were going to think of me."

Her lashes swept demurely against her cheeks. "Oh, Quint, they know this wasn't a case of you taking advantage of an innocent young woman. We're both—" She paused, her fingers instinctively tightening around his. "Responsible adults."

Yes. Responsible. That's why he'd wanted this marriage. To do the proper and responsible thing. So why didn't that rationale feel right whenever it was spoken out loud?

Shoving that troubling thought away, he changed to a more pleasant subject. "I hope you're happy about going to Hawaii for our honeymoon. I know it's a typical spot for newlyweds, but I thought—"

"I've never been to the Hawaiian Islands, Quint. I'm very pleased about going."

"Are you?"

Taken aback by his question, she turned toward him. "You don't sound as though you believe me. Why?"

He shrugged. "To be honest, I wasn't sure you'd even want to have a honeymoon or be in my bed again."

A pained look crossed her beautiful face and then with a muffled groan, she leaned close and rested her palm against the side of his cheek. Her touch was like a piece of sunshine after a hard, cold winter.

She whispered, "Just because I was against us getting married doesn't mean I want the relationship we had to end."

Relief poured through him and with a needy groan, he pulled her into his arms and didn't stop kissing her until they reached the Donovan house.

The honeymoon turned out to be far more lovely than Maura imagined it could be. For two long weeks they enjoyed the tropical climate, the beautiful beaches and each other. Quint couldn't seem to keep his hands off her and Maura had been completely surprised at just how he seemed to enjoy the tropical paradise and her.

But now that they were back on the Golden Spur and a month had passed, the memories of their honeymoon seemed almost surreal to Maura. As soon as they returned from Hawaii, Quint got back to the huge task of building the Spur into a profitable ranch and as each day went by, his attention seemed to grow more and more consumed with work, while Maura was left to keep herself occupied.

After Maura and Quint had married, Abe had quickly insisted that he no longer needed a nurse. His dizzy spells appeared to be a thing of the past and if he did come down with one, he assured them that Jim would be around to see after him.

Maura was glad Abe's health was well enough for him to do without her. She loved him as she had loved her own grandfather and wanted him to be able to actively enjoy his horses and ranch. But she missed being needed by the old man, missed the quiet evenings they'd spent simply talking about nothing in particular. Without any words, she'd understood that Abe liked her, even loved her. With Quint she couldn't quite discern what was going on behind his blue eyes, what was in his heart whenever he touched her. He would come home late and tired, and after a quick supper, generally just wanted to rest, not talk.

With Quint throwing his all into the ranch, Maura got busy creating a nursery in the spare bedroom. The task was a pure joy and she spent hours decorating the walls and windows, filling it with furniture, toys and baby necessities. But once the nursery was completed, she once again found herself puttering around the house, hunting anything to do to keep her mind occupied and off the uncertain bonds of her marriage.

Then one day when Maura was having lunch with Bridget, her sister offered her a light-duty nursing job at her private clinic. Maura was thrilled with the idea and that same evening when Quint returned to the house, she couldn't wait to tell him about her new job offer.

"You want to go to work?" he asked with surprise as the two of them sat down to dinner. "But why? There's no need for you to work."

"There's no need for you to work, either," she parried.

He grimaced as he plopped sour cream on a baked potato. "A man has to have a purpose."

"So does a woman," she argued. "And I'm not the aimless sort, Quint."

"You do all the bookkeeping for the ranch," he pointed out. "That's meaningful."

"At most, that takes me a couple of hours a week. I can't just sit around for the rest of the time. And in my condition, I can't help you with strenuous ranching chores. Nursing is my profession and Bridget needs me to cover another nurse who is taking some time off. And it's just for the next three months or so."

Looking up from his plate, his blue eyes searched her face. "But it's miles from town. You'll have a long drive every day getting to and from work."

She smiled at him. "I'm healthy and have plenty of energy. It'll be better for me to be occupied than sitting here bored."

Frowning, he picked up a steak knife and sliced through a strip of rare beef. "I thought you liked it here on the ranch," he said sullenly.

Seeing he misunderstood, she sighed. "I do like it, Quint. But—"

Glancing back up at her, he said, "Look, Maura, I know this house is old and needs some work here and there. That it's not nearly as nice as what you're accustomed to. But when we came back from Hawaii I offered for us to live at the Chaparral and you turned it down. Are you regretting that decision now?"

Vexed that he was getting so off course of the real issue, she shook her head. "Not at all. This is your home and—"

"It's not just my home. Now that we're married, it's yours, too," he interrupted with a bit of frustration. "If it's not good enough for you—"

She put down her fork and leaned back in her chair. "Quint, please slow down and quit being so defensive. This has nothing to do with the house. I need to have something to do. Are you against women working or something?"

"I'm not a caveman," he said sharply, then released a heavy breath. "I would never try to keep you from working, Maura. I just think—well, we hardly need the money. And we've not been married for very long. The baby is coming and I thought—"

He broke off and Maura waited patiently for him to continue, but instead he stubbornly returned his attention to his plate.

Maura said, "I'd like for you to finish, Quint. What were you thinking?"

He put down his fork and looked at her. Maura was immediately surprised to see a hint of color creeping up his neck and she wondered if it bothered him that much to express his real feelings to her. She hated to think so. Hated to think she was the one person in his life he couldn't talk to.

"This is going to sound stupid, especially since I—" He shook his head. "Forget that. What I'm trying to say is that

I thought you were a woman who would be satisfied with simpler things—a simpler life."

Not like Holly, who'd wanted more and more and not been satisfied until she'd ran off with another, Quint thought bitterly. Not like the women he'd later dated, who'd suggested he build a mansion or use his money to move to some island paradise.

"You're insulting me now, Quint," she said stiffly. "I don't want more or better things. You've seen the way I live. I was at your grandfather's home for a long while and his home is similar."

She was right. He was being insulting. Maura wasn't a spoiled rich girl. She wasn't even close to that. And there wasn't any reason for him to be putting up a fuss about her helping at her sister's clinic. He didn't know why he was behaving this way. Except that the moment she'd told him about the job, he'd viewed it as her drawing away from him, severing the few fragile threads holding them together.

Why he felt so unsure about their marriage, he didn't know. For the past six weeks since the wedding, she'd been like an adoring little kitten in his arms. When he asked her to make love, she never turned away. And yet he couldn't help feeling as though a part of her was vacant, as though that magical thing that he'd first felt between them had slowly and surely evaporated.

"I'm sorry, Maura. I wasn't thinking how it must be with you here most of the day by yourself—with little to do now that you've got the nursery and house in hand. If you want to work at Bridget's clinic, then go for it. You hardly need my permission anyway."

She got up from the table and retrieved a pitcher of iced water from the cabinet. As she refilled their glasses, she said, "No. Just like you don't need my permission whenever you leave the house in the mornings and return home long after dark."

Her voice wasn't exactly cool or sharp, yet he felt cut to the bone just the same. And he wondered sickly if this was already the beginning of the end.

What did you expect, you fool? She only agreed to marry you because of the gossip and the baby. She's not here because she wants to be your wife, to live in the same house, share her life with you. And she's definitely not here because she loves you. So forget it. You can play at being man and wife, but it won't ever be the real thing.

The voice inside him made Quint want to curse aloud. Hell, what did that maudlin, sarcastic part of him know, anyway? He didn't want Maura to love him. He didn't want to love her. All he wanted was for them to be happy. And a person didn't have to have love to be happy. Love only made things complicated and painful. Being together was enough. It had to be. Because living with Maura was one thing, while having her love appeared to be beyond his reach.

Chapter Ten

A few days later, Maura was stripping a used sheet from an examining table when Bridget walked in the small room and took her sister by the arm.

"Okay," she declared in an authoritative voice. "That's enough for today. You've not sat down since lunch." She forced Maura into the nearest plastic chair positioned against the wall. "Before you started this job we agreed you'd have light duty."

Maura waved a dismissive hand at her. "I'm not over-tiring myself. I'm enjoying this."

Bridget rested a hip against the table as she leveled a stern gaze at Maura. "Maybe so. But I want you to go home for the remainder of the day."

Maura glanced at her watch. "It's only three o'clock and you still have several patients to see," she insisted.

"And you have a long drive to the Golden Spur."

"Bridget—"

"If you're going to argue with me, I'll just have to fire you. Besides, you should be happy to get home early and see that husband of yours."

Maura grimaced. These days it was an effort to see Quint at all. He rose and left the house well before daylight and didn't come home until long after dark. The only chance she had to spend much time with her husband was on Sundays when the two of them attended church services together, then shared dinner afterward. Yet even then he seemed distracted and restless, as though spending time exclusively with her bothered him in some way. She understood he was in the process of building a new ranch and she understood that for a while, the project was going to consume his time. But she'd been getting the feeling that he was using his ranch work to deliberately stay away from the house and her. Why, she didn't know. She could only assume that he found it a relief to stay away from her.

"Quint won't be home until bedtime."

"Oh? He has something pressing going on?"

A familiar ache of tears suddenly clogged Maura's throat and she swallowed hard. Being pregnant was making her overly emotional, she told herself. It had nothing to do with Quint's distant behavior.

"No…he—" She broke off and wiped a trembling hand over her face. "I don't know what's going on with him, Brita. He doesn't seem to want to be with me anymore. We sleep in the same bed and we even make love. But a part of him is somewhere else." She turned a miserable gaze on her sister. "I think he regrets marrying me, but he's going through the motions because of the baby." Dropping her head in her hand, she swallowed again as tears now threatened the back of her eyes. "Everything he's done is because of the baby."

"I don't believe that."

Maura sighed. "Well, you'd better start believing it. Your practical sister has jumped straight into another heartache. God, I can't believe I stepped out of one terrible marriage only to turn around and jump into another! What's the matter with me, Brita? Don't I have any sense where men are concerned? I should have stuck to my guns and refused to marry Quint. That would have been better for both of us. Now he's miserable and I'm miserable."

"Have you talked to him about this? Told him your concerns?" Bridget asked.

Maura stared at her. "Why no! How could I? He told me he doesn't believe in romance, that he will never fall in love and doesn't want anyone to love him. I can't put the pressure of my love on him now!"

Bridget was rolling her eyes when a light knock sounded on the door and a young nurse named Michelle stuck her head into the room.

"Sorry to interrupt, Dr. Donovan, but Mrs. Montgomery is in examining room two and working her blood pressure up to the boiling point."

Bridget grimaced. "Okay, Michelle. I'll be there shortly. But kindly remind the woman that she's not the only patient around here."

"Yes, ma'am."

The nurse disappeared and Maura was once again caught in her sister's censuring gaze.

"Maura, you sound ridiculous," she scolded lightly. "You sleep in the same bed with Quint. You're his wife. You'd have to be a robot not to love the man. Surely he knows that."

Maura gave her head a rueful shake. "No. I told him it was only for the sex."

Clearly astounded, her sister's mouth dropped open. "Oh, Maura! You didn't! Why?"

Wadding the dirty sheet into a tight ball, Maura left the chair to stuff the white piece of fabric into a plastic hamper. "Because I—" Whirling back to her sister, she said in an anguished rush, "Look, Bridget, Gil pretty much shattered my self-worth. What he did to me made me feel worse than a fool. He didn't love me. He was using me. For the past year, I was doing my best to get over all that. And slowly I was learning to believe in myself again. Then when Quint came along and showed interest in me, my self-confidence as a woman really started to bloom. I thought that maybe I was still attractive to men. I thought that maybe—" She broke off as the pain in her chest rose up in her throat and she was forced to look away.

"What else were you thinking, sis?" Bridget urged after Maura failed to go on.

"Oh, Brita, before I got pregnant Quint and I were growing close—I mean, more than physically close. And I was starting to believe that maybe he really cared about me. That he might even grow to love me. But then when I told him about the baby, everything seemed to change. He didn't ask me to marry him, he demanded it. He mentioned nothing about caring for me or wanting me in his life. He didn't seem to have any consideration of my wants or needs. He just kept talking about duty and obligation and I was so hurt that I was determined not to let him stomp the last bit of my pride to pieces. I lashed back at him and that's when I told him that I'd slept with him only for the sex."

Bridget groaned with despair. "What a mess! You can't let this go on, Maura. You've got to tell Quint how you really feel about him or nothing is going to get better."

Maura wasn't so sure it could ever get better. But oh, God, how she desperately wanted it to.

Her knees suddenly week, Maura leaned against a work counter lined with first-aid items and medical instruments. "I don't know, Brita. I just don't know. Marriage, the baby—it all seemed to put a cool wall between us. The word *love*...I'm afraid it would only complicate things even worse."

Grimacing, Bridget pushed away from the examining table and headed toward the door. With her hand paused on the doorknob, she said, "Well, I can't see how that could be. But I'm hardly an authority on men and love. This is your life and your happiness. You're the one who'll have to do something to try to fix things—or ultimately regret it."

Back on the Golden Spur, Quint and Jake were riding the creek's edge, heading home after a morning of work that had taken them several miles northeast of the ranch yard.

A few minutes ago, they'd skirted old Chillicothe, and seeing the place where he'd first made love to Maura, even from a distance, had left Quint feeling more than melancholy. That trip with her had been very special to him. That day, for the first time in years, he'd felt excited about living, about the future. About having someone to share it with.

Had he loved Maura even then? For the past few months, he'd been telling himself that everything he did was not for her or for him. It was for the baby. But that wasn't entirely true. He didn't hold Maura in his arms each night only because her body excited him. He didn't want her as his wife simply because she was the mother of his child. He loved her. He hadn't planned on it, was afraid to tell her about it. So what did that make him? The biggest sap in the world?

"What's the matter, Quint? You've been quiet all afternoon."

Jake's question caused Quint's head to swing around toward his longtime friend. "Nothing is wrong. I've just had a lot on my mind. The past few days Gramps has been giving me hell about reopening the mine. He's like a dog with a bone. I tell you, Jake, I wished the damned thing was anywhere but here on my ranch property."

"Well, you just said the key word, buddy. This is *your* property. You can do what you want. If you're against opening the mine again, then put your foot down and tell the old man to quit yammering about it."

Quint grimaced as he contemplated Jake's suggestion. Even though the majority of Cantrell property was a shared conglomerate of the family, Abe had signed papers turning the Golden Spur property solely over to Quint. Yet in Quint's mind, that technicality hardly mattered. Family was family. He didn't want to hurt his grandfather over a blasted hole in the mountain.

"Jake, this ranch is mine because of Gramps. If not for him, I…my father…none of us Cantrells would have anything. Besides," he added glumly, "it's not just Gramps and the mine that has me distracted. Maura is—"

"What? Not feeling good?"

Quint's gaze dropped to the saddle horn as he easily envisioned Maura as she'd looked last night in a thin nightgown that had clung to her body. Her pregnancy was beginning to show and each time he looked at the rounded bump of her belly, he wanted to pull her into his arms and tell her how much he loved her and the baby.

But each time he got close to expressing his feelings, a sick sort of fear rushed over him. His throat clamped shut and his palms turned clammy. Marriage—a marriage only he'd wanted—had changed everything, had erected an invisible barrier between them that he couldn't seem to tear down. Telling her that he loved her might make it even worse.

"Her health is fine," he finally muttered.

Jake let out a long sigh. "I'm sorry, Quint, but you sound about as happy as a man who's just been thrown in jail. Didn't I tell you not to marry the woman? You didn't have to do that to be a good father to the kid. Now you're all glum and moody and worrying if you're gonna lose her."

Quint's head jerked up. "Why do you say that? You think Maura is going to leave me? Does she act that unhappy to you, too?"

Jake cursed as he maneuvered his horse away from a patch of prickly pear. "Worry. That's all a man ever does when he loves a beautiful woman. First he frets about catching her. And then when he does get his hands on her, he worries himself silly wondering if he'll be able to keep her."

Quint hated to admit it, but his cynical friend was right. From the moment he'd kissed Maura at the altar, he'd known that their marriage was a bargain for the baby's sake, not something with a real foundation. How long could he expect it to last?

Once they reached the ranch yard and Quint began to unsaddle his mount, he was still asking himself that same question. But the answer wouldn't come.

When the cell phone in his pocket shrilled loudly, the distraction was somewhat of a relief. Until he saw it was his grandfather calling. For the old man to ring his cell phone, it had to be something important. Or at least, important to Abe.

"Hello, Gramps," he said as he held the phone with one hand and used the other to place a sweaty horse blanket over the top rail of a wooden fence. "Are you all right?"

"Hell, yes, I'm all right! I'm talking to you, ain't I?"

Quint breathed deeply and tried to hang on to his patience. "You normally ring the house phone."

"I've learned that doesn't do anything but waste time. You're never in the house and Maura ain't, either. Now that you've let her go to work," he added with undisguised sarcasm.

Quint led his dun-colored mount, Champ, over to a nearby stall and slipped the bridle from his mouth.

"I don't 'let' Maura do anything," Quint drawled. "She's a grown woman. She does what she wants to."

Abe snorted. "Have you forgot that she's pregnant?"

"You didn't appear to be worried about that when she was working for you," Quint countered.

There was a long pause and then Abe said, "I ain't callin' about Maura. I want you to get over here. I just got off the phone with the big shot of Red Bluff. He's given me some estimates and I want to go over them with you. And not over the damned phone, either."

His teeth grinding together, Quint locked the gate on the stall and started out of the barn. "You went behind my back and called the man?"

Insulted, Abe practically shouted, "Behind your back? It ain't like we haven't talked about this for months. I'm gettin' tired of you bein' so wishy-washy and sittin' on your—"

"All right!" Quint practically shouted. "I'm coming over there right now! We're going to get this mining thing settled once and for all. And this time, I mean it!"

Abe's reply to that was to slam the telephone receiver back on the hook.

Halfway across the ranch yard, Quint met Jake. "Feed Champ for me," Quint told him. "I've got to go to Apache Wells. Once you get the feeding done, you might as well call it a day. I won't be back before late."

Shaking his head, Jake gave him an affectionate slap on the shoulder. "Don't worry about things here, buddy. Just do what you have to do."

On the drive home, Maura wrestled with the idea of having a heart-to-heart talk with Quint tonight. Perhaps Bridget was right. If he understood how much she loved him, then he might view their whole marriage in a different way. If it would even draw him back to the way he'd been with her before she'd told him about the baby, then it would be worth the risk, she decided, as she parked her car at the side of their small ranch house.

She didn't how she was going to approach him or even find the nerve to confess her love, but she had to find the courage somewhere.

Inside the house, she put her things away, then went to the kitchen to see what she could find toward making a special meal for the evening ahead. Instead, she found a note Quint had left lying on the kitchen table, telling her that he'd gone to see his grandfather and not to expect him back for supper.

Terribly disappointed, Maura walked over to the wall of windows and tried not to cry as she stared out at the sea of cholla cacti and sage sweeping to the west. How many days, months, years had she sat at home alone, waiting for Gil to decide he wanted to spend time with her? She couldn't begin to count those lonely, unhappy days and nights. Now, after swearing to never let another man hurt her, she was back on the same path, waiting for a man, even though she clearly knew that man didn't love her.

Was she crazy or just one of those people who couldn't help but walk down a path of self-destruction?

Later that evening, just before dark settled over the ranch, Maura forced down a light meal then went to sit on the front porch. Cuddled in a thick sweater and sipping coffee from a thermal mug, she was suddenly surprised by the sound of a vehicle coming from the direction of the ranch yard. Had Jake or one of the building contractors stayed behind to work late?

Before she could rise to go look, she spotted Jake's pickup truck pulling through the ranch yard gate. Obviously the man had stayed behind to finish an important task and was just now heading home. A place, which Quint had told her, was a small piece of property near Fort Stanton.

Since Maura had come to live on the Golden Spur, she'd gotten to know Quint's best friend and ranch hand a bit better. But she doubted anyone, other than her husband, knew the man completely. Gradually, she'd discovered he was a man of contradictions. On the surface he seemed to take life and himself as a joke, yet there had been moments when Maura had seen him staring off in the distance, his thoughts obviously too deep for him to share.

Lowering her cup, she watched him carefully latch the gate behind him then climb back into his truck. Fully expecting him to turn onto the long dirt road leading away from the ranch, she was bemused to see him brake to a stop in front of the house.

As he walked across the small yard toward the porch, she noticed he was dressed in clean jeans and a starched white shirt. Clearly, he was headed somewhere other than home and had used the facilities in the barn to freshen up.

"Good evening, Jake," she greeted.

Lifting a black hat from his head, he held it politely at his side. "Evening, Maura. I saw you sitting out here and thought I'd stop by. See if you needed anything before I left for town."

"That was thoughtful of you. But I can't think of anything—except for my husband to come home," she added wistfully.

A benevolent smile curved the corners of his mouth. "I think he and his grandfather were going at it over something. I expect he'll be home shortly."

"I hope you're right," Maura said, trying her best to sound lighthearted, but failing miserably. She gestured toward a chair positioned a few feet away from her. "Would you like to sit and have a cup of coffee? The pot is still fresh."

He stepped onto the porch and eased onto the edge of a bent willow chair. "I'll sit for a moment. But I'll have to pass on the coffee. I've got to get to Ruidoso in about forty minutes."

"Looks like you're on your way to a special outing," she observed.

His chuckle was a bit self-conscious and Maura smiled to herself. Apparently, Jake was planning to enjoy a bit of female companionship tonight and she was glad. Like Quint, the man worked far too hard and, as far as she knew, did very little socializing.

"Just a little date with Rita Baxter."

Maura tried to hide her disapproval, but it must have shown on her face because his features crinkled into a comical frown.

"Looks like you don't think too highly of Rita," he said.

Maura made an issue of straightening her sweater as she tried to think of the best way to reply. Jake was such a devoted friend that she hated to hurt his feelings. But Rita was not the right woman for him. True, she was from a well-to-do family and ran a popular souvenir shop in Ruidoso, but she used men for her own benefit.

"Well, have you known her long?"

"Oh. I wouldn't say that I could write her life history. But I've been acquainted with the woman for a while. Ever since she started showing up at the Finish Line—you know, the nightclub out by the track. Before that—well, I never traveled in that rich of a social circle."

She slanted him a droll look. "Jake, you can't get much richer than Quint and you've been traveling in his circle for years."

He batted a dismissive hand through the air. "Shoot, that's different, Maura. Quint might be rich, but he don't act it. Most folks wouldn't know he and his family own half the county unless you told them. But Rita—well, I think she likes flaunting what she has."

Maura let out a breath of relief. "So you know that—"

"She's a man-eater?" he finished with a sly grin.

A blush stung Maura's face. "Well, I wasn't going to describe her quite that way. But since you brought it up, yes. She's out for herself. And I happen to think you could do a whole lot better than Rita Baxter."

He surprised her with a low chuckle. "Thanks, Maura. But you don't have to warn me about her. I know what she is."

Confused now, Maura shook her head. "If you know, then why are you dating her?"

His grin was tinged with wry resignation. "Because I'm not nearly as lucky as Quint. I don't have a good woman like you to come home to every night. I have to settle for something far less."

Maura was so momentarily stunned by his remark she didn't know what to say. After Gil's infidelity, she'd believed she must be lacking, that a decent man would never give her a second thought. Now she could see how ridiculous that sort of thinking had been. She was a good woman. And she had lots to offer Quint and their marriage. If only he would open his heart and accept her love.

"That's nice of you, Jake. But take it from me, don't ever sell yourself short. And most of all, don't let Rita get her hooks into you."

Rising to his feet, Jake plopped his hat on his head. "No chance in that happening, Maura. I've got my eyes wide-open." He stepped off the porch, then gave her a little wave as he headed back out to his truck.

As Maura watched the man drive away, she decided that she finally had her eyes wide-open, too. Her marriage might not have started under the best conditions, but she wanted it to succeed. She wanted it to be real and lasting. And somehow, someway, she was going to make that clear to her husband.

Much later that night, long after Maura had gone to bed, she heard Quint when he walked into the bedroom and, without bothering to turn on the light, began to undress.

Maura glanced at the digital clock near the head of the bed: 12:10 a.m.

"Is Abe okay?" she murmured drowsily as he climbed into bed.

"He's fine," he said curtly. "We had things to discuss."

She scooted closer to his warm body and rested her hand upon his arm. "Oh. What sort of things?"

He lay on his back and though it was dark inside the room, Maura instinctively knew he was staring up at the ceiling. And then his hand reached across and briefly touched her shoulder.

"I'll tell you about it later," he said tiredly. "Right now it's late. We'd better get to sleep."

"Yes. Good night," she muttered stiffly.

Rolling to her side, she squeezed her eyes shut while she tried to push away the hollow disappointment filling her heart. Everything inside her wanted to reach for him, to beg him to make love to her, but he wasn't giving her any initiative and in her emotional condition, she could hardly handle a rejection.

After several long moments had passed and she'd heard his breathing slow, he said, "I'm sorry I wasn't here for supper."

She swallowed as tears threatened to overtake her. There was so much she wanted, needed to say to him. But the timing was rotten and the risk too great, so she swallowed away the words of love and kept it simple. "That's okay, Quint. I understand you have other things to take care of."

"Do you really?"

The doubt in his voice confused and angered her, making her reply come out sharper than she intended. "I like to think I'm an understanding woman, Quint."

"You sure sound like it."

A heavy sigh rushed past her lips. "I missed you, Quint. That's all."

"Look, Maura, you ought to know I'm not trying to ignore you. Right now I'm carrying a hell of a load. I just can't carry any more."

In other words, she and the coming baby had only added to his mountain of responsibilities. She wanted to scream at him, to ask him why he'd demanded that they marry in the first place. But getting into a shouting match in the middle of the night wouldn't solve anything.

"And whose fault is that, Quint? Mine?"

After several tense moments, his head turned on the pillow and she could feel his gaze studying her in the semidarkness.

"Don't say that, Maura."

She bit down on her lip as pain stabbed the middle of her chest. "You can only spread yourself so thin, Quint. Maybe it's time you decided what's most important to you."

His sigh was as heavy as a rock falling into a pool of water. "Yeah. I guess you're right."

The next morning Jake called Quint to say his mother was having some sort of problem with the pump on her water well and he'd be late getting to the ranch. Since he couldn't start much of a project without his right-hand man, Quint used the time to drive down to Ruidoso Grain and Tack and pick up several things he'd been needing, including several pairs of horseshoes and the nails to go with them.

Throughout the drive, he tried to focus his attention on the radio and the local market report, but his mind wasn't having any of it. All he could think about was Maura and the lovely way she'd looked this morning when he'd left her sleeping in their bed.

He didn't know what had made him snap at her last night. He couldn't use exhaustion as an excuse, since he was more often than not dog tired when he got home to the house each night. But something about the disappointment in her voice had stabbed him where it hurt the most. He'd not expected that from Maura. Holly, yes. But not Maura. He'd always thought of his wife as a truly unselfish woman, one who would never make demands on him.

She wasn't making demands, Quint. She was trying to tell you that she's unhappy. And it's time for you to change all of that.

But how, Quint wondered. How could he expect to keep a special woman like Maura happy?

"Maybe it's time you decided what's most important to you."

What had she meant by that? he asked himself. That he give up the things he loved to devote his time completely to her? Or was she trying to say she simply wanted to be included in the things he loved? Oh, God, he wished he knew. He needed to make time to talk to her. To find out what was going on. They couldn't keep going like this once the baby was here.

A few minutes later, Quint picked up the items he needed from the feed store, then at the last minute decided to grab a cup of coffee and a pastry at the Blue Mesa before he made the long drive back to the ranch.

At an outside table, he was draining the last of his cup, when he heard someone call his name from behind. Glancing over his shoulder, he was more than stunned to see Vince Johnson approaching him.

Holly's parents had been gone from Lincoln County for at least five or six years and Quint hadn't spoken to any of the family since the breakup seven years ago. The odds of running in to Vince like this had to be impossible. And especially on a day when he wasn't in the humor for raking up the past. In fact, he wasn't much in the humor for anything. Damn it all, he was having the worst of luck this morning and once he got back to the ranch, he was going to let Jake know he was half the cause of it!

"Quint! I thought that was you!"

Smiling, the older man extended his hand and in spite of being weighed down with frustration, Quint rose politely to his feet and shook it. "Hello, Vince. This is a surprise. I heard you'd moved to Nevada."

The tall, graying man nodded. "That's right, we call Beatty home now. We're just here for a little visit with the wife's cousins. They still live over at Alto." With another wide smile, he patted Quint's shoulder. "How have you been? Still ranching?"

"I'm okay. We lost Dad a couple of years ago. So I'm seeing after the ranches now."

The other man's expression turned rueful. "Yeah. We heard about Lewis passing. I'm so sorry, Quint. He was a good man. Guess that's why he raised such a good son."

Quint glanced skeptically at him, then let out an awkward laugh. "I almost believe you mean that."

Vince Johnson stared straight at him. "Well, hell, yes, I mean it," he said with conviction. "Why wouldn't I?"

"After Holly—"

"Oh, my daughter," he interrupted with a shake of his head. "After she went to Denver I don't think I ever had the chance to tell you how sorry I was about her behavior."

"It wasn't your place to apologize," Quint assured him.

"Well, I just wanted you to know that her mother and I never approved of what she did to you. Damn it, we still don't approve of her behavior. But she's a grown woman and what's a parent to do? Tell her how to live her life?"

"I couldn't say, Vince. I don't have any children." *Yet,* he thought. But soon he would be a father and raising that child to be a decent, honest human being was going to be his first priority in life. That and Maura.

With a tight grimace, the older man glanced around as though to make sure no one close was listening, then settled his gaze back on Quint. "Let me tell you something, Quint, the Lord blessed you when he took Holly off your hands."

The Johnsons used to dote on their young daughter, so it more than surprised Quint to heart Vince talk about Holly in such a negative way.

"You think so?"

"Oh, hell, son, she's not turned out the way that we'd hoped. But then, I suppose me and Joyce made everything too easy for her. Now, she drinks too much and spends money like it's water. Her kids are monsters but what should we expect when they have no supervision? Not with their parents on the road all the time."

"I'm sorry to hear that," Quint said, and he meant it. All of a sudden, he realized that he held no ill wishes toward Holly. In fact, now that he was listening to Vince talk of his daughter, it struck him that he felt nothing except relief that he'd been dealt a far better hand. He now had a beautiful wife who was going to give him a child. Being bitter about the past held no place in his life anymore.

"It's a mystery to me why she had the kids in the first place," Vince went on. "Just to solidify her marriage is my guess. You see, Robert, her husband, was pretty much of a playboy when she married him. I guess she thought the kids would anchor him. Hell, if you ask me the two of them deserve each other."

"But the children don't deserve that," Quint replied.

Vince released a heavy breath. "No. You're right about that. Joyce and I are thinking of bringing them out to Beatty to live with us. We're a little old to be raising kids now, but something has to be done. Let's just hope we don't make the same mistakes with them as we did with Holly."

The faint smile on Quint's face said he wished the man luck. "We all live and learn, Vince."

"Yeah. Isn't that the truth," he said, then clearing his throat, he slapped Quint on the shoulder again. "It's been good to see you, Quint. Why, it was just the other day that Joyce was saying she wished you'd been our son-in-law instead of Robert. I told her you're too nice a young man to be wishing that sort of trouble on."

He chuckled as he finished his last remark, and for a split second Quint stared quizzically at the man before he, too, began laughing. Running into Vince Johnson this morning hadn't been a curse at all, he realized. It was an eye-opener. He'd not lost Holly because he'd done anything wrong. Or because he'd not been man enough to hold on to her. She'd left because of her own self-satisfying interests. And from the things Vince had said about her, it sounded as though she was still chasing around, trying to find something or someone to make her happy.

But Quint didn't have to wonder what made him happy. It was Maura. He'd been fortunate enough to find her, love her, make a baby with her. And somehow, someway, he was going to have to make her see just how important she and their coming baby had become to him.

The two men exchanged goodbyes and Quint walked away from the Blue Mesa, feeling as though he'd just shed a ton of garbage from his shoulders.

Later that afternoon, on the Golden Spur, while Jake and Quint were busy shoeing horses, the ring of Quint's cell phone interrupted their progress.

"You might want to ignore that," Jake joked. "It might be Abe again wanting you to go back over to Apache Wells."

"Not after last night," Quint told the other man. "He was so angry at me he could have spit nails. I figure it'll be a while before I hear from Gramps again."

Stepping back from the horse, Quint dug the phone from his pocket, while hoping the caller ID would be illuminating Maura's name. There had been a few times during her afternoon break at work she would call for a brief chat, but like Abe, after last night she was probably too angry with him to bother, he thought ruefully. All afternoon he'd been tempted to call her and apologize, to let her know he could hardly wait for her to get home. But he feared he'd interrupt her work at the worst possible moment. Besides that, he figured she deserved an apology in person. She deserved so much more than she'd been getting from him and he wanted to be standing face-to-face with her whenever he told her so.

Quickly turning the phone upright, Quint was suddenly jerked from his thoughts of Maura. The caller was Mac, his brother in Texas! What was he doing calling in the middle of the afternoon? First Vince Johnson this morning and now Mac this afternoon. This day was certainly turning out to be full of the unexpected, he thought drily.

"I gotta take this, Jake," he said to the other man, then quickly moved over to a quiet spot in the shade of the barn and flipped open the phone.

"Mac!" Quint greeted. "This is a surprise!"

The other man chuckled. "I have a little coffee break going on and thought I'd call and see how my brother is doing. Do you have a minute?"

Quint glanced across the way to see Jake was still hard at work, fitting a shoe to the horse's hind hoof, but the animal was behaving nicely and Jake could handle the task without Quint's help.

"Sure. We're just doing a little farrier work this afternoon."

Mac chuckled again. "See, when you live in sandy south Texas, you don't have to worry about horseshoes," his brother teased.

"So Alexa tells me," Quint said wryly, then proceeded to ask him about his family.

After Mac had assured him that everyone was doing good, he said, "Actually, I was calling to see how you're doing, Quint. I'm worried about you."

Quint stiffened. "Don't tell me. Abe called and tried to enlist your aid in persuading me to reopen the Spur."

"As a matter of fact, he did call, but we didn't talk that much about the old mine," Mac admitted, then paused for a long moment. "He seems to think you're very unhappy. I told him he must be wrong. You're married to a sweet, beautiful woman and you're going to have a baby. You're getting your ranch shaped up and running—there's no reason for you to be unhappy. Is there?"

Quint let out a long, heavy breath. "Not at all. I'm sorry he bothered you with such an idea, Mac. He should have told you the real reason I'm upset—that's he's hounding me to death about reopening the mine. I told him last night that I flat-out oppose it. But Abe doesn't always hear the word *no*."

"Well, I'm not one to pry, Quint. I just promised the old man that I'd call, so I'm keeping my promise. I'm glad there's nothing wrong with you and Maura. You two seemed very happy at the wedding."

Had they? Their wedding day had passed in a haze for him, yet he remembered the sense of being happy, remembered thinking that having Maura as his wife felt right and good. And even through the honeymoon, he'd felt so contented to have her wrapped in his arms each night.

It wasn't until they'd gotten home that reality had struck Quint like a bolt of lightning. He'd looked around at the ranch he'd worked so hard to build and it had dawned on him that none of it would mean anything without Maura.

And that had scared him. He'd never wanted to be that emotionally dependent on any woman. He'd not wanted his happiness to be wound up so deeply in another human being. But now it was and he couldn't hide from his feelings any longer.

"Mac, I—I'm not being entirely honest," he said with a sudden rush. "I am aggravated about dealing with the mine issue. But to tell you the truth, what I'm really miserable about is Maura and me."

"Why?"

"Because I've realized that I love her. Love her with all my heart."

Mac paused and when he spoke again, Quint could hear a smile in his voice.

"Yeah. I know the feeling. When you think about it, about her, you get kinda shaky and scared and angry all at once. All you can think about is how vulnerable she makes you feel and how awful life would be without her."

Quint let out a breath of relief. "Oh, hell, Mac, will it always be this way?"

"It won't if you'll quit running scared and tell Maura how you really feel," he said, then added, "And if that's not enough to convince you, just think about how much our mother lost, Quint, because she hid her fears from the people she loved the most. You don't want that to happen to you."

Quint stared across the ranch yard to the house. There were still a few hours to go before Maura returned from work. Tonight after she got home, he wasn't going to hold back. Win, lose or draw, he was going to let her know how very much he loved her. But would she believe him? God, he could only hope. "No. Mother—all of us—lost too much," Quint agreed.

"And by the way," Mac went on, "I realize your grandfather can be a handful to deal with. But he has your interests at heart. And you need to remember that he made his fortune by taking chances. It might not hurt for you to take a chance on him."

"And go along with that cockamamie plan of his to hunt for gold?" Quint countered with disbelief. "Mac, I thought you were a practical man."

He laughed with genuine amusement. "Ileana has changed me. Besides, Mom says that before Abe struck oil in Texas, people called him all sorts of a fool. But he stuck to his guns and proved them wrong. Maybe you ought to rethink your decision about reopening the mine, Quint. If it turned out to be a producer, it would be a nice legacy for the baby."

"I'll think about it, Mac. And—"

"Oops, sorry, brother. I gotta go," Mac interrupted abruptly. "I'm on duty and it's an emergency. Call me later."

Mac swiftly ended the call and Quint thoughtfully slipped the phone back into his pocket. He should have been furious with Abe for calling Mac and dragging him into his personal problems. But deep down, Quint couldn't be angry with his grandfather. Somehow Abe had realized that talking with his older brother was just the sort of thing Quint needed.

With sudden resolve, he walked back over to where Jake was finishing the last shoe on Ramrod.

"Don't worry about shoeing the other horse right now," Quint told him. "We'll work on him tomorrow. While there's still some daylight left, I'm going to drive out to the old mine and take a look around."

Jake looked at him with surprise. "The Spur? You need me to come along?"

"No. Go ahead and ride the filly. We need to get her ready for pasture work. I'll be back in a little while," Quint told him.

Thankfully, Bridget's clinic was filled with patients throughout the day and that kept Maura very busy until closing time. While she'd taken blood pressures and temperatures and registered information in charts, she'd tried to focus entirely on her work and not on her husband's cool behavior toward her.

But that was easier said than done and in spite of listening to a drone of aches and pains from the patients, Maura longed to lay her head down in some quiet place and weep her eyes out.

"Maura, wait a minute! You can't leave yet!"

Pausing at the door, Maura glanced over her shoulder to see Bridget hurrying toward her. She'd shed her lab coat and reading glasses and looked more like her little sister than the harried physician who hardly took a moment for herself.

"I peeked in your office to say goodbye for the day," Maura told her. "But you were on the phone."

Bridget grimaced. "Discussing treatment for the Hollister baby. I'm sending him to a cardiologist in Albuquerque."

Maura's hand settled protectively over her growing stomach. Every day, every night, she prayed to God that her child would be healthy.

"Is there hope that the little fella's heart can be fixed?" Maura asked.

Bridget pressed fingers to her furrowed brow. "There's always hope, Maura. And I think his chances to grow up and lead a normal life are good."

Maura sighed with relief. She was familiar with the

Hollister baby and his mother and she desperately wanted things to turn out good for them.

"I'm so glad," she said, then arched a questioning brow at her sister. "Did you stop me for some other reason?"

Bridget caught her by the arm and began leading her back to her office. "I most certainly did."

After ushering Maura into the small room and shutting the door behind them, she said, "We've not had a chance to say more than two words to each other all day. And I want to hear how things went with you and Quint last night. Did you have that talk with him, like I suggested?"

A heavy sigh slipped from Maura. "I didn't have the chance. When I got home Quint had gone to his grandfather's and didn't come home until after midnight. By the time I got up this morning, he'd already left the house."

"I see." She thoughtfully chewed her bottom lip. "Well, I've thought about this a lot since we talked yesterday and I think—" She leveled a troubled glance at Maura. "There's something I think I'd better tell you."

An uneasy chill rippled down Maura's spine. Was something wrong with someone in the family? With Abe? It wasn't like Bridget to be secretive. "Tell me what? Did Quint go to see Abe because his grandfather is ill? Is that why he didn't want to talk to me about the visit?"

Bridget's expression suddenly turned rueful. "No, no. It's nothing like that. It's nothing to do with anyone's health. Except maybe yours," she added bleakly.

Maura sank into the plush leather chair positioned in front of Bridget's desk. "What are you talking about?"

Facing her sister, Bridget rested a hip on the corner of the desk. "All right. A few days ago, during my lunch break, I drove down to the Blue Mesa."

Maura groaned. "Oh, God, Brita, don't tell me you heard more gossip about me and Abe!"

"I haven't heard a word about any of that. What I'm trying to tell you is that on my way back here to the clinic, I saw Quint."

"Quint? Here in town?" It wasn't often that her husband drove into Ruidoso. He wasn't the type to enjoy urban attractions. Even the small-town kind. And if the ranch needed supplies, Jake always drove in to collect them.

Bridget nodded. "I wasn't going to tell you. And it's probably nothing, but well, he was coming out of a lawyer's office. The one down on Sudderth. Phillips, Andrews and Phillips, I think."

Bridget might as well have thrown ice water in Maura's face. She was so shocked, all she could do was stare in stunned silence at her sister. Finally, she asked in a raw whisper, "Quint went to a lawyer? Did you talk to him?"

"No! I was in the car and I didn't stop or wave to him. Actually, I didn't want him to know that I'd seen him. I was concerned that—" She broke off with a frown. "Has he mentioned seeing a lawyer about anything?"

Maura's eyes widened as the pit of her stomach turned to lead weight. "No! But then Quint doesn't do a lot of talking. I— Oh, God, Bridget! Maybe he's already decided he wants a divorce and wanted to discuss his rights to the baby?"

Bridget closed the short space between them and placed a steadying hand on Maura's shoulder. "Don't go jumping to conclusions like that. I happen to think that Quint loves you. But he might be confused about your feelings and—"

Maura instantly shot to her feet. "I've got to get home, Brita! I've got to talk to him. Now! As soon as I get there!"

But as Maura headed her truck toward the Golden Spur, she couldn't help but wonder if she'd waited too long.

Chapter Eleven

Dust fogged in the wake of Maura's truck as she sped down the last mile to the ranch house, then braked to a stop next to Quint's vehicle.

Inside the house, she called his name, then after finding the rooms empty, she didn't bother changing from her green scrubs before she hurried to the barn.

Halfway there, she spotted Jake riding a painted filly in the training pen, so she turned on her heel and walked in his direction.

"You looking for Quint?" he called out to her from atop the nervous horse.

"Yes. Is he at the barn?"

"No. He drove the old four-wheel drive out to the mine."

As Maura reached the board fence of the training pen, she frowned with confusion. "The mine? Whatever for?"

Jake shrugged. "I don't know. He got a phone call from somebody. He didn't say who and then he just took off. Frankly, Maura, I'm worried about him. Quint's made of iron, but a man can just take so much. And Abe—"

"Yes, yes, I know, Jake! I'm going out there now to find Quint. Has he been gone long?"

Jake glanced at his watch. "A couple of hours, at least. Do you want me to go with you?"

Maura shook her head. "No thanks, I can find it."

"Well, if you have any trouble, you have my cell number," he reminded her.

Maura thanked him again, then hurried back to the house. There she quickly threw on blue jeans, a heavy shirt and boots, then jumped into her truck and sped back down the graveled road. Five miles east, another road turned to the left and curved a snaky loop back into the mountains. Maura had never traveled the road, but Quint had told her it was a shortcut to Chillicothe. Since the mine was near the old town, it would be the best route for her to take.

During the rough ride, Maura clung to the steering wheel, while her mind whirled with Jake's words.

Quint's made of iron, but a man can just take so much.

Why hadn't Maura thought of that sooner? For the past year and a half Quint had put in long, endless hours building this ranch. And all during that time he'd been seeing after his grandfather's health, along with the old man's demands. And still recovering from the shock of learning his mother had another family, his sister's pregnancy and then marriage to a Texas Ranger. Then he'd gotten entangled with Maura and suddenly he was faced with a wife and a coming baby. No doubt all of those things together had stretched Quint thin and pulled his emotions in all directions. Instead of her whining and worrying herself about him not giving her the right attention, she should have been busy trying to become a real partner for him, and showing how much his happiness meant to her. To love—really love—meant to give. Not take.

By the time she reached the mine, the sun was dipping toward the horizon, but there was still at least an hour of sunlight left.

The old ranch truck was parked a short distance from the entrance to the shaft, yet Quint was nowhere in sight. After parking her own vehicle, she climbed out and began to search and call his name.

"Quint?" she called. "Where are you?"

Her voice bounced off the mountain walls and echoed back to her, but Quint's voice didn't follow.

Deciding she was wasting time, she pulled out her cell phone and punched his number. It tried to ring once but the sound was erratic and then the connection was cut off completely. After three attempts with the same result, she realized the tower signal was too far away and reaching him by phone was impossible, so she slipped the phone back into her jeans pocket and began to search the narrow canyon that traveled a hundred yards or more east of the shaft entrance.

After several more minutes of searching with no sign of him, Maura began to worry that the only place left for Quint to be was inside the mine. Being underground would have certainly blocked off her cell phone signal to him.

But why would he have entered the dangerous cave? Especially after he'd warned her that it was unsafe? Was he so unhappy that he didn't care if he put his own life in jeopardy? Surely he would think about the baby!

For a moment she considered calling Jake. But she didn't want to alarm the man. Add to that, it would take him at least thirty minutes of hard driving to get out here, so she cast that notion aside and hurried to her truck for a flashlight.

At the mine entrance, she stuck her head just inside the dark interior and called out, "Quint? Are you in here? Please, answer!"

Maura waited for a reply, but all she could hear was a faint *drip, drip*. After a quick search with her light, she could see the source of the noise was coming from the ceiling of the tunnel. Small leaks of orange-and-yellow-tinted water were falling to the rock-strewn floor, creating gummy puddles of liquid minerals that eventually spilled over and made a slow trickle out the open doorway and down the side of the foothill.

After another loud yell out to her husband, Maura decided she had no choice but to go into the cave to search for him. Clearly he'd been gone far longer than what it would take a person to have a simple look over the outside area.

Drawing in a deep breath, Maura aimed the flashlight to the ground in front of her, then stepped inside the dank mine. The air was a tad warmer than outside and smelled of wet rocks and something indefinable like sulfur or some sort of metal. The sound of the dripping water was erratic and each time a drop hit, it echoed like a fire cracker exploding in a concrete canyon.

Beneath her boots, the ground was strewn with huge rocks made extremely slippery by a thick coat of moisture. As Maura carefully made her way forward, she kept her left hand on the wall of the mineshaft to hold herself steady, while her right gripped the flashlight.

As much as she wanted to find Quint, she didn't want to

take the risk of falling. If the baby was harmed, Quint would never forgive her. Nor would she ever forgive herself.

After traveling about ten yards deeper into the cavern, the air grew stuffier and the path ahead abruptly split in two directions. Since one still held the tracks to carry ore cars, Maura followed it and prayed she'd chosen the right one.

With a few more yards behind her, she paused, peered into the eerie darkness and willed him to answer. "Quint? Are you in here? It's Maura!"

Suddenly from far away, the muffled sound of his voice came back to her.

"Maura! Stay there! I'm coming!"

The relief pouring through her was so great she was practically sobbing by the time he finally reached her side.

"Oh, Quint!" she exclaimed. "Are you all right? What are you doing in here? You told me this mine wasn't safe to enter!"

Grabbing her by the shoulders, he tugged her to him. "It isn't! So why are you in here?"

"Because I came out here to find you. When I couldn't, I decided you must have come in here. I was afraid, Quint! If you'd been lying hurt or trapped—" Shuddering, she broke off as tears of relief poured down her face.

With a choked groan, he clutched her tight against him and buried his face in her hair. The intensity of his grip dazed her, made her wonder what he could possibly be thinking.

"Maura, Maura," he whispered. "I'm sorry I frightened you. But you shouldn't have come in here. If something happened to you or the baby—well, I don't even want to think about it!"

Lifting her head from his chest, she searched his face in the semidarkness. "Do you mean that, Quint?"

"Why wouldn't I mean it? You're my wife. You're carrying my child—a child I can't wait to hold in my arms."

Fresh tears spiked her lashes and poured from the corners of her eyes. "I was afraid you wanted a divorce," she finally managed to get out.

Stunned, he shook his head, then grabbed her by the arm. "Let's get out of this dark hole. We'll talk about this outside."

"No! I'm fine right here," she said stubbornly. "And I'm not going anywhere! Not until we discuss this!"

Releasing a long breath, he asked, "Why would you think I wanted a divorce?"

"Since we returned from our honeymoon you haven't seemed too happy to be around me. I've been thinking that you must be regretting that we married. And then—" Biting down on her lip, she glanced away from him and into the darkness. "Earlier this evening, before I left work, Bridget confessed to me that she'd seen you coming out of a lawyer's office. I thought—"

"The worst," he finished grimly, then groaned deep in his throat. "Oh, Maura, can't you see I'd wither away without you?"

Confusion clouded her eyes. "No, Quint. I've been seeing a very unhappy man trying to pretend that everything is okay."

"I guess that's true. But only because after we got home from Hawaii I realized just how very much I loved you. And I knew you didn't feel the same. That you'd only married me because of the baby." His fingers tightened against her back until she was pressed so close to him that she could feel his heart beating against hers, his warm breath brushing her cheek. "Have I ruined every chance for us? Tell me I haven't!"

She said in a strained voice, "Oh, Quint—you haven't ruined anything. I'm the one who's been an idiot."

"Not as much as I've been," he mouthed against her cheek. "I should have told you that I went to see the lawyer to make sure my will was in order. If anything should happen to me there won't be any doubt about my wishes. My whole estate will go to you and our child."

Overwhelmed, she clutched his shoulders and choked back a sob. "We hadn't been together too long when the baby happened. And I knew you weren't looking for a family back then. I felt very guilty about getting pregnant and—"

"Oh, God, Maura, do you know how happy I am that you did get pregnant? That wasn't an accident by any fault of yours, that was dealt by a higher hand. He meant for the baby to cement us together."

Everything inside of her was shaking, trembling with a joy so great she wanted to shout. "Quint, I love you. So very much. As long as you want me as your wife, I—"

"Want you? Oh, darling, I love you! Love you with all my heart." His head bent and his lips suddenly hovered over hers. "I should have told you that from the very beginning. Instead, I kept denying the way I was feeling. I didn't want to be that needy or vulnerable. I told myself it was your body that I was infatuated with and that if or when you decided to get up and walk away from me, I could stand it, I wouldn't be hurt. But when we got back from our honeymoon the reality of being home—of being married—shook my eyes wide-open, made me see that nothing would matter if I didn't have you in my world."

Amazed that he was saying these things to her, she

reached up and framed his face with her hands. "But you've acted so distant and—"

"Because I was scared. I could see you were unhappy and that I'd forced you into a marriage you hadn't wanted. So I dove into my work and tried to pretend I didn't care. God, I've been stupid!"

Her thumbs caressed the lines of fatigue beneath his eyes. "You were right. I've been unhappy, too. I didn't want to get married. Because I wanted you to marry me for love—not just because of the baby. But you never mentioned the word to me."

"Neither did you," he countered. "You said you'd slept with me for the sex. You can't possibly know how much that cut me, Maura."

"I'm sorry, Quint, truly. But after Gil crushed me, I couldn't believe a man like you could actually love me. And I was trying to hang on to what little pride I had left."

His mouth twisted ruefully. "And I was thinking that after three years of being with Holly, of believing she loved me, I lost her. How the hell did I think I could possibly hang on to you? Especially when you didn't want to marry me in the first place."

Suddenly, happy laughter bubbled up inside her and once it passed her lips, the sound rippled through the old gold mine like musical notes. "Holly, Gil. We can forgive and forget the mistakes we made with them, darling. None of that matters anymore. Because you and I have so much more than they could have ever given us. We have each other."

With a growl of contentment, his hand dropped to her belly and as he pressed his hand lovingly against their child, he whispered, "And we have our baby."

"Our baby," she repeated.

Closing the last bit of space between their lips, Quint let his kiss tell Maura how much he loved and wanted her and would until he died.

"Now," he said when he finally lifted his head, "don't you think it's time we got out of this place? It's probably full of rattlesnakes and bats and everything else."

With a sly little smile, she squeezed his hand. "As soon as you tell me why you were in here, we'll leave. Jake said you received a phone call and then you took off for the mine. Did Abe send you out here?"

He chuckled. "I like to please my grandfather, but not that much. We had a huge row about the mine last night. He's adamant that we need to start mining it again. I tried to explain all the reasons I didn't want to do that and told him flat out that my mind was made up. I was going to board this place up and forget it completely."

"Looks like you sure told him how the cow eats the corn," Maura said wryly.

"Well, this afternoon I had a change of heart. My brother Mac called. And he sagely pointed out that I needed to quit fighting my love for you."

"Mmm. Next time I see your brother, I'm going to tell him what a wise, wise man he is."

Smiling, Quint smoothed her hair back and placed a kiss on her soft forehead. "He also implied that I should quit fighting Grandfather's dreams. After all, Abe got what he has by taking risks."

"So you've decided to reopen this thing and let the miners start digging again?"

He nodded. "After I talked with Mac, I felt compelled to come out here. And once I got here, it was like a voice was calling me inside. That's when I decided I'd come in here and see for myself if any sort of structure to the shaft was left. I was surprised to see it's in better condition than I expected. 'Course it will take lots of shoring before actual mining can begin, but Gramps is willing to make the investment and so am I."

"I'm glad, Quint. I think someday you'll see what a gift you're giving your grandfather by going along with this. And we owe him so much, darling, for bringing us together. Don't you think?"

Quint opened his mouth to answer just as an odd rumble sounded a few feet above their heads.

Frowning, Maura asked, "Was that thunder? I didn't notice any clouds when I drove up."

Quint tilted his head to one side as the both of them listened intently. "I don't know what it was," he said, "Maybe—"

He broke off as a grumbling ache suddenly belched through the mine shaft. The sound of cracking wood splintered the air and choking dust showered down from the ceiling.

"Hurry! We'd better get out of here. Hold on to me!"

Grabbing her hand, he rushed her in the direction of the entrance. But they'd hardly taken ten strides when the ground and the walls begin to shake with an intensity that caused Maura to scream and fling herself against Quint.

"Oh, God! It's an earthquake! It's going to collapse on us!"

She'd hardly gotten the words out when a portion of the ceiling above their heads started to fall. Taking Maura with him, Quint leaped to one side of the cavern, then after pushing her to a crouch, he covered her body as best as he could with his own.

Two feet away, a heavy beam broke, to send the jagged

ends stabbing into the floor of the cave. Rocks, dirt and gravel spilled from the gaping hole like a landslide roaring down a mountain. The sound was deafening.

Dust boiled around them so thick they both began to cough and sputter for air. Maura buried her face deeper in the middle of Quint's chest, while she felt the protection of his arms circle tightly around her. And in that moment she knew that no matter what happened in their lives, Quint loved her, would always love her.

After what seemed like an eternity, all went quiet. The dust and rock settled. And Quint slowly raised the both of them to their feet.

Totally dazed, Maura clung to Quint's arm as she glanced around at the rubble piled in the middle of the mine shaft. "Whew! That was close!"

Quint pointed his flashlight toward the heap of ore that had fallen from the cave-in. Some of the rocks and debris had rolled all the way to their feet. But by the grace of God, neither of them appeared to be hurt.

"Close, I'll say," Quint agreed.

While he took off his hat and wiped his grimy forehead on the back of his sleeve, Maura attempted to shake the dirt and pebbles from her hair. She was swiping the grime away from her eyes, when some sort of flash caught her attention and she took a second look at the rocks strewn about their feet.

"Quint, shine your light down here. Something looks—" Frowning, she bent down and picked up one of the larger pieces of ore. "It's sparkling like—"

Excitement flickered, then rushed over her as she yelped out an incredible laugh. "It's gold, Quint! This old mine wasn't trying to kill us. It was trying to tell us it was never empty of riches." She grabbed his arm. "Let's go show Abe what we've found!"

Too stunned to speak, Quint stuffed two of the rocks into his pocket, then reached for Maura's hand.

Finally, he managed to say, "Looks like we've struck it rich, honey. But as far as I'm concerned my treasure is you."

Happy tears stung Maura's eyes as her husband led her out of the darkness of the mine and into the brightness of their love.

Epilogue

A year to the day later, on a bright fall afternoon, Maura and Quint stood on the sidewalk of the old Chillicothe general store, while just behind them, Abe had his seven-month-old great-grandson, Riley Donovan Cantrell, cradled in one arm.

The group of four had just enjoyed a picnic lunch at the same table where Maura and Quint had eaten that day the storm had struck and little Riley had been conceived. Now that the meal was over, Abe insisted they all walk over to the mine site and let the baby watch the large equipment at work.

Once Red Bluff Mining Company had moved in, the crew had quickly gone to work to make the mine a safe workplace. Even going at a rapid pace that enormous task had taken a few months. After the shoring had been completed, the miners had finally gone in to dig and much to everyone's dismay had discovered a rich vein of gold that was expected to reach far back into the mountainside. Geologists predicted it would take years to recover all of the yellow metal inside the Golden Spur.

Maura's older brother Conall, a rancher and business-man in his own right, had agreed to take over the manage-ment of the mine operations, which thankfully left Quint free to do the things he loved to do, which was work with his cattle and horses.

Up until Riley had been born, Maura had continued to work at Bridget's clinic, but now she was content to stay at home and be a mother…a job that more than agreed with her. She'd never been happier or felt more fulfilled, and each time she looked at her husband, it showed on her face. Maybe someday, after their family was grown, she would return to being a nurse. But for now, she simply wanted to be a wife and mother.

As the four of them left the old ghost town and walked toward the low mountain ridge where the mine entrance was located, Quint asked his grandfather, "Would you like for me to carry Riley? He can get heavy."

"Nope. My little cowboy is not that heavy. Yet."

"He will be if you keep stuffing his face with those animal cookies," Quint said drily.

Smiling, Maura glanced at Abe and her young son. Soggy cookie crumbs smeared the baby's plump cheeks and the front of Abe's shirt, but the old man hardly cared about keeping either of them tidy. He adored his great-grandson and had taken to visiting the Golden Spur on a regular basis in order to spend more time with him.

For safety purposes, the entrance to the mine and the excavated area around it was now enclosed with a tall, chain-link fence. As for any cattle that roamed near the mine, Quint had fenced off the outer portion of the working area and the road to the highway in order to keep the animals from grazing too close to the truck traffic.

In a way, the mine had caused more work to be done to the ranch, but the benefits of the gold sales far superseded the cost and trouble. So far the income from the gold had been extraordinary and Quint and Maura were now sharing part of the earnings with both their families and putting the remainder away for Riley and the other children they hoped to have soon. As for Abe, he didn't want any money. It was enough for him to see his dreams come true.

Now as they stood outside the fence and watched the men and equipment at work, Abe said, "I knew all along there was a vein of gold left in these hills. Back in the fifties, when they quit this mine, they shouldn't have stopped lookin'. A man can't stop searchin'. Not when he truly believes in somethin'."

Gazing down at Maura, Quint curled his arm lovingly around the back of her waist. "I'll agree with that."

Seeing the look his grandson was giving his wife, Abe snorted. "Don't go actin' like you findin' Maura and a mine full of gold was all your idea. If I'd left things up to you, you'd still be single and the old Spur would be boarded up and forgotten."

Grinning faintly, Quint shook his head. "Oh. So you think you're responsible for getting me a wife?"

"Damned right," Abe retorted. "Why do you think I hired Maura in the first place?"

Quint winked at Maura. "Because you had dizzy spells."

Abe let out another snort. "Hell, no! I knew how to treat myself for those spells. I wanted her for you." Suddenly his eyes misted over and after clearing his throat, he bent his head and placed a kiss on the top of Riley's sandy red curls. "You see," he said in a voice thick with emotion, "I had big dreams for you, Quint. And I've been blessed to see them all come true."

Except for the first time he'd held Riley in his arms, Maura had never seen Abe get teary-eyed over anything. Seeing his softer side, she couldn't help but get a little blurry-eyed herself. As she watched Abe move away from them and carry little Riley over to the flimsy shade of a pinyon tree, she smiled through her tears. Her son. Her husband. Her family. She had everything she'd ever wanted.

The tug of Quint's hand at the side of her waist brought Maura's head back around to her husband and she glanced slyly up at him. "Has your grandfather always been such a conniver?"

"Yes. But I like to think that somehow, someway, I would have found you in spite of his help." He bent his head and softly kissed her lips. "You know, that first time we went riding together and you made such a big deal out of the cholla blooms was the first time I'd ever looked at the ranch through different eyes. You made me see that I needed to stop and appreciate the beauty around me. And then later, after we married, you made me realize that the Golden Spur wasn't just a place for me to work, to raise herds of cattle and horses. It was a place for us to live and love and raise our children. You taught me how to dream, my darling. And you've made mine all come true. Don't ever forget that."

Sometimes when her husband touched her, she felt so full of love that she was overwhelmed with the urge to show him, tell him exactly how much he meant to her. And then, like this very moment, she knew her feelings were so deep it was impossible to express them. So she simply smiled and pressed her cheek against his chest.

"You know," she said softly, "I think this is the perfect time to tell Abe he's going to be great-grandfather again. Don't you?"

"I think it's the perfect time," Quint agreed.

Hand in hand, they walked over to give Abe the good news.

* * * * *

THE BABY BUMP

BY
JENNIFER GREENE

Jennifer Greene lives near Lake Michigan with her husband and an assorted menagerie of pets. Michigan State University has honored her as an outstanding woman graduate for her work with women on campus. Jennifer has written more than seventy love stories, for which she has won numerous awards, including four RITA® Awards from the Romance Writers of America and their Hall of Fame and Lifetime Achievement Awards.

You're welcome to contact Jennifer through her website at www.jennifergreene.com.

To "my" librarians at the Benton Harbor and St. Joseph libraries. From the start, you encouraged me to write and nourished my writing dreams. You've always gone out of your way to help everyone in the community enrich their worlds through books. You're the best!

Chapter One

Back when Ginger Gautier was a block-headed, reckless twenty-one-year-old, she'd have taken the mountain curves at ninety miles an hour and not thought twice.

Now that she was twenty-eight…well, she couldn't swear to have better judgment.

Unfortunately she was eight weeks pregnant—by a doctor who'd claimed he deeply loved her just a day before he bought an engagement ring for someone else. So. Her judgment in men clearly sucked.

She'd lost a job she loved over the jerk. That said even more about her lack of good judgment.

Some said she had a temper to match her red hair. Friends and coworkers tended to run for cover when she had a good fume on. So possibly her temper might be considered another character flaw.

But she loved.

No one ever said that Ginger Gautier didn't give two hundred percent for anyone she loved.

When she passed the welcome sign for South Carolina, she pushed the gas pedal a wee bit harder. Just to eighty miles an hour.

Gramps was in trouble. And she was almost home.

The eastern sky turned glossy gray, then hemmed the horizon in pink. By the time the sun was full up, Ginger had shed her sweater and hurled it in the backseat on top of her down jacket. When she left Chicago, it had been cold enough to snow. In South Carolina, the air was sweeter, cleaner, warmer…and so familiar that her eyes stung with embarrassingly sentimental tears.

She should have gone home more often—way more often—after her grandmother died four years ago. But it never seemed that simple, not once she'd gotten the job in hospital administration. Her boss had been a crabby old tyrant, but she'd loved the work, and never minded the unpredictable extra hours. They'd just added up. She'd come for holidays, called Gramps every week, sometimes more often.

Not enough. The guilt in her stomach churned like acid. Calling was fine, but if she'd visited more in person, she'd have *known* that Gramps needed her.

The miles kept zipping by. Another hour passed, then two. Maybe if she liked driving, the trip would have been easier, but nine hundred miles in her packed-to-the-gills Civic had been tough. She'd stopped a zillion times, for food and gas and naps and to stretch her legs, but this last stretch was downright grueling.

When she spotted the swinging sign for Gautier Tea Plantation, though, her exhaustion disappeared. She couldn't grow a weed, was never engrossed in the agricultural side of the tea business—but she'd worked in the shop as a teenager, knew all the smells and tastes of their teas, could bake a great scone in her sleep, could give lessons on the seeping and steeping of tea. No place on the planet was remotely like this one, especially the scents.

Past the eastern fields was a curve in the road, then a private drive shaded by giant old oaks and then finally, finally…the house. The Gautiers—being of French-Scottish origin—inherited more ornery stubbornness than they usually knew what to do with. The word "plantation" implied a graceful old mansion with gardens and pillars and maybe an ostentatious fountain or two. Not for Ginger's family.

The house was a massive sprawler, white, with no claim to fanciness. A generous veranda wrapped around the main floor, shading practical rockers and porch swings with fat cushions. Ginger opened the door to her Civic and sprang out, leaving everything inside, just wanting to see Gramps.

She'd vaulted two steps up before she spotted the body draped in front of the double-screen doors. It was a dog's body. A huge bloodhound's body.

She took another cautious step. Its fur was red-gray, his ears longer than her face, and he had enough wrinkles to star in a commercial for aging cream. He certainly didn't appear vicious…but she wasn't positive he was alive, either.

She said, "Hey, boy" in her gentlest voice. He didn't budge. She cleared her throat and tried, "Hey, girl." One eye opened, for all of three seconds. The dog let out an asthmatic snort and immediately returned to her coma.

For years, her grandparents had dogs—always Yorkie mixes—Gramps invariably carried her and Grandma usually had her groomed and fitted up with a pink bow. The possibility that Gramps had taken on this hound was as likely as his voting Republican. Still, the dog certainly looked content.

"Okay," Ginger said briskly, "I can't open the door until you move. I can see you're tired. But it doesn't take that much energy to just move about a foot, does it? Come on. Just budge a little for me."

No response. Nothing. Nada. If the dog didn't make occasionally snuffling noises, Ginger might have worried it was dead. As it was, she figured the big hound for a solid hundred pounds...which meant she had only a twenty-pound advantage. It took some tussling, but eventually she got a wedge of screen door open, stepped over the hound and turned herself into a pretzel. She made it inside with just a skinned elbow and an extra strip off her already frayed temper.

"Gramps! Cornelius! It's me!"

No one answered. Cornelius was...well, Ginger had never known exactly what Cornelius was. He worked for Gramps, but she'd never known his job title. He was the guy she'd gone to when a doll's shoe went down to the toilet, when she needed a ride to a party and Grandma couldn't take her. He got plumbers and painters in the house, supervised the lawn people, got prescriptions and picked up people from the airport. Cornelius didn't answer her, though, any more than her grandfather did.

She charged through, only taking seconds to glance around. The house had been built years ago, back when the first room was called a parlor. It faced east, caught all the morning sun, and was bowling alley size, stuffed to the gills with stuff. Gram's piano, the maze of furniture and paintings and rugs, were all the same, yet Ginger felt her anxiety antenna raised high. The room was dusty. Nothing new there, but she saw crumbs on tables, half-filled glasses from heaven knows when, enough dust to write her name on surfaces.

A little dirt never hurt anyone, her grandmother had always said. Gram felt a woman who had a perfect house should have been doing things that mattered. Still.

A little disarray was normal. Beyond dusty was another.

She hustled past the wild cherrywood staircase, past the dining room—one glass cabinet there had a museum-quality collection of teapots. A second glass cabinet held the whole historic history of Gautier tea tins, some older than a century. Past the dining "salon," which was what Gramps called the sun room—meaning that he'd puttered in there as long as she'd known him, trying samples of tea plants, mixing and mating and seeing what new offspring he could come up with.

The house had always been fragrant with the smell of tea, comforting with the familiar whir of big ceiling fans, a little dust, open books, blue—her grandma had had some shade of blue in every room in the house; it was her favorite color and always had been. Longing for Gram almost made her eyes well with tears again. She'd even loved Gram's flaws. Even when they had a little feud—invariably over Ginger getting into some kind of impulsive trouble—their fights invariably led to some tears, some cookies and a big hug before long— because no one in the Gautier family believed in going to bed mad.

The good memories were all there. The things she remembered were all there. But the whole downstairs had never had a look of neglect before. She called her grandfather's name again, moving down the hall, past the dining room and the butler's keep. Just outside the kitchen she heard—finally!—voices.

The kitchen was warehouse size, with windows facing north and west—which meant in the heat of a summer afternoon sun poured in, hotter than lava, on the old tile table. A kettle sat directly on the table, infusing the room with the scents of Darjeeling and peppermint. A fat, orange cat snoozed on the windowsill. Dishes and glasses and what all crowded the tile counter. The sink faucet was dripping. Dust and crumbs and various spills had long dried on the fancy parquet floor.

Ginger noticed it all in a blink. She took in the stranger, as well—but for that first second, all her attention focused on her grandfather.

He spotted her, pushed away from the table. A smile wreathed his face, bigger than sunshine. "What a sight for sore eyes, you. You're so late. I was getting worried. But you look beautiful, you do. The drive must have done you wonders. Come here and get your hug."

The comment about being late startled her—she'd made amazing time, he couldn't possibly have expected her earlier. But whatever. What mattered was swooping her arms around him, feeling the love, seeing the shine in his eyes that matched her own.

"What is this? Aren't you eating? You're skinny!" she accused him.

"Am not. Eating all the time. Broke the scales this morning, I'm getting so fat."

"Well, if that isn't the biggest whopper I've heard since I left home."

"You're accusing your grandfather of fibbing?"

"I am." The bantering was precious, how they'd always talked, teasing and laughing until they'd inevitably catch a scold from her grandmother. But something was wrong. Gramps had never been heavy, never tall, but she could feel his bones under his shirt, and his pants were hanging. His eyes, a gorgeous blue, seemed oddly vague. His smile was real. The hug wonderfully real. But his face seemed wizened, wrinkled and cracked like an old walnut shell, white whiskers on his chin as if he hadn't shaved—when Cashner Gautier took pride in shaving every day of his life before the sun came up.

She cast another glance at the stranger…and felt her nerves bristle sharper than a porcupine's. The man was certainly no crony of her gramps, couldn't be more than a few years older than she was.

The guy was sprawled at the head of the old tile table, had scruffy dirty-blond hair, wore sandals and chinos with frayed cuffs and a clay-colored shirt-shirt. Either he was too lazy to shave or was growing a halfhearted beard. And yeah, there was more to the picture. The intruder had tough, wide shoulders—as if he could lift a couple of tree logs in his spare time. The tan was stunning, especially for a guy with eyes that certain blue— wicked blue, light blue, blue like you couldn't forget, not if you were a woman. The height, the breadth, the way he stood up slow, showing off his quiet, lanky frame— oh, yeah, he was a looker.

Men that cute were destined to break a woman's heart.

That wasn't a problem for her, of course. Her heart was already in Humpty Dumpty shape. There wasn't a man in the universe who could wrestle a pinch of sexual interest from her. She was just judiciously assessing and recognizing trouble.

"You have to be Ginger," he said in a voice that made her think of dark sugar and bourbon.

"Aw, darlin', I should have said right off…this is Ike. Come to see me this afternoon. He's—"

"I saw right off who he was, Gramps." He had to be the man her grandfather told her about on the phone. The one who was trying to get Gramps to "sign papers." The one who was trying to "take the land away from him." Gramps had implied that his doctor had started it all, was behind the whole conspiracy, to take away "everything that ever mattered to him."

Ginger drew herself up to her full five-four. "You're the man who's been advising my grandfather, aren't you, bless your heart. And that has to be your dog on the front porch, isn't it?"

"Pansy. Yes."

"Pansy." For a moment she almost laughed, the name was so darned silly for that huge lummox of a dog. But she was in no laughing mood. She was in more of a killing mood. "Well, I'd appreciate it if you'd get your dog and yourself and take off, preferably in the next thirty seconds."

"Honey!" Her grandfather pulled out of her arms and shot her a shocked expression.

She squeezed his hand, but she was still facing down the intruder. "It's all right, Gramps. I'm here. And I'm going to be here from now on." Her voice was as cordial as Southern sweet tea, but that was only because she was raised with Southern manners. "I'll be taking care of my grandfather from now on, and we won't need any interference from anyone. Bless your heart, I'm sure you know your way to the front door."

"Honey, this is Ike—"

"Yes, I heard you say the name." She wasn't through glaring daggers at the son of a sea dog who'd try to cheat a vulnerable old man. "I really don't care if your name is Judas or Sam or Godfrey or whatever else. But thanks so much for stopping by."

He could have had the decency to look ashamed. Or afraid. Or something besides amused. There was no full-fledged grin, nothing *that* offensive, but the corners of his slim mouth couldn't seem to help turning up at the edges. "You know, I have the oddest feeling that we've gotten off on the wrong foot."

"You can bet your sweet bippy we have," she said sweetly.

"I strongly suspect that you'll change your mind before we see each other again. I promise I won't hold it against you. In fact, I'm really happy you're here. Your grandfather thinks the world rises and sets with you."

"Uh-huh." He could take that bunch of polite nonsense and start a fire with it. She wasn't impressed. She made a little flutter motion with her hands—a traditional bye-bye—but she definitely planned to see him out the door. First, so she could lock the screen doors after him, and second, to make darned sure he took the dog.

He was halfway down the hall when he called out, "Pansy, going home now." And the lazy, comatose, surely half-dead dog suddenly sprang to her feet and let out a joyful howl. Her tail should have been licensed as a weapon. It started wagging, knocking into a porch rocker, slapping against the door. Pansy seemed to think her owner was a god.

"Goodbye now," Ginger said, just as she snapped the door closed on both of them and flipped the lock. Obviously, locking a screen door was symbolic at best. Anyone could break through a screen door. But she still wanted the good-looking son of a shyster to hear the sound.

She whirled around to see her grandfather walking toward her with a rickety, fragile gait.

"Sweetheart. I don't understand what got into you. You know that was Ike."

"I know, I know. You told me his name already."

"Ike. Ike MacKinnon. My doctor. I mean *that* Ike."

For the second time, she had an odd shivery sensation, that something in her grandfather's eyes wasn't… right. Still, she answered him swiftly. "You know what Grandma would say—that he can't be a very good doctor if he can't afford a pair of shoes and a haircut."

When her grandfather didn't laugh, only continued to look at her with a bewildered expression, she hesitated. She shouldn't have made a small joke.

The situation wasn't remotely funny—for him or her. Maybe she hadn't immediately recognized that Ike was Gramps's doctor—how could she? But she'd have been even ruder to him if she had known. Gramps had said precisely on the phone that the "doctor" was behind it all. Behind the conspiracy to take the land away from him and force him to move.

"Gramps, where is Cornelius?"

"I don't know. Somewhere. Chores. The bank or something." Her grandfather reached out a hand, steadied himself against the wall, still frowning at her. "Ike is a nice man, Rachel. And you've always liked him. I can't imagine what put you in such a fuss. I can't remember you ever being rude to a soul."

She stopped, suddenly still as a statue.

Rachel was her grandmother's name.

"Gramps," she said softly. "It's me. Ginger."

"O' course," he said. "I know that, you silly one. Next time, don't take so long at the hairdresser's, okay?"

She smiled at him. Said "I sure won't," as if his comment and her reply made sense.

It didn't, but since she was reeling from confusion, she decided to change gears. Gramps was easily coaxed to settle in a rocker on the veranda, and he nodded off almost before he'd had a chance to put his feet up. She was free then to stare at her car, which unquestionably was stuffed within an inch of its life.

The boxes and bags weren't heavy. She refused to think about the pregnancy until she was ready to make serious life decisions—and Gramps's problems came first. Still, some instinct had motivated her to pack in lighter boxes and bags. Of course, that meant she had to make a million trips up the stairs, and down the long hall to the bedroom where she'd slept as a girl.

The whole upstairs brought on another niggling worry. Nothing was wrong, exactly. She'd been here last Christmas, and the Christmas before, and for quick summer weekends. But her visits had all been rushed. She'd had no reason or time to take an objective look at anything.

Now…she couldn't help but notice that the whole second floor smelled stale and musty. Each of the five bedrooms upstairs had a made-up bed, just as when her grandmother was alive. The three bathrooms had perfectly hung-up towels that matched their floor tile color. But her grandparents' bedroom had the smell of a room that had been shut up and abandoned for months or more. Dust coated the varnished floor, and the curtains were heavy with it.

There was nothing interesting about dust, of course. As soon as you cleaned, the dust bunnies under the bed reproduced—sometimes doubled—by morning. Ginger had never met a housekeeping chore she couldn't postpone. It was just…a little dust was a different species than downright dirt.

The whole place looked neglected.

Gramps looked neglected.

When the last bag had been hauled from the car, her childhood bedroom looked like a rummage sale, but enough was enough. She opened the windows, breathed in the fresh air then crashed on the peach bedspread. She was so tired she couldn't think.

She was so anxious she was afraid of thinking.

In the past month, her entire life had fallen apart… which she had the bad, bad feeling she was entirely responsible for. She'd been bamboozled by a guy she'd lost her heart to, lost her job, shredded everything she owned to sublet her Chicago apartment, had a completely unexpected pregnancy that she had no way to afford or deal with…and then came the call for help from Gramps.

She'd fix it all.

She had to.

And Gramps came first because…well, because she loved him. There was no question about her priorities. It was just that she was getting the terrorizing feeling that her grandfather's problems weren't coming from without, but from within.

And if anyone was going to be able to give her a better picture of her grandfather's situation, it was unfortunately—very, very, *very* unfortunately—his doctor.

Chapter Two

Still yawning, Ike lumbered downstairs barefoot with the dog at his heels. Pansy had woken him, wanted to be let out. He opened the back door, waited. Pansy stepped a foot outside, stopped dead, let out a howl and barreled back in the house.

Ike peered out. There happened to be a snake in the driveway. A big one. A rat snake, nothing interesting.

"You live in South Carolina," he reminded Pansy. "You know about snakes. You just leave them alone. They don't want to hurt you. Just don't get in their way."

Pansy had heard this horseradish before. It hadn't worked then, either. She continued to dog his footsteps, closer than glue, all the way into the kitchen. He opened the fridge, peered in and had to shake his head.

He must have left the door unlocked again last night. The proof was in the white casserole on the top refrigerator shelf, tagged with a note from Maybelle Charles.

The casserole was her mama's famous Chicken Surprise recipe. On the counter there seemed to be a fancy pie—pecan—anchored on hot pads that he'd have to return. The pie would definitely be from the widow five doors down, Ms. Joelle Simmons. The basket on the front porch held a peck of late South Carolina peaches. Babs, he suspected.

This was possibly the best place for a single man to live in the entire known universe. The whole town seemed to think he was too thin and incapable of feeding himself. The unmarried female population all seemed convinced that he needed a woman to shape him up. The more bedraggled he looked, the more they chased him. No one seemed to worry that he was a natural slob. They'd all decided, independently, that the right woman could fix minor male problems like that.

The food thing had started a day after he'd moved to Sweet Valley—which was more than three years ago. It was the same day he'd taken over old Doc Brady's country practice, the same day he'd found this fabulous ramshackle place just a couple blocks from the center of town. Come to think of it—it was even the same day his parents had expressed stunned horror that he'd failed to take a cardiac surgery option at Johns Hopkins, the way they had, the way any self-respecting MacKinnon was supposed to do. His two siblings had already failed their parents by choosing their own paths, but Ike had been the worst disappointment, because he'd actually decided to follow the family heritage of doctoring. Only he was never supposed to take a job here, in this bitsy town that could barely afford a doctor in the first place.

Everything about Sweet Water was perfect for him… except for the minor issue with all the food. The single ladies expected their plates returned. They cooked and baked and made everything on pretty little girly-type plates that invariably had their names on the bottom. Only when he returned them, he usually had to fight to leave.

He was bushwhacked into a chair, fed something else, made to drink something else, was expected to shell out some flirtation and interest.

Ike couldn't summon the energy to be rude, but he lucked out when Pansy showed up at his door. She refused to leave him, insisted on being adopted and went with him everywhere. She really helped with shortening the visits from all the single ladies.

Upstairs was home. Downstairs was his office—as in open to any and everyone.

Old Doc Brady hadn't run it that way, but Ike did. He'd inherited some help with the place. Bartholomew had some personality issues, but he cleaned the whole first floor at night and loved the part-time work. A retired nurse named Stephie still lived in the area, and always came in if he needed extra help. And the mainstay of the office was sixty-year-old Ruby, who was a wee bit bossy—but she could run a small country without breaking a sweat.

Right now, though, was his favorite time of day. He fetched a mug of coffee and the paper and ambled out to the screened-in back deck. Tuesday he had no scheduled patients until ten. Ruby would shout to let him know when she got there.

Pansy refused to come out. She was still worried about the snake.

Ike was worried about nothing. The morning was cool; he'd had to pull on a sweatshirt. Occasionally he heard the regular sounds of school buses going by, cars starting to congregate behind lights, stores opening and the occasional conversation as people headed for work or breakfast.

He'd finished the paper and started his second mug of coffee when he heard Ruby's voice from the front desk—and then the brisk snap of her footsteps coming down the hall to the back door. Par for the course, her portly shape was draped in a wild flower print, accessorized—her word, not his—by bright pink earrings, shoes and lipstick.

"Lady here to see you, Doc. Ginger Gautier. Cashner Gautier's granddaughter. You've got a ten o'clock—"

He glanced at his watch. It was only 9:10. "If you wouldn't mind, ask her to come on back."

"You mean in your office? Or in an examining room?" More than once, Ruby felt obligated to explain appropriate behavior to him, always tactfully and framed as a question. Still, her tone made it clear that patients shouldn't be seen on the back porch.

But Ginger wasn't a patient. And he knew what she'd come to talk about.

It was always a touchy situation when someone embarrassed themselves. It wasn't tough on the person who'd been the victim—him. But it was usually difficult for the person who'd done the embarrassing thing. Her.

As quickly as Ruby disappeared, he heard Ginger's lighter footstep, charging fast—Ike suspected she'd really, really like to get this meeting over with. From the open door, he could see her climb over the exhausted Pansy and step out onto the quiet back porch. She looked…

Delectable.

The hair was wild. Calling it red didn't explain anything. The color wasn't remotely ginger, like her name; it didn't have any of that cinnamon or orange. It was more like dark auburn, with a mix of sun and chestnut, with some streaks of red shivering in the long, thick strands. She'd strapped it up with some kind of hair leash. In the meantime, she had silver shining in her ears, on her wrist. Today she was wearing greens. A dark green shirt, pale green pants.

There was a lot of blue in those eyes. The same blue as a lake in a storm, deep and rich.

Her face was an oval. The eyes took up a whole lot of space, dominated everything about her face. She had thin, arched brows, gloss on her lips, but otherwise he couldn't tell if she wore any makeup. She had that redhead kind of skin, though…translucent, clear, clean… give or take the smattering of freckles.

As far as the body…well. She looked more like the kind of girl you brought home to meet Mom rather than the kind a man imagined under the sheets. But Ike was nonstop imagining that body under the sheets right now. There was a lot of music, a lot of passion, in the way she moved, the way she did everything he'd seen so far. Of course, he'd been celibate for too long a stretch, so maybe he was dreaming up the sizzle he sensed in her.

That celibacy had probably been dumb. Abstinence had never worked well for him, and he could have slept with any number of ladies in town. Somehow he never had.

Maybe that was because no woman had really enticed him before. Not like Ginger seemed to. Heaven knew he could analyze her body for three, four hours and still want to analyze more. For one thing, she had significantly perky breasts. The breasts themselves weren't all that significant, but the perky was. They were round, firm, pressed just right against the shirt. She had no waist to speak of. But the pants—well, the pants begged to be taken off. They were just cotton, or some other lightweight fabric, but he could see the outline of her fanny, her thighs, her calves. She might be on the skimpy side, weight wise, but she looked strong and healthy, making it extremely easy to imagine her legs wrapped around him, without those pants. Without that blouse.

Damn, but she was refreshing. Challengingly refreshing. Even the resentment in her flash of a smile was disarming. He was getting mighty sick of women smiling at him as if he were slab of meat. Being disliked was a lot more interesting.

"I was hoping you'd come by to talk. Want some coffee?"

She nodded. "Black." She motioned to Pansy. "Does that dog ever move?"

"Rarely. About ninety percent of the day she's in a coma. But don't say the word d-i-n-n-e-r or there'll be hell to pay. And I'm talking relentless." He motioned her to a white Adirondack rocker while he stepped into the kitchen/lab, came back with a mug for her, and a fresh one for him. "How's Cashner doing today?"

"Happy as a clam." She locked her palms around the mug. "But I'm not. Being with him has made me scared to death."

He nodded. "I'm glad you came home."

"I had no idea. I talked to him on the phone—"

"All the time. I know. He told me. He thinks the sun rises and sets with you. And he holds it together in some conversations, especially in the early part of the day. He's always in good humor. Never a complainer. He can talk a blue streak, telling jokes, spinning yarns, talking about the tea farm. It's not always apparent to other people what's been going on."

"He told me…" She hesitated, and he guessed the apology was coming. Or the closest he was going to get to an apology. "He told me his doctor was trying to take the land away from him. Force him to move. That his doctor was behind the conspiracy."

"Yeah. That would be me. The evil doctor. Not about forcing him. That's not my place. But especially in the last couple months, I've been pushing him to believe he could live a lot easier in a place with more help."

"He doesn't want help."

"I know."

"He doesn't believe he needs help."

"I know."

"Last night I found him sitting in the wet grass. Wearing a suit. Around one in the morning."

Ike winced in sympathy.

"He calls me Ginger. And a minute later, he'll call me Rachel. My grandmother's name. And sometimes I'm Loretta. Do you have a clue who Loretta is?"

Ike shook his head.

"And then there's Cornelius. Cornelius was old before I was born. Half the afternoon yesterday, they played cards. Rummy. And canasta. Cornelius was as balmy-headed as my gramps. Nothing's getting cleaned. Cornelius seems to make food sometimes. And forget other times…" At the sudden sound of voices coming from inside the house, she said immediately, "Do you have a patient? I know I should have called first, before stopping by."

"First patient's at ten. Ruby'll let me know when he gets here."

"Okay." She took a breath. "Listen, Doc—"

"Ike," he corrected her gently. "I'm your grandfather's doctor, not yours."

She immediately launched into an emotional sputter. "He was perfectly fine at Christmas and Easter both! He's been fine every darned time I call! I was here in *June* for Pete's sake. I don't understand how he could have changed so much, so fast!"

"Because that's how it hits people sometimes."

She launched into the next rocket round of nonstop sputter. "Well, what exactly *is* wrong with him—and *don't* tell me Alzheimer's. Or that there's nothing you can do. I want to know what tests you've run. If you've sent him to specialists. I may not have a heap of money, but my grandfather can afford the best of any kind of treatment. And I can stay here. I mean…I don't know how on earth I could find a job here. But for however long it takes, I can stay here, live with him. I could make sure he gets everything he needs, nutrition and medicine and exercise or whatever else you think he needs—"

"Ginger." He said her name to calm her. He was watching her face. She was so upset. Naturally. Who wouldn't be, to suddenly find out someone you loved had a fragile health issue? But there was something more going on. He'd seen her take a sip of coffee, and then immediately put the mug down. She'd had peach-healthy color in her cheeks when she came in, but that color was fading, her face turning pale.

Still, he answered her questions. "Yes, Cashner's been prescribed some medications that help a lot of people. There's no perfect medicine for this. I sent him to Greenville for tests, put him in the hands of two physicians I know personally. He's been tested and evaluated and retested."

"Don't you say it," she warned him.

He got it. She wasn't ready to hear the words *Alz-*

heimer's or *dementia.* "I'll give you the other answer," he said patiently. "Old age."

"He's not that old!"

Ike nodded. "I think it's possible he had some mini strokes a while back. He's been on high blood pressure meds from long before I came here. But he's at a point where I'm not certain if he remembers to take them. I set up a schedule for him, to help him remember, conveyed the same information to Cornelius. But sometimes—"

Ruby showed up in the doorway. "Doc. Mr. Robards is here. It'll take me a few minutes to get him weighed in and BP done and then into a gown, but then he's ready."

Ike started to say, "I'll be there in a minute," then noticed Ginger jump to her feet faster than a firecracker. Ruby's interruption had given her the perfect excuse to take off. She either wanted to get away from him, a depressing thought, or she needed to absorb what he'd told her about her grandfather. Alone.

Whatever her reasons, she stood up damned fast. The last pinch of color bleached from her face, and down she went. He barely had time to jerk forward, protect her head and help ease her to the ground. The porch only had matting for a rug.

Ruby rushed through the door, muttering, "Well, I'll be" and "What the sam hill is this about?" and then Pansy pushed through the door. Pansy invariably liked commotion. She jutted her jowly head under Ike's arm, trailing a small amount of drool on Ginger's hair. Ruby hunkered down just as intrusively.

"Ruby. Pansy. She needs air. And I need space."

Ruby took several creaking moments to get back to her feet. "I'll get a damp washcloth. And a BP unit."

"Good thinking. Thanks." He nudged Pansy out of the way, thinking that he'd been hoping to get his hands on Ginger—but not in this context. She was already coming to. Her eyes opened, dazed, closed again. She frowned in confusion—another sign that she was regaining full consciousness—and then she raised a hand, as if her first instinct was to sit up.

"You're fine, Ginger. Just stay where you are for a minute. It's just me. Ike."

No temp. He didn't need a thermometer to be certain. Normal color was flushing back into her face. He brushed his hands through her hair, feeling for bumps or lumps, any injury that might have caused the faint. He pressed two fingers on her carotid artery.

Accidentally, he noticed the rapid rise and fall of her breasts. The softness of her. The scent on her skin—not flowers, not for this one. Some sassy, citrusy perfume. It suited her.

Ruby hustled back with the BP unit. He took it, finding what he expected, that it was slightly on the low side. Again, he took her pulse as he studied her face. Her pulse rate was coming back to normal. And then, when her eyes suddenly met his, that pulse rate zoomed way out of the stratosphere.

Yeah. That was how he felt around her, too.

"If you need me…" Ruby said from the doorway.

"No. She's fine. Or she will be in a minute. Just give Mr. Robards a magazine and tell him I'll just be a few minutes, not long." He never turned his head. Focused his gaze only on her, tight as glue.

He knew a ton of women…but few with the fire of this one. Loyal. Passionate.

Interesting.

Her forehead crinkled in one last confused frown,

and then she seemed to recover herself altogether. She muttered something akin to "Good grief" and pushed off the porch matting—or tried to.

He didn't forcibly hold her down, just put one hand on her shoulder. "I know you're getting up, but let's keep it slow."

"I'm fine."

"Uh-huh. You're pregnant, aren't you?" It was the doctor asking the question, but the man listening for the answer. Most of the time Ike didn't have to separate the two, but for this question, for this woman, he definitely did.

"Say what?" Wow. Those soft, sensual blue eyes abruptly turned glacier blue. Color slammed into her face. "What on earth made you ask that!"

He'd like her to think he was naturally brilliant, but the truth was it had just been a gut call, a wild guess. It was her response that gave away the truth of it. He answered slowly, "Just a short list of clues. Everything about you looks healthy and fit. You asked for coffee, but your hand shot to your stomach when you took a sip. Then you fainted out of the blue."

This time she pushed free and fast, got her legs under her, stood up. He watched for any other symptoms of lightheadedness, but saw nothing. "If you're diabetic, better tell me now. And are you on prenatal vitamins? Have anything prescribed for nausea?"

Okay. He'd pressed too far, judging from the sputter. The smoke coming from her ears. Her hands fisted on her hips. "Let's get something straight right now, Doc."

"Go for it." He eased to his feet.

"You're my grandfather's doctor. Not mine."

"Got it."

"My private life has nothing to do with you."

"Got it," he repeated. "But if you haven't been on prenatal vitamins—"

"What is it about small towns? People leap to conclusions over a breath of wind. No one said I was pregnant. No one has any reason in the universe to think that."

"So there's no guy." He just wanted to slip that question in there, while she was still talking to him.

"Exactly. There's no guy."

"I wondered," he admitted.

Ouch. She was shaking mad now. "For the record—" She punctuated her comments with a royal finger shake. "—I wouldn't fall for a doctor if he were the last man in the country. On the continent. On the entire planet...."

"Got it," he said again. "I'm sure glad we had this conversation."

That was it. She spun around, stepped over the dog, yanked open the back porch screen door and charged down the hall. Ruby peeked her head out of exam room one—then snapped her head back, clearly alarmed at getting in Ginger's way.

Ike followed her exit—mostly by following the swing of her fanny and bounce of her hair—all the way to the slamming of his front door.

Ruby popped her head out again. She didn't speak. Just raised her eyebrows.

Ike shook his head. "Don't ask me what that was."

But Ginger lingered in his mind. He was so used to being treated like a catch.

So many single women in the area fawned over him. Played up to him. They'd been spoiling him rotten, with food and attention and God knows all kinds of subtle and less-than-subtle offers.

It was a nice change of pace to meet a shrew. She was such a breath of fresh air.

He blew out a sigh, headed inside to wash his hands and start his doctor day.

He told himself she was in trouble. That she *was* trouble. That she had troubles.

His head got it.

But there was still hot blood zooming up and down his veins. And a stupid smile on his face when he ambled in to greet Rupert Robards.

Rupert had prostate problems. The next patient was an older lady with a lump on her rump, followed by a young mom with a yeast infection and, last for the morning, a sixteen-year-old kid with hot tears in his eyes and a fishing hook stuck deep in his wrist.

There was no room in the entire morning for a single romantic or sexy thought to surface.

Still. She lingered in his mind.

Ginger had parked the Civic right on Magnolia, but once she stormed out of Ike's office, she ignored the car and kept on walking. She needed the exercise. The fresh air. The chance to think.

He'd made her lose her temper twice now.

Usually she could keep her worst flaws under wraps until she'd known a person awhile. Invariably her temper—and other character flaws, such as impulsiveness—couldn't be kept in the closet forever. But somehow Ike had brought out the worst in her right up front.

It would help if he wasn't a doctor. A damn good-looking, sexually appealing doctor. Scruffy. But still adorable.

Steve hadn't been half that adorable, and she'd still been blindsided. Any inkling of attraction for Ike just seemed to work like a trigger for her. Her stay-away button started blinking red and setting off alarm instincts.

She ambled down Magnolia, crossed Oak, aimed down Cypress. It wasn't as if she didn't know the town like the back of her hand. The big stores like Walmart and Target were located in the new section of town, but Sweet Valley's downtown was still vibrant, filled with shop after shop, restaurant after restaurant.

She'd shut down her life in Chicago and zoomed home so fast that she needed some things. Shampoo. Her favorite brand of toothpaste.

En route to the pharmacy, she accidentally spotted a shoe sale.

By the time she'd tried on and bought a pair of sandals, she'd put her mind off handsome, interfering doctors and had her head back where it belonged. On Gramps.

Nothing Ike told her had been reassuring. He'd only opened up more worries, more concerns. She needed to know the truth. She just didn't know what to do about the situation.

Perhaps by instinct, she found herself standing in front of the Butter Bakery. She'd forgotten—or just hadn't had a reason to remember before—that Gramps had an attorney. Ginger knew the name. Louella Meachams. Ginger must have met her sometime—Sweet Valley was such a small town that everyone about met everyone else at some time or another. But Ginger couldn't recall anything about her, until she spotted the sign for Louella Meachams, Esq., just above the stairwell from the bakery.

She couldn't imagine the attorney would be able to see her without an appointment, but she could at least stop by while she was right there in town, set up something.

The old-fashioned stairwell was airless and dark, with steep steps leading to the upstairs offices. Her stomach churned in protest, partly because she'd always been claustrophobic, and partly because she needed to eat something, and soon. She'd planned to have breakfast right after seeing Ike, but that stupid fainting business had stolen her appetite. Still, she'd immediately started to feel better once she'd gotten out in the fresh air. As soon as she made contact with the attorney, she'd stop and get some serious food before heading home.

Upstairs, she found an old-fashioned oak door with the attorney's name on a brass sign. She turned the knob without knocking, assuming she'd be entering a receptionist and lobby area, not the lawyer's specific office.

"Oh. Excuse me. I was hoping to make an appointment with Mrs. Meachams—"

"I'm Louella Meachams. And just Louella would do. Come in. Sit yourself."

The lady had to be around fifty, had a wash-and-wear hairstyle and a general bucket build. She wore men's pants, a starched shirt, no makeup. Hunting dog pictures graced the walls. The sturdy oak chairs facing the desk had no cushions. Windows overlooking the street below had blinds, but no curtains. The whole office looked like a male lawyer's lair, rather than a woman's. And Louella looked a little—maybe even a lot—like a man herself. She peered at her over half-rim glasses.

"I believe you're my grandfather's attorney. Cashner Gautier," Ginger started. "I'm Ginger, his granddaughter. I just got into town a few days ago. And I was hoping you could help me clarify his situation."

"I know who you are, just from all that red hair.

You were one fiery little girl. And I'm more than will-ing to talk with you, but you need to understand that your grandfather's my client. I not only can't, but never would, break confidentiality with him."

"I understand that. And I'd never ask you to." Halt-ingly she started to explain the situation she'd found at home, how her grandfather wasn't himself, that he seemed to have both memory and health issues, that the place looked in serious disarray compared to the last time she'd been home. Louella leaned back, stuck a leather shoe on a wastebasket for a footrest and lis-tened until she came through with a question.

"As long as I've been Cashner's attorney, I've never been completely clear about his family situation. I know your grandparents only had one child, a daughter—your mother. And that even when your mother married, she kept the Gautier name, which is pretty unusual in these parts. If I have it right, you're now the only close blood kin of Cashner's, because your mama died quite a while ago."

"Yes. Mom was in a terrible car accident. I was barely ten. And that was when I came to live with my grandparents."

"But are there other blood kin? Brothers, cousins? Any relatives at all on your grandfather's side of the fence?"

"No, not that I'm aware of. The Gautiers came orig-inally from France...there may be some distant rela-tives still there, but none I know of. My grandmother had some family in California, but I never met any of them. They were like second cousins or that distance."

"What about your father?" Louella leaned over, opened a drawer, lifted a sterling silver flask. "Need a little toot?"

"Uh, no. Thank you." She added, "My father has nothing to do with this situation. He's not a Gautier—"

"Yes. But he's family for you, so he could help you, couldn't he? Advise you on options you might consider for your grandfather."

Ginger frowned. So far she'd given more information than she'd gotten. Not that she minded telling her grandfather's attorney the situation. Gramps trusted Louella. So Ginger did. "My dad," she said carefully, "is about as lovable as you can get. He's huggable, always laughing, lots of fun. I adored him when I was little. He brought me a puppy one birthday, rented a Ferris wheel for another birthday party, took me out of school—played hooky—to fly me to Disney World one year. You'd love him. Everyone does."

"I'm sure there's some reason you're telling me this," Louella said stridently.

"I'm just trying to say, as tactfully as I can, that my dad can't be in this picture. I love him. Not loving him would be like…well, like not loving a puppy. Puppies piddle. It isn't fun to clean up after them, but you can't expect a puppy to behave like a grown-up. Which is to say…I don't even know where my dad is right now. Whatever problems my grandfather has—I'm his person. His problems are mine. And there's nothing I wouldn't do for him."

"All right. I always heard the gossip that your father was your basic good-looking reprobate, but I never met him, didn't know for sure. I'm glad you clarified the situation. I'm sorry that he's out of the picture for you. That makes Cashner's circumstances all the more awkward. But I still can't tell you about his will—"

"I don't give a hoot about his will. I need to know if he's paying his bills. If he's solvent. Can you tell me who has power of attorney? If someone has medical powers? I need to know if I have the right to look into his bank accounts, make sure that bills are being paid, what shape the business is in, whether he's okay financially or if I need to do something."

Louella harrumphed, looked out the window as if she were thinking about how to phrase an answer. Ginger was more than willing to wait.

At least she thought she was. A glance at an old wall clock revealed it was well past noon. Apparently they'd been talking—and she'd been running around town—a lot longer than she'd expected. Technically time didn't matter; it wasn't as if she was on a schedule. But the queasiness that plagued her earlier in the morning was suddenly back. So was exhaustion. Not exhaustion from doing anything; she just had a sudden, consuming urge to curl up in a ball like a cat and close her eyes, just nap for a few minutes.

She'd never been a napper. Until eight weeks ago. Now she could suddenly get so tired she could barely stumble around. It was crazy. She felt crazy. And in a blink of a minute, she just wanted to go home.

"Well, Ginger. I don't know how to say this but bluntly. Your grandfather needs to move out of that big old place. But he won't. He needs to hire someone to take over the tea plantation before it's in complete ruin. But he won't do that, either. And the best advice I can give you is to just leave him alone. Go on about your life. It's what I'd want, if I were in Cashner's situation. He doesn't need or want someone telling him what to do, where he needs to be, what rules he should be following. It won't help. If you want to help, be a good granddaughter and love him. But then just go on with your own life."

Ginger heard her. Alarm shot sparks straight to her bloodstream. Gramps *was* in trouble, in ways the attorney knew about, separate from the problems Ike knew as Gramps's doctor. Urgency made her heart slam. She rushed to her feet—or she tried to.

For the second time that morning, the world turned green and everything in sight started spinning.

"Well, my word!"

She heard Louella's husky voice. Heard it as if it was coming from a hundred yards away. After that, everything went smoky black.

Chapter Three

When the last patient of the morning canceled, Ruby let him know with a fervent "Hallelujah!"

Ike was still smiling when he heard the front door slam—Ruby did like a long lunch when she could get it. But his mind was really on Ginger, and had been all morning.

There was no question that he'd see her again. She'd seek him out because she had to; he was the best source of information on her grandfather. Ike needed that connection just as much, because he happened to love the old man, and something had to be decided about Cashner before the situation turned into a real crisis.

Still, when the office phone rang, he never guessed it would be Ginger contacting him again this soon. Nor would he have thought he'd hear from Louella Meachams—one of his most reluctant patients. She told him she "had no truck with doctors" every single time he took her blood pressure. Louella was at least part guy. Not gay. Just an exuberantly male kind of female. People trusted her in town. He did, too. She just had a lot of coarse sandpaper in her character.

"Don't waste your time telling me you're busy with a patient, Ike MacKinnon. I don't care if you have fifty patients. I have a woman in my office on the floor. Fainted dead away. Now you get right over here and do something about her."

"Since you asked so nicely, I'll be there right away. But in the meantime...do you know who she is, why she fainted, what happened?"

"I don't care what happened. I want her off my floor. When she went down, it scared the bejesus out of me. I thought she was dead!"

"I understand—"

"I don't care if you understand or not. You get her out of here somehow, someway, and I'm talking pronto."

"Yes, ma'am. But again…" Hell. Ike just wanted a clue what the problem could be. "Do you know her?"

"Her name is Ginger Gautier. Cashner's granddaughter. What difference does it make? The problem is I thought she'd stopped breathing. Almost gave me a heart attack. I don't do first aid. I had a sister who fainted all the time, but that was to get our mother's attention. It was fake every time. This is *not* fake. I'm telling you, she went *down*. Right in front of my desk."

"Okay, got it, see you in five, max six."

"You make that three minutes, Doc. And I'm not whistling Dixie."

If Louella really believed there was an emergency, she'd have called 911—but Louella, being stingy, would never risk an ambulance charge unless she was absolutely positive there was no other choice. So Ike took the time to shove on street shoes, grab a jacket and scribble a note to Ruby before heading out.

He could jog the distance faster than driving it—the lawyer's office was only three blocks over, faster yet if he zigzagged through buildings. Pansy let out an unholy howl of abandonment when he left without her, but sometimes, darn it, he just couldn't take his favorite girl.

Less than five minutes later, he reached the bakery and zipped up the steps to the second floor. When he turned the knob of Louella's office, though, something heavy seemed to be blocking it. "Louella, it's me, Doc," he said as he knocked.

Louella opened it. Apparently she'd been the something heavy blocking the entrance. "She keeps trying to leave. Doesn't have a brain cell in her head. I told her she wasn't going anywhere until you checked her out, and that's that."

"I must have said a dozen times that I'm feeling better—and that I was going straight home from here." Ginger's voice was coming from the floor—but it certainly sounded healthy and strong.

"Yeah, I heard you. And I told you a dozen times that there could be liability issues if you left here in shape to cause yourself or others harm."

"You're the only person I've met in a blue moon who's more bullheaded than I am, bless your heart. But keeping a person against their will is called kidnapping. Or is there another legal term?"

While the two women continued this pleasant conversation, Ike hunkered down—apparently Louella had threatened Ginger with death if she tried to get up before the doctor got there. He went through the routine. Pulse. Temp. Whether she could focus, whether she had swollen lymph glands.

Wherever he touched her, she jumped.

He liked that. If he was stuck feeling walloped this close to her, he at least wanted her to suffer the same way.

He got some extra personal contact—judicious, but lucky for sure—when he helped her to her feet. She didn't wobble. Of course, with his arm around her, she couldn't have wobbled—or fallen—even if she'd wanted to. But she shot him one of those ice-blue looks to indicate he could remove his hands. Now. Right now.

"Okay, Louella, I'm taking her from your office."

"And don't let her come back here until she's fit as a fiddle."

"My. I had no idea that fiddles had health issues. Like whether they could be fit or sick. I had no idea they were alive at all—"

Ike saw the look on Louella's face, could see she was in a rolling up the sleeves to get into another squabble, so he shuffled Ginger quickly into the hall.

He saw her sudden choke when they reached the top of her stairs, so he suspected she was still a little on the dizzy side. He hooked an arm around her, making sure she was steady.

"You don't need to do that," she said irritably.

"Can't have you falling on my watch."

"I'm not on your watch."

"Uh-huh. You know...you *could* have been nice to Louella."

"She wasn't nice to me first!"

"You seriously scared her when you fainted."

"That's an excuse for holding me hostage and not letting me leave? For insulting me? For calling you?"

"Yup. At least, that's how I see it. But then, I don't have your temper."

At the bottom of the stairs, he'd barely pushed open the door before she shot through. She took a step west before he kidnapped her wrist.

"Hey. My car is that way—"

"And you'll be in your car in about a half hour. But first, you need an immediate medical intervention."

"Intervention? What are you talking about?"

The New York Deli was at the corner of Magnolia. Whether anything served had anything to do with New York, no one knew or cared. The place was always packed at lunch, but Feinstein—the owner—always saved a table for Ike. It was bribery, pure and simple. Feinstein was worried about the performance of his boy parts. He'd never had any marital problems with his wife before, but "everybody" knew guys eventually needed a little chemical boost. Which was to say, Feinstein had motivation for taking good care of the town doctor.

Ike never came for the bribe. He came for the food. And Ginger continued to make minor protestations about being herded like a sheep, but that was only until she saw the menu.

Mrs. Feinstein—possibly the homeliest woman Ike had ever seen—advised Ginger on the best choices, and who could have guessed? Ginger agreed without arguing.

Right off, she devoured three pickles. Then a masterful corned beef on rye. Chips. Cole slaw. Since she picked at the crumbs after that, he figured she was still hungry, so he ordered dessert. Apple cake with whipped cream.

Then more pickles.

He leveled a sandwich, too, which took all of a minute and a half. So while her mouth was full, he took the opportunity to start a conversation. "I'm guessing that before the evening news, the whole town will know that you fainted twice this morning, that we're having lunch together...and they'll likely be speculating on whether we're sleeping together."

She dropped her fork, which he took as encouraging. So he went on, "My theory is...we might as well sleep together, since we've already been branded with the tag."

She dropped her fork—again—but then she just squinted her eyes at him. He didn't see temper this time, just reluctant humor. "Hey. Do you usually flirt with women you think are pregnant by someone else?"

"Not usually, no. In fact, never." He retrieved a couple fresh forks from the table next to them, then went back for another couple. Who knew how many she would need before this meal was over. "But I keep finding your situation, well, unique. You came home because you were really worked up about your grandfather. But there's no guy here. If you had a guy, he'd have to be a class-A jerk not to be with you when he knows you need help."

"Wow. That analysis and conclusion is just stunning."

"Yeah, my mama always said I was a bright boy," he agreed with his best deadpan expression. "So my theory is...there's no guy to stop me from moving in on you."

This time she had to chuckle—clearly in spite of herself. "I've been doing a lot of hurling and fainting. Most guys would run in the opposite direction."

"Most guys haven't been through medical school."

"That's an answer?"

"What can I say? A first-year resident loses any chance of being embarrassed ever again in his life.

Some things just come with life. Now what's that expression about?"

She lifted a hand. "I was just thinking. I had this sudden instinct…that you just might be a hardcore, card-carrying good guy." She put a stop sign into another hand gesture. "I'm not accusing you of anything terrible. I just didn't expect to even let a positive thought anywhere near you. So I'm just saying. If I was ever going to trust a doctor again as long as I live—which I'm not—it might have been you."

"Ah. It's the doctor thing that's a problem. You're such a relief."

"Relief?"

"Practically every single woman in this town has been feeding me, taking care of me, fluttering her eye-lashes at me. All their mamas think of doctors as being a terrific catch. You know, dumb as a fish that just needs the right bait to sucker in. You're so much more fun. I'd ask you out…but I'm afraid if we had a good time, you'd quit disliking me, and then where would we be? Not having fun together anymore. It's not worth the risk. Still, I don't see why we shouldn't sleep together. That doesn't have to interfere with your giving me a constant hard time. We could just redirect all that passionate energy a little differently when the lights go off."

She cupped her chin. "Did anything you just said make a lick of sense?"

He didn't care if he was making sense. She'd had a rotten morning—a stressful visit with him, then a stressful visit with the lawyer, no easy answers about her grandfather. And he hadn't known until he'd sneaked the information that the father of her baby was both a doctor and a louse.

She was flying solo. Flying solo with a pregnancy and no help in sight.

But he'd gotten her fed. And teased. And almost laughing. She'd forgotten it all for a while.

Sometimes that was the best a doctor could do. Offer some stress relief. There was no way any doctor could cure all ills…much less all wrongs.

When she glanced at a wall clock, he did, too. He was startled at how much time had passed. Ruby was going to kill him. He was ten minutes late for his first afternoon patient.

"Yeah, I didn't realize how late it was, either. I need to get back to my grandfather."

He put some money down, knowing the Feinsteins wouldn't give him a check, and eventually steered her to the door. There was the usual gauntlet of "Hi, Doc!" and "Ginger, so glad to hear you're back in town" and other ferocious attempts to stall them. He kept moving them as fast as he could.

Outside, the sky was pumping out clouds now. A whiskery wind tossed paper and litter in the air, lifted collars. The temperature was still warmish, somewhere in the sixties, but there was rain in the wind, and the bright sun kept hiding from sight.

"I see your car," he said.

"You don't have to walk me there. You have to be in a hurry to get back to your office."

"It all comes with the service. A lady faints, she gets walked to her car."

"What if she isn't a lady?"

"If a wicked woman faints, she still gets walked to her car. It's in the rule book."

"What rule book is that?"

"The *South Carolina Rules for Gentlemen* rule book.

My mom made me memorize whole passages before I was four. She called it getting ready for kindergarten."

Walking next to her felt like foreplay. It was kind of a test of rhythms.

Whether they could walk together, move together in a natural way. How his height worked with hers. Whether she could keep up with his stride. Whether she wanted to. Whether she galloped on ahead when he wanted to amble.

Fast, too damned fast, they reached her rust bucket of a Civic. She dipped in her shoulder bag for her car key, found it, lifted her head and suddenly frowned at him.

"What?" He had no idea what her expression meant. Even less of an idea what she planned to do.

She popped up on tiptoe, framed his face between her soft palms and kissed him. On a guy's scale of kisses, it was only a two. No tongue. No pressure. No invitation.

More…just a short, evocative melding of textures. Her lips. His lips.

Like a meeting of whipped cream and chocolate.

Or like brandy and a winter fire.

Or like the snug of gloves on a freezing morning.

Or like that click, that electric high-charge surge, not like the million kisses you've had since middle school, not like the any-girl-would-do kisses, but the click kind. The wonder kind. The damn it, what the hell is happening here kind.

She pulled back, sank back, cocked her head and looked at him. Her purse fell.

He picked it up. Her keys fell. He picked those up, too.

When he got his breath back, he said carefully, "Do we have any idea why you did that?"

"I've been known to do some very bad, impulsive things sometimes. Even if I regret it. Even if I know I'm going to regret it later."

"So that was just a bad impulse." He shook his head. "Sure came across like a great impulse to me." Before she could try selling him any more malarkey, he said, "I stop to see your grandfather at least twice a week. Always short visits. He pretends it's not about his health. So do I. Which is to say...I'll see you soon. Very soon. And that's a promise."

But not soon enough. His heart slammed.

Of course, that was the man talking, and not the doctor. Sometimes it was okay to be both roles...but not with her, he sensed. Never with her.

Ginger had barely pulled in the drive when the rain started. It was just a spatter when she stepped out, but the sky cracked with a streak of lightning by the time she reached the porch.

Thunder growled. Clouds started swirling as if a child had finger-painted the whole sky with grays. Pretty, but ominous. Inside, she called, "Gramps? I'm home!" The dark had infiltrated the downstairs with gloom, somehow accenting the dust and neglect that seemed everywhere. Still, she heard voices—and laughter—coming from the kitchen.

At the kitchen doorway, she folded her arms, having to smile at the two cronies at the kitchen table. The game looked to be cutthroat canasta. Money was on the table. Cards all over the place. From the time she'd left that morning, a set of dirty china seemed to have accumulated on the sink counter, but the two old codgers were having a blast.

She bent down to kiss her grandfather. Got a huge

hug back. And for now, his eyes were lucid and dancing-clear. "You've been gone all day, you little hussy. Hope you spent a lot of money shopping and had a great old time."

"I did." The two rounds of fainting and encounters with Ike were locked up in her mind's closet. Her grandfather recognized her. Had a happy, loving smile for her. "Cornelius, you're getting a hug from me, too, so don't try running."

Cornelius pretended he was trying to duck under the table, but that was all tease. He took his hug like a man. Cornelius was smaller than she was, and possibly had some Asian and black and maybe Native American blood. For certain no one else looked quite like him. Ginger had never known whether her family had adopted him or the other way around, but he and Gramps were of an age. Neither could manage to put a glass in the dishwasher. Neither obeyed an order from anyone. And both of them could while away a dark afternoon playing cards and having a great time.

"All right, you two. I'm going upstairs for a short nap."

"Go. Go." She was promptly shooed away, as Cornelius chortled over some card played and both men issued raucous, enthusiastically gruesome death threats to each other.

Apparently the morning had been tough on her system, because once her head hit the pillow upstairs, she crashed harder than a whipped puppy. She woke up to a washed-clean world and the hour was past four. After a fast shower, she flew downstairs to find her boys on the front veranda now, rocking and sipping sweet tea and arguing about a ball game.

When Cornelius saw her, he pushed out of the rocker.

"We was thinking you might not wake up until tomorrow, you were looking so tired."

"I was a little tired, but I'm feeling great now."

Cornelius nodded. "I'm headed to the kitchen. Got some supper cooking. Can't remember what all I started right now, but should be ready in an hour or so."

"That'd be great, you." She planned to head into the kitchen and help him—but not yet. Her gramps's eyes were still clear, still bright. She pulled a rocker closer to him, sat down.

"Gramps. All these years, you had Amos Hawthorne managing the land, running the farm. But no one's mentioned him, and I haven't seen him around."

"That's because he's not here anymore. I had to fire him. I don't remember exactly when it happened. But he stopped doing what I told him. He badgered and badgered me, until I said I'd had enough. Let him go."

Ginger gulped. "So…who's handling the tea now? The shop? The grounds?"

"Well, I am, honey child. Me and Cornelius. We closed the shop after…" He frowned. "I don't know exactly when. A little while ago."

"Okay. So who's doing the grounds around the house? The mowing. The gardens and trees and all."

"Cornelius and I had a theory about that. We need some goats."

"Goats," Ginger echoed.

"Yup. We have a heap of acreage that's nothing but lawn. Goats love grass. Wouldn't cost us a thing. The goats could eat the grass without using a lick of gas or needing a tractor at all."

Ginger was getting a thump of anxiety in her tummy again. "So…right now we don't have a lawn service or a farm manager?"

"We both think goats could do the work. They'd be happy. We'd be happy. Don't you think that sounds like fun, sweetheart?"

"I do. I do." She'd inherited the ability to lie from her father. "Gramps, do you know who did your taxes last year? I mean, do you have an accountant in town?"

"Why, honey, you know your grandma does all that. I always oversaw the business, the farm. But it was your grandma who did all the work with figures. We never depended on outsiders for that kind of thing. Why are you asking all these questions? We can do something fun. Like play cards. Or put out the backgammon board. After dinner, we could take the golf cart around before the bugs hit."

He was right, Ginger realized. There was no point in asking any more questions. Every answer she'd heard so far was downright scary. There appeared to be no one running the place. Not the tea plantation. Not the house. Gramps seemed under the impression that Grandma was still alive, still there with him. The whole situation was more overwhelming than she'd ever expected.

Ginger wondered if she could somehow will herself to faint again. It certainly helped her block out things earlier that day.... Except that fainting brought on Ike, as if he had some invisible radar when anything embarrassing or upsetting was happening to her.

She still couldn't figure out what possessed her to kiss him. He'd been a white knight, sort of. And she'd been starving and hadn't realized it. And a simple gesture like a hug or a kiss just didn't seem like that big a deal....

But it was.

It was a big deal because she already knew she was susceptible to doctors.

She also knew that impulsiveness got her into trouble every time. A woman could make a mistake. Everyone did that. No one could avoid it. But the measure of a woman was partly how she handled those mistakes.

Fool me once, shame on you. Fool me twice, shame on me. She'd been trying to drill that mantra into her head. A doctor might seem like great husband potential for lots of women—but not her. Doctors invariably put their jobs first, their own needs, and played by their own rule book.

Ike for sure played by his own rule book.

Keeping her heart a long, long way away from him was an easy for-sure.

Chapter Four

The next day, by midmorning, Ginger was not only reenergized, but conquering the world at the speed of sound. She'd put both boys to work by wrapping microfiber fabric around their shoes. Their job was to shuffle around the entire downstairs. It might not be the most glamorous way to dust the hardwood floors, but it was good enough. They were, of course, complaining mightily.

She'd hunkered down in the kitchen to clean, and figured she wasn't likely to escape the room for another three years at best. She'd found flour moths. That discovery canceled out any other plans she'd had for the day. She immediately started removing everything from the cupboards. Her first thought was to wash every surface with bleach, but she worried fumes that strong couldn't be good with a pregnancy, so she pulled on old plastic gloves, mixed up strong soap and a disinfectant, then unearthed a serious scrub brush.

The top west side cupboards were completely emptied out when she was interrupted by the sound of a motor—a lawn motor. She glanced outside, and then immediately climbed down and sprinted outside. A total stranger was driving a green lawn-mowing tractor. She'd never seen either the tractor or the man before, but once she chased after him—and finally won his attention—she could at least make out his features. He was an older black man, with a graying head of hair and soft eyes.

He shut off the mower when he spotted her.

"I don't understand," she started with. "Who are you and why are you here?"

"I'm Jed, ma'am."

His voice was liquid sweet, but that explained precisely nothing. "You don't work for my grandfather."

"No, ma'am. I'm retired. Don't work no more."

When she started another question, he gently interrupted with a more thorough explanation. "I stopped working anything regular, but I'm sure not ready for a rocking chair yet, and I have time on my hands. Dr. Ike now, he delivered my grandchild, knowing ahead the family couldn't pay him. So I'm paying it off this way. By doing things he finds for me to do. Not to worry. I'll check the oil and the gas and the blades when I put the mower back in the shop. I know my way around tractors."

She didn't know what to say, and when she didn't come up with anything fast enough, he just tipped his baseball cap and started the noisy motor again.

She stood there, hands on hips, and debated whether to call Ike immediately to give him what for...or to wait. Waiting seemed the wiser choice, because he'd be in the middle of his workday, likely seeing patients. So she went back toward the kitchen, thinking that the cleaning chore would give her time to think up what to say to him, besides.

She checked on Gramps and Cornelius, who'd turned on a radio to some station channeling rock and roll from the 1950s. But they were moving—at least until she showed up, and then they complained that they were too old to do this much exercise, that she was killing them, that she was cruel. She brewed everyone a fresh pot of Charleston's Best—everybody's favorite tea— then sent them back to work.

The kitchen looked as insurmountable as it had when she left it—but it wasn't as if she had an option to give up. The job had to be done, so she hunkered back down. She had her head under the sink when she heard the front doorbell.

She waited, thinking that her guys would obviously answer it—but no. The bell rang. Then rang again. She stood up and yanked off her plastic gloves as she stomped down the hall. A lady was on the other side of the screen door. A plump lady, wearing an old calico dress, her thin brown hair tied up in a haphazard bun.

"I know who you are," she said gruffly. "You're Cashner's granddaughter, Ginger Gautier. And I'm your new cook."

Ginger frowned. "I don't understand. We don't have a cook."

"Well, you do now. I don't do tofu, I'm telling you right off. No sushi, either. You want something fancy, you need somebody else."

Ginger started to speak, but the woman was downright belligerent, particularly for someone who'd shown up out of the blue. Without giving her any chance to answer, the lady pushed open the screen door and marched herself inside, aiming straight down the hall to the kitchen.

"Now just wait one minute. I don't even know who you are."

"My name's Sarah. Just Sarah. And like I said, I already know you're Ginger. Your grandma and I used to help out at church dinners now and then. A great lady, your grandma. Knew the value of a day's work, she did. Good grief."

When Sarah-Just-Sarah reached the doorway to the kitchen, she whipped around with an annoyed expression. "This kitchen is a complete mess. No one could cook in there right now."

Ginger threw up her hands. "I'd have told you that. If it was any of your business. Or if you'd asked."

Sarah ignored her, just propped her hands on her hips as she poked and peered around at the kitchen set up. "Well, here's the thing. The court says I got a problem with anger management. I don't think so. I think you'd be mad, too, if you had a no-count bum of a husband like mine. So the thing is, I got three children to feed. Which means I can't take on jobs where you have to show up for regular hours. My youngest one is on the sickly side, besides. So I'll just show up as I can. I'll get a meal cooking or a slow cooker going or whatever's going to work that day. You'll be able to eat it hot or just reheat. I'm a good cook. Close to a great cook. No one's ever complained about my cooking. Ever."

"I'm sure that's true. If I was looking for a cook. But—"

Sarah-Just-Sarah's chin shot up another notch. "Dr. Ike. He's been seeing my kids since he came to town.

That's almost four years. I paid him when I could, but I could never seem to hold a job, between the kids and my no-good husband. So I'd bring Dr. Ike cookies or a pie, or maybe cornbread with wildflower honey. Anyways, when all three of my kids got sick in September, he didn't even send me a bill. Never even brought it up. And the thing was, I couldn't even try to work then, not with sick kids. So I cornered him, I did. Said I was nobody's charity case, even if I couldn't immediately pay my bill. And he said, 'I could need a favor down the pike.' So I'm his favor. Well, holy moly. You are in a mess in here, aren't you?"

Every word that came out of the woman's mouth sounded angry. Ginger hadn't been able to get a word in, but she was starting to get the picture that Sarah simply talked that way. Mad. And even more mad as she squinted at the scandalized war zone in the kitchen.

It wasn't as if Ginger could help it. She was in the worst part of the mess, of course. Drawers gaped open, drying from where she'd washed inside. Water had sloshed on the floor here and there. Buckets blocked anyone from walking around. Cans from some of the lower cabinets were strewn on the ground while those shelves got cleaned. The dishwasher was running. The table was covered with rolls of shelf paper, which Ginger expected to cover the surfaces—once the place had been disinfected and cleaned and dried.

"There is no possibility I could cook in this mess," Sarah said stridently.

"Well, of course you can't," Ginger said crossly.

"But then, neither could you. So this afternoon, I'll just drop off dinner. Say around six. And at that time, I'll fill out a little schedule for you, so you know what food I'm making and when I'm making it. You'll need to grocery shop. I'm not doing that."

Ginger lifted her fingertips to her temple. She had the oddest headache. "Of course you wouldn't shop for me—"

"But I'll give you a list of what to buy. For the dinners. Whatever you want to eat for breakfast or lunch, that's on you, not me."

"Now you just wait a minute—"

But Sarah ignored her again, said something rude and dismissive, and then just marched for the front door as furiously fast as she'd walked in.

Ginger stared after her, aghast. One crazy encounter that morning had been bewildering enough—but two? In the same day? People didn't behave like that. Not normal people.

It was as if some unseen force had instructed both Jed and Sarah to ignore any attempt she made to say no.

That unseen-force was a three-letter word, of course. *Ike.* But that was precisely the upsetting part. She was in over her head in every way, and was likely to be overwhelmed by messes and problems for a good long time. For just those reasons, she wanted no association with Ike. She didn't want to be thinking about kissing and that look in his eyes and her making an idiot of herself every time she was near him.

She didn't want to think about Ike.

She half turned and faced her wreck of a kitchen again. She didn't have time for a heart attack or a mental breakdown. Maybe later in the day, but not now.

She searched out her guys, found they'd tried hiding in rockers on the veranda. That was okay, they'd done more than enough work for the day. She made sandwiches, took them out on a tray, and by the time they'd finished a makeshift lunch, the boys were nodding off. She headed back to the kitchen.

The war zone finally started to turn the corner. In another hour, all surfaces were scrubbed and sparkling. Cupboards were all lined with fresh paper. She'd saved the worst for last—the very top cupboard shelves to the right of the sink. It was like the mystery shelf in every house—the place that no one could reach—and was inevitably filled with things no one had seen in decades. Dishes with cracks. Dishes that had no function anyone could think of. Teapots—the ugly ones that Grandma had never wanted in the living room collection. Dust. Peppermint schnapps. Tequila—five bottles, all with the worms.

She didn't want to do it. Her back ached. Her fingers and hands felt sore from scrubbing. Her shoulders and arms were whining about how she'd abused them for hours now.

But there was just that one last shelf. And then she'd be completely done.

She crawled up and then stood up on the counter, scrub brush in hand—which was when she heard a rap on the door—for the third interruption that day.

This time, though, she was ready. She climbed down and bolted for the front door. Unfortunately, Gramps and Cornelius were still out on the front veranda. Before she could push open the screen, she could hear her guys and their joyful greetings for the visitor.

She could have raced to the bathroom to freshen up, but what was the point? He'd already seen her at her worst. Twice. And it wasn't as if she was trying to attract the man. So she was wearing plastic gloves and no shoes and her hair hadn't seen a brush in a *long* time, not counting the lack of makeup or the details.

And of course, it was Ike. Ike and the slobbering, mournful hound, who dragged herself up the steps only to fall in a heap in everyone's way.

Pansy only looked half as disreputable as her owner. Ike wore a clay-colored T-shirt that was frayed at the neck, a derelict pair of shorts, sandals that looked to be about a hundred years old. Maybe he'd shaved yesterday.

Still, she felt it. The fever climbing up from her toes, weakening her heart. There were fevers and there were fevers. A fever of ninety-nine, anyone started to feel yucky. A fever of one hundred generally brought her to her knees. A fever of one-oh-one and she knew she was in deep trouble, sick trouble. Only when a fever reached around a hundred and two did some weird factor kick in, and she started to feel euphoric. Goofy euphoric. High and giddy and crazy. All fear gone. All reality dismissed from sight.

That was precisely how she felt around Ike. The wrong kind of fever.

And he was looking at her the same way. The wrong kind of way.

Gramps and Cornelius were still asking why he'd come by.

"Well, I sure didn't come to see you two old reprobates," he said wryly. "I came to see Ginger. Because I figured around now she was planning to tear a strip off my hide, and I might as well get it over with."

"Why on earth?" Cornelius asked.

"Yeah, why on earth," Ginger echoed.

"I suspect you think I should have asked you first, before sending out some help."

"You could have asked me. But then, I needed help. Which you knew."

She saw the slightest frown crease his forehead. Probably he wasn't expecting her calm, amiable tone— not just because of the circumstances, but because he'd never heard it before. "I did know you could use a hand," he agreed. "I also had patients who needed to pay their own way. So it seemed like a good idea to me. Nobody gets hurt. Everyone gets something they need."

"Except," she said gently, "that it was manipulative and domineering. You didn't ask first. You just assumed you knew best. What was best for me. What was best for my grandfather. I asked around, but I couldn't find anyone who elected you God."

"Ouch," Ike said.

She didn't respond, just headed back in the house. She didn't lock the screen door, just gave it the opportunity to close with a decided *thwack*.

Ike winced when the door slammed, then scratched the back of his neck.

"What on earth did you do to that girl to set her off?" Cornelius demanded.

Cashner set his chair rocking again. "She's a firecracker. Always has been. Always will be. If I were you, Doc, I'd steer clear for a while."

Cornelius looked at him. "Don't listen to him. Listen to me. If you let her fester on her own, she'll build up a heap of temper. Then you'll leave and we'll be left here to get the brunt of it."

"Well, I guess that's true," Cashner reluctantly admitted. "Ike, you best go after her. Believe it. We'll both stay out here, out of your way completely."

Cashner was lucid for a change—a good sign. Cornelius was even making sense. So Ike could put those two concerns out of his mind, at least for a few minutes. "Pansy, stay," he murmured, and then aimed inside.

He found Ginger by following the fumes.

She was standing on the kitchen counter in her bare feet. Her goal was apparently to empty the contents from the top cupboard shelf. Two bottles of tequila were open and in the process of pouring down the drain, and she was about to lean down with a third. When she saw him in the doorway, she jumped.

He surged forward at rocket speed, scared she'd fall—a risk that was hardly far-fetched, considering her behavior the other day. Yet when he sprinted close enough to lift his arms to support her, she moved back an inch. Just enough so he didn't touch her. And said crossly, "I wasn't going to fall. You just startled me."

"You startled me, too. Or the smell did. I take it you don't like tequila?"

"I have no idea. But you can take it to the bank, I won't be drinking anything with worms in the bottle. Years ago, Gramps had an employee, worked in the tea, always brought Gramps a bottle at the end of the season. They kept accumulating. Grandma and I just ignored them. She had the same feeling about the worms that I did." Then, "If you came for another kiss, you're not going to get one."

"What makes you think I want to kiss you? You've got a smudge on your cheek. Your knees are all red. Your hair is as wild as a rusty Brillo pad."

"You came for another kiss," she informed him. "Beats me why. I'm a wreck. It's obvious. You can't possibly believe this could go anywhere."

He didn't. At least not exactly. The problem was more confounding than that. He'd been content with his laid-back lifestyle in Sweet Valley for all this time— or so he'd believed until he ran into her. Crazy or not, he felt more invigorated after tussling with her for two minutes than in the whole four years before her. "I'm not admitting anything—except that I might have come back for another kiss. But I also came to find out how much trouble I was in for sending over Jed and Sarah."

"Well, that's a different subject. I'm not sure Jed took to me, but I sure took to him. He knows the front from the back end of a tractor. I sure don't." She crouched down, but instead of jumping to the floor, she just sat on the sink counter. She reached for the last two tequila bottles, opened both and then turned them upside down to pour in the sink. "Now Sarah—I'm not so sure. She sure has an ornery side."

"Well, yeah. But that's why I thought you two might get along. You're two peas in a pod and all that."

She squinted at him. "Are you suggesting that I'm ornery?"

"I would never do that," he assured her. "Stubborn, yes. Temper prone, yes. A spark plug ready to fire, yes. A volcano always ready to erupt at the slightest provoca—"

There. A smile. So reluctant. But the darned woman couldn't just throw out a good sense of humor, even when she was trying her best to stay crabby.

"*Only* because I'm a Southern girl raised with manners, I'll offer you something to drink. Something short and quick."

"What have you got? Besides all that tequila."

"Was that a real question?" She rolled her eyes. "This was a tea plantation. Tea's the only drink we serve morning, noon and night."

"Well, I guess I wouldn't mind a cup of…hmm… tea."

She finally hopped down from the counter, gave him

a single poke in the stomach. "You're not as funny as you think you are."

"You're still smiling."

"That may be because I'm a lunatic." Some habits were clearly ingrained in her, without her having to think twice. Making tea was a ritual in her grandparents' house. The right pot. The right temperature water. The decision about which tea. The smelling of the leaves, the measuring. And finally the wait, while the tea steeped.

Ike had watched her grandfather do it a dozen times. Even where Cashner's other memories were fading fast, he knew how to make good tea like he knew how to wake up in the morning.

So did she.

"Don't ask for cream or sugar. They're both sins in this house. For the right tea, you shouldn't need any extras."

"I figured that out the first time your grandfather served me tea. He almost took my head off when I asked for some sweetener. Got a three-hour lecture on tea. I never made that mistake again."

"I'll be darned. A man who learns. Who knew there was such a thing?"

He winced, watching her pull out cups that matched the teapot. "Speaking of men in your life," he said casually, "Does he know? About the pregnancy?"

"And here I thought we were going to have a nice conversation." She handed him his cup.

"So. You haven't told him. But you must have an idea how he's likely to respond when he finds out you're pregnant."

She poured a cup for herself, but now she immediately set it down. "That's it. Out. Out, out, out. I wouldn't have minded talking to you a little more about my gramps. But not now. Another time. When I'm not so likely to brain you with the nearest hard, sharp object."

"Okay," he agreed. "We don't need any more conversation."

As quickly as he put down his tea, he reached for her. She wasn't expecting it. Being pulled into his arms. Having a kiss laid on her mouth the way a bee zoned on pollen.

He hadn't expected to kiss her, either. It hadn't even been on his mind—until she brought it up—and then he couldn't think about anything but getting his hands on her. Talk about lunacy. She'd been nothing but testy and difficult. She was pregnant by someone else. She had a heap of trouble, and who knew if she'd even stay in this little Southern burg for any longer than she had to. But that was his practical side talking.

Right now the only communication going on was between his mouth and hers. Especially hers. The taste of her, the smell of her skin, the sweetness of her lips put a buzz in his blood that refused to shut off. He was a laid-back guy, by choice. He wanted a small life, not a big one. He wanted time to care, to play, to share, and if that meant a sacrifice in money and possessions, so be it.

But this kiss—her sweet, sweet taste—was stressful on a par with a tsunami. It was all her doing…because she tasted like no other woman tasted. Because she gripped his shoulders and hung on. Because she acted volatile, dizzy, weak, as if he was the sexiest connection she'd ever made, even if it was only for a kiss….

Even if that only a kiss barely, sparely involved the tease of her soft, warm breasts, the look of her eyelashes sweeping her cheeks, the way her slim hands clenched on his shoulders, the way she made a groan. Or a moan. A sound as if she didn't mind this insane rocket ride.

Damn it. It was just a kiss.

Except that he didn't end it. Couldn't end it.

Until she suddenly bolted back, her eyes snapping open, looking dazed and confused. "Ike. I keep hearing drums."

"Me, too."

"I mean…I think I'm really hearing drums."

"Oh. Afraid that's my cell phone."

"Your cell phone. Plays a drumroll." That dazed look was disappearing awfully fast. She'd liked those kisses. As much as he had. But now she seemed to be recalling that he wasn't her favorite person on the planet.

"Yes. And unfortunately, I'm afraid it's Tildey."

"And Tildey is…?"

"Tildey's twenty-nine. Two weeks overdue with her third baby. This time, she got a midwife. Didn't want to pay for a doc and a hospital."

"There has to be a 'but' in there," Ginger said. They'd both moved back. There were inches between them… except where his arms were still wrapped around her. She divested them, one at a time. His right arm dropped heavily at his side. Ditto for his left arm. Both arms seemed to have lost all muscle strength.

"But Tildey never really trusted the midwife from the get-go. She's been calling three times a week for some backup information. And she called this morning, to let me know she was in labor. And that the midwife was already there."

"I'll bet this conversation makes sense to one of us," Ginger said dryly.

"I'm guessing she's around five centimeters by now. And in a fair panic."

"Then you'd better go."

"I need to," he agreed, but truthfully, he still felt shell-shocked. Or Ginger-shocked. How the woman could pack so much zesty, earthy, compelling sexiness into a few kisses…well. She was downright dangerous.

But of course, he had to pull himself back together. And he would. He always did. "Whether you believe it or not, I came by because I thought you might need to talk more about your grandfather."

She hesitated. "I do."

"All right. Next time. We'll do a serious talk. Honest." When his cell did a second, fresh drumroll, he said swiftly, "Would you mind if Pansy stayed here? Just for a little while. Normally I either leave her home or bring her with me. But I don't want to take the time to drive home, and this isn't a household where I can take her—"

"Ike. I don't know dogs. And I definitely don't know bloodhounds. I have no idea what—"

"Thanks. Really. And I promise I'll be back as quickly as I can."

That was the plan. To check on Tildey, make sure the delivery was going okay with the midwife and then leave.

Unfortunately, the midwife turned out to have the brain of a flea, Tildey was in trouble and so was the baby. Her two other kids were wandering around, crying and scared, and definitely too young to be left alone. Tildey's husband had apparently left for the bar when she first went into labor and no one had seen him since.

By the time Ike could finally drive back to the Gautiers', the hour was well past midnight. The bright day had turned upside down; the sky was belching clouds and hurtling lightning and having a noisy, stormy tantrum. Rain attacked him the instant he climbed out of his truck. He raced to the front door—not expecting anyone to be awake, or intending to awaken anyone this late. He just had to pick up Pansy, who he'd assumed would be waiting for him on the porch.

She wasn't. She was nowhere to be seen.

Ike stepped back, looked up and around. As far as he could tell, there was only one light on in the entire house. On the second story, in the far east window, he caught sight of the soft yellow glow of lamplight.

Chapter Five

Dinner was a feast. Ginger never saw or heard Sarah in the house; she just found the lavish feast when she popped in the kitchen after five. The casserole dish had instructions taped to the tinfoil. Chicken in some kind of fabulous cheese sauce filled a big pan, with broiled baby potatoes in another. A loaf of French bread—fresh-baked, still warm—sat on the counter, along with instructions not to overcook the butter beans.

Gramps ate as if it was his last meal.

Cornelius, who rarely stayed for dinner, kept heaping on more helpings.

There were only a couple of problems. One was that Gramps kept calling her Rachel. And the other was the dog.

"Sweetheart, I can't believe you let the dog inside. You've never liked dogs inside," Gramps said.

"I didn't let her inside. She howled at the top of her

lungs when Ike left. There was nothing else I could do." That wasn't the only problem with the dog, of course. Ginger wasn't certain how much the bloodhound weighed, but at the moment a hundred pounds—at *least*—of dead weight stuck closer to her leg than glue.

Apparently the hound felt insecure when Ike wasn't there.

Cornelius kept feeding the dog tidbits of chicken. Gramps had been steadily feeding her butter beans. The hound would eat any and everything, but immediately came back to lean against Ginger.

She also drooled.

Ginger had filled a bowl of water—which the dog had gulped down and she'd had to refill three times now. They'd fed her from dinner because they didn't have regular dog food and didn't know when Ike would be back. It had to be soon, though, Ginger thought. Obviously babies arrived in their own chosen time—but there was a midwife there, he'd said. So he had to be back soon.

She told herself that every time she glanced at a clock. It only took a few minutes to pile dishes in the dishwasher, even with Pansy glued to her side. Cornelius finally took off for his quarters—the small house on the other side of the garage. Gramps lingered a little longer.

"We could sit on the porch for a spell, Rachel."

She started to correct him, then stopped. It didn't seem to help, and when push came down to shove, she didn't really care if he called her Rachel or Loretta or any other darned name he wanted to. "It's turned too cold, Gramps. Temperature's been dropping like a stone, and it smells like the wind's bringing on a storm."

"Will you come in and watch TV with me, then? Our favorite show is on at nine."

"I will, Gramps. Give me a hug."

He stretched out his arms, and snuggled against her for a big, warm hug.

"I love you," she said.

"And I love you right back, sweetheart. What do you say we call Ginger tonight? I really miss her."

Ginger sucked in a breath. Every time she thought she'd accepted the changes in Gramps, something else happened. It hurt, that he could be talking right to her and still not know who she was.

The next couple hours were just as unsettling. She finished the kitchen chores, let Pansy out, let Pansy in, brewed a cup of oolong for Gramps and then asked if he wanted to play a game of backgammon.

"You're ready to lose, are you, honey?"

He loved the game, she knew. When she was a girl, they'd played almost every night after dinner. And he perked up, starting chuckling and teasing, having a good time. It took her a few minutes to realize that he was moving pieces that made no sense. He thought he was playing the game, but he didn't seem to have a clue what he was doing.

By the time he went to bed, Ginger felt shaken. Her grandfather seemed to lose more ground every day. Unsettled and uneasy, she ambled around the house. She found Ike's cell phone in the kitchen—which provoked a sharp, strong memory of his kissing her just hours before. The point, though, was that he could likely have borrowed someone else's phone to call if he thought he was going to be much longer.

She wandered to the front doors, peering out. The evening had turned pitch-black, devil black. Clouds tumbled over each other, racing in fast from the west. The rain had started, not a downpour yet, but it looked like the battalion of clouds beyond had the heaviest artillery.

Her sidekick nuzzled her leg. "Yeah, you want Ike back, too, don't you?" She bent down to rub Pansy's ears. "We need a plan here. You want to sleep on the porch? Or just inside? I promise. He'll be here." Ginger crossed her fingers. She was pretty sure Ike would never leave his dog. "You could lie in front of the door, like you did before. Then you'll see him when he drives in. Doesn't that sound like a good plan?"

Pansy seemed okay with the idea, was coaxed outside, ambled down the steps to pee and then heaved back up the steps and collapsed.

Ginger headed upstairs for the bathtub, and was just sinking into the warm soothing water when a low rumble of thunder boomed from the west. Instantly, Pansy let out a howl that could have wakened the dead. Ginger peeled out of the tub, grabbed a towel, ran downstairs and let the dog in.

"We are not going to do that again. I get it. You don't like storms. No problem. You can sleep inside. But no more howling!"

Ginger closed the big doors but left them unlocked for Ike. Pansy seemed unimpressed with the scolding, and just flopped down in an immediate coma.

Relieved, Ginger headed back upstairs. She dried her hair, yanked on a silky green nightgown, dabbed on some moisturizer, brushed her teeth…and hit the sack.

She fell asleep before her head hit the pillow.

That restful sleep lasted maybe two minutes. The instant lightning streaked the sky and rain started se-

riously drumming on the windows, she felt something
warm and wet and smelly touch her bare shoulder.

"No," she said firmly.

But then the damned dog started howling.

Ike stood in the pouring rain, hands on hips, staring
up at the light in the far bedroom on the second floor.
He suspected he'd scare the wits out of her—and Cashner—if they found a soaking-wet man in their house in
the middle of the night.

But the problem was his dog.

Pansy had chowed down heavily in the morning, so
he wasn't afraid she was hungry.

She also was happy anywhere, primarily because
she spent so much time sleeping and she liked people
in general. There were just a couple teensy problems
with her temperament.

The main one, the worst one, was that she was terrified of storms. At the first shot of lightning, she'd
been known to break through screen doors, let out im-
mortal howls, try to fit herself under a bed. And she
shook. Nonstop.

Bottom line… Well, he didn't know what the bottom line was, but he figured he'd start by seeing if the
front door was locked. If the house was left open, it was
a fair guess Ginger expected him to retrieve his dog.

He mounted the steps, taking off his wet windbreaker
and hat on the porch…then did a rethink and took off
his shoes, as well. No sense tracking in half a lake.

The door gave a slight creak when he turned the
knob, but the sound didn't seem to arouse anyone. The
only sound he heard was the tick of a pendulum wall
clock, somewhere in that formal parlor. Silver rain
streamed down windows, not letting in much light, but

once his eyes adjusted, he could make out the tinkle-light of the hall chandelier, and the glow of a night-light at the top of the stairs.

He whispered, "Pansy!" which accomplished nothing. The dog had a great nose, but lousy ears. Like Ginger's grandfather, the dog could have benefited from a hearing aid.

He scratched his nape. Ike never liked making mistakes. He was ninety-nine-point-nine percent sure that going upstairs—even for the serious reason of reclaiming his dog—was a bad, bad, bad mistake. The only reason it crossed his mind was because the dog hadn't shown up so far. Which meant she wasn't downstairs. Which pretty much meant she was upstairs. Which for damn sure meant Ginger had been stuck with her since the start of the storm.

Amazing, how a man could justify making a mistake.

Still. There was a tiny chance he could retrieve the dog and hightail it out of there without waking her.

At the top of the stairs, he hesitated. Cashner had slept upstairs until a few months ago, when he and Cornelius had badgered him into making a move. The old house had plenty of spare space on the first floor. The room off the kitchen had once been a "sun room," with no particular purpose that Ike could see. A twin bed fit in there fine. A full downstairs bathroom was next door, so the location was ideal for a man getting older and less steady.

But the point was that the light on the second floor could only be coming from Ginger's bedroom. And she was alone upstairs. Which made it even more ticklish for him to go up there.

Out of nowhere, he heard a voice. "*Ike.* For Pete's

sake, would you quit dithering out there and just come in and get your dog!"

The voice was very cross and very impatient. Definitely Ginger. And Ginger was definitely wide-awake, which made his conscience stop feeling so frayed. He quit dithering and hiked as far as the bedroom doorway. He took one look. His response was immediate and instinctual. "Uh-oh."

"Ike. Your dog is a complete and total coward."

"Hey, you didn't have to let her up on the bed."

"Right. I'm lucky she isn't under the covers. She tried." She was scowling at him—a pretty familiar expression, actually.

But he had to hold back laughter. Pansy was stretched to her full length, which meant she was about as tall as Ginger. The hound's face framed by the frothy-looking canopy over the bed was downright hysterical. Further, she was sleeping, eyes closed, snoring…except that her tail was wagging hard enough to shake the house.

She knew he was there.

She just wasn't inclined to move.

Ike could relate. Spooning next to Ginger in a storm on a chilly night… Oh, yeah, that sounded like a good idea to him, too.

He leaned against the doorjamb. "I would have called, but—"

"You left your cell phone in the kitchen."

"No. I mean, yes, I realized that. But I could have used someone else's."

"I figured that, Ike. I was thinking a lot of bad names about you this afternoon. Some of them were even eloquent curse words. But the bottom line is that I knew you wouldn't ditch your dog any longer than you had to. So you must have run into some trouble."

"I did. Tildey had two easy deliveries before, was so sure she didn't need more than a midwife. And I would have agreed with her, except that this midwife happened to be a twerp. Didn't know the umbilical cord was wrapped around the baby's neck. To top it all off, Tildey's two other kids, both under five, were crying and wailing and scared."

"So where was the dad?"

"Apparently he has a pattern of taking off to a bar when his wife goes into labor. Eventually he showed up...but right at the point when Tildey was a few huffs away from delivering. When she saw her husband, she tried to get out of bed, told him that she had a knife and if he ever touched her against she was going to use it."

"Oh, my."

"Then she actually produced the knife. It was in the drawer by her bed. A butcher knife. Belonged to her great-grandma. Made of straight steel."

"Oh, no." Her voice raised an octave. "*Pansy. Do not lick my face. Ever. Ever again.* Okay, Ike, then what happened?"

"The husband—Hamilton is his name—passed out. Crumpled right in the doorway. The midwife tried to step in, and Tildey almost turned the knife on her. She was just out of patience, out of strength, and she'd lost the rhythm of the contractions, just plain got screwed up. When she started crying, the kids started crying and carrying on, too. And that woke up her husband, who was as helpful as an elephant in a china cabinet."

She bunched the pillow under her head, turned more on her side. The window lamp only provided a pale glow. He still couldn't see much of her face. Just talking to her, though, eased the long day's exhaustion.

"Are all your patients this exciting?"

"Actually…yeah. I don't see many gunshots or stab wounds or gang fight scars. Just straight life kind of problems. Anyway. Tildey had a son. Her two other kids are both girls. That's why they came easy as pie, she said. Men are always trouble. Even little men."

"Was the baby okay?"

"Absolutely. Bald as an eagle, a scream worthy of a rock band, a wriggling mass of furious baby boy." He eased into the room. Standing after all this time was exhausting. He just took a corner of the bed. The back corner.

"What color eyes?"

"Blue, silly. All babies are born with blue eyes."

"You think he's going to be cute?"

"Cute?" Ike had to think. "I'm not sure I ever notice whether a baby's cute or not. He looked healthy—and happy—once he'd been cleaned up and put in his mama's arms. Tildey settled down then, too. The kids saw the baby, but by the time the place was cleaned up, they'd cuddled on the couch with a blanket over them. I called the hospital—closest one is sixty-some miles—I didn't think Tildey has to get there until tomorrow, but the baby should be checked out."

"So she'll go?"

"She'll go. But I still couldn't quite leave that minute. She told me I looked like hell, to use the shower off the kitchen, which I did. I always keep clean clothes in the truck. Pretty rare they don't come in handy. I cleaned up as quickly as I could, but it was really late to call, and I was afraid of waking you both…."

"It's all right. I knew something had happened. However…"

"However?"

"Your dog, Ike, has no sense of boundaries. From

the minute you left, she leaned on me as if I were a fence post. She moaned if I tried to go into the bathroom alone. Watched me while I brushed my teeth. And when she heard the first thunder—"

Ike winced. "I know."

"It was one thing for her to want to sleep near a human. I get that. I had nightmares as a kid. But she still wasn't happy until I turned the light on. And then she had to get in bed with me. I had to give her her own pillow, or else she was determined to share mine. If you don't do what she wants, she looks at you with that…face. Those eyes. That expression. As if you'd broken up with her. This is not a *dog,* Ike. She's a full-scale monster."

"I know, Ginger, I know. I didn't want her. When I moved here, she just showed up at the back door. I couldn't get rid of her. Tried to give her to a family down the road that had a bunch of kids. They loved her. But she came back. Tried to give her to the sheriff, thinking she could help, she's got a serious nose and all. He liked her right off…but she still beat me back home, and I swear, she takes all day to walk a mile. So I gave up. Anyway, I'm sorry she was such a nuisance."

"Ike. She thinks we're praising her. She's wagging her tail faster than a metronome."

Ike thought maybe they'd had enough of this chit-chat. "I think she's got the best world she can imagine. Her and me on the same bed. With you. At night. Hell, it's almost foreplay, don't you think?"

The storm stopped. Just like that. No more thunder, no lightning, no silver rain tapping on the windows. The room went still as a stone. Maybe she hadn't noticed before that he'd slowly, carelessly sunk down on the bed. Just at her feet, not next to her. There wasn't room next to her, because of Pansy.

He'd leaned back on an elbow, at some point, because hell, it'd been a long day and it was late. And maybe he'd put a hand on her foot—which was covered up with sheets, of course. And maybe the embroidered sheet up near her neck had slipped a few inches—but only enough to reveal that she was wearing some kind of pale green nightgown.

The lamp by the window, he finally realized, wasn't an ordinary lamp. It looked like an antique, with an old brass base and a mother-of-pearl shade. Ike wouldn't normally notice details like that, except that the lamp wasn't…well…normal.

It had been the beacon that drew him upstairs, into her room, but that wasn't the issue. The lamp had magic. It had to have magic, because that soft glow made Ginger look irresistible in every way. Her skin, impossibly luminous. Her eyes, incomparably deep. Her hair, like copper on fire. And her expression…

"No, Ike," she murmured, but her expression wasn't saying no.

"No, you don't think this little meeting is like foreplay?"

"No. To what you were thinking."

"Ginger. There's a dog on the bed. I couldn't possibly be thinking anything that you'd object to."

"Yes, you could. Apparently no matter how bad I look or what the circumstances are."

"Now, Ginger. You're giving yourself an awful lot of credit for being irresistible."

"I am. Just that. But I learned the hard way that I only seem to be irresistible to the wrong men. Go home, Ike."

"Man. You can be really harsh."

There, that serious expression disappeared. She had to bite her lip not to laugh. "You're sitting on my bed, with this crazy hound, in the middle of the night! I'm not remotely harsh!"

"But it's just *me*," he said plaintively. "And Pansy, of course. It seems really cruel for you to reject a helpless dog."

Rather abruptly, she threw a pillow at his head. That seemed to wake Pansy out of a dead snore. He made a tongue-click sound. The hound's eyes immediately opened, and graceful as a pregnant ox, she leaped down from the bed.

"I'm leaving," he told Ginger, still using his most plaintive voice. "But first, I'll turn the light off for you."

"Thank you. Good night. Goodbye."

He threw her another wounded look—as if she'd hurt his feelings yet again.

He crossed the room, switched off the light, took a second to let his eyes adjust to the sudden darkness. He knew where Pansy was. She never moved if she didn't have to, so she was exactly where she'd jumped down and waited for him.

Easy enough, then, to edge toward the bed.

Ginger sensed it, too. Said, "I mean it, Ike. No."

"Hey. I was just tucking you in." Which he did, shaking off the sand Pansy had brought with her, easing the soft percale sheet under Ginger's chin, the light blanket beneath. Not touching her. Just tucking. And looking at her.

Swiftly—faster than a breath of wind—he bent over and kissed her. Just a light kiss. A texture to texture, taste to taste connection. At least he tasted it. The flavor of all that could be.

Just as swiftly, he lifted his head. "That was just a good-night-sweet-dreams kiss. So don't argue."

Ginger didn't fuss, but she woke up the next morning with a good fume on. By the time she changed the sheets—which happened to have a fair amount of dog hair and sand—she'd added to the day's fume. A shower, hair brush and fresh clothes later, the fume had become one of her best.

Ike was playing with her. Flirting, for lack of a better word—and in the South, there probably was no better word, because the term had always been cherished below the Mason-Dixon Line.

She headed downstairs, reminding herself that she had a grandfather losing his mind, a pregnancy she hadn't even started to deal with, no job or means of supporting herself. So. There was nothing for Ike to be attracted to—which was why she was so certain he was playing. And the truth was, because she was stuck in a quicksand well of troubles, it felt good to do a little playing.

But that was no excuse to be so damned charmed by the man. He was a devil.

A rascal.

She found Gramps in the kitchen, wearing the same clothes he'd had on the night before, holding—for no known reason—a clock.

"Well, aren't you looking pretty this morning, Loretta," he said immediately.

She was in no mood to be patient. Not this morning. "Gramps, this is me. Ginger. Not Loretta. I don't have a clue who Loretta is."

"You don't know where she is?"

She sighed. Made him scrambled eggs and toast,

picked up the morning paper from the porch and sat across from him. "Gramps. Try to concentrate. What happened to Amos Hawthorne?"

"That old son of a sea dog? I fired him."

"Why did you fire him? Do you remember what happened? Do you know where he lives?"

Well, hell. That was clearly too many questions. He lifted his head and blessed her with a beatific smile. "These are probably the best eggs I've ever tasted in my whole life. You're spoiling me, honey, and I like it."

Okay, okay. She started answering to Loretta, got the kitchen cleaned up and tracked down her grandmother's old address book. Naturally, she should have thought of it first—but she quickly located the number and address for Amos Hawthorne. She put on shoes, grabbed a purse and was almost out the door when the landline rang.

Her grandfather picked it up, called out, "Ginger, it's the doctor. Ike. For you!"

She answered back, "Tell him I'm late for a meeting. Can't talk now."

"What meeting?"

"Just tell him, Gramps."

"But where are you going?"

"I told you. I won't be gone more than a couple hours—max. I promise. And you have my cell phone number."

She'd been through this with him several times. Gramps wasn't into technology like cell phones, and he didn't want to learn. Would probably forget it if he did grasp it. But she'd put her number on paper in several rooms so he could reach her whenever she was gone.

She tried calling Amos Hawthorne's phone, but no

one answered, so when she climbed in her Civic, she plugged the address into her aging GPS and took off.

Amos only lived about ten minutes away, farther into the country, the sign for his road barely visible for all the scrappy brush. Once she located the house number on his mailbox, though, the landscape changed abruptly. Amos lived in a tiny white-frame house, but the lawn was manicure-perfect, the windows gleamed and even the driveway looked clean enough to eat off of.

She didn't try knocking at the house, because she could smell the burning brush the minute she climbed from the car. His property was long and narrow, and he'd set up a brush pile at the far back end. It struck her as amazing that he had any brush to burn, when every tree and bush and plant had been pruned to perfection. She'd known Amos from years ago—but he was distant from her life, never at the house, only someone who'd passed in and out of the tea store sometimes.

He was younger than Gramps by a heap, had taken the job when he was fresh out of school, but that was about all Ginger remembered about him. She thought he was tall—likely because she'd most often seen him atop a tractor—but he wasn't at all.

He was raking brush into his fire, and he half turned to fork up another small heap of twigs when he spotted her.

She was probably a couple inches taller than Amos. They probably weighed about the same. He was all wire and bone, with straw-colored hair, and skin prematurely wrinkled from endless sun exposure. He squinted at her.

"I'm Ginger Gautier, Amos. You probably don't remember me—"

"Shore I remember you." His voice wasn't unkind,

but it wasn't welcoming, either. He poked the rake in the ground, leaned on it. Then just waited.

"I need help. My grandfather needs help."

"Cashner fired me. Told me I was the son of Satan. That I'd been messing with his wife." A scowl showed up, hard to discern from the rest of his wrinkles. "Your grandmother's been gone a while now. As if I'd ever have touched a hair on her pretty head. He couldn't have said anything to insult me worse."

"That's terrible, Amos. But my grandfather isn't in his right mind. I'm sure you must have seen changes in him. He really doesn't always know what he's saying."

"That's what you know. But I'll tell you what I know." He stopped the leaning on the rake posture, stabbed the rake into another short pile of brush. When he tossed it on, the flames shot up, and the smoke swirled in restless circles. "I knew he had trouble. And I got into it with him a while back, talked to him with all the tact I had. We needed to shut down the store. No one could handle it. The store was just a fun project for your grandmother anyhow. We could sell on the internet if he wanted to keep up that nature of the tea business. We could hire a kid to set that up. Even the dumbest kids seem to know everything about computers these days."

"That sounds like a wonderful idea."

"You think? Just suggesting that was when Cashner started cussing me out. That was the fight that led him to firing me."

"Would you consider coming back?"

"Why, shore...on the day it rains purple."

Ginger gulped. "What if I raised the salary you had before? And if you weren't working for my gramps, but me. And I'd be happy to accept your judgment on whatever you felt needed doing."

More stabbing brush. More sparks of hot fire. More simmering smoke.

"I don't like to turn down a lady, especially one asking for help. Lots of people with a farming background around the country here. But not many who know tea. But your grandfather treated me wrong. I understand. He's ill, so to speak. But I don't see being ill is an excuse for treating someone bad."

"I don't, either. But he's been calling me all kinds of names—like he thinks I'm Grandma. And some other names, I don't even know who they are. Amos, he's not in his right mind. I don't believe he'd ever have insulted you if he'd been himself."

"I don't know that. And I'm finding plenty to do. Everybody knows I did a good job at your place. That I work hard. Know my way around a wrench and a tractor. So I don't need that job anymore."

"Please?"

"I'm sorry. No."

"Even for a short period? Amos, I can't possibly replace you and really, really don't want to. But right now, I don't know a plant from a weed. Could you work with me for a while, just to educate me on things I should do, get some kind of idea what the place needs? I'd pay you anything you asked."

Ginger rarely met anyone as bullheaded as she was, but Amos wouldn't give in by even the slightest millimeter. She tried every guile and wile and coaxing that she knew. She even tried being flat-out honest. Nothing worked. After he'd given her his final "no" several times, she walked away…but she wasn't about to give up.

Amos had left her no choice but to try going behind his back. She walked the long yard back to the driveway—thankfully her eyes were stinging from the smoke, so her eyes were tearing. She had to look as if she'd been crying. She didn't try knocking on the back door, where Amos could see her, but approached the front door to ring the bell.

Amos's wife showed up, wringing her hands dry on a dish towel. She peered through the screen and immediately opened the door. "Why, honey, what's wrong?" she said. "You're Ginger Gautier, aren't you? I've thought a lot about you since your grandma passed. Did you have an accident? Are you hurt? Never mind, come on in, I'll get us some tea, and you can tell me whatever it is."

Guilt pinged at her conscience. Her grandparents had certainly never taught her to lie…but it wasn't her fault she had to resort to a little shady behavior. A girl couldn't sew on a button if she didn't have needle and thread.

She needed *some* way to coax Amos into working for her.

Chapter Six

Ike regarded one of his favorite—and most difficult—patients. "You know, Amos, it might help if you gave me a call before you were in a world of hurt."

Amos stuck out his chin. "I'm not one to complain to doctors."

"And I respect that. But gout is a mighty painful condition, and we want to address that uric acid before the numbers get so high. There's medicine that helps."

"Well, I know that. But I don't want any dang fool pills."

"Afraid you're going to have to bite the bullet, because I'm writing you a script for some of those dang fool pills. But I'm also going to recommend that we work on your stress level."

"I don't do stress and never will. I'm sick of everyone talking about stress as if anyone had a choice about it. Life's stress. It's just the way it is. And I need to work."

"But you don't need to work seven days a week. I want you to just try it. Relaxing. Take a long weekend with your wife, go up to Whisper Mountain, maybe camp out there or stay in one of the retreats or resorts around there. Sleep in. Take a couple fishing poles. Practice just sitting around and enjoying the view."

His patient looked at him. "Are you plumb crazy?"

Ike nodded. "What can I tell you? That's what they teach us in medical school."

"If I was to go up to Whisper Mountain, it wouldn't be to pay for any dang fool *resort.* There are stills in the hollows of that mountain. Moonshine. Good moonshine. Now *that* might help the pain."

"My family came from Whisper Mountain. My brother, Tucker, still lives up there. I've heard about the stills, but I figured that was just country legend."

"Nope. It's truth. When I was a kid…well, no, never mind. No reason you should hear about the wild things I did as a boy." Amos buttoned his shirt. "You know, this flare-up of gout happened because of the Gautier girl."

"Ginger? What did she do?"

"She went to my wife, that's what she did. Went around my back. I *told* her I wasn't working for the Gautiers ever again and that was that. And like I'd never spoke to her, she went to my wife, started crying, and the next thing I know, my wife is tearing a strip off my hide, yelling and not making dinner and making me sleep on the couch."

"No!" Ike tried to make his tone sound incredulous.

"You don't know my wife. She's kind to everybody in the whole county but me. She says I was being ungentlemanly for not helping that girl. That I was raised better. That her grandmother's passed and her grandfather left his mind somewhere months ago, and when that poor child asked for a little help, what did I do? Turn her down. My Lord. She went on and on. My back almost went out from sleeping on that old couch. There was no living with her until I agreed to help the Gautier girl, and I'm not just telling tales."

"Oh, I believe you. I've heard Ginger can be a little on the strong-willed side."

"She's pretty enough. But bless her heart, she's ornery clear through."

That was his Ginger, all right.

He hadn't seen her in four days, and that was about as long as he could take.

He was overdue a visit with Cashner, anyway.

Three patients later, he grabbed a bite for lunch and then he was free for the day.

Pansy howled when he gave her a fresh rawhide bone—she knew that meant he was leaving her—but a frisky wind was bringing in a fresh batch of clouds. The area needed more rain like fish needed feet, but Pansy'd do better at home in a storm than tearing around the country with him.

He turned onto Gautier property before two. One glance and he could see the place was starting to look better. The long, rolling lawn was freshly mowed, a lot of the tangled brush near the fence cleared out, and a dead tree had been cut down. He was still glancing at all the improvements as he knocked on the door—and then let himself in.

When he didn't immediately see or hear anyone, he ambled inside, aiming for the kitchen. He found a pot of Creole gumbo soup simmering on the stove, and more great smells emanating from a slow cooker. A stew, maybe? The air was rich with the scents of fresh basil and tarragon and pepper. A lot of great food—but still no bodies in sight.

Eventually he located Cashner, taking an afternoon snooze in front of the television. He did his usual prowl-around, checking the tray in Cashner's bedroom, making sure the medication was there and that Cashner was taking his pills. Normally Ike would have taken his blood pressure and pulse, but there was no sense waking him as long as his color was good.

Ginger's old Civic was parked in the drive, so she couldn't be too far. He checked the backyard, glanced around the garages—nothing. For lack of a better choice, he ambled across the road to the farm. A sharp wind bit at his sweatshirt, nipped at his neck. If it did rain, it was likely to be a mighty cold soak…which was probably why he noticed the wide-open door to the tea shop.

He'd never been in the retail shop before, had no reason to, but he knew that the tidy white building housed both the retail tea products and the farm office. Ginger's grandmother had done the landscaping herself, made the place pretty and welcoming from the outside.

When he stepped through the open door, though, he wanted to shake his head.

The inside wasn't just neglected; it was a disaster area. Dust and dirt carpeted every surface. The windows hadn't been washed in years. The stock on shelves was either in disarray or just suffered from an abandoned look. The old-fashioned cash register was gaping wide open. A mouse or some varmint had taken off with string and ribbon. Papers cuddled in corners and odd heaps.

But he'd finally found her.

Ginger.

On the floor, lying on her back with a bunched-up jacket behind her head.

He closed the door—since she hadn't had the sense to—and then hunkered down beside her.

She wasn't asleep. Her eyes were wide open and narrowed on him, her voice as cross as always. "How is it that you manage to always—*always*—show up when I'm at my absolute worst?"

Ike knew better than to answer an estrogen-loaded question like that. Besides, his first priority was to make sure she was okay. It didn't look as if she'd fainted or fallen, more as if she'd taken an impromptu rest.

Her appearance revealed that she'd been up to no good. She was wearing old jeans, dirty at the knees and seat. The white sweatshirt—well, there was a single spot, near her right shoulder, that was still white. The spot was no bigger than a quarter. The rest of the sweatshirt and everything else looked like something his mother would have thrown in the rag bag.

Her chin had some more dirt. Her hair had streaks of white, not from sudden age but dust. At some point she'd wiped her face and eyes with a clean rag—apparently—because there was an almost-clean swatch of face around the eyes.

But the familiar belligerence in her expression was enough for him to conclude she was fine. Frustrated and tired, but pink-cheeked healthy.

"So, is this really your worst?" he asked with pretend curiosity. "Do you promise?"

"Don't make me laugh, Ike, or you're likely to see violence." She closed her eyes tight. "Right now, Ike…I just plain can't see any possible way I could raise a baby."

So they were in the middle of that conversation, were

they? "I don't suppose that maybe you're feeling over-whelmed because you *are* overwhelmed?"

Nah. She didn't like that answer. Didn't even try opening her eyes. "I don't have a job. I don't see any chances of a job here, at least in anything I studied for, and there's no way I could move away from here to find a job. I can't leave my grandfather for a com-pletely unknown period of time. This is a royal, royal mess. And I just can't fix it. Or affect it. Not in a week. Maybe not in months."

He wished he could soften the edges for her, but there was no way. "Okay. What else?"

"Money. I don't exactly need a lot of money here. Gramps has enough coming in from Social Security and his retirement funds to keep him going. I'm not worried about him having enough to eat. It's just…"

"You don't have any spending money."

"Actually, I don't care about spending money. I had savings before I quit my Chicago job, and I have a few investments besides. My grandparents weren't about to raise any dumb granddaughters. But…" She sighed, still not opening her eyes. "But I still see huge debts pos-sibly everywhere. I don't think Gramps filed taxes last spring. Amos says the fields are almost too far gone to bring back, and for sure there was no income last year. The farm could go under. And I don't know what the house needs to bring it back into good shape."

Now she opened her eyes, swung to a sitting posi-tion and sat cross-legged—which enabled her to hold a chin in one palm. "Ike, I need the legal right to pay his bills. To see what kind of financial trouble he's in. That's why I tried to talk to his attorney—crabby old witch that she is."

"She was just as complimentary about you."

"I kind of liked her."

"I do, too."

"But here's the thing. Even if I saw a heap of his records, I'm not sure I'd know what they meant. I've been all through the office in the house. Then I came out here. I was trying to go through everything—the inventory records and the tax records and the sales information and all that—but the place was so dirty, I couldn't even think. When my grandmother was alive, this place was spotless. And I found a bunch of records, but the numbers all started to blur in my head. And between trying to clean and trying to wade through gross and net numbers, I just got completely lost."

He got it. Why she'd been lying on the floor like she was in a coma. Or a wished-for coma. He'd likely have caved on line two of her list.

"Ginger…tell me about tea. This whole place."

"That's just the point. I don't know anything about the business! I keep telling you!"

She crashed back on the floor and closed her eyes again. He clearly needed a new tack. "I don't mean the big picture numbers. I meant…what are all these products on the shelves? White tea and green tea and black tea and all. What makes them all different?"

"They're not different. They all come from the same plant. *Camellia sinensis.*"

"Huh?"

She opened one eye. "You're just humoring me, Ike. Trying to get me in a better mood. Trust me, I'm entitled to a terrible mood. I'd have to be certifiable to be in a good mood. There are no silver linings in any of these clouds."

"Okay. I promise you can go back to your terrible mood—I certainly would, in your shoes. But just tell me a little more. I don't get it. How you'd get all those different kinds of teas from the same plant."

She shot him a suspicious look. But she answered, "You always have to start with *camellia sinensis.* Then the next trick is to have the right climate, and to give the plants the right food and the right handling—to get the best quality tea. No shortcuts. No lazy stuff. No skimping on what the plants need."

"Got it. But you're saying that green teas come from the same plant that black teas come from?"

"Yes. Exactly. One tea plant could be bred a little differently than another. But that isn't what distinguishes the type and taste of the tea. That's about how the leaves are handled. It's about fermenting."

"Fermenting? Are we talking about moonshine and stills here?"

"No, you goof. Tea's never alcoholic. But you get different flavors based on how you handle the leaves. You get white tea from picking the leaves before they're fully open, when the buds are still tiny and young. That makes white tea more rare. It's the most expensive."

"So…white tea is the best?"

"That's just a matter of taste. Green tea has a really light flavor. It takes a whole lot less fermenting—or oxidation—than the dark teas."

"So it's better?"

"Better is just a matter of taste. Green tea, for instance, has a really light flavor. The leaves for green tea aren't fermented—or oxidized—at all. So those people who love green tea think the taste is more fresh, more herbal."

"How about you?"

"Ike. If you're raised a Gautier, all teas are holy. The

worst sacrilege would be to not love tea. The second would be to believe one was better than another."

"Okay."

"So now we're up to oolong. You know what that is. Even if you're not a regular tea drinker, you've undoubtedly had oolong tea at Chinese restaurants. Oolong is between a black and a green tea. It's partly fermented—but not for a long period of time. Black teas are the richest, hardiest teas because they're fully fermented and oxidized."

"But then how do they get the other names? Like mint and jasmine and all that stuff—"

"You can add all kinds of ingredients to the leaves. Like you could add jasmine to oolong to make jasmine oolong. Or you could add mint, if you liked that spice. But if you preferred Darjeeling, for another example... Ike! What are you *doing?*"

Ginger knew perfectly well what he was doing.

The man was loco. Witless. In a complete meltdown. Marbles all lost. IQ dipping into the negative numbers. A major drafty hole between his ears.

He kissed her again, this time his lips just skimming hers before sinking in for a long, slow kiss.

Daft. The man was daft. She was filthy. Buried in dust and paper and discouragement. Hadn't brushed her hair in hours. The tea store was a romantic setting on a par with...

On a par with...

On a par with...

She couldn't think. He suddenly twisted around, shifted them both so that he was flat on the floor now and she was propped over him. It should have been awkward, the sudden tangle of arms and legs, both of them off balance. But his mouth never severed from hers. It was a whole swoosh of sensation, her breasts against his chest, the heat and pressure and throbbing of his erection against the soft cradle of her pelvis.

That gasp of awareness…she wasn't expecting it, had had no idea the fierceness of longing and need were so close to the surface. Longing for him. Need for *him*. How could she have known?

Possibly the real problem was that she was kissing him back.

Possibly he wasn't the only daft one—but she had excuses. She was exhausted. Worried. Anxious. She'd been trying so hard to do the right things, to make something of her life, to stand up for doing what needed doing…and every time she turned around, even more insurmountable problems seemed to show up.

Besides which, Ike was a wicked-good kisser. Crazy. But lunacy didn't affect the parts of him that worked really, really well. He had certain beguiling habits. He surprised, but he didn't pounce. He took, but she just couldn't see it coming. He was a lazy man who brought every ounce of laziness to his kisses, as if every taste, every scent, every sensation needed to be examined and savored. He touched. Her upper arms, her back, into her hair, down her spine, around. Every stroke, every caress, conveyed the tenderness of a man who could soothe a lioness, disarm a wild animal.

She was going to slap him any second.

Pretty soon.

Any second now.

That lazy trick shouldn't have worked. She'd never liked lazy or slow. She always galloped, never walked. Her temper was a brush fire, quick and hot, then over. It was who she was, how she was.

Except with him.

He pushed up her sweatshirt. Slid his hands into her jeans, pressed on her fanny, so she was glued even tighter against him. Still, he pulled kisses from her.

Still, he made her close her eyes, because she felt so shivery and weak. Still, he made sounds, volatile sounds, groans, murmurs that sounded a whole lot like a love song.

"Ginger."

"Hmm?" She lifted her head, but not willingly. She opened her eyes, but only reluctantly.

And there was reality, in the form of his rugged face and unshaved chin and devil-blue eyes. He sucked in some oxygen. Smiled at her.

"I'm all about this," he assured her, and then said it a second time, because his voice didn't seem to carry any volume on the first try. "I'm more about this than you can imagine. But at least the first time…I think we can do better than a dirty floor. A place where anyone could come in. Where there isn't a pillow or a candle in sight."

She pushed up. Scowled at him. "We were never going that far."

"No?"

She sort of straddled his thigh, trying to get off him. Everything that had been so impossibly right…now seemed so impossibly wrong.

Ike told himself he couldn't be falling for her. He just couldn't. She almost kneed him in his privates in an effort to scramble off him.

But damned if she didn't look adorable. Still dirt-smudged. Still rattled. But there was still passion in her eyes, an earthy pink in her cheeks. Women liked him. Women had always liked him. But she sparked something different for him, something dangerous, something compelling. Maybe because she responded to him as if he were the only man in the universe—at least her universe.

"You're not looking happy," he murmured.

She was still straightening, tugging, smoothing. Sunlight streaming from the windows glowed on her face, put fire in her hair. "I'm definitely not," she agreed.

"You mad at me?"

"No. I'm mad at me."

Her voice was still cross, but he relaxed. "I like that answer. I was hoping I wouldn't have to apologize or grovel."

She stood up, pushing a hand through her hair as her gaze swept the tea shop. As awful as it was, Ike could see there were patterns to her messes. One mountain was trash. Paper piles were separated into taxes and receipts and similar records. A trash barrel held broken pottery. Unbroken tins and tea containers were temporarily shelved together.

"I don't suppose you know how to fix a broken antique cash register?" she asked, as if they were in the middle of a completely different conversation.

"If it's old, then it's not electronic. If it's just a mechanical problem, there's a slim chance I can." He uncoiled, stood up. He'd seen the cash register gaping open, just hadn't bothered to wonder why. But now he tested the drawer, and shortly discovered the obvious. Something was caught behind it. He leaned over, tried to reach in. "We're going to need a tool. Knife. Screwdriver. Fork. Something long and thin."

She went on a search, came through with a long-handled spoon.

He took it and she said, "Just be a little careful with it, okay? It's sterling silver."

He rolled his eyes, gave her back the spoon.

"It was all I could find!"

"Think ruler. Tape measure. Fly swatter…"

She found a ruler. He swore. She played cheerleader. He considered asking if she wanted to talk about it… It seemed fairly monumental to him, nearly making love in the least romantic place on the planet, no foreplay, no warnings, just a kiss leading to Armageddon. But then he figured she'd bring it up if she wanted to, needed to.

Eventually—by half killing himself—he managed to figure out the problem. Two acorns. Some shredded paper. Some unmentionables. "You had a mouse make a nest back there."

"Ew."

"That's an elegant way to put it." He tested the drawer two more times, making sure it closed and re-opened cleanly again.

"Ike…it's not easy for me to ask a favor from any-one." She'd thrown out the debris he'd unearthed in the register, pulled hand sanitizer from her pocket and liberally used it on her hands—then offered it to him.

"Well, I like the idea of your asking favors from me. Then you're in my debt. That's always good."

She chuckled, but there was a carefulness in her tone. "I need…well, I need someone with me next Thursday. I have to talk to Amos Hawthorne, on the tea farm, about the tea farm. We set up a time. But since I'm not his favorite person…"

"How could that possibly be? When you're so cute and smart and so easy to get along with?"

A ball of wadded-up paper hit his forehead. "All right, all right, so it might be my fault that Amos isn't too fond of me."

"Because you went behind his back and sicced his wife on him?"

She glared at him. "That could be part of it. But the point is that he's coming to talk on Thursday afternoon. Three o'clock. And you may have patients, I realize. But if you're free, I'd appreciate your being here."

"You feel you need protection? That he might strangle you?"

"Well, I'm hoping it won't come to that. I'm going to practice being meek and agreeable. But just in case I can't pull it off…"

"You'd like backup."

"Yes. If you can. And if you wouldn't mind."

"Well, this is an easy yes. No sweat. I'll be here a few minutes early." He was amazed at the workings of the female mind. At least her female mind. He'd probably have paid gold for the chance to be there for her. And extra platinum for her asking him, specifically him, to play a hero role for her. Casually he mentioned, "You're using me."

"I know. I know. It's not nice."

"That's okay. Feel free to use me whenever you want."

She looked as if she was about to reply when his pager went off. He was tempted to throw the damn thing in the river. Every time they got into an interesting conversation, he was interrupted.

"I have to go," he said. En route to the door, he managed to swoop an arm around her waist and peck a fast, soft kiss on her forehead. "Be good. But only when I'm not there, okay?"

She bristled up, but he just laughed. And dug in his pocket for his truck keys.

Chapter Seven

Ginger paced in front of the farm office at the speed of a Derby contender. Ike was late. He said he'd be here by three on Thursday, and it was three minutes after three.

She'd been ready for Amos Hawthorne's arrival since before lunch. Not that she was nervous, but she couldn't eat anything but a few soda crackers with weak tea. She'd pitched and tossed clothes because she couldn't find a pair of pants that buttoned. She'd still had a waist until that morning! Suddenly the pooch had appeared.

The pregnancy had been on her mind every other second for weeks now—she wanted to make decisions, forge plans, positively hated procrastinating about anything so serious. It was just that Gramps's issues were more immediately overwhelming. He was the crisis. She couldn't be the crisis until she had time to be the crisis.

A truck turned in the drive. An old pickup, which made shards of anxiety twist in her stomach—it wasn't

Ike, but Amos, and she'd so counted on Ike being here first. Clouds clenched and darkened in the west. Since it typically rained a ton in the fall, another shower wouldn't be unusual, but she needed at least an hour with no rain. She needed to win over Amos. She needed the darned farm taken care of so she could go back to the rest of the crises in her life.

She needed an awful lot to go right over the next hour.

Amos pulled into the drive, stepped out. She had the old golf cart with the canopy top all charged up and ready to boogie—which he'd asked for. It was the easiest transportation around the acreage. "Thanks so much for coming," she started to say.

Amos greeted her with a scowl darker than the sky. "My wife sent you a pecan pie, seeing as she thinks the sun rises and sets with you. Just so you know it's from her and not from me. I don't appreciate your going round my back to my wife, missy."

"Please thank her so much for the pie. And I'm seriously sorry, Amos. I know what I did was wrong." Her voice was sincere. She was willing to eat as much crow as Amos wanted. If he'd just help her.

"Yeah, well, when I say no to something, I mean no. The only reason I came is because I thought about it, and realized it was your grandfather that fired me, not you. So I'll fill you in on how things are. Explain some things I know you don't know. Then you can do whatever you want with the information. I'm out of it."

"I'd appreciate any help you could give me." She'd practiced that contrite voice, hoped she sounded subservient and meek.

"Well, let's go." He motioned to the golf cart, took the driver's side, took off the minute she was seated.

His first stop—his priority stop—was in front of the major field of tea plants. "All right. What do you see out there?"

She looked. She'd seen the view a million times. Green as far as the eye could see, that unique rich green of tea plants. Nothing looked dead. The field exuded an exuberantly fresh and unique smell.

"It looks healthy to me," she said carefully.

"Then you never looked real close, did you." Amos didn't phrase it like a question.

"I wasn't ever looking from your eyes, Amos. But it's true. I have no memory of what the fields looked like in October."

"Well, I'll tell you how it looked when I was managing the place. The top of that field should look absolutely even. Floor-even. Table-even. There shouldn't be a branch or a leaf of a limb sticking out anywhere. This is a mess."

She gulped. "I guess my first impression was that the plants looked healthy."

"They are healthy. Those plants will live another few hundred years. Never had trouble with them," he said fondly. "One of the nice things about tea is that you never have to use chemicals like insecticides. No insects anywhere around here. Nobody knows why. Some say that the insects don't like the natural caffeine in tea. But whatever. If you're good to a tea plant, it'll last centuries and more."

"You love them, don't you, Amos?" He was starting to calm down, at least a little.

"You think I worked all those years just for a paycheck? Of course I love it." He started driving again, but slowly, pointing out this and that. "You see a bald eagle over head, you know it's one of the farm's. Bald eagles like it here. There's always at least a pair nesting by the irrigation ponds. When the young are born, they bring them to the tea plants. The plants are so close, the trunks so gnarly, that no predator can get in there. The mama can go out hunting, knowing her babies are safe."

"Gramps showed me a nest one time," Ginger murmured. "I thought those babies were about the ugliest, scrawniest hairless critters I'd ever seen." She hoped to coax a smile, but Amos took off again, his posture stiff as steel.

"You know how many tea plantations there are in the United States?" he demanded.

She shook her head.

"Three. There's one way bigger than ours, right in the Carolinas, a lot bigger name than we have. They make great tea, sell it all over the world—but that's all right. What we had here was our own little taste of paradise. We never wanted to be big, just wanted the best tea in the universe. The best tea is all in the plants. Nurturing them as if they were babies, giving them the perfect food, just the right amount. You have to know every plant as if it was a kid of yours. See any bad behavior, you have to stop it in its tracks. But you have to love it, too."

She looked at him, suddenly realizing that she'd misunderstood the situation completely. She never had to win Amos over. It wasn't about her. It was about the land. And her grandfather should have given Amos a serious piece of the land a long time ago.

"Amos," she started to say seriously, but then stopped. From the corner of her eye, she saw a pickup— a white charger of a pickup—turning from the far, long side of the field. Her heart thumped even before she could identify him. So he was a little late. He'd said he'd come and he had.

He was the lover she couldn't have—which she'd known from the get-go. But tarnation, he did stir her blood like a burst of light after a long dark storm.

Ike, being Ike, took his time getting out of the truck and ambling toward them. He shot her a look—but to Amos, he extended a hand. "How's the gout doing, Amos?"

"Could be better. Could be worse. I'm not complaining."

"Good to hear. And the wife?"

"I thought that cough was going to never stop. The medicine you gave her helped a smidgeon, I have to say."

Faint praise, Ginger mused. Still, it was obvious that Amos trusted Ike. She could see it in the way he shook Ike's welcoming hand, how he stood taller, how a hint of a smile showed up.

Before they'd stood there two minutes, though, Amos drew a line in the sand. "So, Doc, I assume you showed up because you're riding shotgun for Miss Ginger here?"

"Well, I'd have to admit to that…except the truth is, I don't know anything about your business, the tea, the land, any of it. So I'm likely to keep my mouth shut."

Amos turned back to her. "Well, I'm not through telling you things you need to know."

"I'm listening," she said, and added "sir" with all the Southern feminine syrup that she'd grown up with. The sky started spitting rain. It wasn't a lot, wasn't even a drizzle, more like a slow drool with a plop landing here and there. Just enough to make her hair frizz and her neck feel sticky.

Amos abandoned the golf cart and led a walk around the acres that would have exhausted a marine. The greenhouse. The pump. The supply barn. The irrigation setup. The warehouse where the harvest was brought in, first to the withering bed, then to the rotovane, then to the oxidation bed.

"What's wrong in here?" he asked her, the same as he had, at every stop.

The answer was always the same. Her. She was the one who was wrong. Her lack of knowledge was adding up to a college degree in ignorance.

"What's wrong," Amos prodded her, when she failed to express the correct answer, "is that the machinery's just sitting here. Not turned on. This place should be busy and noisy, the last harvest of the season. The greenhouses should be filled with cuttings started during the growing season. There's nothing right happening anywhere on the premises."

She felt a hand at the small of her back. Ike. Who hadn't said a word or offered a question or anything else. He was just…there.

"Amos," she said carefully, "are you trying to tell me the only solution is to sell the property? Is it all so far gone that it can't be brought back?"

"That's your business and your grandfather's. Not mine."

"I would still value your opinion."

"Well, you could sell the place. But not for tea. Not going to find anybody who knows about tea. And as far as selling her for general real estate…she's a pretty piece of ground, so I guess some developer might look at it. In this market, though, I'd doubt you'd get value for your money."

She gulped. So far she hadn't heard any good news.

"All right. So the next question. Is it possible to make it viable again? To bring it back."

"Well, sure. But it'd take a trunk full of money."

"How much money?"

"Honey, I don't know."

"But I'll bet you have a general idea. I suspect you'd know more than the bank would about a problem like that," she added.

"Well, that's another for-sure. People wearing suits don't understand land. About no one understands tea." He pulled a bag from his pocket, looked at her as if silently asking her permission.

She had to shake her head. The bag held chewing tobacco. She was about positive if he started chewing, she'd hurl...and then this whole afternoon would be for nothing. "Please just throw out a general figure. What you think it'd take to bring it back."

"Well, it's gonna take a year of no profit to bring it where it should be again."

"I understand."

"You'll have to pay for the work. And a lot of the work has to be done by hand when it's been let go to this point."

"I understand."

"She could make a good profit. She always has. When you make the best of something, there's always a market for it. But your grandmother had the gift, and she's gone. Your grandfather did his time, but you know he hasn't got the judgment of a rock any more. And then there's you." Amos shook his head. "You couldn't do this, missy. You're too soft. Too much to learn. You're too much a city girl."

She almost bit his head off. She wanted to. She could. She knew perfectly well when she was being insulted—

and she knew exactly how to lose her temper because she did it so often.

But damned Amos. He was telling the truth. It wasn't a truth she wanted to hear, but of course, he was right. She couldn't possibly handle the farm herself. And there was no one else.

Ike spoke up for the first time in a blue moon, his voice casual and easy. "Amos, could you just throw out some kind of dollar figure to Ginger? Just ballpark. Just something that would give her an idea what kind of money it might take to turn this around."

Amos looked at Ike, not her. "I don't know, I'm telling you. I mean I've seen some figures. I know what some things cost. I know what I used to be paid. But I can't guarantee—"

"Aw, Amos. We're not asking for a guarantee. Just a ballpark number. If you were running the place, what would you think it'd take to put the land back on firm footing?"

Amos scratched his neck. "Well, I dunno. But I'm saying a hundred grand easy. That'd be the drop in the bucket. But I'm guessing it'd be more like two."

"Two hundred thousand?" Ginger echoed. All right. It wasn't as big as the national debt, but it might as well have been. For a second, only a second, her eyes squeezed closed. Who knew? Who could possibly have known that she could conceivably feel this sharp-sad sinking feeling of loss?

She'd never dreamed of being part of the working tea farm. Neither had her grandparents. Neither had anyone. She was just trying to find solutions for her grandfather's situation. That's all. But realizing her family could lose it all brought on a heartsick so sharp she could hardly swallow.

She heard a buzz, realized it was Ike's cell. She felt his gaze on her face, hawk eyes, assessing...but he turned around to answer the call.

He flipped the cell shut in less than a minute. "I'm sorry, Ginger. It's the one problem with being the only doctor in town. It's sort of a twenty-four-seven thing."

"You have to go," she said.

"Yeah. Seems a five-year-old had a fall from a jungle gym. Sounds like the child's fine, but the mother's a wreck and a half."

"Of course. You have to go," she said. And meant it. But not really. She'd never wanted to be the kind of woman who needed a man in that capital-*N* way. But right then...well, she did. She wanted to lean on him. On Ike. Not any man. Just on him.

If a woman's world was falling apart, well, then, it was. But she just wanted a little company.

She felt him squeeze the back of her neck, a tender gesture, almost a whisper of a gesture—but then he turned away and hiked toward his car. And she was left to turn around and face Amos alone.

"I want you to thank your wife for the pie, Amos," she said sincerely. "I'll write her a note myself, but please let her know how much I appreciate it."

"I will," Amos agreed, and propped on his straw hat again. Apparently he thought their meeting was over.

So did she. But somehow, words came out of her mouth that she'd never planned on. "Amos, if I could get that money...and add to the salary you once had. Would you be able to bring the farm back?"

"Someone could. If they stepped up now, and no later."

"But you could do it. If we had the money...you could do it."

Amos narrowed his eyes at her. "Don't you go talking to my wife again, missy. You went behind my back
once. I won't forgive it a second time. You can bat those
pretty eyes at the doctor, but not at me."

"Yes, sir."

"The answer is no. And I won't say it again."

"Yes, sir."

By the time Amos left, Ginger wandered back home
in a funk…and the rest of the day deteriorated from
there. Sarah-Just-Sarah had left chicken and dump-
lings, homemade, absolutely delicious—but somehow
her stomach couldn't tolerate it. She lost that, snacked
on soda crackers, which stayed down but were hardly
comparable to a great cook's recipe for anything.

And then there was Gramps. He'd had a good morning, she knew he had. But when she sat down with him
at dinner, tried to talk to him about the land, the tea,
what Cashner believed was happening with the property…her gramps just kept smiling at her, saying that
she looked prettier every day, that she shouldn't be worrying about things like the farm, she should be thinking
about going out dancing with some nice young man…
although he'd beat her at gin rummy if she had nothing better to do.

By eight-thirty, Gramps had retired to his room. Ginger prowled through the empty house for a while, eventually poured herself a Darjeeling, and headed outside
to the porch swing.

The drizzling rain had long stopped, but the dark
clouds refused to move along. The evening was unre-
lentingly dreary—a perfect atmosphere, Ginger figured—to indulge in a good long wallow in self-pity.

It wasn't as if she didn't have plenty to feel sorry for
herself about. She considered crying—nothing she nor-

mally indulged in—but hey, when a girl was miserable, she might as well go for it whole-hog. As she explored how awful things were—how awful her life was, how impossible her entire future was, how she was failing right and left to achieve any of the dreams she'd had as a young girl—she almost worked up to some serious crying.

But then she heard the sound of an engine coming in the drive. She didn't look up. It couldn't be Ike driving in, because fate couldn't be that unkind. Practically every single time he'd seen her, she'd been at her physical, mental and emotional worst. And part of the reason she was considering a long, noisy, blubbering crying jag was specifically him.

She'd wanted him to stay during the confrontation thing with Amos. She'd wanted him to save her. She was sick of being a mature, capable woman. She wanted the prince to charge up on his white horse and make all the awful stuff go away. She didn't care if there was a happily ever after.

She was pretty sure there were no happily ever afters. But she still wanted the stupid prince and the white horse.

While her eyes were still closed, she was forced to realize that an animal had shown up on the porch. Not a white horse. But the bloodhound, who leaped toward her and immediately tried to clean her face with her long, fat tongue.

She reared up, and instead of yelling at the dog, she put her arms around the damned hound and hugged her. Pansy sat down and accepted the affection as her due.

Eventually she had to look up. Or look at. Ike hadn't sat down, more hunkered down to be on eye level with her. Behind the clouds, the sun was dropping, adding more gloom and gray to a night that was already fuzzy and dim. He looked at her as if she was under bright lights, though. As if the only thing in his universe was her.

Because she was a damn fool—hopefully not forever, but for now—all she wanted in that single zinging moment was to make love with him. As if that would solve anything. As if that could mean anything.

"How was your patient?" she asked.

"The kid—Jacob—was fine. The dad almost required a tranquilizer. The mom was visiting family out east. She's pregnant again, and he thought she needed a break, so he offered to take care of Jacob. He's a good dad. He just keels over at the sight of blood."

"Uh-oh."

"After Jacob, I had a snakebite to treat. An old granny who should have known better. Found a copperhead on her front porch and decided she'd just get a rake and move him off."

"Not?"

"Not. Copperheads aren't the most poisonous of the snakes around here, but they're not a dip of ice cream, either. Her blood pressure shot to the moon."

"She's okay now?"

"Yeah. It just took some time. How'd the rest of the meeting with Amos go?"

"Oh, it was even more fun after you left. Amos said it'd take somewhere between one and two hundred grand to put the place in shape. But he wouldn't do it. And no one else probably on this continent really knows much about tea. And he was still mad at me for talking to his wife."

"Wow. I missed all that?"

"What can I tell you? You missed all the best parts."

"Two hundred thousand, huh?"

"Yup. I was thinking of driving into town, picking up a lottery ticket."

"I don't know. Afraid then you'd need two hundred thousand and one."

"Plus gas."

"Yeah, forgot the cost of gas. So. That meeting with Amos make a few things easier for you?"

"Easier?" She kept petting the dog, kept trying not to look at Ike. She'd afraid he'd see the yearning.

"Yes. You never wanted part of the tea plantation yourself, right? So now you know. Selling it's your best option. You don't have to sweat feeling like you lost something that mattered to you. You never wanted to be in the tea business."

She sucked in a breath. Who knew that hearing the words in Ike's gentle, easygoing voice would make her feel slapped? Which wasn't Ike's fault. It was true... she'd never wanted anything to do with the tea farm. Ever. Until Gramps had said someone was trying to take it from the family. And then she'd come here and realized that her whole family history was about to disappear, all the love and family lore and memories of the house and land and people...unless someone else could take it on.

"I'd have to be downright stupid to try to keep it," she said hollowly. "I have a degree in business. Not farming or agriculture. I started out wanting to be in medicine, veered off into business and hospital administration. Might be hard for you to see it, but I was darned good at my job. And loved it besides."

"Hey. I suspect you'd be darned good. You're smart. And you're more than fearless when you take something on."

"Some things, maybe. But not agriculture."

"That issue's moot, isn't it? Since you don't want anything to do with the tea farm."

"I *know* it's moot. I'm just saying…you probably don't think I could handle something like the farm. Because I'm so unqualified and all that."

"Hey. That's like worrying whether you can shoot an Uzi. It doesn't matter since you'd never volunteer to try it."

She had no idea why she suddenly felt it rising. Temper. She'd been depressed and anxious and wallowing in self-pity—but not mad. Not remotely mad. Yet she knew all the symptoms. Bristling energy. Itchiness. Couldn't sit still. And the smell…trouble always had a tantalizing smell.

She pushed off the porch swing, lifted a hand to Ike as if she wanted to say something or make some gesture…and then just didn't. Instead, she stalked off the porch. Pansy, with an extremely reluctant groan, forced herself to her feet and tore after her. For the hound, a walk was a walk. Even if it was an inexplicable hike around the house at seventy, seventy-five miles an hour.

She didn't see Ike get to his feet. Didn't hear his footfalls in the grass. But suddenly she heard his voice just behind her, lazy as the night breeze.

"Did I miss something in the conversation?"

"No, of course you didn't."

"You took off like a bat out of hell. What's wrong?"

"Nothing." She stopped, swatted a bug nipping at her ankles. Took off again.

The backyard glistened with rainy leaves and smelled like a rain forest and was just as dark as her fitful mood.

"Okay. I must have said something to upset you."

"No. Of course you didn't. What could you possibly have said to upset me?"

"I have no idea. That's why I asked." He added kindly, "You seem to be letting out steam from both ears. I'm pretty sure you're ticked about something."

"Well, I'm not. Pansy just needed a little walk." But Pansy, the lazy turncoat, apparently decided that two times around the house was more than enough exercise. She heaved herself back on the front porch and threw herself on the welcome mat.

"That's okay," Ike said in the same annoyingly kind tone. "You don't need the Pansy excuse. I'm up for as many laps around the house as you need."

She stopped dead, parked her hands on her hips. "Would you stop being nice to me?"

"Okay. Just say it, then. What the problem is."

"Which one? I seem to have about five million right now."

"The one about the land, Ginger."

She was tempted to sock him. Even though she'd never hit anybody and was a firm believer in taking out her temper only on inanimate objects. Still, she put some serious fury in her voice. "I can't save the darn land. There's no possibility. I'm too ignorant. The learning curve's too steep. And the day I could convince a bank to loan me two hundred grand will be the same day pigs fly."

"But that's not the point," Ike persisted calmly. "That'll be the point tomorrow. Tonight the only point is for you is to say out loud what you really want to do."

"Good grief, you're exasperating. You want me to say it, I'll say it. I hate to give up the land, the tea. It's my whole heritage. I didn't think it remotely mattered to me...but it does. My grandma loved it. My mom loved it. It's part of who I am. The part I always knew I could come home to. It's home, in a way no other place could be. Now. Are you happy?"

"Oh, yeah," he murmured. "You did good."

And as if the man hadn't behaved like a lunatic since he got there, he suddenly grabbed her. She was half in shadow, half in the porch light. She saw something in his eyes that made her suddenly want to shiver.

And then of all the fool things to do, he kissed her.

Chapter Eight

Ike almost hadn't stopped by. He knew Ginger'd had a challenging day, and he'd been going nonstop since daybreak. But once he turned in the yard...well.

Maybe he'd wanted to be sure she was okay. Maybe in some place in his heart he'd known this was going to happen. A kiss, just like this one.

She fired up faster than a rocket. And he kept telling himself he felt resentful for the way she so easily rocked his world. Everything had been fine until he met her. Now nothing was.

Yet he felt the energy of a superman when his lips touched hers, claimed hers. The kick was fast and potent. It didn't matter that they were standing in the middle of a rain-soaked yard. It didn't matter that Pansy was up on the porch snoring. It wouldn't matter if the sky cracked open and rained daisies.

Nothing mattered when he kissed her. And that was the whole thing.

He felt rich with her. Rich on her. Her lips were expensive, sheer-soft, yielding.

She sank into him when he kissed her, at least when he kissed her until they were both breathless, and that's the only way he seemed to know how. Her body bowed into his, obviously made for him, because all the right parts touched. Breast. Pelvis. Heart.

She gave out a swish of a groan, a woman sound, angry—darn it, the woman was always angry—but it was still another yielding. She liked to be kissed. At least she liked to be kissed by him. That shot up his testosterone level another notch, and desire had already put his hormones in the stratosphere.

"Hey," he murmured, hoping she'd think he still had some sanity left and would listen if she objected.

But she didn't object. And she ignored his token *hey*. She suddenly lost all patience with his shirt, pulling and tugging and wrestling with it. Once her bare palms found the bare skin of his back, though, she slowed down. Just…stroked. Rubbed. Made catlike sounds of pleasure. She snuggled her lips against his neck, nestled in against his bared chest, rocked.

"Ike," she murmured.

"Hmm?"

"I wish you wouldn't do this."

His eyebrows arched. She had a habit of making comments that left him speechless. Maybe he'd initiated the kiss, but she'd responded whole hog, rocket speed, shooting past all the stop signs. He hadn't made her do that. He hadn't made her do anything.

He eased up, not too far. Her hands were still on his back, his hands looped around her neck. Foreheads touched instead of lips. Both practiced breathing.

"There's this really nice lady," he said.

"Oh?"

"Her name is Sandy Joe. She makes me cakes all the time. And cookies. And brownies. She's two years younger than me. Divorced about four years. As comfortable to be with as an old pair of gloves."

"I'll bet there's a reason you're telling me about this woman."

"There is, there is. I like her. She's a good person. Kind. Sweet. She's been waiting for me to ask her out for months now."

"Um, are you hoping I'll give you advice about that? Like 'Dear Abby' or something?"

"No. I'm just saying. I've wanted to ask her out. She couldn't be nicer. And I couldn't figure out why I didn't just do it."

"I'll bet you want me to ask why."

"You don't have to ask. I want to tell you. It's because of you. I didn't realize there wasn't a pinch of chemistry when she comes around. But any time I'm near you, I'm ready to go off like a firecracker. In principle, it doesn't make sense. You've got a mean streak. You're difficult. Contrary."

"Yeah, but you're forgetting the obvious factor, Doc. You know I'm not on the market. It's a whole lot easier to let the sparks bubble to the surface when you know there's no…repercussions. No risk."

"You think there's no risk? Of my falling for you?"

For an instant, he saw the glow of something perilously vulnerable and soft in her eyes. "You didn't say falling. You were talking about chemistry. Sex. Sparks."

"The hell I was," he murmured. He almost turned to walk away. Almost. But it was that vulnerability in her eyes, the disbelief that he could actually care, that sent him in another direction entirely.

He pulled her close, tilted his head, kissed her hard this time. He wanted to give her sugar, not hot pepper. Care, not roughness. She had so much on her plate, so much she was trying to cope with. He wanted to give her tenderness, empathy. He felt those things.

But somehow it all came out with heat and flame. He kissed her bruising hard—she moaned and twisted tighter in his arms, met fire with fire. Everything that was impossible between them came out in an explosion. Her fingers clutched his shirt, then yanked at it, a button popping, her meeting every wild kiss with another, until he couldn't breathe and she couldn't breathe and neither cared.

Soft shadows danced into darker shadows. She pulled him off balance, not intentionally, but he had to twist swiftly in front of her so she wouldn't fall under him. The crash was awkward...silly. But she wasn't hurt. He was the one flattened onto the wet, cool grass, with Ginger scrabbling on top of him. He almost laughed, even regained a pinch of sense, said, "I'm pretty sure that was a sign we should both signal a no..."

But she whispered right back, "I'll let you know when I'm saying no, Doc, and it sure isn't now."

This couldn't happen. He knew it. There wasn't a prayer of their making love, not here, not now, not on wet grass with the night whisking up a chill breeze. It was out of the question.

But when she tumbled on top of him, he assumed she was scrambling to climb off. Instead, she turned the awkward position into temptation, straddling him— straddling him tight. For that first millisecond, her eyes were above his, a silky hint of moonlight illuminating soft, wet lips and the sharp flare of emotion in her gaze. He'd seen the vulnerability before...but not this kind.

This was the naked kind. She was upset and mad—nothing new about that with Ginger—but she didn't seem mad at him.

She seemed to want to lose herself in him. Forget everything else. Ignore everything else. Make the whole darned impossible world disappear. She dipped her head, closed her eyes, took a kiss—and that was a capital-K, estrogen-fueled, woman-wicked of a kiss. Her tongue found his, and her body started rocking against him, inviting, coaxing. He was already steel-hard and hot, and her soft, warm flesh against his was not helping.

Her hands found their way past his shirt, rubbed against skin, ribs, chest. Her mouth took another soul-stealing kiss while those busy fingers of hers sneaked down, lower, below his navel.

There was a line Ike figured every woman ever born knew better than to cross.

She'd crossed it.

He might be on the bottom, but he couldn't wait another second before getting his hands on her. Her top pushed up. Her pants pushed down. She was a long, slow stroke, from her midback to the valley at the base of her spine, to her delectably small little butt. She groaned, softened a kiss against his neck.

"I don't want to hurt you," he said.

"You couldn't."

"Ginger. You're sure this is what you want?"

"I'm sure that I'm sick of trying to do right things. Sick of decisions. Sick of worrying and all that other nonsense. I just want to *live* for a moment, Ike. With you. Feel. Experience. Lose myself. With you. Is that okay?"

For bare seconds, she lifted her head, sought his ex-

pression in the shadows. He didn't answer. Couldn't.
She did look lost. Crushable. A woman who'd had all
she could take, at least for a while. And if she wanted
him to be the answer, hell…

He'd have climbed mountains for her. Given her
probably anything he had and then some.

Making love was an easy yes. In spite of the night's
damp chill, her skin was fever-warm…more so when he
scooched off his jeans, pushed her pants down to thigh
level. A rock dug into his back. His whole backside was
soaked through. Smells permeated the night—the ver-
dant earth, bark, grass, sweet leaves. Her.

He arranged all he could arrange, held her hips in his
palms…whether he slid into her, or she climbed on, he
wasn't sure. Didn't care. Seduction was never all that
fun unless it was an even-steven sport. Her smile was
sudden and glorious, a little shocked—he loved that,
that the feel of him inside her, owning her, claiming
her was rich enough to shock her. She went weak all of
a sudden…but that was more than okay. He felt richer
than Croesus, watched her face, felt her whole body
build up tension and need…and too soon, way, way too
soon, watched her peak with a sharp, sweet cry.

He seemed to be breathing louder than a freight train.
She sank on top of him with all the strength of a limp
noodle, nuzzling her face into his neck. That moment,
that exact moment, was so good. Beyond any good he
could recall. She was his, the way it never mattered
before. He wanted her, no one else. Loved her, like no
one else.

Eventually, she rubbed her cheek against his shoulder and then eased up on an elbow. She touched his lip
with the tip of a finger. Looked about to say something
when they both startled at a sudden voice.

"Annabelle!"

They were deep in shadows, but even so, Ginger peeled off him faster than a gunshot. He jolted aware and awake as fast as she did. Both of them buttoning, zipping, straightening—and sharing a look of laughter.

They were both standing up and reasonably respectable by the time they spotted Cashner, the kitchen light behind him, standing on the back porch in his undershorts and a saggy tee. "Annabelle Marie, you come in the house! You get away from that boy this minute!"

"Gramps, it's me. Ginger."

"And I'm the one out here with her, Cashner. Ike."

"I don't care who either of you say you are. There's a dog howling on the porch. A lovesick hound. Woke me out of a sound sleep. You're grounded forever, Annabelle."

"Who on earth is Annabelle?" Ike whispered.

"I haven't a clue. I think he's adding girlfriends to his imagination. He's not forgetting. He's just inventing people now and then. Most of them seem to be women."

And to her grandfather, she called out, "I'm coming, Gramps. And Ike'll take Pansy with him. Everything's fine. We're all going to sleep now."

Maybe they were, but Ike wasn't.

She thought she was no risk. That he had nothing but sexual feelings for her.

Ginger's father had taken off, or so the town always said. And the doctor she'd fallen for sounded like another take-off-for-where-the-grass-was-greener kind of guy. Somehow she'd started seeing that as a man's default position. When a guy had to show up for more than fun, he took off.

Ike wasn't that way.

He'd never been that way.

But that didn't mean he had any answers for a woman with serious trust issues.

He drove home with Pansy leaning her extremely heavy head on his shoulder, which meant drool slobbered down his shirt—which meant he'd need to shower before climbing in bed. He could have stopped the dog from leaning, of course. But it was Pansy's thing—sticking close when her human was upset.

Ike wasn't necessarily admitting he was upset. He didn't get upset. He'd never had a nervous bone in his body. A guy who had two high-powered surgeons for parents learned the hard way, mighty young, that panic in a tough situation accomplished nothing. But he hadn't liked leaving Ginger after making love. Hadn't wanted to leave her at all that night...much less after a crazy melding in that rain-soaked yard. He wasn't sure what she felt...about making love. About him.

But for darn sure, their whole relationship had abruptly become more complicated and precarious than before.

Minutes later, he pulled in his driveway—and let out a deep, tired sigh. A battered, mud-painted Jeep was already parked in the drive ahead of him. There were times he valued company. This wasn't one of them—even if he happened to love this particular visitor. Pansy lifted her head, but didn't waste the effort of barking.

She knew Rosemary.

Every light in the upstairs was on, the front door unlocked. He could hear his washing machine running, and at the top of the stairs—blocking the way—was a duffel bag stuffed with dirty clothes. It was easy enough to track down his sister. He found her—as always—crouched in front of the refrigerator, taking out covered dish after covered dish.

"About time you got home," she told him. "And man, I should have stopped by a lot more often than this. You must have every single woman in the county cooking for you! Good grief!"

"It's not my fault. I don't know how to stop it. They never ask. They just show up. Or I get home to find a covered casserole on the porch." He claimed his hug, then zipped out of sight as fast as he could. It didn't take him long to shed the wet clothes and pull on old sweats. Rosemary readily picked up the topic of conversation.

"It's just because you're cute. And you're a doctor. Every Southern mama's version of a catch. Except for the hound."

"Hey, Pansy's the best chaperone there is. She starts drooling and the women backtrack toward the door."

"Not me," announced his sister, who not only greeted Pansy with a kiss on the brow, but offered the dog chicken divan. From a fork. She did stuff like that to get his goat, because—she claimed—that's what sisters did. Worked hard to drive their brothers crazy.

Judging from the heap of dishes on the counter, she'd already had sugar pie and a piece of Coca-Cola cake—before heating the chicken divan. She did the same thing to Tucker—the oldest of the clan—showed up when she wanted feeding. But Ike's fridge always had the best goods.

She looked okay, Ike assessed. Her blonde hair was still shorter than grass, her face tanned and freckled, and she hadn't gained an ounce. Late last spring, just days before a big-to-do wedding, she'd called it off and taken off. No one knew what she'd told George, her ex-fiancé, and the parents were still fit to be tied. Just after that, Rosemary had disappeared up on Whisper Mountain. Well, maybe not exactly disappeared, considering she was a botanist and had a two-year grant to study wild orchids in the region.

But she was living like a hermit, out in the wild. There was a mountain-top cabin, adequate shelter but not a place meant to live in. It was rustic, no amenities. She showed up—either to his place or Tucker's—when she needed clothes washed or some serious food. Or, being Rosemary, to reassure her brothers that she was okay.

"You were the one who got the brunt of our absentee parents, weren't you?" he asked.

"Sheesh. Talk about diving into deep waters before we've even done the dishes."

"I'm just saying. Tucker and I are guys. Most of the time we didn't mind fending for ourselves. But you were the girl. Whenever you needed a dress for a prom or the right shoes before school or a permission slip to go somewhere...you needed Mom. Not two brothers who didn't know a curling iron from a lipstick."

"Did you ever hear me complain?"

"No. But you also never told anyone why you really called off the wedding."

"Listen, you." Rosemary had experience pointing a fork at brothers. "I didn't come here to be badgered. I came here to do the badgering. I heard from Tucker a couple nights ago."

"Any news?"

"No. He's still sounding like a lovesick goon. I can hardly talk to him. He's happy about this, happy about that. He started singing on the phone."

"Oh, no. Not that."

"Yeah. Like that. I usually check in with him once a week when I'm on the mountain, but I can't stand listening to all that sweet stuff. And then I checked in with the parents."

That made him pause, study her face. Their parents had been gung-ho on her marrying George and had given Rosemary a major hard time ever since. "So... what'd they have to say?"

"Pretty much the same message I get every time. They're certain I could still make it up with George, still get a wedding going again. If I just called and talked with him."

"And you probably said, *oh, wow, thanks so much for that advice?*"

By then she'd finished gorging herself, spun a kitchen towel into a weapon and smacked him. "So," she said firmly, "what's the deal with you?"

"No deals. Just the usual. My life's good. Love being the town doctor, love that every day's different, that there's always something unexpected around the corner. It's a good place, good people."

"Uh-huh. So who's the woman in this picture?"

"I'll be darned. Did I mention a woman?"

"I'm your sister. I can read between your lines any day." Rosemary cocked her head—her hair looked like a sun-streaked mop, her eyes too-searing blue. "It's not someone from town. I knew you'd never get the itch for a small-town girl. You do the laid-back thing really well, but underneath, we're all stuck with the parents' overachiever genes." Abruptly she jogged over from the sink and checked out his face close up. "I'll be damned. You're actually seeing someone."

"I never said that."

"You didn't have to. I'm looking at your face. Good grief, you've got the same goon expression that Tucker has half the time. You've got that secret smile. You're distracted. You just put a dirty dish away in the cup-board."

"I probably do that now and then."

"No. You don't. Ever. Wow. Wait until I tell Tucker."

"When you were a kid," he said heavily, "I beat you up now and then. I still could, you know."

"That went the way of urban legends. You never beat me up. You were an amazing brother."

He changed tactics. "I agree. I was beyond good to you. So why would you pick on me now?"

"Just tell me her name and I won't ask a single other question, I swear."

"Oh, yeah. I believe that like I believe there's a man in the moon."

"Aha. There *is* a woman in your life. Come on. Spill."

That'd probably happen in one or two zillion years. Ike didn't spill. Didn't talk personal stuff the way his sister loved to do.

But just for a second, he wanted to. All teasing aside, he trusted Rosemary the same way as he trusted Tucker. The MacKinnons had always stood up for each other. He wouldn't mind getting Rosemary's take on Ginger's situation…like whether it was fair for a guy to push—for a relationship, for risk—with a woman who was under so much stress. Whether he was nuts to think the two of them could make it. Whether Rosemary'd think he was even more crazy to have fallen for a lady who was carrying another man's baby.

But he didn't.

There was no point in telling Rosemary. He already knew those answers.

He needed to stay away from Ginger. To let her breathe. Let her figure out what she wanted and needed.

Pushing her—the way he knew damn well he wanted to push her—was wrong any way he said it.

But that was going to be extra hard, if not impossible, after making love with her.

Ginger had barely buttoned her favorite pants—a light green that went with an equally favorite cotton sweater—when the button popped. Actually it popped like a bullet, soared to the far window, ricocheted and then rolled under the bed.

She turned sideways in the bedroom mirror, and there it was again. The new pooch. Not a watermelon or a basketball or anything that huge. But the stomach shape had changed from concave to convex. Just like that.

In case she wanted to postpone dealing with the pregnancy issues, her silhouette was a caterwauling wake-up call.

She retrieved the button, yanked her hair back in a low tail and aimed downstairs. Just like that, on the third stair, she remembered Ike. Ike in the moonlight, kissing her. Ike, like a flash of magic, suddenly spinning her troubled world into a soft, whimsical place, where the power of the right man and the right woman could handle anything, fix anything, conquer anything.

She'd believed that last night.

She could believe anything when she was with Ike... but more, so much more, after they'd made love.

Impatiently she put some steel in her spine. This was a real-life morning. It had to be. And all her life she'd fought allowing herself to believe in dreams and magic—for seriously good reasons.

Her dad had been a nonstop believer in magic, a dreamer who was always sure there could be a pot of gold at the road's end. When she was little, her dad could talk her out of nightmares with his whimsical stories. And her dad was the reason she should never have fallen for a smooth-talking doc. She knew about smooth-talking dreamers.

She just never wanted to be one.

Ike was nothing like her Chicago ex. She knew that. But her twisted, goofy, inexplicable feelings for Ike were darned scary. Steve had introduced her to some strong feelings. Ike—well, Ike was an earthquake, a tsunami, a cataclysmic explosion of emotion. There was no comparison.

Ike was far scarier.

She just needed some space away from him for a while. It wasn't as if she had to invent reasons to be unavailable. She had problems crashing down on her life in every direction.

She grabbed a mug of tea and an apple, then tracked down Gramps. He looked bright-eyed this morning, was standing in the library with binoculars. "C'mere, Ginger. I think I spotted a bald eagle."

"Really? Let's see." Gramps handed over the binocs. The creature was across the road, close to the irrigation ponds, perched on an overhanging limb. It was definitely an eagle. A young one. "She's adorable," Ginger murmured.

"I think it's a boy."

"As if either of us could tell from here." She grinned—Gramps grinned right back—and it was so good to share this kind of moment with him again. They'd always taken joy in the simple things in nature. "You busy?"

"At my age, I don't know what busy means any more."

"Then would you take a short ride with me?"

He had trouble getting into her old Civic, and then

he grumbled about having to wear a seat belt, but it was obvious he liked it—going out with his best girl, as he put it.

"Do we have a destination?"

"Oh, yes," she said. The first stop was for an ice cream cone at Willie's—the best ice cream in the universe, even on a cold morning. And Gramps had always been a sucker for chocolate velvet—Willie's specialty. From there, she drove back home, but instead of turning in the house drive, she turned into the tea plantation.

She'd finished her single scooper, but Gramps was still lapping on his double cone when she put the car in park and turned the key.

"Pretty morning," he said.

He knew something was coming. Knew the minute she turned in the wrong drive. When Cashner was thinking clearly, he was undoubtedly smarter than she was ten times over. "We need a serious talk," she said. "Do you want to stay here?"

"Until I finish my cone."

"Gramps. Don't joke. Is this where you want to be, to live, for the rest of your life?"

"I won't live anywhere else. This is home. It's everything your grandmother and I worked for. Lived for. Every best memory I have is here. And those sure include you, honey."

She nodded. "Same here, Gramps. I love you to bits. But we have some financial issues. If you want to stay here, we have to find some way to make money off our tea again. I could learn all I can, but I don't believe that's even close to enough. If you want to stay here, we have to find a way to rehire Amos."

Cashner finished his cone, wiped his hands on the handful of napkins she'd brought him and shot her a shrewd look. "That'll happen when hell freezes over. He insulted me."

"And from what I hear...you insulted him."

"He tried to tell me what to do!"

She wasn't sure how long she could count on him to have a clear mind. "Here's the whole picture, Gramps. If we're going to live here, two things have to happen. We have to rehire Amos. And we have to find a way to coax the bank into loaning us a boatload of money. They're both long shots."

"Sweetheart—"

"No, please, Gramps. Just listen. If we can't make that happen...then there's still no worry for you. You'll be with me. Wherever I am, you can live with me, stay with me." Those were big promises she was making, Ginger knew well. She hadn't a clue how she was going to make a living, not right that minute. Much less did she have a plan for handling the pregnancy and earning a living at the same time.

On the other hand, first things came first. The most immediate thing that needed securing was Gramps.

He stared bleakly out the window, then turned back to her. "I couldn't leave here, Loretta."

She swallowed. Once "Loretta" or any other name came into play, she knew his mind was fading to a different place. "Every memory you love, Gramps, is in your heart. It doesn't matter where you are. You have all those memories. They're yours forever."

"You're talking foolishness, honey."

Foolishness, she thought, was for that afternoon. She couldn't imagine anyone at the bank responding to her loan request with anything but downright laughter.

By the time she took Gramps home, he was ready for a nap. She tried a light lunch, and then called the bank to set up a time when the bank manager might be free. The response was a sweet trill of laughter.

"Why, bless your heart, but you don't need an appointment around here, sugar. Just come on in. But before four-thirty, mind you."

That pretty much cut out any chance to procrastinate, so she headed upstairs and foraged for clothes. She had a work wardrobe from her Chicago job, but none of that was quite right. She needed lucky clothes. A feel-good blouse. A little jewelry, not pizzazz-y stuff, but maybe one of the gold pendants that had belonged to her mom. And makeup. Afternoon makeup, not going-to-a-party paint, but still. Serious lipstick. Tidy eyebrows. A wink of blue earrings, to go with the wrap-neck silk blouse, black slacks that were slimming and comfortable. She went so far as to force her feet into heels she hadn't worn since Chicago.

She'd barely walked through the front doors of the People's Bank of Sweet Valley before realizing she wasn't dressed fancily enough. The bank manager was a woman. Ginger could smell her perfume all the way from the manager's office, past the tellers, past the lobbies, to just about the front door.

It was a nice perfume. It was just sort of gobsmackingly strong. Lydia Trellace came out to greet her, wearing suede pumps and a two-tone suit. Her champagne coif had been shellacked so precisely that a tornado wouldn't likely bring it down. Diamonds winked from her ears, her watch was a whole circle of them and on a delicate chain at her throat she had another rock that likely made her neck ache by the end of the day.

Lydia's office had also been decorated within an inch of its life. No sterility here. Two massive vases of fresh flowers flanked the desk. On the walls hung a variety of oils, likely painted by locals—or flowers done by someone who had a heavy hand with pink. A pair of chairs was upholstered in a pastel tapestry print, and the carpet was a thick wedge of ivories and pinks.

"I knew when you said the name that you were Cashner's granddaughter, honey. Sit down and I'll pour you a little sweet tea. Tell me what I can do for you."

Ginger perched at the end of the chair. She'd rehearsed something to say at home. Obviously she couldn't come right out and beg for a couple hundred thousand dollars, with no collateral of her own, and her grandfather too not himself to provide any of the management or knowledge the tea plantation needed.

Still. Her stomach was steady. She'd been getting serious rest. She couldn't stop the stress cooker she'd been stirring around, but she hadn't had a dizzy spell since that first week in town.

She was ready, she told herself, but somehow she ended up blurting out, "Lydia, I need a bank loan for two hundred thousand dollars." The response from across the desk was a stunned silence.

Ginger didn't need a crystal ball to suspect the bank manager's response of speechlessness was not an auspicious sign. But once her request was out there, she had to follow through and fill it all in. "Lydia...it's not known in town or anywhere else, but I'm going to have a baby. I want to raise the child here, on the land that belonged to my mom, and her mom, and her mom. I wish I'd known my grandfather was having trouble coping, but I didn't, not until a few weeks ago." The room started spinning. She ignored it. "The farm needs work and money to make it viable, but there's every reason to believe that can happen. The tea plants are strong and sturdy. Until my grandmother passed away, the farm made a great living. It's a special place, not like anywhere else in the country. Once it's gone, all that heritage would be destroyed with it. It'll be at least a year before we can start talking any kind of return. But..."

"Honey, take a breath."

At some point in Ginger's long monologue, Lydia had reached for the desk phone. She called Ike. Who else? There was only one town doctor, and it wasn't as if Ginger could have cut her off at the pass. She wasn't finished talking. She just happened to finish her explanation from the carpet, which was plush enough to feel almost comfortable. The chair really had been spinning. The carpet was staying in place. As long as she didn't close her eyes for too long.

"Here's the thing. From your side of the fence...why would the bank want the farm? In today's economic times? What would you put there that could make you a solid investment? Houses? You know that's not a good idea right now. And the tea...the tea plants can grow for hundreds more years. It only takes a couple people—and of course, all the machinery, but we already have that—but overall, it's a low-cost setup. We can do this. It's a good investment. I know, I know, you're thinking I have no background in agriculture. That I've never spent time in the field at all. And you're probably wondering about Amos because none of this would work without a farm manager, but I think—I'm almost positive—I can get Amos to come around. The thing is, first I have to be able to tell him that we're a go. That the farm is a go. For that matter, I talked to Gramps's attorney. Obviously I can't do anything without having his power of attorney and all that—and I don't yet. But that will happen because it has to. Gramps really can't take care of himself right now or pay his own bills.

Amos is the one who said a hundred thousand, max of two hundred thousand. That's only because it'll take hand labor at the start. I'm sure you'll need a bucketful of paper and past records to give me a positive answer. I understand that. But I still had to initially talk to you, to find out if there was even any possibility of—"

"Ginger," Ike said calmly. "Stop talking. Open your eyes for a minute."

She'd already opened her eyes, the instant she felt his warm hands on her wrist, felt…well, she'd felt his presence. She didn't know when that happened. When she started just *knowing* when he was around. It was a primal thing. A sixth sense. A warming in her bones. A zooming in her blood. Even before she actually laid eyes on him.

"I'm fine, Ike." Except for last night showing up front and center on the big screen in her mind. All it took was looking at him. His being this close.

"Believe me, I think you're way, way, way more than fine." His humor was as wicked as his smile…but the smile faded awfully quickly. "I do think you're okay, Ginger. But we're going to have to do something about the stress load you're hauling around."

"I sure agree. Do you have a magic wand you could wave around, or something like that?"

"Not on me. I'm going to cart you over to the office, though. Do some blood work."

"I'd rather do the wand thing."

He didn't even blink. "We'll get the blood work done, then see if I can cook up a wand from somewhere."

He was so damned adorable. All that gentleness in his eyes, all that easy-don't-worry smile in his voice, all that sex appeal. Even when she was on the carpet.

In a bank. With nothing remotely sexual on her mind. "Ike, I need to finish talking to Mrs. Trellace."

Lydia abruptly showed up in her vision. Apparently she'd been standing by the door since Ike arrived. "Honey, you just go with the doctor now. You gave me enough information about the loan you want. I can put some questions and paperwork together."

"But—"

"There really wasn't going to be much more we could talk about today, sugar. I don't care how big or small the loan might be. I'd need time to work with a financial plan. You just go on with the doc now, honey."

Ginger started to sit up—or tried to.

It wasn't as if she had a choice—but that didn't mean she liked it.

Ginger liked being forced into anything like she liked Brussels sprouts.

Not.

Chapter Nine

When Ike walked in with Ginger under his arm, Ruby was sitting at the reception desk with a phone glued to her ear. She glanced up, took one look at him and then a fast, shrewd look at Ginger. That fast, she put a hand over the mouthpiece and started rattling off information. "I just put Mrs. Barker on hold. I can deal with her. Mr. Black went home, said he'd call you back in a day or so. Merline came up for her blood pressure check. One of those annoying drug people stopped by, wanting you to try their new antihistamine product, put those samples in lockup. George Moon's mother called, she's bringing him in, said he got into another fight and a kid hit him on the head with a rock, he's bleeding."

"Just another day in paradise," Ike said to Ginger.

"You don't have time for me. And I feel much stronger now," she told him.

Yeah. As if he was going to let her loose. He had her

safely tucked against his shoulder, and that's where she was going to stay until he had her upstairs. "We already did the 'I'm okay' conversation, so don't start. Ruby, I'm taking Ginger upstairs, need to do the vampire thing, then put her in a recliner by a telephone. Tell me when George and his mother get here, okay?"

"Will do. Nice to see you, Ginger, honey."

"You, too, Ruby. Although I'd appreciate you telling your boss that he's behaving like a Neanderthal."

Ruby put on a smirk and kept it there. "I totally agree with you, sugar. But you don't know doctors like I do—especially this one. There's no point in arguing over the little things, because your whole day'd turn into a quarrel. With all men, you need to pick your fights, dear. Sitting in a recliner for a few minutes doesn't seem all that bad, does it?"

"Sitting in a recliner is one thing. But what on earth difference does it make if I'm sitting by a phone?" Ginger questioned.

Ike responded to Ruby. "Ginger was just at the bank. In the course of a conversation with Lydia Trellace, she let out that she was pregnant."

Ruby sucked in a breath. "Oh, my." She glanced at the wall clock. "The whole town will know before four-thirty."

"So Ginger's likely going to want to call her grandfather pretty immediately. Get a correct story out there."

"I don't have a story. For heaven's sake. This isn't the Middle Ages. I'm not a scandal just because I'm pregnant."

Ruby looked at her fondly. "You must have forgotten that you're below the Mason-Dixon Line, honey. And Lydia, bless her heart, got an A-plus in plays well with gossips in the sandbox."

"But I don't care what Lydia tells anyone."

Ike slipped in a word. "But you do care what your grandfather thinks. And you don't want him hit with personal family news coming from outsiders."

That silenced her immediately.

Ruby stood up. "I'll bring up the blood tray. Anything else?"

"Nope. And I'll be back down as soon as George and his mom get here. That's all for the afternoon?"

"Martin said he'd stop by after work. No appointment. He wants another refill, thinks he can talk you into it." Ruby added something else, which Ike couldn't hear. Pansy must have suddenly realized he was home, because she let out a bloodcurdling howl of welcome and galloped in from the back porch to greet them, and then tried to trip them going upstairs.

He climbed behind Ginger, with his hands on her waist. He told himself he was worried about her losing her balance, but that was just a politician's truth. He was worried about her. That was more true. He'd already run tests, knew her numbers were terrific…but one way or another, she wasn't fainting again. Not on his watch.

And that was the real truth. Ginger was on his watch. He knew perfectly well that didn't mean as a doctor, but as a man.

He'd fallen for her. Every termagant ounce of stubbornness. Every leap-to-conclusions impulsiveness. Every born-to-argue gene. At the moment her face looked washed out, with none of her normal sassy color. Didn't matter. She was beautiful that way, too. That way. Any way.

"Park," he said, once he'd steered her into the living room and his old leather recliner in the corner. It wasn't a big room, but it had a balcony and enough space for both his leather couch and chair. The flatscreen was on the north wall. Wood blinds closed out the heat or the light when he needed to.

"Well, aren't you the bossy one. Maybe I don't want to sit down right now."

"You need a bathroom?"

"Oh, for Pete's sake. If I did, I could find it on my own."

She was extra crabby when she felt vulnerable. He'd thought that the first day he met her, but he knew it to the bone by now. She sank into the leather chair with a don't-you-mess-with-me-buster expression…but she'd curled her legs under her and leaned her head back about a millisecond after she sat down.

"Blood work first," he said. "Then when Ruby's gone, we talk."

She looked as if she was about to give him another argument, but Ruby knocked and showed up in the doorway with a blood work tray. After that, he started talking about how beautiful, how exotically unique, how breathtakingly exciting her veins were. Ruby started laughing at him, and that provoked Ginger into laughing, too. The blood draw didn't take him more than a couple of minutes, including asking Ruby to send it off to Charleston with his lab order. He did general testing in his own lab downstairs—but not for the fancy stuff.

Not for Ginger.

Once Ruby left, she immediately started talking. "Ike, I want to know what you're testing me for. Do you seriously think there's something wrong with me?"

He answered the question about the tests from the kitchen, where he poured a long glass of sweet tea for her and foraged for some crackers. He juggled the snack on a plate and set it on the table by the landline phone.

Then he hunkered on the ottoman in front of her. "And no, I don't think anything's wrong with you. I also don't like putting pregnant women through unnecessary tests, especially in the first few months. But we need to be sure you're not fainting for a health reason. I'm certain the reason is stress, because that's the obvious conclusion to come to. You're carrying the weight of several elephants on your shoulders. Ginger…"

She took a sip of tea, then snuggled deeper into the oversize chair. "I know. You think I should tell my grandfather about the pregnancy. But I don't agree with you. You know the shape he's in. The last thing I want to do is confuse him with any extra problems."

"I understand. And maybe you're right. But I think there is another way of looking at this. Cashner is increasingly lost in his own little world. You might actually help him by giving him something else to think about, to worry about. Something besides himself."

She fell silent with a frown, obviously considering that idea. He gave her a minute, then slowly pushed into the sticky area he doubted she wanted to talk about.

"Back to the stress subject. Sarah can help take cooking and kitchen chores off your hands. And we can get your outside work done, because Jed could make a jungle look like a manicured golf course. But I have the impression you're trying to save the world here. At least your grandfather's world."

She frowned again. "That's not true—or fair. Decisions have to be made. My grandfather isn't capable of coping. I have to make sure he's taken care of. And that includes what happens to the tea. I can't just leave Gramps with the mess he's in, and there's no one but me who can step in."

"I understand. But let's break this down into more

manageable parts. Do you want this baby, sugar? Yes or no."

She sucked in a breath. "Yes."

He said, lazylike, "You're sure."

"I wasn't sure before. But I am now. Yes."

"So you're not trying to jeopardize the pregnancy by taking on all those elephants?"

Her jaw dropped. "No, Ike. *No.* I didn't ask for any of these elephants. I came here and found them all in the living room, so to speak. I don't know what the right thing is about anything. But I'm trying to face the situation head-on, make whatever decisions have to be made. So if you're criticizing me—"

"I wasn't criticizing you. I think you're a trouper, doing great at figuring it all out. It's just…a ton."

"I know."

Since they were already swimming in murky water, he figured he might as well push a little deeper. "So," he said, "have you told the baby's father?"

She squinted at him. He was coming to think of that expression as her ornery look. He was trespassing where she hadn't opened any gates. "No."

"Why not?"

"Because when I took the first pregnancy test, it seemed too soon to tell anyone. I needed time to think about what I needed and wanted to do before going public. Especially with him. Calling him was never going to be easy. So I wanted my ducks in a row."

"So…that was then. But this is now."

He got another of those looks, and figured he was risking being slapped upside the head. But then…she apparently decided to answer. "This is now," she agreed. "And the man I thought I was honestly, deeply in love with…is probably on his honeymoon with the upper-crust lady he married."

Ike knew the story had to be upsetting. But from his viewpoint, he was relieved to get the past guy finally out of the closet and in the open. How could he know if he had an enemy, a rival or a saint until Ginger was willing to share what happened? "Okay. So he's a royal jerk. But if he's the father, he's the father. You have every right to financial child support. And I would assume he has every legal right to see the child."

Her arms crossed. "Exactly who's asking these questions? Ike the man…or Ike the doctor?"

"Damned if I know. All I know is that we need more of those elephants out of your living room. And this is the biggest one. Our being able to talk about your pregnancy. About your situation. Figuring out what those issues mean for you. And for me. And for us."

"Oh."

"Oh what?"

"I had no idea there was an 'us,' Ike."

Wow. That stab in the gut felt as real as a knife blade. Which was stupid. She'd come here, fresh from a hurtful relationship, doing a complete start-over of her life. She'd never implied she was looking for a serious relationship in any way. He'd come along; they'd slept together. What was this, the nineteenth century? He had no reason to assume she took the two of them as an exclusive pair.

He'd have to be stupid to think that way. She wasn't his girl. His woman. His fiancée. His significant other.

But damn it. He wanted her to be. All those labels and a few more.

"Ike, I can see you don't know what to say. I'm not trying to—"

"Don't sweat it." He knew how that sentence of hers was likely to end. No, she didn't want to hurt him. Yes, she wanted to give him a kick in the teeth…but she wanted to do it nicely. So he'd say thank you.

Thankfully, Ruby paged him. "Get down here, Doc. George is here and he's bleeding all over my desk. And the mother brought the baby and a neighbor's baby, because there was no other babysitter. And they're crying all over the place, too."

"I have to go downstairs," he said to Ginger.

"Of course you do."

"Just keep your feet up for a few minutes. This shouldn't take forever."

He wasn't sure whether she looked more relieved— or he did. But for damn sure that conversation hadn't gone well, and dealing with screaming kids had to be easier.

Pansy usually raised a fit if kids were in the place and she wasn't included, but right then, the turncoat looked perfectly happy leaning her full weight against Ginger's easy chair.

Downstairs…well. George was six. An extraordinary hellion. The kid was scrawny, so the other kids made fun of him, and George had seemed to decide in pre-school that he was resigned to regularly fight. Besides the ripped shirt, the kid had a face full of dirt, scuffed-up knees, a bruise on his cheek and a scrape cut on the back of his leg. Ike liked the kid from the get-go.

Virginia Moon, the mom, was one of those mothers who did the Rock. She couldn't stand still. She was too used to having a baby on the hip or the shoulder, so she automatically seemed to start that rocking motion. "The problem, Doctor, is that I can't even discipline him for fighting. Because he comes home hurt. And

Tom, that's my husband, he says a boy has to stand up for himself, and that's just what George is doing, so I should just leave him alone."

Ike finished cleaning the scrape-gash on the back of George's leg, and then plucked out a tray of assorted Band-Aids. The adults got the boring stuff, but the kids could choose from an array of cartoon and hero character bandages. George knew the drill. He knew where the lemon drops were, too, for the kids who did their best to be brave and not cry. Or cry. Whatever. A kid got a lemon drop if he wanted one.

Then came the problem of addressing tagalong babies. They weren't just crying to drive George's mom crazy, in spite of what she said. The one baby—the one that Virginia was caretaking—had an ear infection, so that mom had to be phoned and a script called in to the drugstore. Once the noisy bunch left, Ruby started closing up and Ike took on the aftermath cleanup.

Ike made it upstairs before five—just before—but as soon as he turned the knob he realized there'd been no need to hurry. Ginger was still curled up in his recliner, with Pansy sleeping at her feet. One of them was snoring excessively. It wasn't the redhead.

He stood, just looking at her for a good long while. Late-afternoon light was a pale wash of yellow, making her hair look brushed with pastel fire. She'd dressed extra businesslike for the meeting with the banker, but curled up, her black slacks showed off the soft curve of her hip, and the blue silky blouse showed her throat and the satin swell of her breast. The tidy hair…well, Ginger's hair was never going to stay sculpted back and tamed for long. Strands and curls were scattered on her cheek, her throat, her forehead.

There was no sign of the ornery Ginger right now.

The fighter. The obstinate, crabby, too-smart-for-her-own-good female who was giving Ike's heart and life fits.

She wasn't everything that was wrong for him now. She was sleeping. He could love her all he wanted and she wasn't likely to give him a lick of lip.

Pansy stirred, opened an eye and spotted him. She should have given a noisy howl of greeting and demanded a solid ten of petting and rubbing before going outside. Instead, the damned dog just put her head back down at Ginger's feet.

Contrary females seemed to stick together.

He was just about to push off his shoes, crash on the couch and just plain watch her for a while…when his private cell phone did a song and dance. He punched it fast, hoping the sound wouldn't wake Ginger, and hustled toward the kitchen, where she wasn't likely to overhear voices.

"It's me," the caller announced…which meant it was Tucker. Two weeks rarely passed without his older brother checking in, but that was before he'd gotten married.

"I hope you're not going to give me an extensive report on the honeymoon," Ike said. "I'm too young for those kinds of details."

"Hey, I gave you the birds and bees talk when you were nine, didn't I? If I recall, you threatened to throw up. You said the whole thing sounded gross and like nothing you'd ever do."

"Sometimes I think it's a good thing the parents were never home," Ike said wryly. "I'm pretty sure their lecture on sex would have been a lot more tame. But in the meantime…is your new wife leaving you for me yet? And how are the boys?"

"The boys are why I'm calling." Tucker already had a ten-year-old and had inherited an extra ten-year-old boy with his marriage. "I was wondering if you could take them on this weekend. Not the whole weekend. Just Saturday and Saturday night."

"You just got home from a honeymoon and now you already need more free time together?"

"Something like that. She has to do a thing with her parents. Her parents are, shall we say, challenging. If I go with her, it'll be better. But the boys would be bored beyond sanity—we could drag them, but…" Tucker suddenly paused. "Uh-oh."

"Uh-oh what?"

"You usually jump at the chance to corrupt my kid. The chance to corrupt two—and spend the night on Whisper Mountain—would usually get a fast yes out of you. So…something new going on in your private life? Don't worry about the boys, I can—"

"Of course I'll take the boys."

"There's only one little extra problem…"

"What?"

"A couple of kittens. It's pretty obvious to me that cats can stay alone for twenty-four hours, but the boys ganged up on me, claimed they're too little, the kittens have to come with the deal."

"You know I have to bring Pansy. And that Pansy is deathly afraid of cats."

"Your dog is deathly afraid of everything. Still. It's because I raised such a smart younger brother that I knew you'd be able to figure it out. Maybe the girl in your life could come along."

"What girl?"

"The one you haven't told me about. I can't believe it. Which one of the two hundred single women bring-

ing you casseroles and pecan pies finally wrangled you
into a date?"

"None of them."

"I should have guessed you'd have to import. Even
in high school, you liked a hot pepper a whole lot more
than you went for sugar."

"That's the most ridiculous thing I've ever heard." He
suffered Tucker's hounding him a little longer, without
telling him about Ginger, at least nothing more than he'd
told his sister. Considering how tight the siblings had
always been, he wasn't sure why he wasn't in a rush to
share everything about her. He had before.

But Ginger wasn't like any woman he'd ever had in
his life—or his heart—before. She was more precious.
The relationship more precarious. His damn heart too
unguarded.

Tucker eventually rang off. When Ike turned around,
he found Ginger standing in the doorway. Her feet were
bare. She looked as if she'd shoveled her hair, her cheeks
had a fresh pinkness, and she was almost smiling.

"I slept like the dead."

"Yeah, it looked like you were out pretty cold."

"For more than three hours, for heaven's sake."

He nodded. "It's the recliner. I swear, it's some kind
of narcotic chair. You turn on the TV, sit in the recliner
and that's it, instant sleep. It's a guarantee." And man,
he thought, she'd needed that serious nap. She looked
like herself again, full of perk and spirit.

She lifted her arms, did something with her swarm
of hair, clipped it somehow—but she was still eyeing
him from the doorway. "It sounded as if you were talking to family?"

"I was. Tucker. Tucker's the oldest, then me, then
Rosemary. Tucker just got married a few months ago,

turned into one of those blended families—he's got two boys now, age ten. And he wanted me to babysit them over the weekend."

"Of course you said no."

He lifted an eyebrow. "You might as well know now. I never say no to kids."

"I'll be darned. Who'd have thunk it? That you were a soft touch for kids and dogs and other vulnerable things?"

"I sense an insult in there somewhere."

She grinned, but it was a short one. "I'm going home. My car's still over by the bank, but it's a short walk."

"You need dinner."

"I do," she agreed, "but thanks to you, I really have to get home. I called my grandfather, and as usual, you were right. That's getting annoying, Doc. How often you're right. It's a very unlikable quality in any man. Anyway…Gramps was over the moon about having a great-grandchild. He was immediately charging off to tell Rachel. My grandmother."

Ike winced.

"Yeah, well…he was happy. No question. Never asked me who the father was, which seems a measure of how far his mind has gone. But honestly, I need to go home, see him face to face, see what's what."

"I understand." He did understand. He just didn't want her gone. He hadn't finished grilling her…and they'd left a serious conversation with thorns still sticking his heart. About how there was no "us." About his place in her life.

Or about the place he didn't have in her life.

"If you wanted to be a good boy, you'd drive me to my car. But it really won't kill me to walk three blocks—"

"Of course I'll drive you," he said, only to hear his pager go off.

She chuckled. "I should have expected that. Well, thanks for saving me, handsome." She hiked over, lifted up on tiptoe, brushed her lips across his. It wasn't an ultra long, ultra deep kiss. But it was long enough, deep enough, for her eyes to close, for the sound of a sigh to mingle with tastes and luxurious textures and the sweet, giving shape of her lips. And then she lifted her head.

She'd called him *handsome*. And she'd kissed him like a dream. And she smiled at him now with pure mischief.

And then she left.

He had to answer his pager. He had to let Pansy out for a serious walk. But for a moment he just stood there, thinking he was never going to survive a relationship with that woman. No way, no how. She messed with his head. There was no rest with her around.

The whole peaceful, stressless life he'd carved out so carefully—gone in a *pffft*. The minute he met her. And it was only getting worse.

When Ginger pulled into the drive, she immediately aimed for the kitchen. Earlier that day, she'd left cash and a vase of garden flowers for Sarah. Sara had taken the flowers, left the money and made some kind of cheesy-crusted chicken and a platter of roasted root vegetables. The baking pans were still sitting on the counter, so the boys must have already eaten. She heaped up a plate, grabbed silverware and carried the dinner with her as she searched for Gramps.

The evening was too cool to sit on the porch, so she figured he must be near the TV. Not. She checked his room, the library, the backyard, the bathroom. Still no

Gramps. Worried now, she climbed the stairs to the second story…and finally picked up the vague murmur of conversation coming from a distance.

The open door to the attic would have been a telling clue, if she'd had reason to believe—in a hundred zillion years—that Gramps could conceivably have climbed all the way from the ground floor to the attic.

"What are you two doing up here?" She was still carrying her plate, but it was mostly empty now. She set it on a dusty crate, narrowed her eyes at the boys. Both Cornelius and Gramps were settled in rocking chairs, talking like kids in a sandbox. Both rockers had spokes or parts of the seat missing, and likely a generation of dust on top.

"Sweetheart! I'm so glad you're home!" Gramps didn't rise from the chair or even try, just bent forward to accept her greeting kiss and hug.

"I've been looking all over for you two. What possessed you to climb all those stairs?"

"Well, I admit we're tuckered." Cornelius spoke up first. "But Cashner here was all excited at dinner. He recalled there used to be some things in the attic here—"

"A crib. A toy chest. A wicker basket. I didn't know what all, but I knew there was a heap of old baby things up here. And we found them. But then we both got tired after all the climbing and decided we'd sit a spell."

She turned around. Saw. The attic was lit by skylights and two hanging bald lightbulbs. In midsummer, a massive attic fan helped chase off the heat, but at this time of year, the space was just stifling and dusty. Ginger remembered fearing all the bogeymen up here—the ones waiting to come get her if she dared go to sleep.

There were no nightmares up here now—just generations of Gautier stuff that no one could seem to throw away. Suitcases and hope chests and steamer trunks. Antique clocks that didn't run, a Jenny Lind couch missing spokes, lamps missing shades. Every which way Ginger glanced, there was more.

And abruptly she spotted the bedraggled guitar case. It was her grandmother's old Gibson. Ginger hadn't seen it since she was a little girl. She crouched down to open it—when Gramps and Cornelius abruptly yanked her back to the present.

"Rachel! Come look at these things and see if you can think there's anything Ginger could use."

She straightened, turned to face her grandfather. "It's me," she said firmly. "I'm Ginger, Gramps."

"Yes, of course." He looked bewildered for a moment, then resumed his rocking. "Well, Rachel and I were talking earlier, sweetheart. She was thinking that the whole upstairs wing is bigger than the usual house. You and your husband and the baby could redo whatever you wanted, make it into a completely independent apartment if you wanted. There'd be room for the baby. And more babies. And more babies. And then they could grow up with the tea, like Gautiers all do. Be part of the land, their history." Cashner frowned suddenly. "Forgive me, honey, but I can't just this minute remember your husband's name."

Ginger pushed a hand through her hair.

"Well, it doesn't matter what his name is. It'll come to me. Anyhow, what do you think of that idea? Cornelius thinks it's as brilliant as I do."

Cornelius nodded from the far rocking chair, where he looked darned close to dozing off. She needed to get them downstairs. Separately. Both looked more frail than the heap of tattered lace hanging from a lamp in the far corner.

But as her gaze was drawn in that direction, she spotted the cache of baby things stored under a rafter. The crib was wood, and undoubtedly wouldn't meet today's safety standards, but beneath it was a toy box, painted with puppies and kittens and baby ducklings. Dirty now, but a true treasure. And the jewel of the lot was buried in the corner—a white wicker basket on wheels, with a crown of organza draping the sides.

It would have to be cleaned up, repainted, the old organza ripped off and a new mosquito netting sewn on to replace it…but Ginger touched the basket and felt a sudden clutch in her throat. It was so clearly a bed for a cherished baby princess. Her mom had snoozed in this basket, and her grandmother in the generation before that. It was so easy to imagine another baby in there, napping, all cuddled up, surrounded by all the family love and history and treated like the princess she deserved to be.

Or maybe it'd be a strapping boy this time—it was about time the Gautiers came through with some smart, sturdy boys. The netting might look a little sissy for a boy, unfortunately. But if the basket could just be cleaned and fixed, Ginger could so easily picture pulling the basket wherever she was, from room to room, so that baby would always be with her.

And just like that, she felt a burst of longing so fierce she could hardly breathe. She wanted the baby more than she wanted her own breath.

She pictured Ike. So far the only way she was keeping her head above water—barely above water—was on his charity. The cook. The gardener. The one to gallop in—maybe not on a white horse, but definitely with a bloodhound in tow—whenever she had a problem.

Only he couldn't save her forever.

She had to find a way to rescue herself. She couldn't talk about loving Ike, about being in love with him—not while she was a charity case. He'd been stuck with her because he was a good guy and she sure needed help. But neither of them would survive a relationship that was so one-sided.

She couldn't just take.

She needed to give, as well.

Chapter Ten

Ike finally pulled into his driveway on Sunday evening. He'd had a blast with his nephews on Whisper Mountain. They'd stayed up late, camped in the high mountain cabin, fished, ate junk food, told ghost stories and of course, made huge fires—everything the boys wanted to do. Everything he loved to do with them, as well…although Ginger was never far from his mind.

He'd checked his home phone and office phone and pager at least a dozen times over the weekend. There were messages. But none from Ginger.

He plunked down his gear from the weekend and headed straight for the shower, thinking that a few days of separation had likely been a good idea anyway.

If she didn't think there was an "us"—or any potential of an "us"—after all they'd shared, then just maybe he needed to cool his jets. He wasn't sixteen anymore. And even when he'd been sixteen, he hadn't panted or drooled after a girl who didn't give him a yes signal. Rejection wasn't fun then, and was even less fun now.

But that didn't stop him from thinking about her.

Monday morning, he woke up to a bright, sunny day and a serious case of determination. Mondays he tried to keep free. He'd see any patients who called in, but otherwise, Ruby had the day off and wasn't there to plague him about paperwork and files. He intended to enjoy the day or die trying.

Before nine, he'd stashed a fishing pole, a blanket and a picnic satchel complete with dog food and a water dish for Pansy. He had a plan.

The same plan he always had.

To not live the way his high-powered parents had lived. He and his brother and sister all had the same roughed-up sores from having parents who were wonderful, fantastic, extraordinary people…but who were never there. They were always too busy, too committed, always on call for complicated surgeries. Ike was the only one who'd gone near a medical career, but he'd done it drastically differently from how he'd grown up.

There was always time to put his feet up. To stick a pole in a creek. To take kids on a camping weekend. To crash in a hammock with a book and a beer after a long day.

"You and I understand laziness," he said to Pansy, who was rarely allowed on the front seat of the truck and was in her glory, riding with the windows down, her best guy next to her. Everything was right in their world. The dog leaned over and smooshed a wet tongue on his cheek.

"I know, I know. You love me. And I love you right back. And we're going to do nothing today. Maybe nap under a cypress tree. Fish a little. Chew on a bone." He glanced at Pansy. "Yeah, I brought you a bone. Made a whole separate trip to the butcher, just for you. But this time, try to remember to chew on it before burying it, okay?"

Pansy, judging from the adoration in her eyes, was willing to follow the entire day's plan without a single howl.

Only something happened. He couldn't explain it, but the truck developed a crazy problem. Instead of aiming south—toward his favorite fishing spot—the darned truck turned east. Ike couldn't believe it.

"What's going on here?" he asked Pansy, who by then had dropped her head to his shoulder and was already on vacation time, snoring between drools and dream snorting sounds.

The truck made another turn. Then another.

"This isn't happening," he told Pansy. "The GPS must be broken. Or the steering column."

Of all the damned…Ike scowled as the Gautier house came into view. For damned sure, he hadn't planned to see her. Or think about her. This entire day was supposed to be a playing-hooky agenda. He didn't want or need another slap in the heart from Miss Gautier.

He muttered a few more aw hells before parking and turning the key. He left the door open for Pansy, who wasn't immediately inclined to get out. Ike's gaze riveted on another vehicle in the driveway. A shiny black convertible. A rental, he could see from the plates.

An indulgent toy, that car. Wasteful. The convertible top rarely useable. Only two seats and no space. How impractical was that in real life?

Ike had always wanted one. They were just so damned…sexy. The immediate question, of course, was whom the car belonged to.

Since three days rarely went by without his checking on Cashner, Ike took brisk, self-righteous steps up the porch to the front door. Knocked, then poked his head inside.

"Just me!" he called out. "Just going in this direction, figured I'd stop by and sponge a mug of tea…"

It was his traditional greeting, and when he paused in the kitchen doorway, he put his hands in the air. In another life, he really could have made it as an actor, no matter what his family said. "Well, darn, I didn't realize you had company. I don't want to interrupt—"

"Nonsense," Cashner said, his response as predictable as sunshine. "Sit down, sit down. Ginger hid some of my best black teas, said I was overdoing it, but I've got a good green mint brewing. Steve, this is Ike MacKinnon. He's my doctor. And Ike, this is Steve Winters. He's here from Detroit."

"Chicago," the visitor immediately corrected.

"Yeah, I always get those two mixed up. Steve's waiting for Ginger. They worked together up north. Or they were both at the same hospital or something. He's a doctor like you. So I guess I can call you both Doc, and then I don't have to worry if I forget your names, huh?"

Ike got his own mug and poured his own tea—in case the stranger happened to notice that he knew his way around the Gautier place. Still, it took a minute before he could finally sit down and take a serious look at the jerk.

"So…where is Ginger?" he asked amiably.

"She just left a bit ago. Doing a grocery and bank run. I swear she left the drive about the same time Steve drove in. They could have passed each other. But anyways, like I told him, nothing in Sweet Valley is too far a drive. Ginger'll be back before lunch, for sure. I'd think before eleven."

"So you're Cashner's doctor," said the Chicago turd. "Sure am."

Ginger hadn't said the creep's name was Steve. But the father of her baby was a doctor, and she'd been in Chicago, and now the son of a sea dog showed up here out of the blue, and with that car. Ike didn't need a calculator to add up the clues.

The guy's external appearance alone was beyond offensive. Chinos with a crease. Loafers, the kind of butter-soft leather that had never seen an ounce of dirt or a puddle. A navy-blue polo shirt, short sleeves, the kind that showed off serious upper-body muscle and toned arms. The idiot was tanned.

Ike struggled to find something to like, but that was sure a tough sled. The guy had a shave so fresh the razor was probably still dripping. Square jaw. A smile that showed off lots of money in orthodontia. Eyes such a cool blue that he probably had contacts. Brown hair. Lots of it. Not straight or curly, just sort of thick and wavy. Had a Dartmouth class ring. Broad shoulders, clean-cut smile. The whole package was tall, lean, smooth. Oh, and cultured.

Talk about a scuzzball.

"You're a long way from your neck of the woods," Ike said. "Or do you have family or friends in this area?"

"No, no. Only one I know is Ginger. But she called me on Saturday night. And after talking to her…" Another of those blinding-white smiles. "Well, I hadn't seen her in a while. I knew she was from here. She often talked about the tea plantation, her grandparents. So…"

"So she's expecting you?" Ike asked, his voice reeking careless interest.

"No, no, it's a surprise. After talking to her…well, I got it in my head that I had to see her. Took a bit to make arrangements—"

"I'm sure it did. You're a surgeon?"

"Yeah, how'd you know?"

"I didn't. Or I guessed from something someone said. That you spent most of your time literally at the hospital, so it was easy to—"

"Yeah. Cardiovascular." He paused, as if making sure the importance of that sunk into Ike. Then he added, "And you're, like, the town doctor here?"

"Yes."

"Get a lot of scraped knees and flu and chicken pox?" Scuzzball smiled genially, as if to make sure Ike understood he was joking.

He wasn't joking. Ike understood full well that they might both be doctors, but in the jerk's view, Ike was low class and Scuzzball ruled the universe. *Maybe* he'd let Ike shine his loafers some day. *That* kind of smile.

Abruptly Ike heard a howl, then a growl of thunder, then the thunder of hooves. Pansy showed up in the doorway, wild-eyed.

"Oh, my God," said God's Gift to Women.

"Yeah, she's a bloodhound. C'mere, girl. It's just a little rain. Nothing to be scared of. And if you broke through Cashner's screen again, I'm gonna have to shoot you."

"She doesn't break through the screen anymore," Cashner said. "Ever since we put that different latch on the door, she can push it down herself, get in on her own."

Pansy, being Pansy, had to smell anything new in her realm, so she abruptly forgot about the storm the instant she spotted Steve. Ike watched the jerk's eyes widen.

Since a response was obviously required of Ike, he immediately said, "No, no, Pansy."

Pansy responded to serious commands—at least most of the time. Well, some of the time. In this case, she was too busy to listen and put out her big old wet, drooling muzzle and sniffed up Steve from ankle to knee to leg and—almost—to crotch.

"Oh, my God," Steve said again.

"Aw, man. I'm so sorry." Ike slowly stood up. "Pansy. Go lie down. How could you do that to a visitor? Hey, I'll take care of it." He ambled toward the sink, soaked a dish towel, brought the sopping cloth back. "It does dry. Won't look so much like snot when it's dry—"

"I'll do it." The perfect smile slipped. Suddenly there was a little acid in the eyes, a narrowed look, as if Scuzzball was starting to realize he wasn't exactly among friends.

Outside, there was a sudden burst of noise and commotion. A car door slammed. Pansy started a joyous howl and tail thump. Cornelius's voice mingled with the sound of Ginger's laughter. They seemed to be arguing about who was carrying in the grocery bags—and both of them were winning.

The commotion only took a few seconds—but long enough for Ike to figure out something he didn't want to figure out. If Scuzzball was here, after a phone call with Ginger, then she'd likely told him about the pregnancy. And if he responded by showing up, it didn't sound likely that he thought his relationship with Ginger was over and done with.

Ginger charged through the back door, carrying a couple of light sacks, and almost fell when Pansy rushed to greet her. Cornelius, just behind her, carted an overflowing grocery sack that appeared to be splitting. A ball of lettuce fell, bounced on the floor. Then a small bag of oranges.

Ginger was still laughing, but she seemed to forget the groceries altogether when she looked up. Her eyes went soft. "Ike," she said, and probably would have said something more—until she glanced around the table and recognized Scuzzball. She did a double take. "Steve? Why on earth are you here?"

"We needed to talk."

"We did talk."

"On the phone. I knew we needed to talk face-to-face."

The minute she put down the two sacks, her hand flew to her stomach in a protective gesture. "Maybe we do. But I wish you had called before showing up here."

"Honey," Cashner said, "I think you're not being very welcoming, especially when someone's come all this way to see you."

Ike blanked out most of that awkward chitchat while he debated his options.

He could knock the guy's block off. For sure, that was his favorite choice. He'd never had much violence in him, but for Scuzzball, he could manage some serious steam.

A second option was to stay quiet, but maneuver himself carefully between Ginger and the jerk. Just to make sure nothing happened that she didn't want. To protect her. Or to tell Pansy to attack, if all else failed. Pansy wouldn't have a clue what that meant, but the jerk would be distracted.

Ike liked all those options. Except for the one option he really, really didn't want to do.

Ike didn't sigh, didn't kick a chair, didn't do anything to indicate that he was not happy. "You know what?"

he asked, in a loud enough voice to garner attention. "Cashner and I are going for a little drive. Maybe get some lunch. We'll be back here, say, in an hour and a half. Max."

He wanted to look at Ginger. He wanted to talk to her, wanted just a few minutes—even one minute, one short minute—before he left her alone with the bozo. He could even feel her eyes on his back…but nothing he wanted seemed remotely relevant just then.

It took energy and persuasion to get Cashner to his feet, to steer him from the kitchen, find a light jacket for him, find his shoes, get him outside and into the truck. There was a light rain falling by then. Cashner was not of an age to be comfortable climbing in and out of a truck. And then there was Pansy.

Pansy, of course, wanted to go with them. Pansy couldn't imagine Ike leaving in the truck without her. But handling both Pansy and Cashner in the front seat was impossible, besides which he wanted her with Ginger.

Pansy gave him The Eyes—the desolate, abandoned, sad eyes—when he told her to stay.

Somehow by the time he started the truck engine, he felt as if he'd run a marathon. Dark clouds scuttled in front of the sun, changing an overcast day into an ominously gloomy one. Cashner didn't care. Once he finally settled himself in the truck, he was all about an outing. Happy as a clam, he said in a conspiratorial whisper, "Did you know Rachel and I are going to have a baby? Can you believe it? She's over the moon!"

Oh, man. It was going to be a long hour and a half.

Talk about feeling deserted. Cornelius peeled out the back door almost as fast as Ike hauled Gramps out the front. She was stuck not only with Steve in the kitchen, but a disconsolate hound trailing every move she made—and sacks of groceries to put away, most of which were perishable.

"I still don't understand why you're here," she repeated. She stashed milk, butter, cheese and eggs in the fridge, then closed the door to face him again.

He was just as good-looking as he'd always been. He had the same intelligence and perception in his eyes— qualities that made him an outstanding surgeon. It was just a shame he didn't have as much perception and intelligence in his character. He didn't look ill at ease now. He never looked ill at ease. Steve could walk into any place, any group, and never fear he couldn't handle himself.

"Did you think," he asked, "that you could just call, tell me you were pregnant and think I'd have nothing to say after that?"

Ah. One of his best tricks. Putting her on the defensive. "I absolutely expected to hear from you. But not yet, and not here. I know my telling you about the pregnancy had to be a serious shock. And I assumed you'd want time to think. Not that you'd suddenly show up here."

The next grocery bag held freezer stuff. Peppermint-stick ice cream. Peach-and-cream frozen yogurt. Blueberry-swizzle ice cream. Double vanilla.

This past week, she'd somehow wanted ice cream with every meal. Even breakfast.

Since Steve didn't immediately comment, she filled up the freezer, then turned around, looked at him and zoomed straight to the counter for a mug of fresh tea. "It was all right with what's-her-name that you came down here?" she asked.

"Audrey. We broke up." Steve hadn't budged from his chosen seat at the head of the table. His gaze tracked her as relentlessly as Pansy did. "I missed you."

Okay. So this meeting never had much potential to go well, but now she was pretty sure it was going down ugly. She sat at the far end of the table with one hand on her mug of tea and the other on Pansy...who finally quieted once she could lean against Ginger.

"Nothing was the same after you left," he said with the same searing look in his eyes that she'd once taken for sincerity. "I was more or less pushed into that engagement. It was a joining of families, schools and ties we'd both had forever. It wasn't about feeling anything for her, the way I did for you. The way I still do feel for you."

It was all she could do to not toss the hot tea on his head. To not give him a good piece of her mind, including expletives and swear words and a good loud tongue-lashing. She'd always let loose when she was angry or upset.

But this time...well, this time was just different. She couldn't put rain back in a rain cloud. The milk had already spilled, the egg had cracked and all those other metaphors. She wasn't angry with him anymore—which was a strangely reassuring realization.

He just didn't matter enough to waste her temper on. Steve, though, seemed encouraged that she wasn't giving him more lip. "Having a child together changes everything. I always thought we had a lot going for us—until I messed it up. I know I hurt you. And I'm sorry. I know it'll take time for you to forgive me, to trust me again, but—"

"Hold it." Not expressing her temper was one thing. Listening to his drivel was another. "This child is yours.

I expect support from you. And I expect to listen if and when you put out a plan to be part of the child's life. But those aren't issues for today. We don't need to talk about those things for quite a while."

"I want—"

"I don't much care what you want," she said pleasantly.

"Love doesn't just die, Ginger—"

"Oh, yeah, it does. The man I fell in love with didn't exist. I saw qualities in you, character in you, that weren't real. You're smart. You're a brilliant surgeon. There are lots of reasons why a child with your genes has every chance to turn into a terrific human being. But to love or trust you again? Never. You'll cheat the first chance you get. No matter who you marry."

"That's not fair."

"I'm not interested in fair. I'm not interested in having any more conversations with you. The only tough thing for me was deciding whether to call you and let you know about the pregnancy. I decided I had to. That you had the right to know. But I'll never have a relationship again with you, Steve."

"We were good together," he began.

"We had pretty good sex—when it conveniently fit into your busy schedule. At the time, it never occurred to me that everything we did revolved around your needs, what you wanted—but you don't have to hit me over the head with a bat twice. I got it."

"Losing you changed me. Changed how I thought about love and what I wanted in my life."

She refrained from a noisy, inelegant snort. But barely. "Are you losing your hearing? I don't care."

Some of that rotten character he kept hidden so well finally showed through. "You think I'm going to pay child support without any say in the child's upbringing? You'd better think again. I could sue you for full custody and get it."

She glanced down. "Pansy, did you smell a threat in the air? Or was that just gas?"

"You're not funny."

"Go home, Steve. We can have many civil conversations in the years ahead about the baby. But there's nothing pleasant either of us has to say to each other today."

The charm, the coaxing and endearing expression on his face that she knew so well, slipped off. His eyes turned glacier. "I have more financial resources than you could in a lifetime, and more connections than you could ever dream of. If I want custody of the child, Ginger, don't doubt for a minute that I can get it."

She'd been holding her own, feeling sure of herself until then. Nothing exactly changed. She'd figured out that he was a rat before this. But it still hurt…that someone she'd cared for had such an ugly side. That she hadn't seen it before this. That she'd given freely of herself to someone who could turn around and treat her like dirt.

Maybe it was a crazy moment to realize she'd fallen in love with Ike.

The current mountain of trouble on her head…she'd never really doubted that she could claw her way to the top of it. She was strong. She'd always stood up on her own two feet. She'd never wanted to ask a man into her life out of need.

But once all the trouble was sorted out—if that wildly crazy magic was still there with Ike—well then, she was likely to go after him with all she had.

She hadn't known that was the plan, the goal, her heart's dream…until she lost it.

Steve had put her down in a way that she'd never thought she could be put down. She'd chosen once upon a time to give her heart to him, a man with this much venom in him. A man with no respect for her, or respect for what she'd given him.

A man who made her feel small.

She felt like a flower that suddenly closed up tight to protect against frost.

Chapter Eleven

When Ike brought Cashner home, the first thing he noticed was that the black Eclipse was nowhere in sight. That wasn't absolute proof the jerk was gone, but it seemed a good sign.

He pulled up next to the porch, making it easier for Cashner to negotiate the path from his truck to the door, and then hustled around to the passenger side to help him out.

"I want to check your blood pressure before going home," he told Cashner.

"You just want to see my granddaughter. And get your dog."

"Right on both counts, but we're still going to do the BP."

"You're a pain, Ike. I don't know why I like you," Cashner grumbled, but his cheeks were pink. The fresh air and outing had done him good.

He stumbled getting out, but Ike was right there, and Cashner regained his balance almost immediately. Ike glanced around, not exactly looking for Ginger, but definitely expecting Pansy to give out a howl of a hello.

Nothing. Nada. Not a sound. Once inside, he settled Cashner in a kitchen chair to check his pulse and blood pressure. Both numbers were good. Cashner wasn't a spring chicken, but the only thing really wrong with him was a fading mind.

"I think I'm going to hole up for a little rest, Ike."

"Good idea. I'll track down Pansy, and then we'll be on our way. You're doing great. Let's do another outing like that soon."

"You bet."

Cashner was already yawning as he waved a goodbye and ambled toward his room. Ike did a swift pivot, trying to figure out from the clues in the kitchen where Ginger was. A single sandwich plate sat on the counter, an opened bag of Oreos next to it. A water dish sat on the floor—with a place mat under it, forcing Ike to chuckle in spite of himself. His dog wasn't exactly a tidy drinker, but he'd never thought of using a place mat to control the slobber.

Ginger knew his dog. And his dog loved Ginger. But no clues he'd seen so far were enough.

He hiked through the dining room, the hall, poked his head in the living room. It wasn't as if he was worried about either one of them. He just wanted to find Ginger, preferably in the next three seconds. He needed to know how the powwow with her ex had gone. He wanted to know if Mr. Flake needed to be tracked down and given the punch in the jaw Ike had been playing and replaying in his head. He wanted to know if she was okay.

Only by accident did he glance out a side window in the back hall. An old-fashioned hammock was tied between two tree limbs, swaying in a winsome breeze. It wasn't hammock weather. It was jacket weather—and it had been damp this morning besides. But there was a foot hanging out of the hammock, with some kind of shoe that tied in a bow.

And below the hammock was his dog. Pansy was sleeping, which was nothing unusual. But she seemed to be sleeping with—almost—her entire head in an empty ice cream container.

No wonder the dog hadn't roused when he got here. Pansy always had her priorities straight. Ice cream came above all else.

He slipped outside, down the step, past the magnolia tree to the two oaks. This wasn't the first time a hammock had been tied between the two trees—the hammock looked almost as old as they did. He crouched down to stroke Pansy's head, which motivated the dog to immediately roll over to demand a tummy massage.

Ike had an eye-level view of Ginger from that angle. She'd put a red blanket under her, zipped up an old white fleece jacket, brought out a poofy pillow for her head and pulled a light blue blanket over her. The foot sticking out was clad in an old-fashioned sneaker, a crazy green-and-yellow plaid with a bow for a fastener. She had a little foot. A delicate ankle. And in spite of the mounded blankets, she looked no bigger than two bits.

His gaze wandered up…the humid air had made her hair curl up, making him think of a cinnamon-colored steel wool after being hit by lightning. Her face, skin that bruised far too easily, was lighter than cream and that soft mouth was beyond-temptation kissable…at least it was for two seconds. But then he realized she'd opened her eyes.

"No," she said.

"Why are you saying no? I didn't ask you a question."

"I'm just saying no, this isn't fair. I am very, very tired of you always seeing me at my worst."

He cocked his head. "You don't seem your worst to me. In fact, you're looking pretty darned edible."

A vulnerable flush climbed her cheeks, but she was still sending out a Ginger scowl. "I meant your stopping by when Steve was here this morning. Your taking Gramps out so he wouldn't hear an argument. Your saving me. Your thinking I needed saving. Your coming through."

"Damn. I can sure see why you'd be annoyed at me for that. Did you have a good nap?" He had to try changing the subject, since his being a nice guy and a good friend seemed to temporarily disgust her.

"A great nap."

"I always sleep great after having ice cream, too. Who had more of that half gallon, you or Pansy?"

"We didn't eat a whole half gallon! There was only a third of a gallon in there! And we both needed ice cream. It was a stressful morning."

"I hope it was even more stressful for your visitor." He added genially, "I was glad to get a look at him. Helped me get an idea what kind of guy appealed to you."

She pulled the blanket over her head. "Go away. I don't want to talk to you any more today."

He tugged on the blanket, then gave the edge to Pansy, who was more than willing, always, to take a length of blanket and run with it. Once the thief had her loot, she sank yet again on the ground to snooze, leaving Ginger blanketless—although she still had on the white fleece jacket and old chinos. And those shoes.

"You know who Steve reminded me of?" he asked.

"I'm afraid you're going to tell me."

"My parents."

"Say what?" She started to sit up, with the obvious intention of getting out of the hammock, but when Ike saw the empty space, he plopped down next to her.

The hammock temporarily rocked precariously—there was a serious risk of both of them being dumped on the ground—but eventually it settled down. As far as Ike was concerned, his settling next to her was an ideal position, because their hips and shoulders were glued. A fair number of her body parts were trapped against him, just as a fair number of his were against her.

Life was good.

She shot him a look. Okay, so they weren't exactly all that comfortable. But he was next to her. For a few minutes he needed her attention. So having her snuggled against him was still a bonus.

"I know I already mentioned that my parents are both surgeons. If you met them, I know you'd like them. They're not just brilliant at what they do, but they're devoted to their patients, to saving lives. They make no end of sacrifices to save those lives."

She squirmed once, trying to find a less glued-on-him position, but really, the hammock had them trapped close. She lifted her head. "This may amaze you, but I don't have a clue what your parents have to do with Steve, other than they're all in the medical profession."

"But it's what first drew you, I'm guessing. That he was a great doctor. The kind of person who sacrificed to save lives. And who does save lives, doesn't just talk about it."

"Well…" She hesitated. "Yes, you're right. I did admire him. Some doctors get a frosty reputation with other hospital staff, but Steve was decent to everyone. No temper tantrums. No arrogance on the surface. No God complex that anyone saw."

"I think," Ike said carefully, "that high-powered people, driven people, the really seriously high-achiever people…just have some things in common."

"Like?"

"Well, you can't say a doctor's selfish when he sacrifices so much for his patients and gives up so much of his personal time. But that skill becomes more important than anything else. More important than a spouse or kids or anyone else in their personal lives. Maybe…" He hesitated. "Maybe there's some glory in being so special, so different from so-called normal people. I don't know. But I do know they expected other people to cater to their needs."

He waited.

And waited some more.

She'd given up battling for distance, and instead, just leaned her head against his shoulder and gave in to the closeness. He couldn't see her expression, but she was listening.

"Well, that was very like Steve," she said finally. "The glory thing. If he was in a hurry, he expected others to get out of the way. If he was a no-show, he expected others to understand. It didn't seem egotistical to me…until I finally realized that's how it always was. His life was more important than anyone else's." She added wryly, "I thought you'd be pretty disgusted by the four-hundred-dollar loafers and no socks."

"What? You think I'm that superficial that I'd give a damn what the guy looked like?"

"No, no," she said immediately.

It's not like he'd ever admit that Scuzzball's whole look—and good looks—had given him a heart attack. Ike didn't give a damn about appearance issues like that. But if they mattered to Ginger, well, it wouldn't have been a good sign. "So," he said, "somehow I suspect he showed up to talk you into going back with him."

"He did."

"Since he didn't call you first, he must have been afraid you'd say no. He thought he was more likely to persuade you, if he saw you in person."

She hesitated, but then her response was quick enough. "Yup. You're getting all the square pegs in the square holes."

"And…then what happened?"

"In a nutshell…I said no, I wasn't going back with him. He insulted me. I told him to leave. He threatened me. I lost my temper." She shrugged. "Just your everyday melodrama."

She apparently wanted him to see the humor in it… but he didn't. It just seemed like one more traumatic thing thrown at Ginger when she'd had a nonstop heap of them in the last month. "So…I'm guessing the subject of the baby came up?"

"Oh, yeah. Which, I have to admit, threw me. Obviously he was unsettled when I first called and told him. But I just assumed there was no reason to have another conversation until after we both had time to consider all the implications. Instead…well, it didn't take long for him to go on the attack. I mean…I told him upfront that he had a legal right to be part of the child's life. But instead of being nice back, he seemed to get more angry. He threatened to sue me for total custody."

Ike had another mental picture of himself punching

out the jerk. But he kept his voice even, not wanting Ginger to stop talking. "What happened after that?"

"That was pretty much the end of it. He left, and Pansy and I galloped straight for the ice cream."

She fell silent after that. He wanted to know more, but she'd answered the one killing issue that had been rug-burning his nerves. She was over the hotshot doc. Maybe the breakup had been fairly recent, but Ike hadn't heard a hint of warmth in her voice, seen any in her eyes.

And since she'd gone limp on his chest, he relaxed, too, just let the hammock sway in a slow, lazy rock. The sun tipped past a cloud, warmed their heads in spite of the damp chill in the air. A bare breeze ruffled the grass, sifted the scents of wet leaves and somewhere, a brush pile burning. A dog barked in the distance, not loud enough to wake Pansy, just a canine greeting its owner from some other property down the road.

"Ike?"

"Hmm?"

"I don't want to say anything about your parents, because I've never met them. Or any more about Steve, because I've had more than enough of talking about him. But…" She hesitated. "I can see the other side of the fence. People who have the gift and the skill to save lives, to stand up for people who can't help themselves…that's a great thing, not a bad thing. But it also makes them different, whether they want to be or not."

"So what's your point?"

She put a palm on his chest. "The point isn't about my ex-guy or your parents. It's about you. You have those same issues. Your pager is always on. That's who you are. It's a good quality. Not a bad one."

"I'm *nothing* like them. I'd never put my job over a spouse or kids."

"Yeah? Well, I've been with you these last few weeks. When the pager makes noise, you're on your feet in two shakes. You go. You don't think twice. You don't need to. It's just who you are."

"Ginger. It's not the same thing. I'm a low achiever, not a driven type in any way."

"Uh-huh."

"Hey. My exam rooms don't have clocks. I wear sandals in the office. The dog goes with me on house calls. Does that sound like someone with a high-stress gene?"

She made a sound. He had a bad feeling it was a chuckle. "Ike, I don't care whether you wear wing tips or sandals. You still run when someone needs you. You're dedicated and you're driven. That's just the way it is."

The hammock quit rocking. "You know, you can be really annoying," he mentioned.

Instead of taking offense, she leaned forward and looked at him with an amused expression. "That's the real problem, isn't it? Because even when you're annoyed…like now…you still want to kiss me."

"More than kiss you," he immediately corrected her.

Out of nowhere, she turned into an estrogen grenade. "Damn it, Ike! Did it never occur to you that that's what I want, too? Only there's a huge difference between what I want and what I can have! And you're just making it harder!"

She took off from the hammock and stomped to the house, going out of her way to let the screen door slam behind her. He stared after her, dumbfounded.

He was the one who should be mad, not her. He was the one who'd been offended, not her. It bit like a steel trap that she'd compared him to Scuzzball Steve…and, for that matter, to his parents.

"Pansy. Go truck." He didn't snarl, because he never snarled at his dog, but the dark, snarly mood followed him the whole rest of the week.

Ginger thought he was *driven?* That he wore the "dedicated" halo that her egotistical ex did? Not. Never. He'd been called to medicine, yeah, but he didn't have a driven bone in his body, and had done everything but stand on his head to avoid a pressure-cooker practice.

His parents valued their reputations, their status. For damn sure, Dumbo Steve did.

Not him. It hurt. That Ginger didn't know him better than that by now. And all week, he made a point of choosing attire that reflected his true personality. Frayed chinos. Shirts dug out of the back of his closet, the ones where you could see threads in the collar—if anyone looked, but why would they? They were soft as butter, old friends, still had plenty of wear in them.

He saved on shaving cream for seven whole days, too.

He saw Ginger all week, because that's how it was in a small town. You had to be careful about having a fight, because you couldn't avoid running into anyone for long—like at the bank window, in line at the grocery store, driving into a gas station just as she finished filling her gas tank.

They waved.

He fumed. He'd get around to talking to her again. As soon as he figured out what to say—and really, that wasn't particularly tough. It was true, he carried a pager.

True, he lived with interruptions all the time.

But in his heart, his life, he believed that family came first. If a patient was in a car accident, yeah, he'd let that interrupt breakfast. But if someone he loved needed him, then that mattered more than a patient calling for allergy medicine. It was about balance. The balance his parents never had. The balance her ex wouldn't understand if it bit him in the butt.

By the following Tuesday, Ike had finally simmered down. He even let a few of her comments leak through his rock head. She'd admitted wanting him. She'd just said she couldn't have what she wanted.

How come he hadn't remembered she'd said that before? That he could handle. Midmorning Tuesday, between patients, he put in a quick call to Sarah.

She answered, sounding crabby and tired—the way she always did. "How're the kids?" he asked first.

"They're for sale. The youngest is cheapest. But you can name your price."

He laughed. "That little squirt's my favorite, you know. I take it you're having a time-out kind of morning?"

"Yeah. I used to give a time-out to the kids. Now I give myself a time-out, sit on the porch with a cup of coffee, let them tear up the house while I get a break."

"Good thinking." He cleared his throat. "Sarah, I called because I need to ask you a favor."

"You know I owe you the moon. Whatever it is, it's a yes."

"Well, I have an idea. But to make it work, I need someone—not me—to gang up on Ginger. Would you be willing to bully her for a good cause? Seriously ruffle her feathers?"

"Are you kidding, Doc? That'll probably be the most fun I'll have this week."

That was exactly what Ike hoped she'd say. And for

the first time since the quarrel with Ginger, he felt his spirits lift. Not soar, but lift.

You couldn't win a war—or woo a woman—without weapons. He'd forgotten what a fighter she was. But then, maybe she didn't realize that he was a fighter himself—especially when it came to someone he loved.

Ginger thought she heard the back door slam, but Gramps and Cornelius were at the senior center for the whole morning. She'd used the promise of quiet to turn the dining room into a temporary office. The house had two offices and a library, all of which had desks, but none with a space as big as the dining room table.

Since that dreadful morning with Ike, she'd buried herself in paper, all tidily organized in heaps. There were piles of tax records, expense records and agricultural resources on tea. The next group had lists of historical buyers. Tea tasters. (Who knew there was a degree in tea tasting from certain universities?) Then came the corral of folders. A folder for investment strategies, another for monthly spreadsheets, cost basis, market graphs, profit and loss projections.

At the moment, she was pretty close to crying—not because she was overwhelmed. She'd worked in hospital administration, so she knew how to develop projections and put a plan together. It was just that the dynamics of an agricultural enterprise were worlds different from a hospital setup.

Besides which, she needed to know everything all at once.

She had a clear goal, had figured it out the morning they'd argued. There was no thinking about Ike until her life crises were fixed—which meant that she needed to create a business plan to take to the bank. She needed a presentation that would knock Lydia Trellace's socks off. She needed the numbers to be true, the ideas defensible—a plan that she could defend up one side and down the other.

And she'd been studying all these files of information for days. She just didn't have a plan together yet.

A thud and a swear word in the kitchen made her jerk her head up. A clatter of pans followed.

"Who's there?" Ginger rose to her feet in a scatter of paper.

"Who do you think's here? How many people do you have cooking in your kitchen, anyway?"

Ginger immediately relaxed. She'd have known Sarah's surly voice anywhere, even if she rarely saw the woman. She searched through the heaps of paper on the dining room table, found one of her empty teacups and carted it into the kitchen.

Sarah glanced up, but continued banging and clattering and slamming.

"I've wanted to tell you for ages how much I appreciate your cooking. You're so good. I've loved everything. So has my grandfather."

"Huh. No surprise there. I told you I could cook."

"Um…smells good in here already."

"Not likely. I haven't opened a single package yet."

It was like trying to talk to a porcupine. Yet Ginger liked her…possibly because she could be a wee bit like a porcupine herself sometimes. "I've been leaving you fresh flowers from the garden and some cash. Somehow you always leave the cash."

"Should be obvious. I'm no one's charity case. And I'm paying off my debt to the doc. I didn't ask for anything more than that." Sarah shot her a look.

It was the only look she ever gave her. Annoyed.

Roll the eyes, couldn't believe how stupid others were in the universe, generically disgusted. Today she was wearing dark gray twills and a steel-gray sweater. The clothes washed out her face, but they certainly suited her personality.

Then she turned around, and started slamming things on the counter—including a menacingly sized knife. "Could be," she said spritely, "that I thought it was about time someone told you a thing or two. Since you appear to be dumb as a rock, bless your heart."

Ginger blinked. "Um, you're offering me advice?"

"Advice you shouldn't need." Sarah took some round steak from the refrigerator and started beating it with a mallet. It seemed an ideal occupation for her. "Way I hear it, you got to do something about the farm. Got to do something about your grandpa. Got to do something about the young 'un in your belly. And you got Amos Hawthorne in a snit, which seems something you're unusually good at. So…"

"So?"

"So, where were you raised, girl? You're in South Carolina. When you want Southerners to do something, you feed 'em. That's how it's done. How it was always done. How it always will be done."

"You mean like…have a party?" Ginger couldn't fathom the idea—much less the cost of feeding a large number of people.

"I don't mean an ordinary party. I mean a *tea* party. Don't you know nothing about your own upbringing? You treat people like dirt, they act like dirt. You treat people like you care about them, they care back. Can't very well be mean to you if you put on all your manners and Southern charm for them." Sarah stopped pounding. "Assuming you have charm. I haven't seen any of it, myself."

Ginger was thinking. "It's not a bad idea. But honestly, I don't see how I could afford to…"

Sarah snorted. Finished pounding the round steak, and started cutting up potatoes as she'd had experience with a machete in a war. "I know you're a college girl, so I try to forgive your ignorance sometimes, but I swear it's a challenge. Everything isn't about money. You do the tea. Jed, now, his wife makes the best lemon meringue pie you ever ate. The Feinsteins that run the deli, they can make finger sandwiches to die for. Not free. Not them, they wouldn't do nothing for free. But you could think of something you could do in trade— like stock their restaurant with your best teas for a while. And then there's Ruby."

"You mean Ike's Ruby?"

"I know. She dresses a little floozylike. All that color and makeup. But honey, she could straighten out the Middle East if anyone ever had the brains to give her the job. You got all those fancy teapots and containers all over the house. You could put on a party like no one's ever seen. Ruby'd know how to do the decorations, the invitations, how things should look. You'd just have to ask her."

Ginger kept thinking she already had too much on her plate without adding another responsibility. "I love the idea. I really do. People have been great to our family over the years, and just as wonderful since I've come home. But…I can't see how to throw a party just to ask people for help, or for money—"

"Thank the Lord your grandmother never heard you say that." Sarah put butter in a huge cast-iron frying pan, waited until the butter was spitting hot, then dumped in the potatoes with the same violence with which she did everything else. "You don't ask for anything at the party. You never mention money. You just do the party and be a hostess. They'll be waiting for you to ask for money, because they know you need it. But you don't. You just smile and make 'em feel welcome and be gracious."

"Gracious," Ginger echoed.

"You don't have more than a bump, but I'd still go buy a maternity top, because you'll look more helpless. This isn't a time to look strong. This is a time to look delicate. You buy it in a color that's light and soft. You know. Something that's nothing like you. Something a sweet woman might wear."

Ginger leaned an elbow on a counter. "Is it some kind of challenge for you? To insult me every few minutes?"

"Challenge? It's no challenge. You're as easy to insult as anybody I ever met. Course, I don't enjoy insulting just anybody."

Ginger got it. That Sarah was giving her a compliment—an exceptionally back-door compliment—but an expression of friendship nonetheless. She shook her head. "Would you mind my giving you a hug?"

Sarah recoiled. "I got work to do here. Kids waiting for me at home. No time for any more talking."

"Okay, okay. I'm going back to work, too. But…if you want to bring your kids with you, I just want to say they'd be welcome here. Lots of yard to run around in. A lot of steps to run up and down and make a lot of noise. Wouldn't bother anyone here."

Sarah responded with an impatient, "Hmmph." Ginger figured that was the nicest thing she'd said so far in the whole discussion, and headed back to the dining room and her business headaches.

But Sarah's tea party idea hung in her mind, took frame and shape until she couldn't let it go. It was a good idea. Her first instinct was to run it by Ike…but she quelled that impulse.

Ike had helped her more than enough.

Chapter Twelve

Two afternoons later, when Ike pulled into the Gautier driveway, he told himself he'd waited as long as he possibly could. He never failed to check on Cashner less than twice a week. And Sarah had related how Ginger had bought the tea party idea, so naturally he wanted to see how the plans were coming along.

Besides—if he waited any longer to see her, he was likely to go out of his mind.

Above him, a pitiful excuse for a sun had finally shown up—he wasn't complaining. In the rainy season any sun was better than none. Still, it was cool as he hiked up the porch steps, did his brisk double rap on the front door, and poked his head in. "It's just me. Ike. Checking in."

The time was going on four. He'd wanted to come earlier, but a young man with a bad burn had taken a major bite from the afternoon.

Cashner called out a greeting from his bedroom in the back, where Ike found the boys sipping sweet tea and swearing over a canasta game. The small bedroom TV had a court show on, but both men could talk over it. "It's a horrible thing when a grown man has to hide in his bedroom. We've lost control of the house, Ike. The shame is almost more than either of us can handle."

"Oh, the pitiful goings-on around here." Cornelius picked up the song, accidentally filching a card from the pile as Ike pulled out his blood pressure kit.

"What's so terrible?" Ike said nothing about the cheating. They both did it, every game; it seemed to be their favorite part of playing together.

"It's all about the party next week on Tuesday. Ginger's got the whole household in an uproar."

"What party?" Ike asked in his most innocent voice.

"The *big* party. I think I first heard it was a tea party, but then I heard it was potluck. Doesn't matter to either of us what it is. The problem is, she's cleaning everything. It's not normal. If you sit down anywhere, she'll be scrubbing you with bleach or assaulting you with a vacuum. It's a bad thing when a man can't find peace in his own house. And she wants me to wear a bow tie."

"Oh, no. Not that."

Cashner whispered, "She's having more fun than I've seen her in a long while. Not the worst thing, having to dress up. But don't tell her I said so."

He checked Cashner's blood pressure, pulse, the sore right shoulder, made sure the sweet tea wasn't spiked, glanced at the medicines to make sure they were being taken. All that took no longer than two shakes of a lamb's tail, and then he was free to track down his redhead.

He found her in the middle of the living room, in a cyclone of a mess.

The Gautier living room was long enough to bowl in, but the kind of place that a kid—especially a boy—was terrified of. All the wall space was taken up with china cabinets and sideboards and casework furniture and breakfronts. Ike couldn't remember the proper furniture names, but basically all the pieces had glass fronts, for the purpose of displaying tea stuff. There were at least a hundred zillion teapots, and even more zillions of little bitty cups and saucers.

It looked to Ike as if a man could break things if he failed to tiptoe…and Ginger had all the glass doors open. Card tables were being set out, and were covered with all those millions of teapots and zillions of the cups and saucers and paraphernalia.

He hesitated in the doorway, thinking that an elephant would be stupid to risk walking any closer. Besides, he wanted a look at her before she spotted him.

Temporarily, she was on her hands and knees, her head almost buried in the lowest shelf of some kind of credenza. She'd scooched her hair back at some point, but strands and curls had done a jailbreak and were tumbling every which way. She'd lost her shoes; her socks were the color of dust, and she was wearing an astoundingly large Clemson University tee—so big Ike figured the garment had room for triplets in the ninth month. Not the sexiest attire he'd ever seen, but it struck him that way.

It was her, of course. She could cover herself from head to toe. She could dye her hair purple. Paint her face in tiger stripes. Wouldn't matter. His blood started sizzling, just from looking at her.

"Hey, Red. Got a minute?"

Her head popped out, swiveled toward the sound of his voice. A brilliant smile of welcome greeted him first…but faster than a snap, the smile dimmed to cordial. The tilt of her head, her sudden careful posture reflected that she wasn't as easy with him as she'd been before. Now there was wariness, defensiveness. Pride.

He knew damn well he'd caused the change.

"To be honest, I really don't have time," she said. "You must have heard about the upcoming tea party— not just because you got an invitation, but because your Ruby's been a godsend at doing a lot of the organizing."

"Yup. I've been hearing about it somewhere around sixty times a day. Ruby was beyond thrilled that you included her in the whole arranging." It helped, Ike mused, that so many people had gotten involved. Hopefully she'd never guessed that he'd sneaked the idea to Sarah behind her back. He motioned around the room. "So…what's all this about?"

She sighed. "The whole idea of giving a tea party was about inviting the community to see what the Gautier Tea Plantation is about. You can't give a serious tea party without serving it with the appropriate china. We have a museum-worthy collection here. But—I don't know how—somehow it all got mixed up. The pattern of teapot should be with its matching service pieces. Instead, they're all over the sam hill place."

He didn't give a damn about china patterns, but she was talking to him. Naturally talking, the way she had before. "Could you use some unskilled labor?"

She looked at him, and then laughed. "I wouldn't mind some help, but honestly, Ike, I don't think you could handle this."

He didn't bristle. Didn't take offense. Ginger had

ways of putting him down that no other woman ever had, but hey. He had tough skin. "Try me," he said.

She chuckled again, then lifted her hands in a give-in gesture. "You can try, if you really want to. But it's okay to cry uncle and beg off when you've had enough."

He'd do that—cry uncle—on the day it rained moonbeams. "Just tell me what you need me to do."

"Okay. You asked. The china just has to be matched... the teapot with the same pattern service pieces. Each pattern is different, see?" She lifted one to illustrate. "This is called Old English Rose, dates back to nineteen forty. This one is Rose Chinz and this one's Pansy. You can tell them apart, either by looking at the flowers—you know roses from pansies, right? But there's also a signed label on the bottom of each piece."

"This is supposed to be tough?" He figured they'd have this licked in ten minutes flat.

The song on her cell phone temporarily interrupted any further conversation. She tracked down the phone in the front hall, and from what little eavesdropping he could manage, he guessed she was talking to the bank manager.

Once she used Lydia's name, he realized it was a serious call, so he dove into the grunt work. Right off, he realized that sorting the patterns was only half the job. All the dumb dishes would have to be washed. They weren't germ-dirty, just plain old dusty, so he scooped a bunch on a tray and carted them into the kitchen. Piece of cake, he figured.

He rooted under the sink for some dish soap, started filling the basin, then went back to get another load of cups and stuff. Ginger was facing the far window in the living room, still talking—he couldn't make out the words but she didn't sound stressed, so he headed back to the kitchen.

The first cup he pulled from the soapy water to rinse was somehow broken. Chipped in two places. He looked at it in horror. Then pulled out another cup—and found the handle broken off.

For Pete's sake, he'd been careful. He knew china stuff was expensive. In itself that didn't matter, because he'd replace it no matter what the cost. But to let Ginger think he'd been careless with something important to her?

Guilty as a thief, he wrapped the two broken cups in paper towels and buried them way deep under the trash. He checked the rest of the china in the soapy water. All okay. But he still jumped half a foot when Ginger entered the kitchen.

"That was Lydia Trellace on the phone," she said immediately. She came up behind him, saw what he was doing and foraged for a fresh linen dish towel to dry. "I gave her a proposal for a business plan a few days ago. She called to say that she'd talked to Louella Meachams—that's Gramps's attorney. Apparently I have to go to court—through Louella—to get legal and medical and financial rights over Gramps's life before we can really deal with the farm plan. Lydia said that Louella said that wouldn't be a problem. It just has to be done. She couldn't give me a yes or no on the business plan until then. *Sheesh,* Ike."

"What?"

"You really did a ton of work during the short time I was on the phone."

"Hey, I'm not just a pretty face."

That started her chuckling. "You're coming to my tea party, aren't you?"

"That depends."

"On whether you have patients, or whether you have to dress up?"

"Why would I have to dress up? I could come, and just say that I was fresh from some medical emergency, so that—"

"Nope. No excuses. I'm talking real shoes. A shirt with a collar, preferably white. Dark pants. Haircut. Shave."

He looked at her, aghast.

"I know it's tough, but just like you said, Ike, you're not just a pretty face. You're more than capable of going the long mile."

"That's just mean," he grumped. "A white shirt? I don't think I own a white shirt."

"It's a *formal* tea."

They were bickering like married people, he thought. Her being bossy. Him making out like dressing up for her was an imposition.

He reached for her—not in a big physical way, more like pulling her into his arms for a dance. A slow dance. Married pairs had that advantage. They could use sex to tease their partner into a better mood, to offer a smile, an argument, a sense of fun, a sense of wonder— everything and anything—just not with words. With touch.

She knew that slow dance. Her arms slowly slid around his waist. She tilted her head up. His lips fit just right on hers, no frantic crazy rush, no push, just the kind of soft kiss that evoked memories. He knew her lips. She knew his. He knew exactly what made her eyes close. She knew exactly what knocked him to his knees.

And she did. Knock him to his knees. It was the way she yielded, the way she shared, the things she promised, the things she feared. She opened her heart to him with her kisses. Making it impossible for him to stay sane or sensible or careful.

But then she stepped back, opened her eyes, took a long breath and said softly, "I can't do this, Ike."

"Can't do what?"

"Love you. Be in love with you. When this whole town knows I'm in trouble."

"The town has nothing to do with us." He wanted her back in his arms. And she was close enough to grab her, to pull her in. To claim her again. But the anxiety in her eyes stopped him.

"You've been rescuing me since I got here. And I sure as sam hill needed rescuing. You're a white-knight hero through and through, Ike. But I didn't know, at the start, that I was going to end up living here. Or that the whole town would be watching us, have eyes on us."

"I couldn't care less."

"I know. You don't care what people say. And I wouldn't normally, but there's a difference between us. You're already a hero for them. So if I stayed with you—especially once my stomach started to seriously pooch out—if you even considered marrying me, they'd assume you were doing the right thing. I'd be stuck with the role of damsel in distress. Only I don't do damsels. I need to build my own reputation, my own way. I need to earn respect, Ike. Theirs. And yours."

"You're nuts, Red. I do respect you."

"I'm not sure of that. I don't know how to be sure of that. You've seen me at my worst, over and over. But I haven't had one chance, even the slightest chance, of being at my best when I'm around you."

He frowned. "Ginger, you don't need to change anything about yourself, in any way, for me to respect you.

I don't know how I could have given you any other impression."

She was so ready with her response. "Unlike all the other doctors in our lives, Ike, you don't put yourself first, ever. You put others first. But right now, I feel I'm lumped in with those others. If you want us to be together, in any way, I want to stand next to you. I don't want to be carried by you."

Well, if that wasn't the dumbest thing he'd ever heard. But when he opened his mouth—not that second certain whether he wanted to talk or kiss her—his pager abruptly went off.

He said hoarsely, "Just hold for one short second." He listened to the message, feeling his gut squeeze acid-tight, looked miserably at Ginger as he punched it off. "It's a kid. Practicing football after school, collapsed out of the complete blue. I—"

"Get out of here. Right now. I don't need the details. Go."

"Ginger—"

"I told you. I totally get it. You need to go. But I need you to understand me the same way. I have to stand up on my own, Ike. I'm not ashamed of making mistakes. But I can pick myself up. I can't be a leaner."

"You're not." But then…damn it. He had to go. "It's a kid," he said again.

As if giving up trying to talk to him, she just motioned him toward the door.

When Ginger climbed downstairs, it was twenty minutes before the guests were scheduled to arrive, and she was more nervous than a trapped mouse. She'd checked everything she could check, prepared everything she could prepare, but she still wanted to give it all one last run-through.

She stopped at the antique mirror in the front hall. Except for the worried eyes, nothing looked wrong about her appearance, at least yet. She'd opted for a soft ivory top and her grandmother's favorite pearls, the knotted single strand. The black slacks didn't button anymore, but no one could see that under the loose top. Subtle makeup was obviously the only choice for a formal tea party, but she'd done her best to make her hair behave with a pair of ivory combs—also her grandmother's.

The toughest thing to shape up had been her hands— all the cleaning had destroyed her nails—so she'd been stuck wasting time on a manicure that morning.

Good thing, since Gramps insisted she wear her grandmother's cameo ring.

That was another lucky omen—or so she was determined to believe.

She traipsed around the downstairs, fretting, checking, fussing.

Gramps and Cornelius were stationed in chairs at the front door, both wearing white shirts and bow ties and shined shoes. They had two jobs: to greet everybody and to behave. They couldn't wait.

Outside—just to make the party more worrisome—a storm hovered over the coast, bringing swirling winds and ominous dark clouds. Ginger turned off overheads, switched on soft lamps in every room. This morning the house had been crazy-busy, with people showing up to help or bring food or participate in any way they could see.

Ginger had been stunned with all the help. She hadn't felt part of the town since she left years ago—she'd believed then that she was leaving, for good. It was startling to hear that folks considered her one of theirs.

Still, she'd set up most things herself—because she needed to. Every space in the downstairs had a function. Every room had different displays. The living room had a station for a formal Japanese tea ceremony, where thick cushions were placed on the floor around a low, round inlaid table. In the opposite corner, an old card table had been judiciously draped with red velvet, where Ruby—when she got here—was going to "read tea leaves."

She glanced out the front door side windows again. No Ike. No one yet. She pivoted around and started prowling again.

The front hall had a massive display of various tea implements—like yixing teapots and infusers, tea cozies and the *guywan,* which was the Mandarin Chinese word for the traditional tea bowl with no handle. A collection of caddy spoons and sugar tongs was displayed on ivory felt. Lydia Trellace had sent over four massive bouquets of fresh flowers. Louella Meacham had literally sent over a man, whom she'd hired to participate in the washing and later cleanup.

By accident, Ginger glanced outside again, just in case she might see Ike driving in.

Still, there was no one—just more clouds and gloom, more thunder.

Well, she had more to check on. Specifically the food—the most terrorizing threat to put together. The kitchen was set up for a breakfast tea—strong black tea, Gautier Breakfast blend—augmented by pastries served with local wild berry spread and a cherry French toast casserole, sliced in small squares.

She'd used the library to set up a traditional afternoon tea—which meant it was by far the most elaborate. There were a half dozen choices of fragrant teas—all Gautier-grown, of course—and then tiers of accompanying food choices: cucumber and cream cheese finger sandwiches, fresh fruit, lemon meringue pie and strawberry tarts, scones and clotted cream. Since she'd done all the last-minute arrangement less than twenty minutes ago, it didn't look any different than the last time she checked.

A flash of lightning in the west made her jump. It was five minutes to four. What if no one came? Where was Ike? What if they lost electricity?

What else could she find to worry about?

She touched, straightened, fussed. There'd been no place left to set up an evening tea, so she'd just shaken out an Irish linen tablecloth and used some of her favorite teapots with the oolongs and greens. Everywhere she could, she'd set out little parchment cards for those who wanted to know more about tea in general, Gautier tea specifically, or anything and everything about tea customs. Truthfully, all that prep had been fun.

She still thought it was a good idea, for the guests to be able to mill around from setup to setup, not be trapped in any one spot. They could sample as much or as little of anything they wanted. She'd wanted to illustrate what her family had been up to for the last couple hundred years—the teas, the culture, the background and tradition.

Would Ike be proud of her? Or would he be bored out of his mind?

What if everyone was bored?

"Would you stop fussing?" her grandfather grumped. "You look beautiful. The place looks beautiful. There's enough food to feed an army. A big army." He glanced out. "And there we have it. The first car's coming up the drive. And oh, my. I'm afraid there is a pile of cars coming all at once."

She flew to the window. Gramps was right. Cars were turning into the drive, filling every spot on the driveway and onto the side. Naturally, the sky took just that moment to open. Rain came pouring down, sloshing down in noisy buckets. People ran, raincoats over their heads, all laughing as they came inside.

But still no sign of Ike.

A frenzy followed. Thirty people must have kissed her in the next few minutes as she greeted them and took their wet coats and showed them around. She tried to put Ike out of her mind. He'd never promised to be early. He could have been caught up with patients. And it wasn't as if she needed him. It was just that once, just once, she wanted him to see her as a capable woman and not such a needy one.

The house filled up…and then filled up to nearly bursting. Ginger kept watching the door, not just for Ike but for Ruby—who'd been so excited, and planned to dress gypsy-style, as she played the role of reading the tea leaves.

And just that second she saw Ruby pelting through the door—hustling two strangers with her.

"I was worried something may have happened," Ginger said as she took Ruby's jacket—and got a wet hug in return.

"Something did happen. Ginger, I want you to meet Ike's mom and dad. They just arrived unexpectedly. They're on their way to Charleston, hoped to visit a bit with Ike—but Ike is nowhere to be found. I couldn't track him down. So—"

"I'm *so* glad you brought them. Dr. and Dr. Mac-

Kinnon, I'm delighted to meet you!" That was honestly true—although Ginger felt a fresh qualm of nerves after all Ike had told her about his parents.

The nerves didn't last long. Ike's parents were as easy to be with as old friends. Walker MacKinnon was ultra tall, with keen eyes and a tenor voice. June had glossy auburn hair and sharp blue eyes and a gorgeous smile. They were wearing traveling clothes, comfortable shoes—good quality all, but nothing pretentious or fancy.

"Delighted to meet you, too, dear." June took both her hands in greeting. "Thankfully Ruby filled us in that you've been seeing Ike. He never said a thing to us."

Ruby added, "His last patient was at two-thirty. One canceled after that. It's the last I've seen of him."

Walker added, "I hope we're not intruding. We could have waited at Ike's place. He's bound to come home sooner or later. So if we're in the way—"

"Nonsense. I'm absolutely delighted you're here. Please come on in, make yourself at home…."

They were nothing like she'd expected. They'd met many of the townspeople before, were equally friendly to rich and poor, young and old.

Walker admitted, "We don't often call before coming to see Ike. I'm sure that seems odd. But his reality is the same as ours. We're all so busy. So if we get a few days free, we generally try to get away, pop in, see if any of the kids have time for us. If we call ahead, then the kids feel they have to do something, clean, get in food, make a fuss."

"I think it's a great idea. And Ike should be coming here…so it makes great sense for you to just relax, enjoy yourselves."

An hour passed. Then almost another. Nothing went

as she expected. First, because she never dreamed so many people would show up, be so interested. And then because she assumed people would wander around, stop out of curiosity, take in some food, be on their way. Only no one left.

Nothing could possibly have gone better...except for Ike's absence.

And then, just before six, an unexpected visitor arrived who changed everything.

When Ike ushered out the last patient for the day, he hit the ground running. He had a plan—a plan he'd been refining and revising for days. The first step was to unlock the back garage where he kept the Volvo—the truck was his regular vehicle because of Pansy. But the cherished old Volvo was his baby.

His siblings had teased him to no end about Volvos being cars for fuddy-duddies. He'd thought so, too, until riding in this one. The engine purred, she loved curves and she hid a whole lot of passion and power inside the modest exterior. Last time she'd been out, he'd been doing a favor for Tucker...that was a few months ago. She wasn't that dirty, but he still washed and polished and rubbed her to a sheen.

That took longer than planned. Unfortunately, he didn't get back upstairs to his place until after four. He'd never expected to be early for her tea party, anyway. He wanted to be late.

He needed to be late. He wanted everyone to see what he was doing. He wanted to prove—to Ginger, to anyone who happened to look—that he wasn't with her out of kindness or responsibility. He was certifiably, hopelessly in love, desperately hooked, crazy about her.

Next, he took a good shower, did a serious shave,

then went the extra mile. He had shirts, but he'd still bought a new white one, one that looked starched and formal. Did the real shoes thing—the kind that actually had to be buffed. Chose pants that weren't jeans or chinos.

That took another heap of time. Who knew he was normally such a slob?

He couldn't find the guy cologne. He knew he had some somewhere, but it was past five now, and he still wasn't done. Then there was the tie issue. He'd worn a tux for his brother's wedding, but otherwise hadn't had a suit and tie on since…hell, he couldn't count that far back.

Still, he had a tie collection at the back of the closet, most dating back to high school or college or Christmas presents from relatives he didn't know. Every single one was ugly, but he had to pick.

By the time he drove through town, hardly anyone was about. Ike figured they were all at Ginger's by now. Ruby had certainly spread the word far and wide, and the whole town had developed an interest in Ginger, in what she was going to do about her grandfather, about the house and tea farm. The coming baby, everyone knew about. All the work she'd done—everyone knew. They knew about her conniving Amos Hawthorne into working for her again, knew about her fainting all over town, knew about the Scuzzball showing up unexpectedly. They hadn't shown up for tea. They'd shown up to show her exactly what she needed to know.

That she was valued. By everyone who'd come to know her.

He wanted to show her that he valued her, too. But in a different way. A very different way.

The next stop was the florist. Naturally they closed

at five, but Rhonda White had arranged to wait for him, met him at the back door in the alley. "You know how much this is going to cost you, sugar?"

"I know. I don't care."

"She's going to love it."

"Could you promise that?"

"Don't you worry. She is. Trust me."

It took a huge number of roses to fill up a car with petals. Who knew? And because Ginger wasn't much on pink, he figured he should get coral. Or that's what Rhonda called the color.

After that, he had to stop at the jeweler's. That trip, thankfully, only took a few minutes.

The rain had finally stopped by the time he pulled into her drive. He was shocked at the number of cars—must have been a hundred people inside. The last he knew, Ginger was inviting somewhere around thirty. Ruby'd said that no one wanted to be cut from an invitation so she'd "slightly" altered the original plan. But they weren't all supposed to come. People always canceled.

He parked in front of the porch—double-parked, truth to tell—but he had no other choice. He had to be able to get in and out. Fast.

Chapter Thirteen

Ginger was running on fumes. The party was a success, by any standard she could measure, but her nerves were frayed. It didn't matter if everything had gone wonderfully. The potential for disaster was still very real and all too possible.

She needed the party over, the doors locked, the lights off and the chance to hide under a table where no one could find her.

Instead, the craziest thing kept happening. Guests started to leave…but within minutes of exiting the house, they came right back in. They'd find her, beam, say they "just couldn't get enough" of all the tea lore and "were having such a wonderful time."

She introduced everyone to her father, of course—although she still hadn't recovered from the shock of his showing up. Heaven knew there was no point wasting any surprise on her dad—he'd always come and gone, all her life, on his whim.

He'd walked right in and loved the party. No surprise there, either. Her dad's black Irish looks—blue eyes, cream skin, a thick head of dark hair—were still extremely attractive. He also had charm to spare and a way with the ladies. He introduced himself to everyone as Sean, Ginger's father—as if he was a Gautier by birth. He'd always loved his association to the "landed gentry" status of her mother's family.

Some of the seniors in the crowd knew him from a long time ago, but no one let on there had ever been a problem. Wherever he walked, wherever he stopped to talk, there was laughter—a brash of laughter, smiles, someone being hugged or touched.

Ginger would have survived the visit just fine, except that Ike's parents—Walker and June—quickly strode over to meet him, which was enough to give Ginger a near heart attack. Where was Ike? How come she got stuck with parents on both sides when their meeting had so much potential for disaster?

Her dad could be irresistibly charming, but it was doubtful he could spell *ethic* even with a dictionary, and for certain he had no clue what a responsibility was. Sometime between his first effusive hug and Gramps calling him "John," he'd mentioned being "a little down and out" and that he'd put a suitcase upstairs. Ike's parents had overheard him. So did others.

Which probably meant the whole town knew—in three minutes or less—that the scoundrel was back in town and likely hitting up Ginger for money.

Abruptly she noticed her dad heading for the living room—both Lydia and Louella were in there—which meant there was a risk of some serious harm. She spun on a heel, planning to go after him, when Amos and his wife—who'd just left the party—abruptly reentered through the front door.

Amos's wife looked at her, shot her a big grin and a thumbs up and a wink.

All right. Ginger had no idea why the guests were behaving so strangely, but something seemed to be affecting them when they went outside. It was hard to guess which was the scariest crisis—her father and Gramps's attorney in the same room—or checking out the scene outside. Probably because she was desperate for some fresh air, she decided to whip out on the porch for a minute.

She'd barely opened the door before a swish of silk covered her eyes.

"Don't be scared. It's not a robber or a murderer. It's just your personal kidnapper."

"Ike…" Of course she knew his voice. She felt his hands tying a knot behind her head, trying to secure the silk blindfold. "I don't understand—"

"Everybody's in on it—so you don't need to worry about leaving the party. Ruby's got a whole committee to do the shut-down and cleanup."

"But what—?"

"Nothing's going to happen that you need to worry about. I just need you to come with me, be with me."

She couldn't get his attention. "Ike. Your parents showed up."

His hands stilled.

"And then my *father* showed up, out of the complete blue. I haven't seen him in more than two years."

He finished the knot. "I want to meet him."

"Maybe you really don't." She never meant for him to hear a quaver in her voice. She hadn't realized it was even there. It was just…she'd so badly needed this day to go well. It wasn't about the tea party. It was about feeling competent, competent on the inside. Maybe the lawyer and the banker and everyone else involved would end up saying no to her. Maybe she couldn't save the tea farm. But she needed to give it the lion's try, for the community and Ike—especially Ike—to see that she was more than a young woman with problems, that problems didn't define her.

It all just caused a quaver, that's all.

And Ike must have heard it, because he suddenly snugged the silk blindfold on tighter. "We'll deal with parents another time. Right now we have far more serious priorities. Like your kidnapping. If anything goes wrong with this, I'm afraid the whole town will blame me."

"You're making me uneasy—"

"Good."

"Ike!" Okay, she couldn't help but laugh. "If you think you're kidnapping me, what's the ransom?"

"It's extremely expensive."

"How expensive?"

"All the marbles." His voice…she didn't know what was in his voice, but it made her suddenly shiver. He'd been steering her, hands on her shoulders, blindfold secure, down the porch steps, into wet grass that tickled around her ankles. Probably ruined her shoes, too, but she didn't care.

This was crazy. Goofy. But for the first time in a long time—since they'd made love, she suspected—she felt her heart lighten, not because it was empty, but because it felt full. Full of love and hope both. Full of anticipation. Full of…

Happiness.

She couldn't remember the last time she'd thought that word, much less felt it.

He opened a door, but it didn't sound like the creaky truck door…and suddenly there was a scent. The soft, velvety, unmistakable scent of roses. Everywhere.

"What—?" she started to ask.

"I'm afraid where we're going is a little drive. Under two hours, so it's not that far…but far enough away that no one in town will know where we are. Now…"

Ike was still talking, but she was too distracted to pay attention. He steered her into a car, the passenger seat— but a passenger seat that had been adjusted to a lie-flat position. When he closed the door—obviously to come around to the driver's seat—he'd secured her seat belt.

He started talking again, the moment he entered the driver's side, but temporarily her senses were consumed with textures and scents. There weren't just roses in the car. There were rose petals. Heaps and heaps of them. Her passenger side was a mattress of velvet, unbearably soft petals, the scent alluring and unforgettable.

"I knew this wouldn't work," Ike was saying, "if you were worried about your grandfather. So I set up a group of people to check in on him, be with him, from Sarah to Amos to Lydia—all of them volunteered. Then I know you're worried about the business plan, the loan…and that you have legal issues you're waiting to hear about, like medical and legal powers for your grandfather, so that you can pay his bills, protect his interests. Louella had a word with me yesterday— you know her, she wouldn't give away your secrets or cross any ethical lines. She just made it bluntly clear that you won't have trouble getting what you needed. And again, on your grandfather, old Doc Brady—the doctor I replaced? I'm sure you knew him from when you were a kid. Anyway, Doc Brady and Stephie, his retired nurse, will both be on call for the next few days. No strangers. No one your grandfather doesn't already know and feel comfortable with…."

She pulled off the scarf and turned her head to look at him. Really look at him. She'd never seen him nervous before, but he was. His fingers were drumming on the wheel, couldn't keep calm. And there was a rose petal on his shirt, another in his hair.

He looked darned silly with a rose petal in his hair.

"Where we're going is Whisper Mountain. The MacKinnons have always had a place there. Actually, we have a couple of the places, but there's a cabin up on the highest ground. Pretty rustic, so don't be expecting too much—but we'll be alone. No anxieties, no intrusions, no interruptions. My sister Rosemary's been hanging there for quite a while—since she broke off an engagement—but she's taking a month off right now, doesn't need the place in any way. She's got Pansy, if you wondered, so don't be worried about that, either—"

"Ike." She wasn't sure he was going to stop talking. If he was even capable of stopping. As far as she could tell, he hadn't even stopped for breath.

He glanced at her, noticed she'd taken off the silk blindfold and shot her a worried look—but his gaze was drawn immediately back to the road. The pavement snaked in wildly sharp curves, too dangerous for a driver to look away more than seconds.

"There's a legend about Whisper Mountain," he said. "You'll laugh, it's that corny. But there's a legend that the mountain whispers—really whispers. But the only people who can hear it are those in love. I haven't a clue how the story got started, but even my great-grandparents—"

"Ike," she interrupted again, this time in a soft, low voice.

This time he heard her. Shot her another quick look, worried look, but had to return his attention to driving.

"Now don't object until you've seen it," he urged her. "It may be rustic, but it's not—"

"Ike, I don't need to hear a mountain whispering to me. I already know. I love you."

"Just go with—what?"

"I love you. With all my heart," she said simply.

He jerked the car so hard she feared they were diving straight down a mountainside. But Ike, being Ike, pulled them both out of trouble. For a couple seconds there, though, he was in an extraordinary fast hurry to stop the car.

Ginger woke up slowly, feeling more luxuriously rested than she had in weeks, just wanting to snuggle deeper into the pillow and blankets. For long moments, she didn't open her eyes, just savored the scents and sounds and textures around her.

Warm sunlight blessed her closed eyelids. The smell of pines and cedar drifted close; even closer was the crackle of a cherrywood fire, the softness of a down pillow, the whisper of cinnamon and roses in the air....

Only...

She didn't have a down pillow. There were no pines or cedar trees anywhere near her bedroom, and she couldn't imagine a reason in the universe for how or why she could be smelling cinnamon.

But her eyes popped open when she caught the scent of roses. The scent of roses was real for her in every way.

She shot up on an elbow, wide-awake that flash-fast, and took in the rest of the unfamiliar room. Rustic cedar beams. A slanted ceiling. The four-poster bed she'd slept in was bigger than a boat. Across the room, a stone hearth had a grate full of sharp orange embers, and a tidy stack of fresh cherrywood on top. The top blanket covering her was a handmade quilt—it had that heirloom sort of look—and the wood floor was varnished, shiny as a mirror.

Nothing was familiar. Even remotely.

Except for Ike.

He was reading, from a giant-size upholstered rocker by the hearth, his stocking feet up on an ottoman. Maybe he'd slept, but it didn't look it. He was still wearing the white shirt he'd had on yesterday. He'd pushed off shoes, at some point brought up a tall glass of something, and his chin sported a fresh crop of whiskers. Now, too, she could see drifts of roses, one on a sock of his, some on the floor, some on the blanket…a regular Hansel and Gretel trail, leading from her.

To home.

Ike was home.

"Hey, kidnapper," she murmured. "Did you sleep at all?"

His head shot up. He immediately put down the book, and once she could see his face, she knew the answer. The intense lines on his brow, the gray shadows under his eyes…no, he hadn't slept.

But his answer was a simple, "I got enough." He didn't move, but looked her over as intensely as she'd studied him.

"What time is it?"

"Around one."

She lifted her eyebrows. "How could it be one? There's sunlight outside—"

"That's because it's one in the afternoon, lazy bones. Which is partly why I didn't try to sleep. You needed—really, really needed—a block of rest. I got you up a couple of times—pregnant women invariably can't make it many hours without a bathroom run. But I think you were half in a coma, didn't really wake up even for that. There's some food downstairs. I made cinnamon rolls. Well. At least, I followed the directions on the container. And there's eggs. I can either do an omelet, or scramble up a bunch. You have to be hungry."

"I am. Near starved." She crooked a finger, inviting him closer. "I just need to talk to you about a couple of things first."

"I can talk from right here."

"No. I don't think so. I have a problem that I need your help with." She hadn't thought up a problem yet, but she knew what motivated Ike. If he thought she needed him, he'd be there faster than jet speed.

And as expected, he pushed out of the rocker immediately, came forward immediately, sat on the bed immediately. But Ike—who always moved with a lanky, boneless rhythm—approached with a careful, robotic stiffness…and she hated the wary expression in his eyes. He carved a seat on the bed near her side, but he didn't attempt to touch her.

She was pretty sure he wasn't afraid she had cooties. So it had to be something else.

"I have a feeling you were watching me sleep for quite a while," she said.

"Maybe. I just didn't want to leave you alone in a strange place. I knew how badly you needed the rest."

"I did. But watching someone sleep has to be unbelievably exciting…on a par with watching grass grow."

That won almost a smile. Not a full smile, but a teensy untensing of all those taut muscles.

"Maybe I find watching you sleep unbelievably exciting."

"Ike?"

"I'm right here. What?"

"Come clean. What's wrong?"

"What could be wrong?"

There happened to be four pillows on the giant bed. She flapped his head with one of them. And there. She caught the ghostly but unmistakable hint of a real grin.

"It's possible," he said delicately, "that you might wake up from a sleep this sound and forget what you said to me last night."

"You mean...about loving you? About being in love with you? Specifically about being crazy in love with you?"

He looked out the window, then back at her. "I never thought I'd hear you say those words. The love words. But as much as I wanted to hear them...I was kicking myself."

"Kicking yourself why?"

"Because I was afraid my plan, what I thought was my great, romantic kidnapping plan, could have backfired. I suddenly realized that you could have felt... pushed. Pressured. Because so many people saw the car, the rose petals, me dressed up like a stranger."

"Wearing a tie, even."

"Wearing a tie, even."

"And without Pansy."

"And without Pansy. Ginger, I didn't want to put you on the spot. Didn't want to make something hugely private to me—to us—to come across as something to be shared in public. It wasn't like that. What I wanted was for you to know—for everyone to see—that I was in love with you. That I wasn't with you because of the baby bump or your grandfather or the tea. It was about you. Being the woman I wanted to fill up the car with rose petals for. Do you remember what you told me?"

"Which thing?" Her voice was thick, from hearing what he'd planned, how he felt.

Hearing her vulnerable man lay himself bare.

"You said that respect was something you had to earn. You didn't expect it for nothing. But you wanted to earn that respect—from me. From everyone."

She pushed back the covers. Even though she'd loved all the cuddling warmth, suddenly she didn't need the blankets. Didn't need the pillow. She just needed to be closer to Ike. "I do feel that way. That respect has to be earned."

"So that's where the whole rose petal idea came from. Because you were pregnant, you were afraid the people in town—neighbors, friends—would assume I was with you out of honor or responsibility or some idiotic nonsense like that."

"Yup. That's exactly how I feel about honor and responsibility."

He didn't seem to hear her teasing attempt at humor, just went on. "So I wanted them to know—I wanted you to know—that I loved you over the top. Loved you in ways that have nothing to do with the baby or honor or responsibility or because you may or may not need someone. I never thought you needed anyone, Ginger. You're strong as a rock. You are a rock."

"Man. Is there an insult in there? Because I feel I should have a chance to brush my hair and put on some makeup if you're going to insult me."

"Quit it, Red. I need you to hear me."

The look in his eyes made her heart ache. "I wasn't trying to make jokes, Ike. I'm listening."

"You *are* a rock. That's the point. People do respect you. I respect you. You proved that from the first day you came back to town. You lit into anyone like a firecracker if you believed they were a threat to your grandfather. People just assumed that you came back because you had to—but that you'd take five minutes with Cashner, close down the place and lock him up in an institution."

"Yikes. That hurts. That anyone thought that of me."

"They hadn't seen you in a lot of years, Ginger, except in passing. They only knew you as a girl. Your mom had been dead a long time. And while some saw your father now and then..."

She nodded quickly, sadly. "I know...they assumed that I had some of my father's blood. I've had that misconception bite me in the heart before. It's partly why respect—real respect, earned respect—has always been so important to me."

"Well, from the day you came home, you threw off anyone's preconceptions like that. You were nothing like your father. You came out fighting for your grandfather's rights. For doing whatever you could to give him the best life he could have. And you sure argued with anyone who tried to stand in your way."

"Okay, okay. Enough about me." If he kept talking, conveying how proud he was of her, how he perceived the things she'd done, she was afraid she'd cry. And dagnabbit, she never cried. "Let's get into one of the real problems here. What are we going to do about your reputation, now that the whole party saw you kidnap me in the car with all the rose petals?"

He sighed. "I'm afraid you'll have to marry me. I'm

afraid the kidnapping…well, I didn't think of all the consequences. My practice will likely be shot. My patients will all think I've cracked, that the common-sense M.D. they knew must have become deranged and derailed somehow. And I can't even defend myself, because it's true."

"You think?" she asked tenderly.

"Ginger, I'm crazy for you. The baby's no burden. I'd love to be her father. Or his father. I'd love to give you a whole basket of babies, both genders…" He hesitated. "But to be honest, I'd prefer little girls with gorgeous eyes and terrible tempers."

"You want *ornery* children?"

"I do."

"Oh, Ike." Clearly, she had to save him. No one else would ever realize he was in such bad shape but her. She pushed back the last of the covers and more or less dove. Not as if she were diving into a pool or a lake, of course, but still, launching herself at Ike, on Ike, so that he simply had to fall into the mounds of down covers and mattress.

He went down. And stayed down. Like a fighter who knew when he was licked—which Ike most certainly was.

It killed her that he'd been so unsure. That Ike, who had so much natural confidence and common sense, could be lain low by worries about her. Of course, Ike wasn't so self-aware. He still didn't realize that he was just as driven as the other doctors in his family, to be there for others in need, to stand up…particularly when normal people would be running for the nearest exit.

While she had him prone, she dipped down and kissed him…no teasing, no playing, not anymore. This kiss conveyed the real thing—that her being in love with him was the real thing. No pretense, no caution, no holding herself back. This was it, a plain old naked kiss, coming from her heart, eyes closed, pulse thumping like a rickety hiccup, love spilling out a deluge of desire and need before she could even try to get it under control

Eventually, at some point, she let him up...seeing as they were both gasping for breath. The tension in his muscles was completely gone, except for one specific area.

The wariness in his eyes had completely disappeared, too.

He got it—that she was going to save him just as zealously as he'd saved her.

Still, being Ike, he had to push. "Would you mind my taking a turn at being on top, Red?"

She wanted to laugh, but her heart seemed to spill a more honest answer. "Any time you want, lover."

When he kissed her this time, she closed her eyes and felt awash with wave on wave of fierce tenderness.

There was so much they had to sort out and fix and work with. But not now. Right now Ginger had no doubt that she and Ike could conquer the world together...as long as they had each other.

* * * * *

AN ACCIDENTAL FAMILY

BY
AMI WEAVER

Two-time Golden Heart® finalist **Ami Weaver** has been reading romance since she was a teen and writing for even longer, so it was only natural she would put the two together. Now she can be found drinking gallons of iced tea at her local coffee shop while doing one of her very favourite things—convincing two characters they deserve their happy-ever-after. When she's not writing she enjoys time spent at the lake, hanging out with her family and reading. Ami lives in Michigan with her four kids, three cats and her very supportive husband.

This is Ami Weaver's fabulous first book for Mills & Boon!

For the Wicked Muses: Chelle, Jodie, Marcy and Rae.
Thank you for all your help. I love you all.
And for Dale, who believed. xo

CHAPTER ONE

THE STICK WAS pink.

Lainey Keeler squeezed her eyes shut, lifted the test with one trembling hand, then peeked with her right eye only.

Yup. Definitely a pink line. Maybe she needed to check the instructions to be sure....

Oh, God. How had this happened?

Okay, so she knew the technicalities of the how. In fact, she knew the when. Lord help her, that was the kicker.

Her eyes swam and her stomach rolled as she reached for the test box anyway, knowing what she'd see there. Knowing the result would read the same as the four other sticks—all different brands—in the garbage.

Knowing she'd been screwed in more ways than one.

So this was the price she paid for one night of lust infused with a heavy dose of stupidity. She slumped on the cold tile of the bathroom floor and let her head thunk on the vanity door. Hysterical laughter bubbled in her throat and she pressed her fingertips to her temples. Did it count, fifteen years after graduation, that she'd finally bedded the star quarterback? The same one she'd nurtured a killer crush on all through high school?

And managed to conceive his baby?

"And here I thought I had the flu," she said to her calico

cat, who observed her from the doorway. Panda's squinty blink in response could have meant anything. "Why didn't being pregnant occur to me?"

Single and pregnant. Right when she was starting a new business and her life couldn't be more unstable.

What would her parents say? She winced at the thought. At thirty-three, she was supposed to be burning up the career ladder. Instead, much to her family's chagrin, she burned *through* careers.

Chewing her lower lip, she took a last look at the pink line, then tossed the test stick in the trash with the others. Five pregnancy tests couldn't be wrong, no matter how much she wished it. She needed a plan.

"A plan is good," she said to the cat in the doorway. Panda meowed in response. Shoot, what was she going to do? She stepped over the cat and hurried into the small hallway, facing straight into her pocket-sized bedroom. Panic kicked up a two-step in her belly. She'd need a bigger place. The cozy one-bedroom apartment above her shop, The Lily Pad, worked beautifully for one person and an overweight cat. But adding a baby to the mix…? Babies needed so much *stuff.* She laid her hand on her still-flat belly. *A baby.*

Good God, she was going to be a mother.

She clenched her eyes shut and willed the tears away. What kind of mother would she be? Her ex and her family told her over and over she tended to be flighty and irresponsible. A baby meant responsibility, stability.

What if it turned out they were right? She certainly hadn't demonstrated good judgment on the night of her reunion.

The thought sliced her to the core and she took a deep breath. No time to cry. Not when she had a shop to open in a few minutes. Beth Gatica, her friend and employee, was already downstairs. She swiped at her eyes, tried to think.

"Where do I start?" she wondered aloud, trying to get her head clear enough to think.

A doctor. She'd need a doctor. Her usual doctor happened to be a friend of her family's, so she'd definitely have to head over to Traverse City. Since she felt better with something to do, she reached for the phone book.

"Lainey?" Beth's voice came through the door connecting the apartment to the shop. "Are you okay?"

Lainey fumbled the phone book and caught sight of herself in the small mirror next to the door. Dark blond hair already escaping from her ponytail? Check. Dark circles under her eyes? Check. Pasty skin? *Yikes.* Wasn't there supposed to be some kind of pregnancy glow? "I'm fine," she called. "Be right there."

"Okay, good. Because we've got a problem."

Well, of course they did. Lainey marched over and yanked open the door, almost grateful for the distraction. "What kind of problem?"

"Come see." Beth turned and hurried down the stairs, long dark curls bouncing. The fresh, cool scent of flowers hit Lainey as they entered the workroom. Beth tipped her head toward the older of the two walk-in coolers. "It's not cold enough, Laine. It's set where it's supposed to be, but it's nearly twelve degrees warmer in there."

"Oh, no." *No.* She needed the cooler to last another year—like she needed the van with its iffy transmission to last another six months. Preferably twelve. A headache began to pulse at the edges of her brain at the thought of her nearly empty bank account. Using only one cooler would mean reducing inventory, which meant possibly not being able to meet the needs of her customers. Which meant less income. And she couldn't afford to lose a single cent at this point.

To say The Lily Pad operated on a shoestring budget was to put it optimistically.

She pulled open the door, even though she didn't doubt Beth. She could feel the difference as soon as she walked in. She tapped the thermostat with her finger. Maybe it was stuck somewhere? She should be so lucky.

"Call Gary at General Repair," she said to Beth. "See if he can get us in today."

"On it." Beth hurried to the phone.

Lainey headed to the working cooler to do some rearranging. Some of the more delicate flowers would have to be moved over.

She tamped down the spurt of fear and worry that threatened to explode. No point inviting trouble, and Lainey figured she had enough to fill her personal quota. She closed her eyes and inhaled the fresh, green scent of the flowers, with their overtones of sweet and tangy and spicy. It always, always relaxed her just to breathe in the flowers.

But not enough, today, to rid her of her worries. About choking coolers. About babies. Lainey smothered a sigh. If she'd stayed home two months ago part of her predicament wouldn't be here. She'd invited trouble. Or, more accurately, trouble had invited her.

Of course she hadn't turned him down.

"Gary will be here at eleven," Beth said from behind her. "Want me to help move things?"

Lainey glanced at her watch. An hour and a half. "Sure. We'll just move a few for now. Let's group them by the door so we can open it a minimum of times." The colder it stayed in there, the better for her bottom line. She couldn't afford to lose a cooler full of flowers.

"Are you okay, Laine? You're awfully pale," Beth commented as she lifted a bucket of carnations out of the way.

Lainey sucked in a breath. Should she tell Beth? They'd been friends for years. Beth wouldn't ridicule her for her mistake with Jon. It would feel so good to tell someone....

"Lainey?" Beth's head was cocked, her brown gaze worried. "What's going on?"

"I'm pregnant," she blurted, and burst into tears. Beth hurried over to her, nearly knocking a bucket over in the process.

"Honey, are you sure?"

Lainey nodded and swiped at the tears. "Pretty sure." Five separate pink lines couldn't be wrong. Could they? "I'll have to go to a doctor to confirm it, though."

"Oh, Laine." Beth hugged her, stepped back. "How far along? I didn't know you were seeing someone."

Lainey closed her eyes. *Here we go.* "Well, I'm actually not. I'm about eight weeks along." She'd let Beth do the math.

"So that's—oh." Beth drew out the word and her eyes rounded. "Your class reunion."

"Yeah." Lainey couldn't meet her friend's gaze. Her poor baby. How could she ever explain the circumstances of his or her conception?

"So who's the daddy?"

"Jon Meier." Lainey could barely say his name. "We… ah…hit it off pretty well."

Beth gave a wry chuckle and opened the cooler door, a load of calla lilies in her hands. "So it seems."

"I have to tell him, Beth, but he lives so far away. Plus the whole thing was pretty forgettable, if you know what I mean. We used protection, but obviously…" She shrugged and swiped at her leaking eyes again. "It didn't work." An understatement if she'd ever heard one.

"He's not father material?"

"I don't know." It wasn't as if they'd discussed things like personal lives. "Plus he lives in LA. He's in some kind of entertainment industry work. He's not going to pull up and move back to Northern Michigan." He'd made his contempt for the area crystal-clear.

"Sometimes having a kid changes that," Beth pointed out.

"True." Lainey didn't want to think about it. "But I think we were pretty much in agreement on how awkward the whole thing was." So much for sex with no strings attached. The baby in her belly was a pretty long string. The length of a lifetime, in fact.

She wanted to bang her head on the wall. What had she been thinking, leaving with Jon that night? Was her self-esteem so damaged by her divorce she had to jump on the first guy who smiled at her?

Best not to answer that.

"I think you'll be a wonderful mom," Beth said, and Lainey's throat tightened.

"Really?" She couldn't keep the wobble out of her voice. Beth's confidence touched her. Her family would look at her being single, pregnant and nearly broke and lose their collective minds. She shoved the thought aside.

"Of course. You're wonderful with my kids. Now, let's get this finished before Gary gets here."

"It could go at any time?" Lainey could not believe she'd heard the repairman correctly. A year—she only needed twelve measly months. Why, oh, why was that too much to ask? "Are you sure?"

"Yes. We can cobble this along for a few more months. But you are definitely going to need a new unit." Gary's lined face wasn't without sympathy.

She took a deep breath. "Do what you have to, Gary. I need it to last as long as possible."

The repairman nodded and returned to the cooling unit.

Beth stood at the counter, ringing up a large bouquet of brightly colored carnations. A great sale, but not nearly enough to buy a new cooler. Or even a used one.

"Thank you. Have a great day," Beth said to the customer as he exited the shop. To Lainey she said, "What's the news?"

"We're going to need a new cooler. Sooner rather than later, probably." Exhaustion washed over her and she sank down on the stool behind the counter. "Even used, that's not something I can swing yet." Or possibly ever. No cooler, no business. No business, no cooler.

No business, no way to provide for the baby.

A wave of nausea rolled through her at the thought. Another failure. This one could be huge.

"Oh, man." Beth leaned on the counter. "Well, let's see. We've got the Higgins wedding coming up. We need more weddings. The funeral business has been picking up. That's good. Maybe…."

She hesitated, and Lainey knew what her friend hadn't said.

"Maybe if my mother sent business my way we wouldn't be in this predicament," she finished. "I know. I agree. I've asked." The answer, while not in so many words, was that the florist her mother used had been around a lot longer and wasn't in danger of folding. The implication? Lainey would fail—again.

Beth winced. "I know you have. I just wish she'd support you. I'm sorry I brought it up."

"It's okay. It's the truth. I don't know what will change her mind." Lainey stood up. "Let's finish getting the deliveries ready."

As Lainey gathered flowers and greenery she wondered if she'd let her business go under rather than ask her parents for a loan. They'd give her one, with plenty of strings attached, and she'd have to crawl to get it. This was supposed to be her chance to prove she could make something of her life without advanced degrees or a rich husband.

Right about now it didn't seem to be working.

Gary came out of the cooler, toolbox in one hand, invoice in the other. "You're all fixed up, Ms. Keeler. Can't say how long it'll last. Could be one month. Could be six. I'm sorry I don't have better news."

"The fact it's running right now is wonderful," Lainey said. "Thank you. I appreciate you coming on such short notice."

"Anytime. Have a good day, ladies." He left the store and the bell above the door chimed, its cheerful sound mocking Lainey's mood. She looked at the amount on the invoice and sighed.

She'd known when she bought the shop nine months ago there were no guarantees on equipment. Even in her current financial bind she didn't regret taking the plunge. This shop felt right to her in a way none of her other jobs ever had. Right enough, in fact, that she hoped to someday buy the building outright.

Working steadily throughout the morning, they completed their orders. The repair seemed to be holding for now, thank goodness. Lainey slid the last of the arrangements into the back of the van and closed the door. "All set, Beth. Hopefully we'll get more this afternoon."

"Fingers crossed." Beth climbed in and turned the ignition. She leaned back out the window. "I'll stop at Dottie's Deli and grab lunch on the way back. I think we've each earned a cheesecake muffin after this morning."

"Mmm." Lainey perked up at the thought. Everyone

knew the calories in Dottie's heavenly muffins didn't count. "Sounds wonderful. Thanks."

She held her breath as Beth thunked the old van into gear and drove off. Relief washed over her. After this morning she'd half expected the thing to go belly-up out of spite.

"Don't borrow trouble," she reminded herself as she turned and went inside.

The chime of the door caught her attention and she hurried to greet the customer.

Fifteen minutes later she started on a new arrangement, this one for a new mom and baby at the hospital. They really needed more of this kind of business—more happy occasions like...

Babies.

Pregnant.

Lainey gulped and gripped the edge of the worktable, her eyes on the array of delicate pastel flowers she'd gathered. She only had about seven months to stabilize her shop and get ready to be a new mom herself. A *single* new mom.

Seven months.

No one could ever accuse her of doing things the easy way.

Ben Lawless pulled into the driveway of his grandmother's old farmhouse and stared. Same white paint, black shutters. The wide porch was missing its swing, but two rockers sat in its place. The two huge maples in the front yard had dropped most of their leaves. Funny, he'd been gone for so many years but this old house still felt like home.

He frowned at the strange car parked behind his grandmother's trusty Buick. Last thing he wanted was to talk to anyone other than his grandma, to deal with friendliness and well-meaning questions. Acting normal was exhausting.

He pushed open the truck door, stepped out and scanned the layout of the front yard. Plenty of room for a ramp, though some of the porch railing would have to be removed, and it would block one of the flowerbeds lining the house's foundation. He kicked at the leaves littering the cracked walkway. The uneven concrete posed a hazard even to an able-bodied person. Why couldn't Grandma admit she needed help?

Why did you assume she didn't need it?

His self-recrimination didn't get any farther as the front door opened and framed his beaming grandmother in her wheelchair. He tried not to wince at the sight. She'd always been so tough, strong and able, and now she looked so small. He moved up the walk and the stairs to the porch.

"Grandma." He bent down to give her an awkward hug in the chair, afraid to hold on too tight. "How are you?"

She hugged him back firmly and patted his face. "I'm good. Making the best of this, I hope." She studied his face for a moment, her clear blue eyes seeing too much. "I'm so glad you're here. Not sleeping well?"

He straightened, not surprised by the observation. "Good enough."

She gave him a look, but dropped the subject and rolled back into the house. "Where are my manners? Come in, come in. I want you to meet a very good friend of mine."

Ben braced himself as he followed her across the familiar living room to the kitchen. Hopefully this friend wasn't one of the mainstays of Holden's Crossing's gossip mill. Last thing he needed was word getting out and people asking him questions or making accusations. He stopped dead when he looked into the cool blue gaze of the gorgeous—and young—blond at the kitchen table.

"Ben Lawless, meet Lainey Keeler. Lainey, this is my grandson. The one who's a firefighter in Grand Rapids." The pride in Rose's voice made Ben's stomach twist. "Lainey was a few years behind you in school, Ben."

No way. *This* was his grandmother's friend? Long dark blond ponytail, a few strands loose around a heart-shaped face. Clear blue eyes, smooth creamy skin. Full breasts a snug pink tee didn't hide. He gave her a brief nod, forced the proper words out. "Nice to meet you."

Her smile curved, but didn't reach her eyes. "Same here. Rose has told me so much about you."

"Did she?" He tensed at her comment, then forced himself to relax. It didn't mean she actually knew anything. He rested his hand on his grandmother's thin shoulder. "Grandma, I'm going to bring in my things, okay?"

Lainey rose. "I'll walk you out." She leaned down to plant a kiss on his grandma's cheek and gave her a hug. "I'll see you in a couple of days, Rose."

"Don't work too hard, honey," Grandma said, and Ben nearly laughed. If he remembered correctly, none of the Keelers had to work. They'd been given anything and everything on the proverbial platter.

Ben caught a whiff of her scent, something floral, as she moved past him. Since he'd gotten boxed in, he followed her out into the cool early October night.

Once on the porch, she turned to him with a frown. "She's glad you're here."

"And you're not."

Those big blue eyes narrowed. "I'm not sure. She's been struggling for months now. Where were you then?"

Temper flared at the accusation in her tone. He'd felt bad enough once he'd realized how much help his grandma needed. He didn't need this chick sticking her nose in, too.

No matter how hot she was. "She isn't big on admitting she needs help." Seemed to run in the family.

Lainey gave him a look that said he was full of it and stomped off the porch. "She's in her eighties. How could you not come visit and check on her?"

Guilt lanced through him. "She always said she was fine, okay? I'm here now." Why did he care if this woman thought he was a total heel?

She shrugged. "You still should have checked on her. How far is it up here? She's so proud of you. But you never bothered to visit."

Even in the dim light he saw the sparks in her blue gaze, the anger on his grandmother's behalf. "I'm here now," he said, his own temper rising.

"Till you leave. Then where will she be?" She spun around and strode across the yard.

God help him, he couldn't pull his gaze off her tight little tush. She climbed in the little car and slammed the door. The spray of gravel that followed her out to the road said it all.

Well, great. He'd managed to tick off his grandmother's hot little friend.

Ben shook his head and stepped off the porch, walked to his truck to get his bags. He'd done something far worse than that. His best friend was dead, thanks to him, and any problems with Lainey Keeler were not even on his list of important things. It made no difference what she thought of him.

Back inside, his grandma frowned at him. "Why were you rude to Lainey?"

But of course it would matter to Grandma. He scrubbed a hand over his face. "I'm sorry. It's been a long day. I didn't know you two were friends."

"We are. We met awhile back when she volunteered

for Senior Services and just clicked, as you young people say. She comes out every Wednesday. More if she can. I didn't think you knew her." His grandmother's eyes were sharp on his face.

"I don't. Just knew *of* her. She was four years behind me in school, as you said. How are you feeling?"

She studied him for a second, then seemed to accept the change of topic. "Every day is a little harder. I'm so glad you're here and can make this old house a little easier to live in. I don't want to leave it."

These last words were spoken in a soft tone. Ben knew this was the only home she'd lived in with his grandfather, her husband of fifty years. Her best friend.

The kind of love and relationship he'd ended for Jason and Callie.

Pain pounded at his temples and he closed his eyes. He shoved it down, locked it back into the deepest part of him he could. Thing was, that place was nearly full these days.

"You won't have to leave, Grandma. You'll have to tell me what you'd like done besides the ramp. Even in the dark I noticed the walk out front has seen better days."

Her smile was rueful. "A lot around here has seen better days, Ben."

"We'll get it fixed up, Grandma. You won't have to leave," he repeated.

"I know. I'm very grateful to you." She maneuvered the chair toward the living room. "Let me show you to your room. Well, partway anyway."

Ben started to say he knew where it was, but of course she'd have taken over the downstairs bedroom after the arthritis in her hip got too bad. "Which one?" There were three upstairs.

She stopped at the base of the stairs and looked up, the sorrow and longing clear on her face. "The back bedroom.

It has the best view and is the biggest room. Lainey freshened it up for you. Dusted, clean sheets, the whole shebang. The bathroom is ready, too."

His grandparents' old room.

"Okay. Tell her thanks for me."

Grandma backed her chair up and gave him a little smile. "You can tell her yourself. Didn't I mention she visits a lot?"

He stared at her. *Uh-oh.* "Grandma. I'm not interested."

She slid him a look and her smile widened. "No one said you were."

He'd walked right into that one.

Smoke filled the room, smothering him, searing his lungs, his eyes, his skin. God, he couldn't see through the gray haze. A cough wracked him, tearing at his parched throat. He couldn't yell for his friend. Where was Jason? He couldn't reach him. Had to get him out before the house came down around them. A roar, a crack, and a fury of orange lit the room. The ceiling caved in a crash fueled by the roar of flames. He spun around, but the door was blocked by a flaming heap of debris. Under it, a boot. Jason. Coming to save him.

Ben woke with a start, his eyes watering and the breath heaving out of his lungs as if he'd been sprinting for his life. Where the hell was he? Moonlight slanted through the window, silver on the floor. The curtain stirred in the faint breeze. He sat up and pushed himself through the fog of sleep. Grandma Rose's house. Had he cried out? God, what if she'd heard him? Shame flowed over him like a lava river. He stepped out of bed, mindful of the creaky floor, and walked down the hall to the bathroom near the landing.

No sound came from downstairs.

He exhaled a shaky breath and went into the bathroom.

He'd been afraid of this—of the nightmare coming. He had no power over it—over what it was, what it did to him. No control.

He turned on the squeaky faucet with unsteady hands and splashed cold water on his face. There'd be no more sleep for him tonight.

CHAPTER TWO

LAINEY WALKED INTO Frank's Grocery after closing the shop and pulled out her mental shopping list. Nothing fancy. Just sauce, pasta, shrimp, some good cheese. If she had more energy she'd make the sauce from scratch, but not tonight. So far the hardest thing about being pregnant was being so tired at the end of the day. She grabbed a basket from the stack and headed for the first aisle.

She came to a dead stop when she spotted the tall, dark-haired man frowning at the pasta sauce display.

Oh, no. Ben Lawless.

She didn't want to chat with Rose's grumpy grandson. He'd made it pretty clear he wasn't interested in being friendly. Since he stood smack in front of the sauce she needed, though, she'd have to talk to him.

He glanced up as she approached. For a heartbeat she found herself caught by those amazing light green eyes, by the grief she saw searing through them.

What the heck? She cleared her throat. "How are you?"

He tipped his head in her direction, his expression now neutral. "Fine, thanks."

His uninterest couldn't have been clearer, though his tone was perfectly polite.

"I just need to get in here." She pointed to the shelves in front of him. He stepped back, hindered by a woman and cart behind him, and Lainey slipped in, bumping him in the process. A little shiver of heat ran through her. "Sorry," she muttered, and grabbed the jar with fingers that threatened to turn to butter.

She managed to wiggle back out, brushing him again, thanks to the oblivious woman behind him who kept him penned between them. She plopped the sauce into her basket and offered what she hoped passed for a smile. "Um, thanks."

"No problem," he murmured.

She turned around and hurried out of the aisle, unsettled by both the physical contact and his apparent loss. So Ben had a few secrets. That flash of grief, deep and wrenching, hit her again.

Rose had never mentioned anything. Then again, why would she? She'd respect her grandson's privacy. It was one of the things Lainey loved about her friend.

It only took a few more minutes to gather the rest of the ingredients. Her path didn't cross Ben's again, and she unloaded her few purchases at the checkout with relief.

Outside, she took a big breath of the cool night air, and some of the tension knotted inside her eased. Fall was her favorite time of year. A mom and small daughter examined a display of pumpkins outside Frank's and her thoughts shifted back to her baby. Next year she'd be carving a pumpkin for her five-month-old. Oh, sure, he or she would be too small to appreciate it, but despite the precariousness of her position the idea gave her a little thrill.

She deposited the bags in the trunk and slipped into the driver's seat to start the car.

Click. Then nothing.

Oh, no. Maybe if she tried it again....

Click.

She leaned forward, rested her head on the steering

wheel, and fought the urge to scream. Not owning any jumper cables, she'd have to go back into Frank's and find someone who did. While she was at it she'd hope like crazy the problem was simply a dead battery, and not something expensive. She yanked the keys out of the ignition, grabbed her purse and got out of the car. One thing was for sure—she'd push the stupid car home before she'd ask her parents for help.

She nearly collided with Ben coming out of the store.

"Whoa," he said, checking his cart before he ran her down.

Before she could think, she blurted, "Can you help me?" Her face heated as he stared at her. "Ah, never mind. I'll find…" She gestured vaguely behind him but he shook his head.

"What do you need?"

"My car won't start. I think the battery's dead. The dome light's been staying on longer than it should and it didn't go off at all this time. I don't have any jumper cables." Realizing she was babbling, she clamped her mouth shut.

He nodded. "Where are you parked?"

She pointed. "There. The silver one." Which he no doubt already knew, since he'd seen her in it the other night. "The space in front of me is open."

"Okay. Give me a minute. I'll pull around."

He walked off and she stared after him. *Shoot.* Why hadn't she found someone else? On the other hand, the whole process wouldn't take very long. Then she could be on her way back home to fix her dinner and curl up in her bed.

The wind picked up, skittering dry leaves across the parking lot, and she tucked her hands under her arms to keep warm as she went back to her car. She propped the hood open as a big black truck rumbled into the empty spot.

Ben got out, cables already in hand, and went to work on her battery. Even though she knew how to hook them up—her mother would be appalled—she let him do it, because it was easier than having his carefully bland gaze on her.

He glanced up. "Do you know how to do this?"

Something in his tone made her bristle. She lifted her chin just a bit. "Actually, I do. I can even change a tire."

His mouth twitched in what could have been a prequel to a smile. "Good for you."

Before she could reply, a voice shrilled nearby. "Lainey? Lainey Keeler, is that you?"

Ben returned to the battery and the fragile moment was shattered. Lainey internally groaned as she turned to see Martha Turner, one of her mother's best friends, hurrying toward her.

"Hi, Mrs. Turner."

"Goodness, what are you doing?" The woman peeked around Lainey and frowned. "Do your parents know you have car trouble? I just left your mother at the Club. Have you called her yet? I'll never understand why you traded in that cute little coupe your husband bought you for—for this." She fluttered her hands at the car.

Not offended, Lainey bit back a laugh. She had to be the only person who'd ever traded in a new car for a used one. "Of course I didn't bother either of them, Mrs. Turner. It's really not a big deal. Just a dead battery."

Behind her, Ben cleared his throat. "Sorry to interrupt, but I need to start the truck now. It's loud."

"Okay." She gave Mrs. Turner an apologetic smile. "It was nice to see you."

Mrs. Turner's gaze went to Ben, reaching into the cab of the truck, then back to Lainey. "You too, dear. Take care."

Lainey could almost see the wheels turning in the other woman's head and imagined her mother would get a phone call before Mrs. Turner even made it inside Frank's. She sighed. She'd get her own call in a matter of minutes after that, and spend a half an hour calming her mother all over nothing.

So much for a relaxing evening.

Ben came back around and stood, hands in pockets, staring at her engine. Finally he lifted his gaze. "What did you trade in?"

Not exactly sure how to interpret his tone, she spoke carefully. "A Mercedes. After my divorce."

She didn't mention the sleek little car had been a bribe—an attempt to keep her in the marriage. Getting rid of it had been a victory of sorts. One of the very few she'd managed.

She caught a glimmer of amusement in his eyes. "That's funny?"

He rocked back on his heels. "Not the divorce. The car. I wouldn't think—" He stopped and she frowned.

"Think what?"

He looked at her, amusement gone, and seemed actually to see straight into her. The full effect of his gaze caused a funny little hitch in her breath. "I think you can start the engine now," he said, and she swallowed a surge of disappointment.

Which was crazy. She didn't care what he thought of her.

She slid into the car and tried not to notice when he braced one arm on the roof of the car and the other on the top of the door. When he leaned down she got a tantalizing glimpse of the smooth, hard muscles of his chest through the gap in his partially unbuttoned shirt.

Her mouth went dry.

"Go ahead and see if it'll start."

His voice slid over her skin and she gave a little shiver. She caught a whiff of his scent—a yummy combination of soap and spice. A little curl of heat slipped through her belly. She reached for the ignition and hoped he didn't notice her shaking hand. The engine turned over on the first try.

"You should be all set now," he said, straightening up. "Drive it around a bit to let the battery charge up."

"I will. Thank you," she said, and meant it. "I appreciate it."

He shrugged and stepped back. "No problem. I'd have done it for anyone."

Her little hormonal buzz evaporated. Of course he would. After all, she'd practically attacked him when he came out of the store.

"Well, see you around," she said, and he gave her a nod and then disappeared around the front of her car.

She sat for a moment, waiting for him to unhook the cables, and gave herself a reality check. She was two months pregnant. Being attracted to a man right now couldn't be more foolish—and she'd learned the hard way what a poor judge of men she was. She'd paid dearly for that mistake. Her focus was her shop, her baby, and making her life work without her parents hovering over her, waiting for her to fail.

Clearly these pregnancy hormones threw her off balance.

The hood of the car dropped with a thud and the sudden glare of headlights made her blink. With a little wave, in case he could see, she put her car in gear and backed out of her spot, then drove the long way through town back to her apartment. Ben stayed a respectable distance behind, but the thoughtful gesture gave her an unwelcome frisson of warmth.

Under his gruff exterior, Ben Lawless was a gentleman. Somehow that made him more dangerous.

Lainey let herself in to her apartment, not allowing herself to glance after Ben's truck as he drove on by. Her phone rang. She dug it out of her bag and checked the display. Ah, here was the call she'd been dreading.

"Hi, Mother," she said into the phone, as a purring Panda wound between her feet.

"Hi, dear," Jacqui Keeler trilled. "I'm almost there. Let me in, love."

That hadn't taken long. Mrs. Turner must have really run up the alarm if she was getting a visit, too. Lainey dumped her bags on the counter with a little more force than necessary. "Here? Why?"

"Can't I simply visit with my daughter?"

Oh, if only. "Of course, Mother. I'll be down in a sec."

She dropped the phone back in her purse and glanced around her cozy space. Her apartment was neat, for all the good it did. It would never meet her mother's standards, no matter what. She'd learned that years ago.

She hurried down the front stairs to unlock the street-level door just as her mother walked up.

"Lainey." Jacqui kissed her cheek, her usual cloud of sweet perfume tickling Lainey's nose. "You look tired."

She bit back a laugh. If her mother only knew. "Thanks," she said dryly as the trim older woman swept past her up the stairs. Jacqui, as always, was impeccably groomed. She wore a pale pink suit and her smooth blond hair swung smartly at her chin. Lainey ran her hand down her pony-tail and tried not to feel inferior in her non-branded jeans and tee shirt.

Damn it. She'd given that life up. But, oh, sometimes she did miss designer clothes.

"Have a meeting tonight, Mother?"

"I did." Jacqui tucked her monster-sized bag securely under her arm, as if she expected to be robbed right there on the stairs. "For the Auxiliary at the hospital. The gala."

No surprise there. For all their differences, Lainey still admired her mother's energy. "When is it?"

"Two weeks. Don't forget you are expected to be there."

Right. Just what she wanted. "Who did the floral arrangements?"

"Gail, of course. She does a lovely job."

Implying that The Lily Pad didn't. Disappointment clogged her vision for a moment. Lainey opened her mouth, snapped it closed. Frustration rushed through her. She'd never get through to her mother until the woman took her seriously. When would that be? What would it take?

"You really should move back home, honey," Jacqui said, her gaze drifting around the living room. "We have plenty of space. You could have your old room back. We'd love to have you."

Lainey stifled a sigh. More like they'd love to micro-manage her life into one that met their standards. Been there, tried that, failed spectacularly.

"I know you would. I'm very happy here, though." Lainey saw her mother's hand twitch, as it did when she was stressed. "Can I get you something to drink?"

"No, thank you." Jacqui perched on the edge of the sofa, the monster bag set primly on her lap, and Lainey sank down on a nearby chair. "Now, I received a disturbing phone call from Martha this evening. You had car trouble? Why didn't you call?"

Lainey smoothed her hand on her jeans. "It was nothing. Really. A dead battery. Not worth bothering you over. Rose's grandson Ben helped me out."

Jacqui's tone turned chilly. "Yes, Martha said you were with a man."

Lainey nearly choked. "Standing in a parking lot while someone was kind enough to jump my battery is hardly being with a man." Though she'd certainly had visions of another kind of jumping, but those were best kept to herself.

"If you'd kept the car your husband bought you—"

"Ex-husband," Lainey said through clenched teeth.

Unperturbed, Jacqui continued on. "If you'd kept the car, and the husband, you wouldn't need strange men to help you in the parking lot. Men who may have less than honorable intentions toward you."

Lainey tried to count to ten and gave up at three. "Excuse me? How does being nice equal intentions of any kind?"

Jacqui glared at her. "Do I need to spell it out for you? Your father's political connections are extremely valuable. Some people will use you for them. You don't always have the best judgment, Lainey."

Ouch. Direct hit. "Like Daniel did?" Lainey shot back. "You weren't concerned then, about my judgment *or* my connections, since he came from the right family. I can't see what need Ben Lawless would have for political connections, or how he thinks he'd get them when we only had ten minutes together."

"Martha said you looked awful cozy."

"Martha was wrong," Lainey said flatly. "Trust me, Mother. Please."

Jacqui made a noise in her throat. "I talked to Daniel earlier."

Betrayal sliced through her, sharp and quick. "What?"

Jacqui sent Lainey a look full of reproach. "He said you never call him. Why ever not, Lainey? He's a good man."

Lainey sucked in a breath. She'd worked so hard to get free of her ex-husband. "I can't think of any reason I'd ever have to call him." Not even if hell froze over. Twice.

Her mother looked at her as if she were a bit daft. "He misses you, dear."

Not a chance. She knew Daniel. Her ex-husband missed the perceived gravy train.

Lainey had never filled her family in on all the reasons behind her divorce. She'd been afraid they would take his side—a fear only reinforced as she looked at her mother now. Her parents adored Daniel. She'd dated him in an effort to be the daughter they wanted. They'd been over the moon when she'd succumbed in a weak moment, perhaps blinded by the three-carat princess-cut ring, and agreed to marry him. She'd thought she could make it work and earn her parents' respect in one fell swoop.

She'd been wrong.

"Why would he miss me now? We've been divorced more than a year," she said, and wasn't totally successful at keeping the bitterness out of her voice. Jacqui didn't seem to notice.

"I gave him your cell phone number and I've got his for you," she said, fishing in her bag. "He said he'd give you a call."

Anger propelled Lainey to her feet. "What? Mother, how *could* you? I don't want to talk to him. Ever. My life is none of his business now." He'd never cared when they were married. Why would he now?

Surprise crossed her mother's face. "Lainey, you were married for seven years. Those feelings don't just go away. He can help you out of this mess you're in. You're barely hanging on. Everyone knows it. You need his help."

Nausea rolled over Lainey. There lay the crux of the matter for Jacqui—the possibility of another public shaming by her wayward daughter and the offer of salvation by a man deemed worthy, no matter the cost.

"I most certainly do not." Telling her parents the truth of her marriage to Daniel would only prove how good she was at failing. "I don't need him or anyone else to make this work. I'm doing perfectly fine on my own." Well, except for the fact her shop was in the red and she had a cooler and a van on the fritz. Oh, and she was about to become a single mom. Still… "I'm happy, Mother."

Jacqui sighed, shook her head, and gestured around the apartment. "Oh, honey. You can't possibly be happy living like this, after how you were raised and how well you married. Talk to him when he calls. Maybe you'll get lucky and he'll give you a second chance."

Lainey shuddered. God help her. "I'm not interested." Those years she'd spent with Daniel were ones she'd never get back. She wasn't going to repeat the mistake of chaining herself to a man. No matter what.

"You should be." Jacqui glanced at her watch. "I'd better get going. Lovely to see you, dear. Come visit us soon."

Lainey bit back a sigh. Typical. Her mother would act as if nothing had happened. "I'll walk you out."

The next evening Ben looked up at the crunch of tires on the gravel drive. He recognized the silver car, and he already knew Lainey Keeler was coming over to visit his grandmother.

He wondered again at her modest choice of car. Somehow that intrigued him. He'd bet there was more to that story than she'd let on.

It would be flat-out rude not to make sure the car was running okay after he'd helped her yesterday. He'd be polite, then get back to his prep for the wheelchair ramp. He leaned the piece of wood he'd been about to cut against the wall and walked out into the twilight.

As he approached the car the door opened and he watched as Lainey planted one slim denim-clad leg, ending in a high-heeled black boot, on the ground. He tried not to notice how long that leg was. She appeared to be struggling with something so he went over to help.

"Evening," he said. She jumped, yelped, and nearly lost her grip on what he could now see was a pizza box. Big blue eyes swung his way and a pretty pink stained her cheeks. Her lips parted slightly and his gaze zeroed in on her mouth. *Very nice.* He shoved the unwelcome thought away. "Can I get that for you?"

She shook her head and her long hair shifted silkily on her shoulders. "I've got it. Thanks."

He stepped back to let her exit the car. "Is it running okay?"

She glanced up at him. "Yes. Thank you again." Her tone was cool, polite. She bumped the door shut with her hip, but her keys fell to the ground. Ben bent and retrieved them for her, pressing them into her palm. A quick zing of heat flashed through him at the contact. He pulled back quickly. *Hell.*

"Um, thanks," she murmured.

"You're welcome." He turned toward the garage. He needed to get away from her before he started to *feel.*

"Ben." Her voice—hesitant, a little husky—flowed over him. He turned back and she tipped the pizza box slightly toward him. "There's plenty here if you want to join us."

"No, thanks." The words came swift, automatic, but he caught a flash of hurt in her eyes. *Damn it.* "I'm in the middle of a project," he amended. "I'll try and grab some in awhile." Why did he feel the need to soften the blow? Since when had big blue eyes affected him? Since last night, when she'd narrowed her eyes and told him she could change a tire.

She shrugged. "Good luck. Rose and I love our pizza."

He slid his hands in his front pockets. "I'll keep that in mind."

She turned to go and he couldn't tear his gaze off the sway of her hips as she walked up to the house.

Double hell. He couldn't risk forging any type of connection. No way would he allow himself the luxury. How could he, when he shouldn't be the one alive?

Turning, he headed back to his project, tried to ignore the feminine laughter floating through the kitchen's screen door. Lainey's throaty laugh carried, teasing at the edge of something he'd shut down after Jason's death.

His phone rang before he could start the saw. A glance at the display revealed the caller to be his boss. Nerves jolted through him, but he kept his voice steady as he answered.

"Hi, Captain."

"Ben." The concern in the older man's voice carried clearly and Ben shut his eyes against the guilt it stirred up. "How are you, son?"

"I'm getting by," he replied.

"Just getting by?"

"Pretty much." Ben paused. He didn't need to paint a rosy picture for his boss. He'd already been ordered to take leave due to the stress of Jason's death. It couldn't really get any worse than that.

"Still having the symptoms, I take it." Not a question.

"Yeah." When the dream stopped, would he be free of the pain? Did he want to be? Wouldn't that be disloyal to the friend he'd loved like a brother?

After all, Ben was alive. Jason wasn't.

The Captain sighed. "It won't do any good for me to tell you again that it was an accident and not your fault, right?"

"With all due respect, sir, you're wrong." The words caught in Ben's throat. "It was my call. I made a bad one, and a good man—a family man—died because of me."

"That's not what the investigation found," the Captain reminded him softly.

It didn't matter. The investigators hadn't been there—in the inferno, in the moment. "I don't give a damn." Ben shut his eyes against the waves of guilt and pain that buffeted his soul, tried not to see Callie's grief-ravaged face. "I know what happened."

"Ben—"

"Please, don't."

There was a pause, then another sigh. "Then I won't. This time. Son, when you heal, come back and see us. There will always be room for fine firefighters such as yourself and I'd be honored to have you."

Heal. Ben swallowed a lump in his throat. He didn't know if it was possible. "Thank you, sir. I'll keep it in mind."

He disconnected the call and the emptiness he'd been battling for the past six months constricted his chest. He could never work as a firefighter again. He no longer trusted his judgment, his ability to read a situation and respond appropriately.

Without those skills he was nothing.

"Ben?"

He looked up sharply, feeling exposed. Lainey stood in the open door with a plate, uncertainty on her beautiful face. He cursed silently. How much had she overheard?

"Rose thought you might be hungry." She lifted the plate slightly.

He rubbed his hand over his face, afraid the rawness of

his emotions showed too clearly. He needed to get them back under control—fast. "Thanks." He shoved the phone in his pocket and walked over, not wanting to look at her and see pity. Or disgust. He'd seen plenty of both over the past couple of months. She handed him the plate wordlessly, then laid her hand on his forearm before he could move away.

His muscles turned to stone even as the heat from her simple touch sought the frozen place inside him. His gaze landed on hers, despite his best intent. He saw no pity, only questions, and he couldn't take the chance of her asking them. Not now, with everything so close to the surface.

He cleared his throat and she stepped back quickly, taking her warmth with her when she removed her hand. It was a much sharper loss than he'd like. "Thanks for the pizza."

"Sure." She hesitated and he held his breath, afraid she'd ask. Perversely, he was almost afraid she wouldn't. She gave him a small smile. "Eat it before it gets cold."

Then she turned and walked into the night before he could tell her how very familiar he was with cold.

And what a lonely place it was.

CHAPTER THREE

AN IMPERIAL SUMMONS was never a good thing.

Lainey had long thought of her mother's invitations to dinner as such a summons—and more often than not they included some well-meaning but completely off-base idea of her parents' to "improve her life."

She'd met her ex at such a dinner. And apparently she was the only one who saw it for the farce it had turned out to be.

Now, if Daniel had been a man like Ben maybe things would have been different. The thought wasn't as shocking as it might have been, considering she'd been unable to get Ben and the haunted look on his face out of her mind for the past two days. She hadn't overheard enough of his conversation to find out what was eating him alive, but she'd heard the pain layering his voice, each word laced with more than the last.

Still, Ben struck her as a fundamentally honorable man, not one who would marry for money without dumping his long-time girlfriend first. Like, say, her ex-husband. The good thing was her heart hadn't been involved—but her pride and self-worth had taken a beating.

Lainey sighed and turned through the thick stone columns into her parents' driveway. Since her parents were expecting her, the black iron gate stood open. She wound her way up the drive and parked in front of the massive log house that managed to be both rustic and majestic.

Lainey turned the car off and got out. On the plus side Grace, the cook, always put together fabulous meals, so she'd make sure she enjoyed that even while avoiding the bombs that were likely to be lobbed over the table. The front door opened even before she made it all the way up the carefully landscaped walkway.

"Lainey!" her father greeted her in his big voice.

"Hi, Dad." She allowed herself to be drawn into a hug. Tall and trim, Greg Keeler cut a handsome picture with his dark, youthful looks, a perfect foil to Jacqui's petite blond paleness. Even in their late fifties, they looked every inch the power couple they'd been for as long as she could remember.

"Come on in. We're in the family room."

He turned and Lainey followed him into the large room off the foyer, with its high ceilings, thick carpet and fireplace. While the outside screamed North Woods, inside the only concession to the house's rustic roots were the thick beams soaring overhead.

Lainey walked across the luxurious carpet, its velvety pile the color of cream, with nary a stain in sight. She tried to picture a baby crawling around in here and failed. Nothing about this room said *family*—even with the professionally shot family photos on the mantel. She vowed to make sure she raised her baby in an environment that was warm and welcoming, not precious and impersonal.

Her mother perched on the edge of a chair near the fire. A manila folder lay on an end table next to her.

"Hello, dear." Jacqui rose and offered her cheek to Lainey, who came around the end of the sofa to place the obligatory kiss.

"Hi, Mother."

"Have a seat." Her dad gestured toward the sofa and turned to the mini-wet-bar. "Can I get you anything to drink?"

Well, no. I'm pregnant. She swallowed the words. That would get this little pow-wow off to a roaring start. In fact it might create stains on the carpet from dropped or flying liquor. "No, thanks."

He raised an eyebrow but said nothing as he mixed his drink quickly and took the seat opposite Jacqui.

Lainey flicked her gaze between both of them. There was no reading her parents. Whatever they'd done, they wouldn't be smug, since they'd consider it a necessary move. She might as well get it over with. "What's going on?"

Jacqui frowned a little. "Wouldn't you rather eat first? Grace has a lovely roast chicken prepared."

Lainey's shoulders tensed at the deflection. "I'd like to know what's going on." She looked at her father but his expression was unreadable. "Dad? Please?"

He down set his drink—a screwdriver, no doubt. "Might as well cut to the chase. Lainey, we want to help you."

Oh, no. Her stomach lurched. She threaded her fingers together in her lap to keep from shaking. She kept her tone measured. "Help me how?"

"With your little shop, honey." Jacqui reached for the folder and the hairs went up on the back of Lainey's neck.

"My little shop? What have you done, Mother? Dad?" She heard the note of panic in her voice. She'd been safe, had rented the business from Esther Browning, what could they possibly—?

Jacqui beamed. "We thought you'd be pleased to know we bought your building."

The room tilted a little and Lainey gripped the arm of the chair, struggling to focus on her mother's clueless face. She couldn't have heard correctly. "I'm sorry—what? Why?"

"You're having such a hard time getting this going, and Esther was worried about making ends meet. You know she needs the rent to live on, dear."

My parents are now my landlords. The realization swept through her, followed closely by rage. "I've never paid late. Not one single payment." She bit off each word. If nothing else, she prided herself on that. She knew her elderly landlord depended on that income, and made absolutely sure those payments went out on time.

Her father cut in. "Of course not. But there's reason to believe you might have a hard time making them, so we thought this would help both of you out."

Lainey sucked in a breath. Poor Esther. The prospect of having the building all paid for, most likely in cash, must have been powerful. She'd done what was best for her, and Lainey refused to fault her for that.

Keeping her voice even, she asked, "But you didn't think maybe you should ask me? See how I'm doing?" Of course the documents would have been anything but reassuring, but still… Betrayal rose in her throat, the taste bitter, and she swallowed hard. Why was it too much for them to think to include her in the decision making?

Jacqui looked surprised. Or would have if the Botox hadn't been working so well. "Well, we already know how you're doing. The whole town does. We've got your best interests at heart, dear. Always."

Lainey shut her eyes. How often had she heard that little line? When would it actually prove to be true? "How exactly does this help me?" She braced herself for the kicker.

"Well, you won't have the monthly payment anymore. We won't make you pay rent. And you can live here now. We'll rent out that little apartment." Her mother sounded pleased, as if she'd truly solved a problem. Her father nodded in agreement as they exchanged a look.

She sucked in a sharp breath. "No. I can't live here." *How am I supposed to puke in private every morning? Hide my rounding belly? Raise my child here?* Panic seized her and she jumped up as her father's phone rang. He checked it, and rose.

"I've got to run. Lainey, we'll talk more later. But for now we feel this is the best thing for you."

He kissed her cheek and strode out of the room. Lainey stared after him, floored because both of her parents seemed to think this was a done deal and hadn't bothered to truly consider *her*. "Why did no one ask me? Has no one noticed I'm an adult? I'm not moving back home." Where she'd go, she didn't know. But it wouldn't be here.

Jacqui set her snifter on the table. "Of course you are, dear. That little place isn't good for you. We've got plenty of room. We can remodel your suite if you'd like. Daniel agrees you should be here."

Lainey whipped around so fast she nearly got dizzy. "He has no say in my life. None. We're divorced, remember?"

Jacqui leaned forward, her gaze earnest. "You were wrong, Lainey. He loves you and he's willing to give you a second chance. What is so bad about that? Now you don't have to struggle anymore. We've taken care of it."

Lainey stared back. Her mother really believed it. She could see the sincerity in the other woman's gaze, hear it in her voice. They didn't understand it was Lainey's problem and she wanted to be the one to solve it—or not. That had been the whole point of taking over the shop—to make it work by herself. Now the choice was gone.

She lifted her chin and met her mother's expectant gaze. "I'm not coming home." Each word came out crystal-clear and Jacqui's eyes widened. "I'm happy where I am. I love my job, my shop. My apartment. I'm not going to give it up, give you control of my life, because you can't accept I'm an adult and haven't chosen the path or the man you wanted for me."

Jacqui frowned. "Lainey, please be reasonable. You needed help. We gave it to you."

"Yes, but at what cost to *me*?" Despair rose and Lainey fought it back, preferring anger. There was really only one option here, since she wasn't going to walk away from the shop she loved. "What do I have to do to get it back?"

Jacqui sat back. "Pardon?"

"I want it back," she repeated. "I'll buy the building flat out from you. And you'll have to completely butt out of my life."

Jacqui frowned, as if this wasn't going the way she'd planned. "I don't think—"

Lainey stood up, the words she should have said years ago boiling out of her. "I'm not letting you force me into this. And there's no hope for Daniel. You have no idea what my marriage was like. *None*. I'd hope you'd want better for me, even if it's not what you would have chosen." She picked up her purse with shaking hands. "I'm going, Mother. I'll find somewhere else to live. And don't worry. I will make those rent payments on my shop. They will be on time. I'm never late."

Pulse roaring in her ears, she walked away before Jacqui could say anything else.

The nerve. Lainey pulled over a couple of miles past the house and sat for a minute, tears of rage pouring down her face. *The nerve.*

Poor Esther. Lainey hoped they'd at least given the woman a fair price. But while apparently not above blackmail, her parents weren't cheats. One small thing in this whole mess to take comfort in.

What she needed was a plan. One that could get her the money, and the time, to solve this herself—which was all she wanted. Just to prove she could do it—run a business, be successful on her own terms without any help from her family.

To show them she wasn't a screw-up, but just as worthy of being a Keeler as they were.

She fished a napkin out of the glove box and wiped her face. Crying wasn't going to solve anything. She put the car back in gear and headed for the public park at the lake. She'd spent many hours here as a kid, and later as a teen when she'd needed space. Sure, there was a private beach at her parents' home, but the park had swings and a playground, now upgraded to a fancy plastic playscape. They'd kept the old metal merry-go-round, her favorite thing in the park.

The gathering twilight and chilly breeze off the water ensured the park itself was empty, though a couple cars parked nearby indicated joggers still out on the loop that ran next to the water.

Lainey pulled the hood of her jacket up and settled on a swing. She scuffed her feet in the wood chips, then backed up, ready to swing. Back and forth she went, pumping her legs, stretching out in the swing until her hood slid off and her hair fell in her face when she leaned forward. The moon hung over the quiet lake, full and incandescent, a bright star to its left. *Star light, star bright, first star I see tonight.* A small laugh escaped her, followed by more tears. She'd gone way beyond childish wishes, even if as a kid she'd believed in the power of the first star. The tensions of her parents' betrayal slid away in the stinging wind, into the encroaching darkness. Finally she stopped pumping, let herself glide through the cool evening air, slowly coming to a stop.

A motion to her left caught her eye and she turned her head.

Ben Lawless sat on the merry-go-round, watching her. Her belly clutched. Oh, no. What was he doing here?

"Did it work?" Despite his low tone, she heard him clearly.

Caught, Lainey forced herself to meet his gaze. "Did what work?"

"The swinging. The tears. You looked like you were trying to get rid of something."

She tilted her head so it rested on the chain. No point in denying it. She didn't want to. "For the moment, maybe." Though the ache under her heart hadn't gone away.

Her parents had bought her building. She squeezed her eyes shut as another wave of betrayal washed over her. How had she not seen it coming?

When she looked back over at Ben he stood up from the merry-go-round, gave it a small shove with his hand. It wobbled in a slow circle. "For the moment?"

Lainey scuffed her foot in the wood chips. Was that an opening for her to talk, no matter how reluctantly issued? She almost laughed. Where would she start? With her parents? With her baby? With her ex-husband? With the father of said baby? "I don't know. Can we not talk about it?" The very thought of trying to explain the twisted mess her life had become exhausted her.

Ben laughed—a quick deep flash that sent tingles though her body. "As long as we don't talk about me."

His grief-stricken face flashed across her memory. "Deal." She hopped out of the swing and her balance shifted a bit. No doubt an effect of her pregnancy. She started toward the water, simply needing to move.

She was surprised when Ben caught up to her. He walked beside her, his arm almost brushing hers. Even without the contact she could feel the heat from his big body as hers seemed to be *way* too tuned in to him.

This was bad.

Distracted, she stumbled a bit on the uneven sand. He caught her arm—pure reflex, she was sure—especially because he let go of her almost as soon as he touched her, as though she'd burned him somehow.

"Careful," he said, his voice low.

"Thanks," she murmured, keeping her eyes on the ground. His scent, a yummy mix of soap and fresh air, drifted over to her. She curled her fingers into fists and shoved them in her pockets so she didn't do something stupid—like reach for him and bury her face in his chest.

Even as the urge confused and scared her she knew Ben wouldn't lie to her, use her, or treat her like a wayward child. Even with his secrets, he came across as sincere in a way she so wanted to believe in.

Except she was done with believing.

They stopped when they reached the lake. The water was almost mirror-still. Perfect for skipping rocks. When was the last time she'd done that? The moon was bright enough that she could see pretty well, so she started to hunt for flat stones. She didn't look at Ben, but could feel him watching her.

Strangely, not talking felt right. She didn't feel she needed to fill the night with chatter—after the bombshell her parents had laid on her that was a good thing—and he seemed to be quiet because he was more comfortable without words.

She picked up a rock—a flat disk, smooth and cold in her hand. She lined up and let it fly over the still water, counting twelve skips. She couldn't resist a little fist pump. She still had it after all these years.

"Not bad." Ben fingered his own rock. "My turn."

"Good luck," she said politely. She'd always been a top-notch rock-skipper. One of her many under-appreciated talents. She couldn't smother a small sigh. No doubt her mother would be appalled.

His rock flew over the water. Thirteen skips.

"Hmm." Glad for the distraction, Lainey narrowed her eyes when he turned to her, eyebrow raised. "I can beat that."

A small laugh escaped him and he looked surprised at the sound. Her heart tugged. Had he really gone so long in sorrow he'd lost laughter?

He leaned toward her, not close enough to touch, but close enough to see the challenge in his eyes. "You're on."

His warm breath feathered over her cheek and her little shiver had nothing to do with the chill in the air. "Good luck," she said again. The words came out a little husky, and she turned away quickly to look for more rocks. What was wrong with her? What was it about Ben Lawless that drew her in? It was wrong on so many levels. She was pregnant, for God's sake. And her life was a mess. There was no room for a man. Especially one with issues of his own.

It took everything Ben had not to ask why she'd been crying. The tracks from her tears were dry now, but even in the light of the moon he could see her beautiful blue eyes were red-rimmed. An unwelcome protective surge caught him off-guard and left a sour feeling in his stomach.

He couldn't protect anyone. He knew that. But tonight he'd been drawn in by her obvious distress. Since she was a friend of his grandma's it had seemed wrong just to walk away until he knew she was okay.

Yeah, that was all it was. A favor to Grandma.

Riiiight...

Choosing to ignore his inner voice, he let his gaze follow her as she searched for rocks along the water's edge. The moon's light turned her hair to silver as she lifted potential candidates, weighed them in her hand, then discarded some and slipped others into her pockets. That unfamiliar smile tugged at his mouth. She took this seriously. He'd do the same.

He picked up a few rocks of his own and was ready when she came back. Determination sparked in her eyes. He swallowed hard. "You ready?" If she noticed the rasp in his voice she didn't show it.

"I'm ready. I'll go first."

She stepped forward to the edge of the water and Ben allowed himself to admire her slender figure as she let the rock fly and stood, as if she were holding her breath, until it sank, leaving an expanding ring of ripples on the water's surface.

"Ten skips."

"Not bad." He moved up next to her. "But let me show you how it's done."

He was rewarded with an eye-roll. He bit back another grin.

He took his turn and after nine skips she turned to him, her glee barely contained. "*That's* how it's done?"

In spite of himself he laughed again, the feeling foreign after so many months of not being able to. It felt—good. But scary, too. Here in the moonlight, with a beautiful woman who wanted nothing from him, playing a silly game, he was almost relaxed.

Back and forth they went, and after six stones each Ben sent her a look. "This is it. Winner takes all."

She arched a brow and pulled out her final stone. "Really? What does the winner get?"

"Bragging rights."

"Good enough." She pulled out her final stone and readied herself. She let it fly and Ben watched it, counting the skips until it sank.

"Fifteen skips." Triumph filled her voice. "Beat that, Ben."

He took his turn and they both watched as his rock sank after twelve. "You win."

She did another fist-pump. "Yay. I like to win." Then frowned. "No offense."

He shook his head. "None taken." He hesitated. "Better?"

She nodded, but he saw the shadow that fell over her features. "Yes. Thank you for staying."

He turned with her to walk back. "No problem. You're my grandma's friend."

There was the tiniest of hitches in her step. "Right. Of course."

He forced himself to ignore the hurt in her tone. He needed to build the distance between them back up. But when she turned those big blue eyes on him something long buried inside him cracked. "Lainey—"

She gave a little shake of her head as she reached her car. "Thanks again."

To hell with it.

Ben turned her around as she fumbled in her pocket for her keys. Her eyes widened and her lips parted, but before she could say anything he dipped his head and covered her mouth with his.

After a heartbeat her cold mouth opened and let him into her warmth. God, it had been so long since he'd felt anything, *anything*, and she was warm and soft and so, so sweet. He fisted his hand in her hair, to angle her head so he could go deeper, and her moan lit fires inside him that had long been dormant.

For a reason.

He broke the kiss and stepped back, his ragged breath catching in his chest. God, what had he done?

She blinked up at him, her gaze smoky and slightly confused. Then her eyes cleared and a look of pure horror crossed her face.

"I've got to go," she said, yanking her keys out of her pocket.

"Lainey, I'm sorry." As soon as the words were out he knew they were the wrong thing to say.

Her back stiffened as she unlocked the car. "It's forgotten." She got in the car and slammed the door.

He stood in the cold and cursed as her taillights disappeared out of the park. Hell. He'd just made a huge mess of something he had no right even to start.

And he had no idea how to fix it.

CHAPTER FOUR

"THEY DID WHAT?" Beth's words ended on a small shriek. The look on her face would have been comical if Lainey could muster the energy to laugh. "No way. Is that even legal?"

"Unfortunately," Lainey said as she selected a few silk 'mums for the centerpiece she was working on.

"They're kicking you out," Beth breathed. "I never thought—"

"It's not technically a kick out," Lainey corrected her. "It's a very strong suggestion I move in with them." And a heck of a way to do it, too. Though where in the budget she'd find the money to rent a place plus continue to pay her parents she didn't know.

How had it not occurred to her parents that their "helping" would put her in this kind of bind?

Beth frowned. "Are you going to? How would that work with the baby?"

A chill ran through Lainey. "I can't think of anything I want less than to live there. Especially since my mother is apparently in cahoots with Daniel. I'm going to ask Rose if she knows of any rental houses. I know she owns a couple."

Maybe she'd get lucky and one would be open. On the other hand, that would make Rose her landlord, and she wasn't sure she wanted to risk extra contact with Ben.

The kiss flashed through her mind and a delicious little shiver ran through her. It had been a mistake, which he'd acknowledged. She had to agree. But a small part of her was hurt. She'd spent much of her adult life being made to feel everything she did was a mistake. To hear it after something as sweet as that kiss, on top of her parents' antics, had cut deep.

"Wow." Beth shook her head and cut a length of ribbon. "I'm just floored."

"Yeah, me too." Lainey fitted the 'mums into the floral foam and stepped back. "These look nice. Let's get them in the window."

It took a nice chunk of time to redo the front windows with a fall theme geared toward Halloween. Lainey was pleased with the result. She glanced at the clock. Almost noon. "I need to call Jon and tell him."

Beth came around the counter. "Do you need me there?"

Lainey gave her friend a hug. "Thanks, but, no. I'll be fine. I just need to get it over with."

She climbed the stairs to her apartment with butterflies roiling in her stomach. She and Jon hadn't even bothered to exchange contact info. It had been pretty clear how forgettable the whole thing was—or would have been except for the baby.

Her hands shook as she sat down at the computer and pulled up the website she'd found for Jon's company. Since California was three hours behind Michigan it was early morning there, so she hoped she had a chance of catching him at his office.

It took two tries to dial the number correctly, but amazingly she got through. His assistant sounded about twenty and possessive, and Lainey bet Jon valued looks over work ethic. How could she have such poor judgment when it came to men?

"Jon Meier." His crisp voice sent a chill over her skin.

"It's Lainey Keeler. We—ah—met at the reunion." She stumbled a bit over the words. How exactly did one phrase *one-night stand* for polite company?

A pause. "Lainey. What's going on?" His tone was wary.

Lainey stared at the ceiling of her living room. It seemed there was only one thing to say and one way to say it. "I'm pregnant."

The silence roared in her ears. She gripped the small phone tighter.

"Jon?" she ventured after a few seconds.

"I'm here," he said, sounding slightly strangled. "Are you sure it's mine?"

Indignation spiked. "Of course it's yours. Who else's would it be?" Like she was some slut.

He said a clear and succinct curse word and Lainey winced.

"I'm sorry," he said, his voice low. "But there's something you should know."

Her heart kicked up in a pattern of dread. Those words never meant anything good. "What's that?"

She heard him exhale roughly. "I'm married."

Nausea hit Lainey like a freight train. Oh, God. *Married?* How had she not known? He was just like her ex-husband. Her stomach rolled and she sank down on the floor, hand pressed over her mouth. *Oh, no. No, no.*

"Lainey? Are you still there?"

I'm married. The words almost physically crawled over her skin. She'd played a role in the betrayal of a marriage. *What Daniel did to me.* "Oh, my God. How could you? You cheated on your wife." She couldn't keep the horror and disgust out of her voice.

There was a rustle of paper. "Well, in my admittedly weak defense, we were going through a rough patch. She doesn't—she doesn't know. I can't have her know. I can pay to take care of it, though, if you'd rather not have it."

It took her a second to sort through the numerous atrocities in those sentences. "Are you—are you offering to pay for an abortion?"

"You're what? Eight weeks? Early enough. Listen, Lainey—"

"No." The word came out furious and flat. Temper rose like bile in her throat, a sharp burn.

"I can't be a father to that baby, Lainey. My wife—she's pregnant, too. I can't risk—"

"Can't risk what? Her finding out what a slime you are?" She couldn't help the angry words. Not because she wanted him in her life, or the baby's, but because she'd given her child this kind of man for a father. The same kind of man her ex was. She pressed her hand over her eyes, willing the tears of anger and frustration away.

He let out a sigh. "Something like that. Listen, I haven't been the best husband, okay? I get that. But we are finally getting on the right track again. I can't—I just can't risk it."

Lainey sucked in a breath. The depth of his deception hit her hard. She couldn't get involved in his mess, though. She and her baby would stay above this.

She couldn't keep the disgust out of her voice. "I want you to sign off on all parental rights. I don't want you in my child's life."

"I'll talk to my lawyers," he said after a moment, and she allowed herself to breathe again. "I don't see how I could be involved even if I wanted to be. My wife..." His voice trailed off. Then, "I'm sorry, Lainey. I really am. But—you understand?"

Your poor wife. Lainey truly felt for her. She could see her own ex-husband pulling this exact same stunt. For all she knew he had. The thought made her even angrier.

"What I understand is you are a cheating, lying bastard. When will I hear from you?"

"End of the week," he said, apparently unfazed by her description of him. "I'll need your contact info. I'd prefer to communicate through email, if we need to discuss anything further."

"Fine with me." She gave him the relevant information and hung up, mind whirling. The sick feeling wouldn't recede. Most likely she'd get what she wanted, but at what cost? What could she tell her baby? The loss here was truly Jon's, but her baby deserved a father.

She dropped her face into her hands. Given her track record with men who seemed great on the surface but were total losers, she wasn't sure she could trust herself to know a good man when she met him. She pushed herself off the floor and went to get a glass of water.

Ben flashed across her mind. He was a good man. His kiss. His quiet playfulness last night. Even though it had seemed as if he was coming out of a deep shell, for that scant hour she'd spent with him he'd been more real than her husband or Jon had ever been. Maybe it was because he hadn't wanted anything from her. Maybe it had to do with the other two men being cheaters. Another wave of nausea flowed over her and she put her head back in her hands. She'd been with a married man. How had she not known? How could she know, with no ring and no mention of a wife?

She went back downstairs. A couple of months ago her life had been pretty simple. Keep her shop open and stay out of her parents' line of fire. Period. Now she was looking at single motherhood and her parents buying their way into her life and pulling her ex along—not to mention her odd connection to Ben.

Maybe one of these days she'd do something the easy way, instead of somehow making everything as difficult as possible.

* * *

Lainey called Rose that evening and at her friend's invitation went over to her house. She didn't want to see Ben, seeing as how the awkwardness level there would be epic, but she wasn't going to avoid her friend. Plus, being with someone who didn't want to manipulate her sounded wonderful.

She didn't see Ben's truck, which was both a relief and an unexpected disappointment. Ignoring the disappointment part, she saw he'd been busy. The framework for the ramp was already in place. It touched a little sweet spot in her that he took his grandma's issues so seriously.

Rose opened the kitchen door with a concerned look. "Hi, honey. Come on in. Everything okay?"

She stepped in with a smile. "Yes. Just a little tired." She didn't ask where Ben was as she slipped her jacket off. She told herself she didn't care. Not to mention it was very important that Rose did not realize Lainey's conflicted emotions regarding Ben. She didn't want any matchmaking attempts, and she doubted Ben would appreciate it, either. Possibly less than she did, if his aloof manner was any indication.

But, oh, the man could kiss.

"Dear, you look a little flushed. Are you sure you're okay?" Rose wheeled over to the table.

Her face heated even more. She couldn't very well tell the older woman she'd kissed her grandson, so she took a seat at the table and filled Rose in on her parents' bombshell.

Rose frowned when she'd finished. "I'm sorry, Lainey. I understand they mean well, or think they do, but they really don't take you into consideration, do they?"

Lainey stared at the table, a small knot in her throat. It was the truth. "Not really."

Rose reached over and squeezed her hand. "Well, as it happens I've got a little place you can rent." Her surprise must have shown on her face because Rose chuckled. "I do. I've got a little rental house over by the lake. The same couple has rented it for—oh, goodness—decades. Thirty years or so? Anyway, they moved out a couple weeks ago. Decided to retire in Florida."

Lainey opened her mouth, then closed it. Hope surged through her. "I—wow. Really?"

"Of course. Two bedrooms. Nice backyard. It's a little Cape Cod. Not real large, but plenty big for you and your cat."

Relief rushed through her. "It sounds wonderful."

Rose reached for the phone. "It needs a little work. Nothing major. Just some freshening up and some minor repairs. Why don't you go take a look? Ben's over there now, assessing what all needs to be done. He seemed to think it could be ready in around a week or so. You can even pick your paint colors."

Ben was there. Anticipation zipped through her, too quick for her to stifle. She didn't see a way to refuse without raising Rose's suspicions. "All right. I'd love to see it, if you're sure?"

Rose waved a hand. "Of course I'm sure. I can't think of anyone I'd like more to have for a tenant than you. Let me call him real quick and you can head over."

Lainey followed Rose's directions to the house, which was on the other side of the lake from her parents' place, a block from the water. The little white house was charming, from what she could see as she pulled in the driveway behind Ben's truck. It had a garage, a front porch, and the backyard was fenced. A little shiver of excitement ran though her.

"It's very cute," she said aloud as she walked up to the front porch. The light was on. She knocked, then stuck her head in. "Hello?"

She'd been hoping somehow that Ben wouldn't be here, or that someone else would be here, too. Anything but just the two of them. Not that she couldn't control herself—of course she could—it was just the last thing she needed was another complication in her life. As Ben appeared in the living room archway she couldn't help but wish all complications could be so hot.

"Lainey?" Ben said, looking behind her. "I'm sorry. Grandma said there was a potential tenant coming to check the place out."

In spite of her nerves, Lainey laughed. *Oh, Rose.* "It's me. I'm the tenant."

"You?" His brow shot up. "I thought you lived above your shop."

Lainey closed the door behind her and unzipped her jacket. She couldn't quite keep her voice steady. "Not for long."

She saw understanding dawn in his eyes, but all he said was, "I see."

Awareness sparked between them, hot and deep, and she knew while he didn't mention it he was thinking about *the kiss.* Lainey pulled her gaze off him and focused on the wall behind him. He looked so good, even with the wary expression he seemed to wear perpetually. Except the other night, when he'd actually laughed. And kissed her.

Darn it. She shut her eyes. *Not helpful.*

"You okay?"

She opened them again and gave him a small smile. "Peachy." She gestured with her hand. "Can I look around?"

Ben stepped back out of the doorway. "Sure. Kitchen—

dining room through there—" he pointed to his right "—bedrooms. Bathroom that way. I'll be in the kitchen if you need anything." Then he disappeared.

She took a minute to wander around the room she stood in—a good-sized living room, with two large windows and a fireplace, flanked by two smaller, higher windows over built-in bookcases. The former tenants' drapes remained, but otherwise the room was bare. The floor was hardwood, scuffed and worn and in need of being redone. She rubbed the toe of her shoe on it. How would a hard floor be with a baby? Maybe she could get some thick rugs. The paint color was an odd shade of pinkish tan, but maybe that was the light from the overhead fixture, which was a little harsh. Still, it had charm and lots of potential.

She walked across the floor and it creaked under her feet. She heard banging and swearing from the direction of the kitchen, so she detoured that way down the short hall.

Ben was on his knees, bent over, half in the cabinet under the sink, and her gaze locked on his very fine butt and flexed thigh muscles. The back of his shirt had ridden up, exposing an inch or so of an equally nice back. She blinked and forced herself to refocus.

"Is there a problem?" she asked.

He scrambled back out from the cabinet, whacked his head and muttered another choice word. She winced.

"Sorry," she said. "Are you okay?"

"Fine." He stood up and rubbed the back of his head. "Need something?"

"Um…no. I heard some noise and thought I'd see what was going on in here." She looked at the array of tools and wet towels on the floor. "Maybe you need a plumber?"

Ben stared at her, then let out a sharp bark of laughter. "What I need is another wrench." He bent over and she tried very hard to keep her eyes off his butt and failed. She very much wanted to chalk it up to pregnancy hormones, except for the little fact she wasn't attracted to any other man but this one. He pulled out two pieces of what had been a wrench and held them up.

"Oh. That's not good."

"No kidding. Are you parked behind me?"

He was going right now? The little stab she felt couldn't be disappointment. It had to be relief. "Yes. I'll move my car."

He turned away to wipe his hands on the towel lying on the counter. She glanced around the room, noting the old but serviceable appliances, the Formica counters that were a bit worn, the old linoleum on the floor. The cabinets were in good condition. It was a nice size. It would work well for her.

"Not what you're used to, I'm sure," Ben said and she blinked at him.

"What isn't?"

He swept his hand out, indicating the room. "This."

It took her a second, then anger spiked. "Oh, for God's sake. Why would you think that?"

He just looked at her and she shook her head, sadness chasing the anger away. Just because she'd been raised in a wealthy household it didn't mean those things mattered to her. "You don't know me. At all. I'd appreciate it if you'd keep your judgments to yourself. I'll go move my car to the street."

Ben shut his eyes as she stomped off. He'd achieved his goal, which had been to drive her away, but he felt no sense of victory. Only shame. She'd looked way too hot, standing there in her jeans, boots and sweatshirt, with her hair up in a ponytail. None of it was even particularly form-fitting, but it was enough. Worse, he'd wanted to touch her, to feel her hot, responsive mouth under his again. That was dangerous. *Wanting* was something he tried to keep a lid on, along with feeling. He saw her headlights flash across the wall as she backed out of the driveway.

Now he needed to apologize. Whatever had prompted last night's crying jag had brought her here today, and it wasn't right for him to make it harder for her just because he was attracted to her. Or to lose a tenant for his grandmother.

So he went into the living room and didn't back down under the cold glare she leveled at him when she came through the door. "I'm sorry. I was out of line."

She considered him, her blue eyes cool. Finally she nodded. "You were. But I accept your apology. Next time don't assume you know anything about me."

I know how you kiss, he wanted to tell her. *I know how you feel in my arms, how soft your skin is under my hand. I know how your breasts feel against me.*

She must have read his thoughts on his face because her gaze skittered off his and she jingled her keys in her hand. He cleared his throat, trying to bring his thoughts back around.

"Okay, then. I'm going to go. If you leave before I get back you can lock the door behind you. Also, if you're considering renting this place, start thinking of paint colors. The sooner you can get them to me, the better. I can get started as soon as I finish a few repairs."

She nodded. "I will. I like it. So far I think it'll suit us just fine."

"Let me know." As he escaped out into the night, he wondered, *Who's us?*

CHAPTER FIVE

LAINEY SHUDDERED OUT a deep breath when the door closed behind him. There had been no mistaking the look on his face when she'd said he didn't know her. Odd that he could know her a little physically but not at all as a person.

It seemed to be a pattern. Her ex-husband had never attempted to really get to know her. He'd had his secretary take care of gifts and things. She'd allowed herself to pretend it was because he was busy, but she knew it had been because he'd never cared enough to find out.

Lesson learned.

She shoved all the thoughts away and walked down the hall to the bedrooms. Two of them, both of which were bigger than her bedroom at the apartment, plus a decent-sized bathroom. Another door led to an open and clean attic.

She went back to the kitchen, where she found a small pantry, an entryway by the back door with hooks for coats, and stairs to the basement. A quick scout revealed it to be clean and apparently dry, and she found the laundry hookups. At some point the space might make a good play area, if there was a way to cover the cement with carpet.

Back upstairs, she mused over paint colors as she went back to the bedrooms. She hadn't decided yet if she wanted to know if she was having a boy or a girl. Then she frowned. Either way, probably better to go neutral. That way she could forestall any questions for longer.

With a groan, she rested her head on the doorjamb. It wouldn't matter. Her little secret would out itself in a matter of weeks. Her pants were already feeling a little snug, and she had taken to wearing slightly baggy tops to cover up.

That wouldn't work much longer.

Her phone rang and she fished it out of her pocket. Seeing Rose's number, she answered.

"What do you think?" There was excitement in Rose's voice and Lainey had to smile.

"I love it."

"I knew it." The smugness in her friend's tone made Lainey laugh. "Come on back tomorrow and we'll sign a lease."

Lainey hesitated. "How much are you asking?" She'd told her parents she'd make rent payments anyway, and to add house rent on top of it would seriously stretch her already tight budget even more.

Rose named an amount that Lainey knew had to be way low, considering the size of the house and the location. "Rose, are you sure? That's not much."

"The house is paid for," her friend said, then added impishly, "And don't you dare argue with your elders."

Lainey laughed and flicked the light switch off in what would be the baby's room. "Well, when you put it like that…"

"You can help do some of the work if you want," Rose said. "Painting and such."

"Sure," Lainey said. How would that work with being pregnant? She'd have to make sure it was safe before she cracked open a paint can.

They talked a few more minutes, then Lainey hung up.

She locked the door behind her after one last look around. She would make a home here, for herself and her baby. But to get it she'd have to work with Ben.

Ignoring the little thrill that gave her, she started her car. She needed to remember Ben would leave. She was going to be a single mother. He was clearly struggling with some kind of issues of his own. None of that held hope for any kind of relationship.

And the very fact she'd even thought the word *relationship* in regard to Ben was troubling.

"So, I've found a place to live," Lainey told Beth as she carefully unpacked the latest shipment of flowers the next morning.

"Really? That was fast."

"Yep. It was perfect timing. Rose has an empty rental house."

Beth snipped the ends off a handful of lilies before plunging them in the water bucket. "Hmm. Will this put you in contact with her very appealing grandson?"

Lainey's face heated. Of course Beth *would* make that connection. "I wouldn't call him appealing," she hedged. *Liar.* "She wants me to help with the cleaning and painting and stuff. Which Ben is doing."

Beth set her scissors down, arched her brow. "Hmm. Is there something you're not telling me, Lainey?"

Lainey busied herself breaking down an empty box. Then she gave up. Her friend would figure it out anyway. "He kissed me."

Beth's mouth dropped open. "Holy cow! When? Was it amazing?"

Amazing? Lainey recalled the tender yet hot way his mouth had moved over hers and her whole body buzzed.

"Um… After the thing with my parents. And, yes, I guess it was."

"You *guess*?" Beth's eyes bugged out. "He doesn't look like the type to rate 'I guess' on the kissing scale."

She had a point. "Okay, yeah, it was amazing."

Beth grinned. "I knew it. So. Spill. What happened?"

Lainey filled her in on her visit to the park and finding Ben there. She finished with, "But it was a mistake. It won't happen again."

Beth shook her head. "Why not?" The front doorbell jingled and she pointed a finger at Lainey. "Don't go anywhere. We're not done here." Then she hurried out front and Lainey heard her greet the customer.

Lainey's phone buzzed in her pocket and she pulled it out. She didn't recognize the number, but answered anyway, tucking it under her chin as she reached for the next box of flowers. "Hello?"

"Lainey?"

Her blood froze. She'd recognize that smooth voice on the other end of the line anywhere. Flowers forgotten, she gripped the phone so hard it hurt.

"Daniel." His name fell like a razor off her tongue. "What do you want?"

He chuckled—a low sound that sent chills up her spine. How had it ever thrilled her? "Why, to talk to you, baby. It's been a long time. Can't I talk to my wife?"

"Ex-wife," she corrected, because it had been hard-won and it mattered.

"Whatever," he said, and she pictured him waving away her words with a sweep of his hand, like so many pesky flies. "It's just details. Can we get together soon? I'd love to see you."

She nearly dropped the phone as rage rolled through

her. "No. Way. I've got nothing left to say to you." As if he'd ever listened, ever heard her.

"Laine. It's been so long. I miss you. I made a mistake." The seductive tone of his voice made her skin crawl and she shivered.

"Yeah, so did I," she muttered. Her marriage had been one big fat mistake from start to finish.

"Lainey, please." Now he sounded almost pleading.

"No." Oh, it felt so good to tell him that. "I can't talk right now, Daniel. I'm at work."

He sighed. "So I've heard. Some little flower shop, right? It's not going well. Your mother said you're having some problems—"

"Having some problems?" she sputtered. His condescending tone had her teeth grinding together. This was the Daniel she knew. "It's a new business. I'm still getting it off the ground."

"Yes, but it's been—what?—nine months? It was an honest try but it's not getting better, Lainey. You need to face reality."

Hearing him voice her own fears made her stomach churn.

His tone turned slightly wheedling. "I'd love to help. I think we could make it work this time."

"Did she dump you?"

A beat, then, "I'm sorry? Who?"

"You don't want me, Daniel. You never did. You want what you think I stand for. Calling me and belittling my shop and the life I've built without you is not going to change my mind. Nothing will," she qualified. Fueled by her chat with Jon, she added, "You cheated. You used me. Don't call me again."

"Lainey, for God's sake, just listen. You can't do this."

His anger snapped through the connection and for a heart-beat she froze.

"I am doing it. Goodbye, Daniel." She clicked the little phone shut as hard as she could. Oh, for the days when a phone could be slammed in a cradle.

She dropped the poor phone on the worktable and leaned forward on her palms, head down, tried to settle. He was right. It had been nine months and she was still struggling. Hearing him voice her fears, in that awful tone, had tears burning her eyes. What if the scumbag was right?

More than that, couldn't he see if he'd really loved her he'd want her to succeed? Couldn't he see she knew what he really was?

More than all that, though, *what if he was right?*

Beth came in and started toward her in alarm.

"Lainey! Are you okay?"

"I'm fine," she said, and wished she meant it. "Daniel just called."

Beth sucked in a breath. "What? Wow, he's got some nerve."

She gave a sharp laugh. "Daniel's got nothing *but* nerve."

Her feelings must have shown on her face because Beth leaned in. "Listen to me. Don't you dare let him get to you. Look at what you've done here. It took a lot of guts to divorce him and buy this place. To keep your parents at arm's length despite their meddling. It hasn't been easy but you're doing it. Don't let them derail you now."

Lainey stared at her friend. "I never—you see it that way?"

Beth leaned over and gave her a one-armed hug. "Of course. And you should, too."

Lainey had never thought of it that way. Oh, she did what needed to be done, but usually well after it should have been done to begin with. Long after she'd been taken for a fool. It didn't strike her as something to be proud of.

The chime of the front door saved her from answering. "I'll get that," she said, and slipped past Beth.

Her friend's words were kind, but Lainey could only hope she was right. There was too much riding on her being able to make this work.

Ben wouldn't admit it to anyone, but he'd been listening for her car.

When he saw her park at the curb he tried to squelch a completely inappropriate spurt of anticipation. He told himself he didn't want this, didn't want her, but every time he saw her it got a little harder to believe it. So he'd rather be anywhere than here, having her help him paint. Just having her in the same house made his skin feel too tight.

Before, he would have asked her out. Seen where it went. But that was—before.

Now he needed to keep his distance—something he wasn't doing very well at.

He heard her come in the front door and turned his attention to finishing taping the bedroom so she could paint. Heard her quick, light steps coming down the hall. He tensed even more as she came in the room.

"Hi." Her voice was slightly tentative, as if she expected to be shot down.

He turned and simply took in the sight of her in old jeans, an oversize sweatshirt, her hair pulled up in a ponytail. She plucked at the sweatshirt uncertainly and he realized he was just standing there, gaping at her like a fool.

He cleared his throat. "Hi. You ready?"

She moved into the room a little farther. So as not to spook her, and to give himself some space, he busied himself popping the top off the paint can.

She came to stand beside him. "I can't wait to see this."

She'd gone to the hardware store on her lunch hour to pick the colors. He'd gone in later to pick them up. Efficient.

She made a little humming noise in her throat. "That's a little pinker than I thought."

"It'll look different once you get it on the wall. It will dry darker. They all do." He set the can off to the side. "You know how to do this?"

He looked up in time to see her shake her head.

He stood up. "You can change a tire, but have never painted a room?"

She looked a little sheepish. "Ah. No. My skills are a bit scattered, I'm afraid."

He didn't want to find that sweet. Or charming. *Damn it.* He turned back to the paint cans and cleared his throat. "Lucky for you, it's easier than changing a tire."

She laughed. "I hope so."

He stirred it and tipped the can to pour into a paint tray. He handed her a paintbrush. "This is pretty simple. You'll do around the trim first. I taped in here already."

He explained the method and showed her how to make small, careful strokes, taking care not to touch her. But she seemed to take equal care not to touch him. She smelled so good it was hard not to give in to temptation.

"When that's done you can do the rest. The roller's pretty simple. Just don't get too much paint on it. You'll be okay in here? I've got some other things to finish up."

Translation: he needed some space. Quickly.

She gave him a small smile and moved the ladder over by the open window. "I'll be fine. I'll call you if I need you."

Dismissed. He walked down the hall toward the kitchen, rubbing his hand over his face. He needed to get this house finished quickly, before the woman in the bedroom back there drove him out of his mind.

When Ben returned to check on Lainey it had only been a half-hour. He'd stayed away as long as he could, which was pitiful. He found her on the ladder by the window, carefully painting under the crown molding. He took a moment to admire the long, lean lines of her legs and the curve of her ass, which was hugged nicely by her soft jeans. Her sweatshirt lifted when she extended her arms up to paint, but not quite enough to give him more than a small but tantalizing glimpse of skin. He tried to shut the feelings down—kissing her had been a mistake because it had unleashed a whole torrent of feelings he didn't want. Couldn't afford. And he was now swamped with them.

This was bad.

She shifted then and he stepped fully into the room. The last thing he wanted was to get caught staring and make things even more weird. "Lainey—"

She turned quickly on the ladder and upset it enough to lose her balance. With a little cry, she fell awkwardly on her rear on the hard floor.

He crossed the room in about two strides. "Lainey! Are you okay?"

She twisted to sit up, wincing. The floor was hard and he imagined it had been quite a landing. She grabbed her ankle with a sharp hiss.

He knelt beside her, worry clouding his vision. "Honey. Are you okay?" When she shook her head he pulled up her jeans leg to see her ankle starting to swell. "We'd better get that checked out. You might need an X-ray."

Her gaze swung to his and he saw the horror and worry there. She shook her head. "No. No X-rays." She gave a forced little laugh. "I'm just clumsy."

"Your ankle—"

"No."

He sat back. "Lainey, listen—"

"I'm pregnant," she whispered and he drew back to stare at her.

The word rang in his head. *Pregnant.* And he'd been kissing her and wanting her—someone else's woman.

She must have seen the expression change on his face because she grabbed his arm. "The father—he's not in the picture. I'm in this alone. My balance is off. That's why I fell. And X-rays might be bad for the baby."

"What kind of man walks out on his responsibility?" he said, not really expecting an answer, but outraged on her behalf.

She gave a humorless little laugh. "One who misrepresented himself. I'll be fine." She tugged her pant leg back down. "I have to ask—no one but my friend Beth knows this yet... Please—don't say anything to Rose. I'll tell her, but..." She hesitated. "I didn't mean to tell you."

"I understand. I won't. But the father—" For some reason he seemed to be stuck on that fact more than anything.

She cut him off with a slash of her hand. "He knows. He's not on board, so to speak."

A surge of anger welled in Ben. A baby should have a father. And here was a man, apparently alive and well, not willing to take on the responsibility for the little life that he'd created. A responsibility that a good man, like Jason, hadn't been able to keep even though he'd wanted to. "His loss."

Her gaze shot to his and she grimaced slightly. "Damn straight. Can you help me stand?"

"Let me check that ankle first." At her confused expression, he added, "I'm a firefighter and an EMT. I'm not a substitute for a doctor or an X-ray, but I may be able to tell if it's broken."

"Oh." She extended her leg slowly and inched up her jeans.

He removed her shoe carefully but didn't miss her wince. With careful fingers he probed her slim ankle. Her skin was smooth and soft and he was a total heel for his completely unprofessional physical response to touching her.

"I don't feel anything broken," he said. "Let me help you stand."

He got to his feet and took both of her hands in his, trying not to feel the heat her soft touch generated in him. He gave a gentle pull and she hopped up on one foot, overbalanced, and landed on his chest. His arms went around her before he could stop them and he looked down into her beautiful, upturned face. There was confusion and pain and heat and wanting in her blue gaze, and his groin tightened at the press of her breasts against his chest.

He cleared his throat. Kissing her was *not an option. Not an option, not an option,* chanted the loop in his brain, but he wanted so badly to lose himself in it, in her, in this—

Pregnant woman.

He cleared his throat and loosened his hold but didn't let her go fully. "So…um…how's the ankle?" His voice was a little rough.

She rested it on the floor and pulled back a bit, putting a little weight on it. Her wince spoke volumes and he steadied her with his hands on her waist. "Lainey. Please. I know I didn't feel anything broken but some types of breaks I wouldn't necessarily feel. Do you need to go to the hospital?"

She gave a little hopping motion and moved backwards.

"No. I'm okay. It's sore, but I can take acetaminophen for it. I want to finish this."

Somehow she hadn't upended the paint when she fell off the ladder, even though she'd dropped the brush on the drop cloth. He took the tray off and poured the paint back in the can so he wouldn't reach for her again. She'd felt far too good in his arms.

But she was pregnant. And even with the father out of the picture he couldn't risk a relationship with her or her baby. He wasn't that kind of guy. Not anymore.

"We'll finish tomorrow. Right now you need to get that ankle up with ice on it. Don't argue," he added when she opened her sexy little mouth to do just that. "And I want you to promise me you'll go in tomorrow if it's worse or not getting better."

She pressed her lips together, then nodded. "Okay. You're right."

"I'll drive you home. You'll need help up to your apartment, right?" He'd get her home, get her settled. It was the least he could do for her, for his grandma's friend. "Tomorrow I'll bring you your car. Leave me your key."

He saw all the arguments cross her face. "I don't want you to go to any trouble—"

"No trouble." He caught her chin, unable to stop the action. The surprise in her eyes licked him like fire. "Lainey. You need a little help. You need to be careful so you don't hurt the baby."

That got her attention and she nodded. "Right. Okay. Thank you."

He swung her into his arms. She let out a little, "Eeep!" and her arms went around his neck.

He gave a little chuckle, surprised by the sound. "Relax. I've got you."

The scary part was how damn good she felt in his arms.

How right. How oddly protective he felt of the baby. He hadn't seen the swell of her belly, but her sweatshirt prevented that.

He cut his thoughts off right there. There was nowhere for this to go that could end well. He would be leaving as soon as he had his grandma squared away and his confidence back. He'd only hurt Lainey and he couldn't bring himself to risk it.

CHAPTER SIX

WHAT WAS SHE thinking?

Lainey winced as she buckled her seat belt and Ben walked around the truck to get in. Holy cow. She'd just blurted out her secret to this man, and she hadn't even told his grandma—her friend—yet. Somehow her filter kept shutting off and then her mouth took over.

"I'm not the type who sleeps around," she blurted as soon as he got in the truck. *Ack!* There went the filter again. Maybe it was the pain in her ankle? Yet for some reason it was very important he understand.

He fitted the key in the ignition. His jaw was tense. "I didn't say you were. Things happen."

Yes, they did. She was living proof that *things* tended to happen to some people more than others. She stared out the window, not wanting to see him even in profile, lit by the dash lights. It wasn't his fault he kept showing up when she was falling apart, though it had happened with alarming frequency since she'd met him.

The drive home was tense but Lainey had no desire to talk. Her ankle throbbed and she tried to focus on that rather than the fact she'd told Ben about the baby. Told an almost perfect stranger who'd kissed her, for God's sake. There was a kind of intimacy that they were both pretty good at ignoring. And she'd just added to it by blurting out that she was pregnant. A little panic raised its head. It had been far, far easier to tell him than it should have been. What was it about him that made her spill her secrets? Was it because he was so different from her ex-husband? She frowned. Even that didn't fully make sense, since she barely knew him. But something about him spoke to her, soothed her. Almost as if she recognized him somehow, on a deeper level.

She gave herself a mental shake. Wow. That really didn't make sense. Maybe she'd somehow managed to hit her head when she fell. Or the pain in her ankle was making her a little crazy.

Ben pulled in front of the shop and she reached down to unbuckle the seat belt. "Well. Thanks for the ride," she said brightly. "Sorry to put you out."

He caught her hand. In the dim glow of the streetlights, he looked as surprised as she was at the contact. "You could never put me out. Stay there. Please. Let me help you down."

"I can—"

"Of course you can," he interrupted. "But you don't want to risk a fall that might hurt the baby or further damage the ankle. And you might need some help navigating those stairs."

Darn it. He was right. "Okay."

He gave her a small smile before he slipped out of the truck. "It's okay to need help, Lainey."

She watched him walk in front of the truck through the wash of the headlights and couldn't help but think he wasn't totally correct. Needing help didn't make her weak, but it left her open to people like her parents and their manipulations. It was safer to rely on herself than sort through the motivations of others.

He opened the door and reached for her. It was a little

awkward to slide out into his arms, and she was surprised when he didn't put her down, instead settled her into his arms. She didn't want to admit how good the hardness of his chest felt against her side, how incredibly good he smelled.

"This is easier if you relax a little," he said close to her ear.

She looked up to see humor spark in his eyes. The humor died, though, when his gaze fell to her mouth and his arms tightened perceptibly around her.

She caught her breath at the dark heat she saw there and an answering one rose in her. It wouldn't take much, just a slight shift…

A car drove by and the spell was snapped. He cleared his throat and started for the door.

Her face burned. Good Lord, what *was* this?

She forced herself to relax into his solid chest. Weird moments aside, it felt good to lean on someone. Just for a minute. His heart beat faster against her ribs. Its rhythm matched that of her own and she wondered if it was from the moment they'd shared or the exertion of carrying her. The coolness of the evening did nothing to counteract the warmth he generated in her.

He got her upstairs and she unlocked her door.

"Sit," he said as he steered her gently toward the couch, and she sank down gratefully.

He put a pillow under the ankle. She couldn't help but notice how he sucked all the air out of the room and made her small space seem even tinier.

"I'll get you ice and some acetaminophen. Where do you keep it?"

"Bathroom, in the medicine cabinet," she said, adjusting the pillow. Not because it needed it but because then she didn't have to look at him and see—what? Or maybe, more accurately, he wouldn't see what kind of effect he had on her.

"All right." He went in the kitchen. "Hey, kitty," she heard him say, and her heart tilted just a bit. Then, in a louder voice, "Where are the glasses? And do I need to feed the cat? She's looking at me like she expects something."

She swallowed a laugh. "She does. There's a can of food in the fridge. You can put the rest of it in her dish. And glasses are in the cupboard to the right of the sink."

She listened to the sounds in the kitchen, the low murmur of his voice as he talked to the cat, the opening and closing of the cupboard, the rattling of ice. She rested her head on the back of the couch and shut her eyes. No one had ever taken care of her before. Such a little thing—ice for her ankle, feeding the cat, water for the pills. Not earth-shattering. Yet it was somehow.

He appeared with the items and placed ice, wrapped in a towel, over her ankle. "That okay?"

The gentleness of the action nearly undid her. She swallowed hard. "Yes. Thanks."

"Here's the water. Hold on while I get the pills."

He headed down the hall, looking first to the left—her bedroom—then to the right—her bathroom. Where she'd thrown bras she'd hand-washed over the shower rod. She shut her eyes in mortification. There was a brief pause as he entered the bathroom—no doubt he'd gotten an eyeful—then the rattling of the pill bottle. When he came back down the hall he didn't actually make eye contact. Then again, neither did she.

"Here you go." He plopped the pills in her palm. Was it just her, or were his fingers slightly unsteady? "Can I call anyone for you?"

She almost laughed. "No. I'm all set, thanks."

He cleared his throat. "All right, then. I'll bring you

your car tomorrow. If you need anything, call me. Where's your phone?"

She tugged her purse over and pulled the phone out. He took it from her and added his number. "Now you have no excuse. I'm serious. Especially if you need help with those stairs in the morning." He handed the phone back and this time their fingers lingered for a heartbeat.

Breathless, she tried to smile. "I will. Um…thank you. For everything."

He stepped back. "No problem."

When the door shut behind him she flopped back on the cushions and pressed both hands over her eyes, unsure if she should laugh or scream.

She was in way deeper trouble than she'd thought.

Ben stared at the game on the TV above the bar. He couldn't have told anyone who was playing, much less the score, and he was only vaguely aware it was a hockey game. All he could see was Lainey's perfect mouth forming the words *"I'm pregnant"*.

They still packed a punch. It wasn't even his kid, and he'd never meet the baby—no doubt he'd be long gone by the time Lainey gave birth. In fact, it was most likely he'd never talk to her again, unless they ran into each other though Rose somehow. So why the hell did it matter?

He shifted on the stool. Lainey was dangerous. The kind of dangerous that made him want what he couldn't have. It wasn't fair to Jason—or Callie, for that matter. What right did he have even to think about pursuing a woman—Lainey—when Callie's husband was gone?

He took a swallow of the beer he couldn't even taste. He was pretty sure the bitterness in his mouth came from his own feelings rather than the drink in his hand.

Pregnant.

He'd felt a stab of jealousy straight to his soul when she'd looked at him with those big blue eyes and whispered those words. No use passing it off as anything but that.

What could he offer her? He didn't even know if he could do his job anymore. That anxiety was ever-present, hovering in the back of his mind. Shading everything he did. It mixed with guilt into a potent brew of shame and sorrow.

So, no, he wasn't in any shape to pursue her. Therefore, being jealous was a complete waste of time and energy. Still, he'd felt a roaring protectiveness when she'd fallen. And far more than that when he'd walked in her bathroom and seen those lacy, sexy bras lined up on the shower rod.

God help him. He was getting in way over his head and all he'd done was help her. But something about her drew him in and he couldn't seem to walk away. All those feelings he'd walled off…? Yeah. He was in danger of drowning in them if he didn't get them under control fast.

It didn't matter. He set aside his half-empty beer, since he couldn't even taste it, and signaled for his bill. He wasn't getting anywhere having a pity party and it was a waste of time anyway. Might as well go home, where there were at least projects he could do to stay busy.

He entered the house quietly, but his sharp-eyed grandma was in the living room, knitting. He couldn't tell what it was but her hands flew and the needles clicked together sharply. She looked up when he came in.

"So. How was it?"

Ben sat down opposite her, since it seemed rude to stand and talk when she was all settled in. He outlined the progress he'd made on the house, then hesitated.

Rose arched a brow. "What?"

He debated how much he could say and keep Lainey's secret safe. "She twisted her ankle," he said finally. "Stepped wrong off the ladder."

Rose's hands stopped moving. "Is she okay?"

"I checked it out," he said. "She was adamant about not going to the hospital."

"She needs an X-ray," Rose muttered and Ben sighed.

"I suggested it but she shot me down." True enough.

Rose sighed and her needles started moving again. "I bet."

"I offered to call her mother, but she said no." He wasn't fishing, exactly, but he was curious as to why Lainey seemed to think she was on her own when she had family nearby.

Rose snorted. "That woman doesn't have a maternal bone in her body. And that ex of hers—" She pressed her lips together tightly. "Well. Anyway. I'd better call her—make sure she's okay. I wish you'd brought her back here."

Ben was pretty sure Lainey didn't want Rose to figure out about the pregnancy. As Rose dialed Lainey's number he took a good look at the knitting project on her lap. The soft colors and small size looked an awful lot like a baby blanket. But he wasn't going to ask any questions.

They'd each keep Lainey's secret.

He hung around, fixing himself something to eat he really didn't want in the kitchen, but he wasn't going to admit that. When he went back in the living room Rose was hanging up and frowning.

That protective instinct reared back up and he forced himself to keep his voice level. "Is she okay?"

Rose's gaze flicked to his. "She's hurting."

Ben started to stand. "I can go—"

Rose shook her head. "She won't come. Thinks she has to be strong." She gave him a pointed look. "Like someone else I know."

He opted not to touch that comment. "I've got to get her car to her tomorrow."

"That's good. Then you can see if she's okay in person. She's likely to not admit it over the phone."

She had a point.

He cleared his throat. "Sounds good. You need anything before I go take a shower?"

Rose shook her head, her hands flying once more over the blanket. "Thank God for DVR. Got one more show to watch. I'm all set, thanks."

He chuckled and walked toward the stairs. She said his name softly. When he turned, she looked at him, her faded blue gaze serious.

"She needs someone like you."

Ben froze as the words pinged around in his heart. "No. No, I'm not what she needs."

"Ben." Her voice was sharp. "You are exactly what she needs. Don't sell yourself short."

He had nothing to say to that. As he went up the stairs his heart was heavy. He wasn't what Lainey needed. He was too damaged to be enough for anyone.

Still. He regretted not being able to have the chance.

Where there's smoke, there's fire.

Ben could see the black plume of smoke the next morning from the front porch of his grandma's house, where he'd been working on the ramp. It was coming from the other side of town. *Lainey's side.*

That thought bumped him into action. He'd go check on her, make sure—just make sure. Since he had to take her car back anyway, this gave him the excuse. And she wouldn't be moving real fast after that fall, so no one would think twice if he checked on her.

"I'm going to take Lainey's car back," he told his

grandma, who was in the kitchen with her Sudoku book. "You need anything while I'm out?"

She tipped her glasses down her nose. "Everything okay?"

He hesitated. "There's a fire."

She gave a small nod. "We've got good people here, Ben. Maybe you should be one of them?"

He opened his mouth, then shut it again. He shook his head, grabbed his jacket from by the back door and hurried to his truck.

It only took a few minutes to drive to the other house. From this angle it was hard to tell precisely where the fire was, but he could smell the smoke. He flexed his hands on the wheel as he turned onto the street and pulled into the rental house's driveway. He started Lainey's car and headed for downtown.

He whipped the car into a spot down the block from Lainey's shop and jogged across the street toward the smoke. He needed to see, to know if he could handle it. Now he could see ash floating in the air, and he heard the wail of sirens. Tension built in his shoulders and he rolled them in an effort to release it.

He took a deep breath of the smoky air and coughed as he turned down a side street to see a fully engulfed building. He stayed well back from the cordoned-off area. Fire didn't fascinate him the way it did other people. It was an enemy, a force, a beast to be tamed and conquered. Seeing it lick gleefully at the building gave him no thrill.

He watched the firefighters doing their job—*his* job— and swallowed hard. This was what he was born to do, but he wasn't sure he could ever go back. God, but he missed it. He missed it like he'd miss his arm if he'd lost it. Missed the adrenaline, the teamwork. The battle. It could be grim work—messy, and damn hard—but, hell, there wasn't anything else he'd rather do.

When the roof caved in with a shower of sparks and the flames leapt higher he shut his eyes as nausea rolled over him. For a second he couldn't breathe. Finally he turned and walked away, disappointment lodging in his gut like a rock. He'd wondered—now he knew. He wasn't ready. Would he ever be?

He stopped in front of The Lily Pad, its bright windows and festive decor drawing him like a beacon through the cool, smoky air. He didn't want to examine his relief at finding her shop okay or his anger at himself for his reaction to the fire. Or the real reason the shop pulled him: the woman inside.

Every step closer tangled everything tighter inside him. He pushed it all away and walked through the door.

Lainey looked up and gave him a small, startled smile. He didn't miss the flash of pleasure that crossed her beautiful face.

"Ben."

He tamped down his own reaction and pulled her key out of his pocket. "Thought I'd stop by and give you this." He moved forward and shook his head when she started to get up. "No, sit. How's the ankle?"

"Better today." She held out her hand and he pressed the key into her palm. Her skin was warm under his cool fingers. Her eyes widened slightly at the contact and he wondered if she felt it, too. The heat, the spark.

Sparks.

"Did you see the fire?" She shook her head as she slipped the key into her pocket. "Of course you must have. I can smell the smoke on your jacket. You said you're a firefighter, right?"

He cleared his throat, suddenly having trouble breathing. "Yeah. I did. I was." *Was.* His voice stuck a little on the word. Was he or wasn't he? Could he ever go back? What if he couldn't?

"Ben?" The concern in her voice made him wince. "Are you okay? You looked a little lost there for a moment."

Lost. That was a good word for him. "I'm fine. Sorry."

She studied him, and for a second he thought she'd ask him more questions. But her phone rang. She glanced at it, then at him.

"I'll get out of here." So he wouldn't touch her, he put his hands in his pockets. "Your car's down about half a block."

"Thank you," she murmured as the phone rang. "I appreciate it."

He didn't hang around as she answered the phone, but he did pause at the door and look back. Her eyes were on him and she blushed just a little as her gaze caught his. He swallowed hard and walked out into the smoky fall air.

Lainey let out a shuddering breath as she hung up the phone from an order. She'd managed to get all the information, but it had been hard, seeing Ben through the windows as he'd walked, slightly hunched against the wind, past the windows of her shop. She'd hoped—foolishly— he'd look back at her one more time. *Silly.*

She entered the last of the order information into the computer and stretched. While her ankle needed to be propped up, the position was uncomfortable for her back.

Beth breezed back in, to-go bag from the café in hand. She shook her head as she placed it on the counter. "Was that Ben I saw walking by? Was he here?"

Lainey took the offered sandwich and set it carefully on a napkin. "Just for a minute. He brought my car up here."

Beth waggled her eyebrows. "Is that all?"

Lainey sighed. His face—so closed up today, after how sweet he'd been last night. He'd shut down even farther when, in her apparently misguided quest to make conversation, she'd asked him about being a firefighter. Clearly a sore spot. "Yeah. That's all."

Beth clucked her tongue. "Too bad. He's hot. And the two of you would be so cute together."

She thought of how easily she'd fit in his arms last night, and the heat in his eyes, and a little shiver passed through her. "That's silly."

Beth shrugged and snagged a French fry. "Maybe. Maybe not. But you have to start somewhere, Laine."

She stared at her sandwich. No, she didn't. Not really. And Ben wasn't interested in her. Well, actually, that wasn't true. He was clearly interested in her. But he wasn't willing or able to take it anywhere.

And neither was she.

CHAPTER SEVEN

THE DOOR CHIMED and Lainey walked carefully out of the back room, not wanting to admit the little skip in her pulse was the hope it was Ben coming back, no matter how unlikely that was. She'd decided to ask him to her mother's gala, and didn't want to lose her nerve.

It was a complete surprise to see her brother. "Kevin?"

"Hey, little sis," Kevin greeted her with a smile. "What's going on? Mom said you're moving."

Lainey looked at her brother, still in his scrubs. He looked tired, and there were definite lines around his blue eyes, but his smile was warm.

She gestured to him. "Come on back. You stopped in to ask me that?"

"Well, I was on my way to Mel's Café for lunch and thought I'd stop in." When Lainey opened her mouth, he held up his hands. "No, I'm not here to convince you of anything. I'm just asking."

Lainey moved to the worktable and pulled out a length of pumpkin-colored ribbon she was using for a silk centerpiece. Kevin had rarely, if ever, been on the receiving end of their parents' ire. He was a surgeon, lived in an appropriate condo, and drove a nice car. No wife yet, but that wasn't held against him. "Did they tell you what happened?"

Kevin leaned on the table. Now his expression was concerned. "No."

She took a deep breath. "They bought this building."

Kevin cocked his head. "Doesn't it help you out?"

She stabbed a floral pin in with a little more force than necessary. "Kevin. They didn't ask me. They showed me the deed and said I had to move back home."

Kevin swore softly under his breath. "I'm sorry, Laine. Did they say why?"

"Of course. I'm not doing well here. Yet. It's been a struggle. And I guess they don't think that reflects well on them." She didn't mention Daniel. No point in muddying the waters.

"Are you?"

"Am I what?"

"Moving back home?"

She gave a sharp little bark of laughter. "God, no. I found a nice little house a friend of mine owns. I'm moving there—this weekend, in fact."

He chucked her under the chin, a gentle and brotherly gesture. "Good for you. I'm glad you stood up to them."

Emotion flooded her. She'd never really expected him to watch her back. "Thank you."

He stepped back. "Do you need help? I'm on call this weekend, but I can come over if I'm around."

She hesitated. Why not? Beth and her husband were helping, but she could use the extra pair of hands. "Sure. That'd be great."

"All right." He turned to go. "I'll be here at nine unless otherwise noted. That okay?"

"See you then," she said, and watched as he disappeared through the workroom door. Strange to have him in her corner. Maybe she'd walled herself off from her brother with her own feelings of inadequacy and inferiority. If so, shame on her. It seemed Kevin might actually be an ally.

God knew she could use one.

That evening, Ben looked up from the whine of the saw to see Lainey standing there, her eyes hooded in the dim light of the rental house's garage, her hands twisted into knots in front of her. He hit the switch on the saw and silenced it.

"Hey."

She swallowed hard. "Hey."

He came toward her and she tipped her head back to look at him. He saw anxiety swimming in her eyes and he closed his hand into a fist to keep from stroking her face.

"Let's go outside—out of the dust." He took her elbow and lightly steered her toward the porch.

"What are you doing in there?"

"Repairing one of the cabinet doors. Do you need some help with the painting?"

She shook her head and her hair bounced lightly on her shoulders. He caught a hint of a lightly fruity shampoo. "Actually, I need you."

The words stopped him cold, even as a spear of heat shot through his belly. It would be no hardship to have her need him, but of course she hadn't meant it that way. He cleared his throat. "For what?"

She paced across the front lawn, kicking at the leaves. "I feel so stupid. I wouldn't ask you if I wasn't desperate."

Ben was pretty sure that was his ego, flying away in shreds. "Desperate?"

"Oh!" She spun back around and her cheeks were bright pink—a huge improvement over the paleness they'd held a few minutes ago. "I didn't mean— I just meant—"

"It's fine," he interrupted. "What do you need?"

She stared at the sky for a minute and he wondered if she was looking for a lightning bolt.

"A date."

He couldn't have heard her right. A date? He didn't date—even casually. If he did date, it definitely wouldn't be a woman who was in danger of making him feel things again. He opened his mouth to tell her so but she rushed on.

"My mother hosts this fundraiser gala thing at the hospital every year. I need to go, and I don't have a date. I was hoping maybe you'd come with me."

"When is it?" God, was he actually considering it? He'd meant to say *no way.*

"Next Thursday." When he said nothing she turned even pinker and turned to walk away. "You know…this was a bad idea. I'm sorry. I'll just go alone."

He crossed to her in two steps. "Black tie?" Hell, he hated black tie.

She swallowed. "Yes."

"I'll go." Holy hell, what was he thinking?

"It's okay—" she started, then stopped as his words sank in. Her eyes widened. "You will?"

He nodded.

"Oh, thank you," she breathed, and flung her arms around him for a brief, tight hug. "Thank you."

He couldn't resist teasing a little. "Only because you're desperate." Hell. He was getting soft. He couldn't possibly be letting her get to him. Right?

She pulled away, but he looped his arms around her back and held her against him, wanting to feel her for a moment. Her gaze caught his and the world fell away for a minute. Heat wove around them, lazy and slow, and his gaze dropped to her mouth. The memory of that kiss in the park hung between them—her warm, sweet mouth and hungry response. He wanted it. Especially now, with her pink cheeks and slightly parted lips tempting him to claim them.

She made a little sound in her throat and he let her go, setting her away from him. Her gaze refocused, then bounced away, landing anywhere but on him.

"So…ah…I'll get going," she said, edging toward her car. "I'll see you later."

"Yeah." He marshaled his thoughts away from kissing her. It took way more effort than he wanted to admit. "What time for the gala?"

"It starts at seven—so say, six-thirty?"

"All right," he said, and she hurried to her car and hopped in. As he watched her drive down the road he wondered where the hell he'd find a tux by next Thursday night.

He strode back to the garage. Then he fished his cell out of his pocket. First things first. He wouldn't let Lainey down.

It seemed the harder Ben tried to keep his distance, the more he was drawn to Lainey.

It wasn't good.

He locked the little house up behind him. Lainey had gone home after painting. They'd managed to avoid any more awkward moments like they'd had outside. It seemed the best thing he could do was bump up his timetable. He'd finished the ramp for his grandma just today, and he was nearly done with this rental house. So there weren't any real reasons to stick around once he'd gotten his grandma squared away. It would be best to get away from Lainey before he got any more involved with her.

Which was why it had floored him when he said he'd go with her to that party. That wasn't the way to keep his distance.

He scrubbed a hand over his face with a sigh. While he wasn't ready to go back to firefighting yet, there was really no reason not to go back to Grand Rapids.

Well, there was Callie and her broken family. He blew out a breath. He couldn't go back yet. He wasn't ready. He couldn't even return Callie's phone calls. Eventually she'd quit trying. One more thing to add to the morass of guilt.

He'd finish up the house, go to the gala, and that would be the end of the contact he had with Lainey. He'd make excuses and leave when she came to visit. It would be easier on both of them. She wanted to see his grandma, anyway, not him.

He cleaned up his mess and drove back to his grandma's house. As he got out of his truck a car turned in the driveway behind him. Grandma—coming home from her knitting group, he thought. She had a very full social calendar, which amused him no end. And pleased him, too.

He walked up to the car and opened her door. She beamed up at him. "Hello, Ben."

"Hi, Grandma."

He went around back when the driver popped the trunk and pulled the wheelchair out. Then he held it steady as his grandma moved from the car to the chair. As much as he hated to see her like this, he had to admit she handled it with grace and humor.

"Thank you," she said, and waved at her friend. Ben helped her wheel up the ramp into the house.

"This ramp is wonderful," she said as they came in the door. "I can't tell you how much easier it is going to make my life. I appreciate it so much."

Ben shut the door behind them, uncomfortable with her gratitude. He didn't deserve it. He'd been gone for too long, and she'd needed him. Lainey had been right about that when they'd first met. "I'm glad," was all he said.

She wheeled around to face him, a frown on her face as she put her knitting bag on the floor by her favorite chair. "It was an honest compliment," she said quietly. "It's okay to accept it."

He shoved his hands in his pockets. "I know. I just feel like I should have been here long before now."

She sighed. "I could have let you know, Ben. I was very clear that I didn't want to worry you. This isn't all on you. As you can see, I've got a very solid support system. I've been managing. And I am very grateful you took this time to help me out. That is all I meant."

He knew that, but it was hard to let go of the self-recrimination. He'd held on to it like a shield for the past week or so, using it to keep his distance.

"So," she said. "Is the house ready for Lainey?"

Grateful for the topic-change, he said, "Pretty much. I'm still working on some minor repairs. But, yes, it's otherwise ready."

She gave a little nod. "Excellent. She's moving this weekend, then?"

"Far as I know." He opted not to mention yet that she'd asked him to the gala. That might put ideas in Grandma's head he didn't want her to have. She liked Lainey, and he didn't want to get her hopes up.

Or your own?

Choosing to ignore that particular thought, he shoved his hands in his pockets. "It'll be all ready for her. You can call her and firm up the date and time."

Rose cocked her head. "You've got a truck," she said thoughtfully. "It might go faster if you offered to help."

Ben swallowed hard. Of course it would. Lainey's car wasn't nearly big enough to haul furniture. And he wasn't going to *not* help her because he was so damn terrified of her. "When you call her, tell her I offered."

She didn't push. "I will. Thank you, Ben."

"Sure," he said, not adding, *I'd do it for anyone*. Because he was afraid that wasn't true.

Lainey's cell buzzed. The number was the same area code as she'd dialed for Jon. Her stomach instantly fell. Beth had left for deliveries so she was alone. She took a deep breath and answered.

"Hello?"

"Lainey. It's Jon." His voice was crisp. "Wanted to let you know we've drawn up the paperwork to begin the process for me to terminate my rights. It's been overnighted to you."

Lainey froze for a moment. This was what she wanted, but somehow saying *thank you* seemed both wrong and inadequate. "I—okay. I'll look out for it."

There was the slightest of pauses, then he cleared his throat. "Best of luck to you, Lainey."

She turned and stared out the window at the cars passing by. "You too. You're going to need it far more than I will."

He barked a laugh, even though she hadn't been trying to be funny. "Don't I know it? From here on out if you have any questions refer them to my lawyer."

"I can't imagine I'd have any need," she said. "But okay."

She clicked the phone shut in her hand. Slowly the import of the conversation began to sink in. She was well and truly a single mother now. Relief mixed with sorrow that it had gone this way. That she'd given her baby a man like Jon for a father. A man who would sign his rights away rather than tell his wife. Instead of a man like Ben.

She sighed and slipped the phone in her pocket. Ben would leave, too. He'd been clear that he was only here for a short time, and even more telling, that his attraction to her was reluctant at best. Something he couldn't help rather than something he actually wanted.

She'd do well to keep that in mind.

"Geez, sis, what do you have in these boxes?"

Kevin's grumbled question on Saturday morning made Lainey smile.

"Rocks—just for you," she teased, and saw Kevin frown out the window. "What?"

"You expecting someone? Big truck. Tall guy. Wait— is that Ben Lawless?"

Lainey's heart skipped. "Yes." It was a good thing he could help, since Beth and her husband hadn't been able to come after all.

"Our job just got easier. He's got a lot of room in that truckbed. Let's get these boxes out of the way so we can move the furniture."

Ben came up the stairs and Lainey tried very hard not to flush or otherwise react in case her brother picked up on anything. As it was, she'd taken care to dress in clothes that hid her slightly rounded midsection, without being obvious about it. She couldn't take the chance that Kevin's doctor eye would spot what she wasn't ready for him to see.

Ben's greeting was a nod, before he turned his attention to Kevin and they launched into a moving strategy discussion. Feeling oddly left out, Lainey slipped into her bedroom, where she'd left a couple boxes of fragile items she didn't want mixed in with the rest of her things.

It only took a few trips. It was a little depressing that her life had been reduced to a couple of car and truckloads, including the furniture. Now it was all in her new house, somewhat willy-nilly, though the guys *had* asked her where she wanted things. Kevin had left after the last trip, and Ben was coming back with a few miscellaneous items.

Lainey went in the kitchen. If she started in there she would be able to at least eat a bowl of cereal or soup. When the front door opened her pulse kicked up. She'd managed to keep Kevin between them. Not too hard, considering they were the ones doing the heavy lifting. But now she and Ben were alone.

She ripped open the box closest to her and found her dishes. She heard Ben's steps in the hall and rose from the floor to greet him. He leaned on the wall and surveyed the mess.

"You've got your work cut out for you," he observed, and she took the opportunity to turn and examine the chaos.

"Yep. It will take me a couple days, but I'll get it all done." Not sure what to do now, she hesitated, then stuck out her hand. "Thank you. I appreciate your help."

He paused just a heartbeat before he took her hand in response. His palm, warm and rough, sent shivers up her arm. What would it feel like on her skin?

She released his hand and stepped back, willing the thoughts away. He shoved his hands in his pockets. She didn't know how to make the awkwardness stop—wasn't even sure it was the best thing to do.

He cleared his throat. "Grandma's invited you to lunch at Mel's Café. She'll be there—" he glanced at his watch "—in about fifteen minutes."

"Oh. That's wonderful, but I think I need to get cracking on this." Practically on cue, her stomach growled loudly and he arched a brow.

"What are you going to eat? One of these boxes?"

Humor glimmered in his eyes and it took her breath away because she knew how rare it was to see it.

"I—well, yeah. Maybe with peanut butter?" She grinned at him and was rewarded with a small smile. Which for him was an ear-to-ear grin.

"We can do better than that," he said dryly. "Come on. I'll drive you."

Unable to think of a suitable excuse—and really she didn't want one, she was hungry—she grabbed her purse and followed him out the door, which she locked with her new key. He opened the passenger door and she climbed in.

"How is Rose getting there?" she asked when he got in the other side.

"A friend took her to get her hair and nails done this morning. She'll drop Grandma off."

Lainey frowned. "How will she get home? This truck is awful high." His expression was shuttered and she realized he'd taken it as a criticism. "I didn't mean that as anything other than a statement of fact," she added stiffly.

He didn't touch her comment. "She's got something else going on after lunch."

"Oh." Lainey stared out the window, mentally kicking herself for her thoughtlessness. It seemed every step they took forward was quickly followed by three back. Such an awkward dance they were doing—trying to be ultra-polite while pretending there was nothing between them.

It was exhausting.

She unbuckled when he'd parked at the café, just down from her shop and her now-former apartment. Once they entered the café she saw Rose at a table by the window. The older woman waved and Lainey waved back. She slid into the seat across from Rose and was surprised when Ben sat next to her. Until she realized Rose had taken over the second seat with her coat and purse. In spite of herself, she wondered if it had been intentional. Was Rose match-making? She wouldn't put it past her friend.

"Love your hair," Lainey said, admiring the soft curls, and Rose patted it.

"She did a good job, didn't she? Makes me look good."

Lainey laughed and caught Rose's hand. "What color is this?" It was a deep pink, a perfect shade for her skin and her silver hair. It occurred to her *she* hadn't had a manicure since she'd divorced Daniel. Not that it mattered, but was one more sign of how much her life had changed.

"I can't remember exactly. It had peony in the name."

"Did you order?" Lainey asked, and Rose shook her head.

"Not yet. But I know what I'm getting."

The waitress came over and Rose ordered a club sandwich, Lainey a turkey sandwich, and Ben something big with roast beef.

Rose sat back. "So. Did you get it all moved?"

She glanced at Ben. "Yes. Ben and Kevin made it look easy. I guess it helped I didn't have that much stuff."

Ben stretched his legs out in front of him and bumped her thigh in the process. She sucked in a breath.

"Sure seemed like a lot for one woman and a cat."

His low, teasing tone gave her goosebumps. She smacked him lightly on the arm, trying desperately not to respond to him. *Rose is here.* The mental reminder didn't work.

"Not that much," she said with a laugh, and saw Rose watching them with an expression that could only be described as thoughtful. Lainey sighed inwardly. The undercurrents between them were on full display.

So much for not feeding the matchmaking fire.

CHAPTER EIGHT

LAINEY'S WEEKEND PASSED in a flurry of unpacking. While the end result was a little sparse, she wasn't worried. One thing she'd always loved was finding treasures at places like thrift shops and garage sales. One more thing her mother had never understood. So she'd keep an eye out for what she might need.

Well, after baby needs, of course. That was her next project. Setting up the nursery.

In fact she stood in the room in question right now. Nothing was in here yet. She'd left it empty on purpose. She needed a crib, a changing table… Maybe she could find a dresser that could do double duty. A rocker for the corner. A bookcase for toys and such. She left the room, a smile on her face, and walked back though the house. Being here felt right. Panda sat in a spot of sunlight on the kitchen floor. While the cat hadn't been pleased about the car ride, she'd settled in once she'd found her food and water bowls, as well as her litter box. Lainey was hopeful come spring she could let the cat out into the fenced-in backyard.

She padded into her bedroom to get dressed. And frowned when her low-rise jeans didn't snap. Yesterday they'd fit—albeit a bit snug. Today, no dice. That meant two things.

One: full-time maternity clothes.

Two: telling her family.

Lainey shut her eyes. The moment of truth was here. Her father was out of town, so she'd have to tell her mother alone. She'd do it after work, when she returned the apartment keys.

She left the house with a little fizzle of joy as she used her new key to lock it up behind her, and drove to the shop. As was her habit now, she checked the cooler temperature first thing. It was running a tick above where she wanted it, but it had been holding fairly steady.

Beth walked in a few minutes later. "Hey, Laine. How was the move?"

"Pretty smooth," she answered.

"Was it just you and Kevin? Aw, Laine. I'm so sorry we couldn't be there. We should have—"

"You should have gone to visit your father-in-law, just like you did. It all worked out. Ben helped, too," Lainey said quickly. "I think Rose asked him to."

A small smile tugged at the corners of Beth's mouth. "Really?" she said, drawing out the word. "How was that?"

Lainey rolled her eyes and stomped over to open the cash register, pretending not to catch her friend's meaning. "A lot of work—what else?"

Beth's low laugh followed her across the room. "Mmm-hmm. Do you think Kevin noticed anything? Lainey, it's pretty obvious there's chemistry with you guys."

Oh, she hoped not. "I don't think so. He's a guy, so he can be pretty oblivious. Plus, I really didn't see Ben that much. They just loaded and unloaded. They were together more than we were." Then she realized what she'd just admitted. "Oh—"

Beth wrapped an arm around Lainey's shoulders and

squeezed. "Now all you have to do is stop fighting it. Let yourself just give in."

She stepped away, her point clearly made, and Lainey busied herself with the cash drawer. It wasn't as easy as *just giving in*. There was too much at stake to *just give in*. Why couldn't Beth see that? She wasn't sure she could give in if she wanted to. She was aware of how quickly things could go wrong. Once you'd had your wings clipped, it made it awful hard to get off the ground.

And she was scared to try and fly again.

Lainey turned down her parents' street and her stomach fluttered. Silly, really, since she was an adult. But those old habits of wanting to be a good daughter were hard to break. She'd decided to go in quick, say her piece, and get out. She'd send for the housekeeper if her mother passed out.

The thought made her giggle just a little hysterically. The unflappable Jacqui—completely flapped.

Her mother's car was parked by the garage—a sure sign she'd be heading back out later. Lainey parked in the circle and took a second to brace herself. While it was time, it would be nice if she had someone to back her up, and she almost wished she'd asked Kevin to come along. He'd know how to manage their mother.

She rang the bell and waited. Jacqui answered after a minute, brow arched high. "Lainey. This is a nice surprise. What brings you here?"

She stepped aside and Lainey entered the foyer.

"I need to talk to you for a minute." Her voice was calm, not betraying her nerves. Good.

"Of course. I've got a meeting in a half-hour. Will this take long?"

"I don't think so," Lainey said.

She followed her mother's trim form into the living

room and took a deep breath. Once again she tried to imagine a baby on the floor, or pulling itself up on the velvet-covered furniture. She couldn't picture it. Was that because she was afraid her parents wouldn't want her and the baby in their lives? Wasn't that part of what had made her so reluctant to tell them?

It didn't matter now. She took a deep breath. "I have something important to tell you."

"I see." Jacqui crossed to the mini-wet bar. "Well, then. Something to drink? Will you be joining me for dinner?"

Not likely. "No, Mother."

Jacqui turned, a can of ginger ale in her hand, an expectant look on her face. "Well, then, what do you need to tell me, dear?"

There was no point in beating around the bush. "I'm pregnant."

Jacqui gasped, and the color leached from her face as the pop can slid from her hand and landed on the carpet with a fizzy hiss. The golden liquid splashed all over her legs and feet. Frozen for a heartbeat, Lainey leapt up and grabbed a handful of paper towels from the wet bar, almost grateful for the distraction.

"Are you sure?" Jacqui's voice was faint.

Lainey didn't look up from blotting at the mess. She wasn't sure she could look at her mother just yet. "Positive. I'm a little more than two months along." Her hands shook as she dropped the first mass of sopping towels in the garbage under the bar.

Jacqui let out a long exhale. "Good God."

That about sums it up.

"Are you getting married? Who's the father?"

Lainey winced. "No. And the father is no one you know." True enough. Jon wouldn't have been on her parents' radar.

"Ben Lawless?" Her mother nearly spat Ben's name.

Lainey bobbled the paper towel roll. What did her mother have against Ben? "No. Of course not. He'd *want* to be involved in the baby's life." The truth of those words batted against her heart.

"And the father doesn't?"

Lainey couldn't speak over the wave of shame that rose in her. She pressed her lips together instead and shook her head.

Jacqui sighed and stepped out of her sticky heels. "Oh, Lainey. You need to get married, pronto. I wonder if Daniel would be willing to marry you with you carrying someone else's baby? Lainey, *damn it.* I think you just ruined any chance you had with that man!"

Lainey sat back on her heels, temper snapping at her throat. "I already told you I don't care, Mother. I'm not getting married. I will be a single parent. I don't give a damn what Daniel thinks. I'm sure he has kids somewhere. He did enough sowing of the seed, as they say."

Jacqui gasped. "Lainey!"

"Well, he did. If it wore heels, he chased it. He almost never slept with *me*, thank God—who knows what I could have come down with?—but he did with other women. At the end he was bringing them into our home, did you know that?" The humiliation burned though her all over again. "I'd be gone, or maybe not. The basement was his little playboy cave. He could have cared less about me— about our marriage. He married me for you and Dad— for your money, for where your name could take him. So when I grew a spine and divorced him it really threw him. He's not back here for *me*, Mother. He wants to get back in your lives."

Jacqui stared at her, jaw dropped. "Lainey—" she said finally, then lapsed into silence.

"But you knew, didn't you?" Lainey said softly. "Some of it, anyway. And it was okay, because he had the right connections, the right amount of money. You were willing to look the other way, like you've done with Dad." The truth arced through her, sharp and hot.

Jacqui stood very still. "Be very careful, young lady. You're on dangerous ground now."

Lainey couldn't stop. It was too important. "He's always been very discreet—unlike Daniel. I'd have thought you'd want better for me than you had. I know I do."

The truth hurt. She loved her father, but she knew his weaknesses. Daniel was just like him, only without the intelligence or compassion. She also knew her father loved her mother, despite his failings. And that was between them. Not her business.

She stood up and threw away the last of the paper towels. "I'm going to go now," she said quietly. There was nothing more to say. It wasn't as if her mother was going to embrace her and squeal with joy at the thought of grandchildren. So the lump of disappointment in her throat was useless. She turned and walked toward the door.

"Lainey—wait."

She paused and turned.

Jacqui asked, "Who else knows about this?"

Lainey laid her hand on her belly and saw Jacqui flinch. "Only Beth knows about your grandchild." There wasn't any reason to tell her Ben knew as well. It would only make things worse.

"Okay, good. We need to make this spin positive somehow. I'll get on it and let you know the plan." Jacqui, clearly perked by the thought of something to do, padded across the carpet on sticky feet.

"No."

Jacqui stopped. "Excuse me?"

Lainey shook her head. "You can plan all you want, but it's not going to make it go away. Not going to make it any more or less than it is. I'm not going to go along with any plan. My baby. My life."

Jacqui's mouth flattened. "Your store—"

"I know. It's at your mercy." Lainey grabbed her purse. "You keep telling me. Now you know why I won't let it go under. I need to succeed so I can support myself and my child. Can I call anyone for you before I go?"

Jacqui shook her head. "No. I don't—I need to talk to your father first. He's going to be so disappointed," she added, more to herself than to Lainey. "Plus it's an election year."

Lainey stared at her. "Mom, I'm thirty-three. Not a teenager. Not even close. So what if I have a baby on my own?" She nearly laughed. As if it was such an easy thing to do. Maybe she was crazy. "Women do it all the time."

"But not women in *your* position," Jacqui said.

She kept her voice steady with effort. "And what position would that be?"

"Women whose lives are under scrutiny," she said, and Lainey's jaw nearly dropped.

"I'm hardly under any kind of scrutiny. Besides, I don't think this is any worse than my divorce," she said dryly. "And it's a much happier occasion."

Jacqui shook her head. "Don't make a joke of it. You don't understand. You never have."

Lainey hesitated, then simply turned and walked toward the door. There wasn't anything else to say. Behind her, she heard her mother on the phone with the housekeeper, telling her to come clean up the mess.

Outside, she took a deep breath as she got in her car and drove out of the driveway. Then she pulled over. She reached for her cell and called her brother.

Amazingly, Kevin answered.

"You're not in surgery today?"

"Nope. Office visits all day. I've only got a few minutes, though. What's up?"

Lainey fiddled with the steering wheel. "I just came from home."

"Oh? How's Mom?"

Lainey stared out the window, not seeing the rain on the windshield. "I kind of shocked her, Kev. She's not happy."

"You told her you're pregnant?"

Tears stung her eyes. Even though she'd suspected he knew. "How did you know?"

He sighed. "I can just tell. Where are you going for your OB?"

Lainey filled him in on the details.

"Is Lawless the father?"

Oh, she wished. Of the few men she'd been involved with, he was the most honorable, hands down. "No," she whispered.

He made a noise that could have been anything. "I caught him looking at you a couple times on Saturday. Really looking. Not how a brother wants a guy to look at his kid sister."

She nearly laughed, and tried to ignore the spurt of pleasure and pain his words caused. "Wow. I'm pretty sure you're wrong. And don't ask me any more about the father, okay? It's not—he's not interested in being a father."

"That's too damn bad," he growled. "Do you need me to hunt him down?"

Now she *did* laugh, at the vision of her respectable surgeon older brother beating the hell out of Jon. It would be quite a match, but her money would be on Kevin. "No. But, thanks."

A pause. "That's not right, Lainey. He shouldn't leave you—"

"It's okay," she interrupted him. "We're better off without him."

Kevin sighed. "All right. And, little sis? You'll be a hell of a mother."

His words and his faith in her warmed her. It was so nice to have him stand up for her. But still… "I don't want to be like our mother," she whispered. There it was…her deepest fear.

Kevin snorted. "You won't be. She somehow flat-out missed the maternal gene. You've got it in spades. You feeling okay?"

"Yeah. Just a little tired. Thankfully I don't have much nausea."

"Okay, good. I've got to run. I'll stop by and see Mom after I get out of here. Let me know if I can help, okay? You don't have to do this alone."

His words brought tears to her eyes. "Thanks, Kev. I will," she promised, and disconnected, feeling a little better. Kevin would smooth out what Lainey couldn't, but she doubted either of them could make Jacqui see this as a good thing.

She tucked the phone back into her purse and sat for another few moments. Her mother's reaction hadn't really shocked her. Jacqui would spin and spin, but in the end it was what Lainey did that mattered, and she'd make it work on her own. Again, if things were different— But they weren't. Whatever was going on with Ben, it had him clearly reluctant to make even the slightest commitment. She needed someone reliable.

So far the only reliable one was herself. The irony of that wasn't lost on her.

* * *

Lainey stood in her new backyard the next day after work and stared up into the nearly empty oak tree, then down at the ground where she stood ankle deep in yellow-brown leaves. Yesterday they'd all been on the tree. Today they were all on the ground. Clearly it was time for a trip to the hardware store to buy a rake.

She trudged through the leaves, hearing the crunch under her feet, on her way out front to her car. Her trip to the hardware store, where she purchased a rake, leaf bags, and a pair of work gloves, took less than half an hour.

She went out back, rake in hand, and tilted her face to the sun. She had a couple of hours before it would be too dark. Might as well make the most of it.

She hadn't been going for more than ten minutes when Ben's big truck pulled in the driveway. Her pulse kicked up and she gripped the rake a little harder. She walked over to the gate to greet him.

"Hi," she said, when he emerged from the truck and turned her way. She tried not to devour him with her eyes. She wanted to curl herself into his embrace, feel his warmth through the black fleece jacket he wore—

Wait. No, she didn't.

"Hey," he said, coming closer, his expression neutral. His gaze dropped to her belly. "Is this okay, in your condition?"

"Of course. I'm not doing any heavy lifting, so I'm fine," she said. "I can do pretty much anything as long as I don't overdo it."

He lifted his gaze to hers. "I can see you overdoing it."

She smiled and shook her head. "I'm very careful. I'm not going to put the baby in any danger."

"Of course you won't. I'll help."

She tried not to stare at the rear view as he walked to the

bed of his truck. How could she not notice how those worn jeans hugged his rear and thighs just right? She cleared her throat. "Do you just carry a rake in the back of your truck for emergencies?"

"I was here earlier and saw what had happened," he answered as she stepped aside for him to come through the gate. Before she could ask, he nodded to the garage. "The light in there was out. I put in a new bulb."

"I'm going to get spoiled—all this personal landlord service," she teased, and saw his back stiffen. "Not to worry. I can change my own lightbulbs."

He sent her a grin. "Does your mother know?"

"Shh," she murmured. "She'll hear you."

He laughed and started raking.

They worked in relative silence for a bit. Lainey kept sneaking glances at him. He'd unzipped his jacket and, while the tee shirt he wore underneath wasn't exactly skintight, she could still see the play of muscles underneath it when he raked.

She exhaled. It had certainly gotten hotter out here since he had shown up.

They raked a big pile over the next little while, and a slight breeze stirred the remaining leaves on the tree and several came floating down. He reached out and plucked a piece of one out of her hair, his fingers lingering on the strands. Her mouth went dry at the intense heat in his gaze and her pulse kicked up when he dropped his gaze to her mouth. Lainey stopped herself from leaning forward, from pressing her mouth to his. He stepped back and offered her the leaf with a small smile.

She took it and twirled the stem in her fingers. "Wow, thanks." She held it up, looking at the red and green threaded in with the yellow. "Pretty, isn't it?"

He closed his hand over hers. She looked up into his gaze.

"Gorgeous," he murmured, drawing her closer and she knew, with a flutter deep inside, that he wasn't talking about the leaf anymore.

He settled his mouth over hers. With a sigh, she melted into him, opening, letting his tongue slip in. When the kiss became deeper, hotter, she fisted the front of his jacket and he gripped her hips, drawing her closer, before plunging one hand into her hair, angling her head to thrust his tongue even deeper.

Fire skipped through her veins, burned along her nerve-endings, sent heat arrowing into the depth of her belly. She pressed closer, feeling his hardness against her and the answering heat of her response.

Suddenly he broke the kiss, though he didn't pull away from her, but rested his forehead on hers. Their breath mingled as she tried to calm her breathing. Every time he touched her she craved more. It wasn't enough. But it was all there was. Frustration welled and she squeezed her eyes shut.

"Lainey," he murmured, his voice raw and rough. "I told myself I'd stay away, but…" His voice trailed off as he stepped back, and she shivered from the loss of his heat. "We'd better get to work."

Shaking, Lainey bent to retrieve her discarded rake. She needed to pull back, keep this kind of thing from happening.

But the real question was, did she want to? In her heart, she feared the answer was no.

CHAPTER NINE

IT DIDN'T TAKE all that long to make a huge pile. Ben pulled some sticks out. "When was the last time you jumped in a leaf pile?"

Shame flushed Lainey's cheeks. "Well, never."

He stared at her. "No way? All those trees on your parents' land and you never played in a leaf pile?"

"No. My mother—you'd have to know my mother. She's not big on dirt." That sounded sad, but it was the truth.

"Oh." There was a wealth of understanding in the word. "I see."

She looked at him in surprise. "You do?"

He nodded. "You need to experience it before the baby gets here. Let me make sure all the sticks are out."

He poked in the pile and she watched with a combination of amusement and exasperation. After extracting a few more sticks, he fluffed the pile with his rake and turned, the satisfaction on his face making her laugh.

"Does it pass muster?" she teased gently.

He nodded. "You're not too far along for this, are you?"

On impulse, Lainey unzipped her vest and ran her hand over her very slight baby bump. The tenderness in his eyes as he watched made her breath catch. "Am I jumping out of a tree?"

His gaze jerked up. "Of course not."

"Then I'll be fine." She leapt lightly into the pile, landing on her knees. The crackle of the leaves and their fresh scent invigorated her. She laughed and threw an armful of leaves in the air, then tried to cover her head when they came raining back down.

"Incoming!" Ben called, and before she could scramble too far over he came crashing into the pile with her. He gave her a big grin—the first she'd seen with no shadows, no pain in his eyes—and tossed a handful of leaves at her. "So, what do you think?"

She threw some back at him. "It was worth the wait."

He laughed. "Yeah? Awesome." He turned and flopped back, folding his hands under his head. "I'm guessing you never looked at cloud shapes either?"

"Stop reminding me how deprived my childhood was," she scolded him with a laugh, and he snaked out a hand and pulled her head down to his. The sweetness of this kiss after the passion of the earlier one threw her.

When she pulled back, searching his face with her gaze, he touched her cheek, twining his fingers in her hair. "I'm sorry," he said.

She arched a brow. "For what?"

"For all you missed. I assumed, growing up as you did, you had everything."

She shrugged and pulled a leaf out of his hair. "I had everything material you could want. Only I didn't actually want it. I didn't get time with my parents. But I see now my mom didn't know how to raise us. She was so caught up in perceptions that just letting me be a kid wasn't possible. She meant well, but..." She sat up in the leaves. "We turned out okay, Kevin and I. Him more than me," she added with a little sigh, thinking of her struggling shop, her pregnancy and her money woes.

Ben frowned. "Don't do that."

Startled, she looked at him. "Do what?"

"Put yourself down like that. You're living life on your terms. How is that not okay?"

"Oh." She nibbled on her lip while she thought. "You're right. I hadn't thought of it like that. I guess I just want to prove I can do it."

"You are. You will." He stood up and extended a hand to her.

His quiet confidence warmed her down to her toes and her heart tipped dangerously.

"Let's get this done."

She grasped his warm, callused palm and let him draw her to her feet. "Okay."

They managed to load about half the leaves into bags before it got too dark. Lainey's arms and back were screaming, and it was with an incredible sense of relief that she dropped her rake on the ground to stretch her back.

"Did you overdo it?" The concern in his voice made her smile.

"According to my back and arms, yes. But none of that will hurt the baby."

"Go on in," he told her. "I'll put these things in the garage. I'll finish tomorrow."

She hesitated before starting toward the house. "Do you—do you want to come in? For coffee or something?"

"I'd like that," he said softly. "If you think you aren't too tired?"

"No, I'm fine. Come in when you're done."

She hurried into the house and started the coffee maker. A quick trip to the bathroom revealed wild hair and a nose bright red from the cold.

Oooh. Sexy.

Though Ben clearly hadn't minded. He'd kissed her. Twice.

Would there be a third time?

She shook her head at her reflection. *Stop it*. She detoured to the living room to switch on the fire. While the walls were bare in here, as she hadn't had a chance yet to deal with artwork, she'd gotten the furniture arranged like she wanted and unpacked pillows and a couple throws. It was comfy enough for the moment. Ben would understand.

When she got back to the kitchen she caught a glimpse of him coming out of the garage. For just a heartbeat she was a wife and a mom, waiting for her man to come in.

The thought threw her. She'd been a wife, and had given up waiting for her man to come in pretty quickly. She was going to be a mom—and that terrified her. But she'd never felt for her ex-husband what she felt for Ben—and she wasn't even in love with Ben.

Not yet.

Reeling from that thought, she opened the cupboard to take out coffee mugs as Ben came in through the back door. She gave him a bright smile. "It's decaf. That okay?"

"Sure," he said, and shrugged out of his jacket.

She poured his and handed it to him. "Let's go in here," she said and led the way to the living room. She settled on the couch with him across from her.

"Something wrong? You look a little pale."

Ben's casual comment threw her. She certainly couldn't tell him *he* was part of what was worrying her. "I'm not ready to be a mother," she blurted. "But I'm committed now."

He looked genuinely surprised. "Why do you think you're not ready?"

"I'm still getting my shop off the ground. I'm not in the best place financially." He just looked at her and she shut her eyes. "I'm not. My parents are wealthy, yes, but there was no trust fund or anything. It was kind of understood

I'd either get a fantastic career or a loaded husband. Or both." She stared at his shoulder, unable to meet his eyes. "I managed to do neither."

"You say that like it's a bad thing," he said softly.

She looked at him and the misery in her eyes nearly had him reaching for her. He wanted to tuck her under his arm and hold her against his chest, where he already knew she fit perfectly.

"I know it shouldn't be. And my ex-husband is a real doozy. Seven years of my life I'll never get back. But somehow it is—in my family. I'm happy where I am. I'm just—"

She stopped and he saw the sheen of tears. "Just what?"

"So worried. Because I don't want to be a bad mother," Lainey blurted, and covered her face with her hands.

Now he did reach for her, and caught her wrists and gently pulled her hands away. "Why would you think you would be?"

She gave a harsh little laugh and looked down in her lap. "My mother has no maternal genes. None. Zero. We aren't close, even though it seems like I see her all the time. I don't want my baby to feel like he or she doesn't matter."

Anger washed through him. "You feel like you don't matter?"

She stood up and walked over to the fireplace. She stared into the dancing flames. "I— Yes. I've never really been a part of the family. I always felt like just a prop, I guess. The black sheep."

He came up behind her and slid his hands down her arms. "You are going to be a wonderful mother, Lainey." When she shook her head, he leaned down and pressed his cheek to hers, inhaled her sweet scent. "Listen to me. I haven't known you long, but what I see is a warm, compassionate, giving woman who cares deeply about those who matter to her. You're strong. You're sweet. You're funny. All of that is going to translate naturally to motherhood."

She turned in his arms and looked up at him, her eyes huge in the soft light of the lamp and the fire. The uncertainty in her eyes killed him.

"You think so?"

He'd meant every word. He touched her face, unable to stop himself from feeling her soft skin. She leaned into him just slightly, eyes closed, and he swallowed hard but couldn't step away even if he wanted to. Which, God help him, he didn't.

"No. I know so."

Her eyes fluttered open and he gave in, lowering his mouth to hers, hearing her sharp inhale. He hesitated at the last second. Her breath feathered over his and she closed the gap, coming up to meet him. He slipped his hands in her hair, even though they really wanted to roam farther south. All he wanted to do right now was feel.

Lainey. Only Lainey.

The kiss grew more urgent quickly, and she opened to him with a little growl in her throat that only served to fuel his internal fire. When her arms went around his neck and she pressed her length against him he was lost.

No. He was found. He hadn't wanted to be, and he wouldn't be able to stay. But she'd managed to lay waste to all his defenses.

He broke the kiss before he accidentally toppled her into the fireplace and rested his forehead on hers. She didn't move away, though he felt the tension return to her body. "I didn't want you to end up in the fire."

She blinked at him, then a small smile curved her mouth. "Thoughtful of you."

"Isn't it, though? Gentleman through and through." He savored her laugh as he took her hand and led her to the couch. If she knew how badly he wanted to take her to bed, to feel her move beneath him, to make love to her, she'd know he wasn't any kind of gentleman.

And those thoughts weren't helpful.

Trying to bring them back around, he asked, "How are your shoulders?"

She rolled them and winced. "I'll be feeling this for a couple days, I think."

He pulled her down on the couch and sat so he was behind her. He began to knead her shoulders gently. "Wow. You *are* tight. Relax and let me see if I can help with that."

She let her head fall forward. "Mmm. That feels wonderful."

Yeah. It did. But touching her like this, on top of the kisses earlier, was sending all his blood south. And when she moaned his breath shortened. He leaned forward and kissed her neck, still massaging, but letting his hands slip over her shoulders to brush the tops of her breasts through her shirt, then moving them back up to her shoulders. Her little inhale prompted him to do it again, this time slipping his hands under her breasts to cup them in his hands, brush his thumbs over her nipples. Was this one of the lacy, sexy bras he'd seen that day in her bathroom?

"Lainey…" he murmured against her neck, and she tilted her head to the side, her breathing shallow. He kissed her neck one more time and she shifted out of his arms. He let her go, instantly feeling her loss, but she just turned around and settled on his lap, wrapped her arms around his neck.

"Stay," she whispered. "Please."

"Lainey." He rested his forehead on hers, struggling for some semblance of control. "Are you sure?"

She slid off his lap and held out her hand. It was trembling slightly and he could see uncertainty warring with desire in her eyes. She was offering him a gift and she was afraid he wouldn't take it.

This might be his only chance. A few hours of heaven he knew he didn't deserve.

But Lainey did.

He took her hand without ever breaking eye contact and stood.

Smoke filled the room, smothering him, searing his lungs, his eyes, his skin. God, he couldn't see through the gray haze. A cough racked him, tearing at his parched throat. He couldn't yell for his friend. Where was Jason? He couldn't reach him—had to get him out before the house came down around him. A roar and a crack, and orange lit the room. The ceiling caved in on a crash fueled by the roar of flames. He spun around, but the door was blocked by a flaming heap of debris. Under it was a boot. Jason coming to save him.

Ben woke up, gasping, to find Lainey's terrified face over him.

"Ben?"

The concern, the worry, was too much for him, and he clamped both hands over his face so she couldn't see the pain, the anger, the shame seeping from him like tears.

Her hand was soft on his arm. "Ben?"

He shook her off. "Lainey—don't. God. I—it's just a dream." He sat up, cursing himself for falling asleep, for allowing the intimacy at all, for thinking maybe it would be okay.

She drew back, a sheet pulled up over those glorious breasts, her gaze steady and worried. "If it's just a dream why are you so rattled?"

She saw too much. Too damn much. He was stripped

emotionally bare after their wonderful night together—all that emotion which he hadn't expected.

"I can't explain it now," he said, weary. "Go back to sleep. I'll see myself out."

Her quick intake of breath lanced him. No point in telling her he wouldn't sleep anymore, anyway. Better she knew as little as possible. Better he didn't give her the chance to soothe him, to connect, while he was vulnerable.

She said nothing as he pulled on his pants in the dark, fumbled with his wallet.

"What ever it is, running isn't going to make it go away."

Her words, though soft, hit him as hard as if she'd shouted or thrown glass shards at him.

"It's not going to make it stop."

"I'm sorry," was all he could say, while he thought, *Yeah, but all I can do is run.* If she knew what he'd done she'd never speak to him again. Bad enough now she'd see him as weak.

He paused in the doorway, looked back. She'd lain down again, her back to the door, covers pulled all the way up. He ached to go back to her, but he knew it was for the best.

"Go if you're going to," she said, her voice raw, and he did, leaving her in her warm bed and slipping into the chilly night.

Beth stopped in her tracks as soon as she entered the shop the next morning. "Wow. You look tired. What happened?"

Lainey winced, then sighed. It was true. Between Ben keeping her awake and then leaving after the nightmare she'd gotten pretty much no sleep. "Ben happened."

Beth cocked her head. "If you were glowing, I'd guess the lack of sleep was due to happy times with Ben," she said. "But I'm guessing not so much?"

"It ended badly," Lainey said finally. "I'm not sure what happened. We were—well, we…" She paused as her cheeks heated and Beth's brow rose as a grin stole across her face. "I guess I don't have to explain it to you. But he just left." She shrugged as if it hadn't hurt. After how wonderful everything had been, she couldn't *help* but be hurt.

It infuriated her.

"Just walked out as in thanks and bye?" Beth's tone was incredulous.

"Not quite that crass, but, yeah." Lainey couldn't tell Beth about Ben's nightmare. He seemed to be ashamed of it, and it wasn't her place to tell anyone. "I really don't want to talk about it."

Beth sent her a sympathetic look. "Love is messy."

Lainey nearly dropped the bucket she held. No one had said anything about love. Especially not with a man who was clearly keeping something from her. "We've just got really good chemistry."

"Chemistry is good," Beth said cheerfully. "And, all told, this is a huge improvement over last week, when I told you to go for it and you looked like I'd kicked a puppy." Her voice sobered and she threw an arm around Lainey's shoulders. "Seriously, though, I see more than just chemistry. The way you say his name—"

"Oh, Beth." Lainey interrupted before this got any worse. "I do *not*. Obviously I like him a lot but that's all. There's no more than that."

Except the slight twist in her belly told a different story. The way he'd loved her, cherished her. The way he made her feel important. The way he stood up for her, even to herself. How crushed she'd been when he shut her out last night.

Oh, no.

Beth looked at her steadily. "If you say so."

Lainey forced a smile. "I do say so." As she forced herself to walk casually to the back room, gripping the bucket handle so hard it hurt, she was afraid Beth was right. This whole thing, at least for her, had tipped well past mutual chemistry and into dangerous emotional territory.

Clearly she'd learned nothing from her past.

But Ben wasn't Daniel or Jon. And, really, how would she know love? She'd never been in love before. It most certainly couldn't happen this quickly.

Could it?

Ben sat at the Rusty Hammer bar, a burger with all the trimmings before him. Best damn burgers anywhere, but it could be cardboard for all he could taste it. Still, the owner was looking at him, so he gave it a shot.

Someone settled on the bar stool next to him. A quick glance revealed Kevin Keeler. The other man nodded in acknowledgement and Ben did the same. Fantastic. Just what he needed.

"What can I get you?" The owner had come to stand in front of Kevin.

Kevin inclined his head toward Ben's plate. "One of those and a beer, please."

"On the way." He drew the beer, placed it in front of Kevin and headed for the kitchen.

Kevin took a long draw. He set the glass down with a thunk and half turned to Ben, who braced himself.

"So. What are your intentions toward my sister?"

Ben nearly choked on his burger. Kevin thumped him on the back. "It's probably a good idea to do that in front of a doctor," he observed dryly.

Ben shook his head and grabbed his beer. Was this a trick question? Did Kevin know he'd slept with her? He doubted it. Lainey would never kiss and tell to Kevin. Besides, big brothers weren't inclined to be friendly when you messed with their little sisters.

"Nothing. No intentions. She needed a date and invited me to the gala. That's all." His words were hollow but he hoped Kevin wouldn't pick up on it. He'd never intended anything to go as far as it had, physically or otherwise. She'd filled holes in him that had desperately needed filling, as hard as he'd tried to avoid it.

Kevin tapped his glass. "It doesn't look like *all*," he said. "You were looking at her pretty seriously. With her being pregnant, I need to know what your intentions are."

Ben picked up his beer and took a deliberate swallow. "Like I said—"

Kevin leaned in. "She deserves better than a guy with *no intentions*. A hell of a lot better. She's been through hell and back with that idiot of an ex-husband, not to mention our selfish, clueless parents."

Ben met the other man's serious gaze. "I completely agree. That's why I have no intention of getting tangled up in her life." *Anymore than I already am.* "She asked for a favor. I agreed. She's an amazing woman and I wish her all the best."

Kevin sat back with a frown. "She's got feelings for you."

"I hope not," he said quietly, but he knew Kevin was right. The hell of it was, he had powerful feelings for her, too. "Like I said, I can't give her what she needs." The truth was painful and he gripped the bottle tighter. "So. My intentions are to walk away and let her live her life." The words were like ash in his mouth.

Kevin nodded at the owner, who'd delivered his burger. "I'm not sure if you're smart or a coward."

Ben barked out a laugh. "Truthfully? Me either."

Actually, that wasn't true. He did know. He was keeping Lainey safe, and that wasn't a cowardly move.

Was it?

For all his not wanting to be part of a family, for not wanting home and hearth and kids and a wife, he knew underneath it all he was a sham. He wanted all of it. He wanted what Jason and Callie had had. He didn't know how to open himself up to have it. But if he could— Lainey was a good woman. She'd be a wonderful mother and wife to the right man.

Just not for him. .

CHAPTER TEN

Lainey hurried home after work on the day of the gala. Of course her mother *would* schedule this party on a Thursday. And, being only her and Beth at the shop, Lainey couldn't exactly take the afternoon off. So she was left with an hour to do all the primping required for a black tie affair.

Her nerves wouldn't settle. She hadn't seen Ben since he'd left that night. She took a deep breath and tried to focus on her hair and make-up, which were thankfully simple. Even with a redo of eyeliner due to her shaking hand. She got the dress on and tried to suck in her belly as she turned to study herself in the full-length mirror. Then she relaxed. The black fabric draped low over her breasts and gathered gently at her stomach, so the pregnancy wasn't obvious.

She eyed the black heels lying on the floor of her room. Sparkly and sexy, they absolutely killed her feet.

She'd make the sacrifice.

The doorbell rang and she scooped up the shoes and made a quick stop in the bathroom. She tried to examine her make-up in the mirror, but all she could see was flushed cheeks and sparkling eyes. She'd piled her hair on her head in an elaborate updo the likes of which she didn't have a reason for too often anymore.

For someone who'd insisted repeatedly this night meant nothing, she'd sure spent a lot of energy stressing over it.

Hearing the bell again, she took a deep breath and hurried over to open the door.

She simply lost her breath.

The tux emphasized Ben's broad shoulders and slim hips. His hair curled a little over the collar, and she took a step back so she didn't reach out to run her fingers through it.

His gaze swept over her in the way a man's did when he appreciated a woman he was interested in. Her nerve-endings sizzled, as if he'd actually caressed her. Heat ran down her spine and he gave her a rare, slow smile.

"You're gorgeous." The words were simple, heartfelt, and she felt her heart stutter at the raw edge in his tone. Daniel had never looked at her like that or said anything so simple—and meant it. Something inside her shifted.

"Thank you," she managed. "So are you."

She stepped aside to let him in. The butterflies in her stomach had grown into bats.

She cleared her throat. "I've just got to get my shoes on."

"All right." He studied her while she sat down and buckled them on her feet. When she stood he must have noticed her wince. "Why do you wear them if they hurt?"

No point in being cagey. "They look great." She lifted the hem of her dress over her ankle so he could see. "See?"

He lifted his gaze from her ankle to her face and she felt the heat of it. She was very glad she'd decided to paint her toenails a sexy red.

An answering sizzle ran through her as he cleared his throat. "Lovely." His voice was still a bit hoarse.

A visceral shudder ran through her at the memory of his hands on her the other night. How wonderful they'd been together. Until he'd left.

She swallowed and grabbed her clutch. "I'm ready."

He rested his hand on the small of her back as they went out her door. The touch was familiar and intimate. "What do women carry in those things anyway?"

"This?" Lainey held up the silver clutch. At his nod she continued. "Well, I've got keys, phone, lipstick, a couple of tissues. A couple of make-up things. The usual girl stuff, I guess." Other than things like tampons, of course. Pregnant girls didn't need those.

"Keys? In there?" He stepped aside so she could lock the door.

"Well, off the ring. Just for the door— Oh!" She turned around and stared at the black coupe, an exact replica of the one she'd owned a year ago. Daniel's gift to her. Recovering before he could notice her shock, she added, "Nice ride."

"Thanks." He opened the door for her and held it while she got in. The rich scent of the buttery leather and the new carpet hit her. A few seconds later he was sliding in the driver's seat. "I didn't think my usual ride was appropriate for tonight. I figured you'd be in a fancy dress and it might be hard to climb in and out of the truck."

Her heart caught. He'd done it for her. Even though she'd ambushed him with it less than two weeks ago, he'd come through. "Thank you," she said after she got her voice back. "It was very thoughtful of you."

"More what you're used to," he said, without looking at her.

Oh, so *that* was how it was. "Ben, you see what I drive now."

He said nothing and she sighed. "It's in my past. And I'm happier without it." The full truth there. That car had symbolized her ultimate failure and catalyzed her ability to do something about it. She gave the dashboard an affectionate little pat and heard Ben's low chuckle.

The full moon hung huge and silver in the obsidian sky as they drove to the Lakeside Country Club. As she looked at it, shining over the lake, she couldn't help but wonder if her mother had managed to call in a favor from somewhere to arrange for the moon.

The club, of course, was gorgeous. What had to be miles of twinkle lights outlined the building, luminaries lined the walkways, and through the wide glass doors she could see a roaring fire in the fireplace. Ben pulled up to the port-cochere and a valet glided forward to open the door. "Good evening, sir and madam," he said as Ben held his hand out and helped Lainey out of the car. She was perfectly capable of exiting on her own, but with Ben it didn't feel like a grand gesture for the sake of it but more as if he wanted to touch her any way he could.

So she let him.

The valet closed the door and took Ben's keys. He cocked his arm at her. "Shall we?"

She tucked her hand in the warm crook of his arm and enjoyed the little fizzy feeling touching him gave her. She took a deep breath and had to keep herself from turning into him to just breathe him in. "Yes. Let's."

After stepping inside and taking care of her wrap, Lainey proceeded with Ben to the hall where the gala was being held. It was early, so the room was little more than half full, and they perused the tables until they found theirs. With her parents, of course. And Kevin.

"Lot of people here already," Ben commented, looking around.

"Yes," Lainey agreed. "Mother does a wonderful job with this." Credit where it was due. Her mother knew how to throw a party.

Lainey spotted her mother heading toward them, a vision in designer gold. On anyone else the form-fitting gown would be tacky. On Jacqui it was perfect.

"Lainey." She offered her cheek and Lainey dutifully kissed her, then offered her own.

"Hi, Mother." She laid a hand on Ben's arm, felt the heat of him through his sleeve. "This is Ben Lawless. Ben, this is my mother—Jacqui Keeler."

Jacqui gave Ben an obvious once-over. He held out his hand with a smile and she took it.

"Nice to meet you," he said.

"Likewise," she said, and turned to Lainey. "Now, honey, you two mingle for a bit before you take your seats. And no leaving until ten o'clock." Someone must have signaled her mother, because Jacqui turned abruptly to leave before Lainey could say a word. "I'll see you at dinner." And she was gone.

"Sorry," Lainey said immediately. "My mom's a little intense. Don't take it personally." What Jacqui could find lacking in the smoking hot package that was Ben, Lainey couldn't fathom. Because he wasn't Daniel? Couldn't give her what her mother deemed most important—money?

"I see that," Ben said as he steered her toward a buffet table piled high with sinful goodies. "And I'm not offended. Let's get something to drink."

Along the way they got pulled into several conversations—people who knew Lainey, or thought they did. The whole process was as exhausting as it always had been to smile for her mother or stump for her father. Tonight was a bit of both.

"Here." Ben pushed a golden flute into her hand. "I know your…situation. But I think you need this. Just carry it if nothing else."

The champagne bubbled in the flute and Lainey took

a tiny sip. It fizzed in her mouth and slid down her throat. Ben was right. Just having it in her hand was enough. She didn't need anyone questioning why she refused to drink. "Thank you. It hits the spot."

Ben bent so his mouth was next to her ear. She could hear him over the band, which had just started up. "You're welcome."

Lainey hoped he didn't notice the little shiver that skittered down her spine at his warm breath on her skin. She was so, so lost to this man. And he didn't even know it.

He moved away slightly and she felt the immediate loss of contact. She chided herself for letting herself get caught up in this even for a moment. Despite her decision to enjoy tonight, it wasn't real. It didn't change anything.

"So, what's good here?" Ben asked her as they surveyed the table loaded with *hors d'oeuvres* of every persuasion. There were tiny *petit-fours*, as well as fancy little things that looked like shrimp, mushrooms, cheese. All high end. No mini hot dogs for this party.

"I'd say all of it," she said. "My mother doesn't skimp on this stuff."

He smiled and handed her a plate. "Not surprised."

Lainey took a few small things and put them on her plate, and Ben did the same. Her brother approached them and Lainey braced herself.

"Laine," Kevin greeted her. She noticed he was dateless, and frowned.

"Kev, where's your date? How did *you* get away with coming stag?" Realizing how her words sounded, she quickly turned to Ben.

He just nodded at Kevin and said, "I see someone I need to talk to. I'll catch up with you in a bit, okay?"

"Um, okay," Lainey said, feeling like a total heel.

"Nice job," Kevin commented, lifting a flute of champagne from a passing waiter. "You've got a way with men, sis."

Lainey sent him a sour look, even though he was right. "I didn't mean it how it sounded." Still, she'd hurt Ben with her thoughtless comment. And after he'd gone to such trouble for her tonight. She tracked him with her eyes and noticed he'd stopped next to a tall, gorgeous, slender blond. Who couldn't possibly have natural boobs. Lainey frowned.

"And you're not listening to anything I say," Kevin said, amusement in his tone. "You can't take your eyes off the guy, can you? Does Mother know?"

"Does Mother know what?" Jacqui materialized next to them and peered critically at Lainey's plate. "Be careful, dear. I know you're—" she glanced around and lowered her voice "—pregnant, but you don't want to gain a lot of weight."

Lainey looked at her and for the first time saw an unhappy, brittle woman whose need to control everything had nearly estranged her from her children and whose marriage had taken a serious toll on her self-worth. Instead of being insulted by her thoughtless words, Lainey felt only pity.

"No worries, Mother," she said smoothly, and selected a prosciutto something from her plate. She was eating for two, right? Might as well do it tonight. "Lovely party, by the way."

Effectively sidetracked, Jacqui glowed. "It is, isn't it? Almost time to get seated for dinner. Lainey, get your date. Kevin, thanks for coming. I know you have to get back later."

Lainey's gaze lasered to Ben as her mother hurried off. Now he was laughing with the blond, his dark head near her golden one. Something sour curled in her belly. Couldn't be jealousy, could it? Despite their night together, and all her feelings for him, she had no actual claim on him. None at all.

So it was silly and petty to be jealous.

As if he'd felt her watching him, he lifted his head and locked on her gaze. The sour feeling was replaced by something much, much sweeter.

Kevin stepped closer, into her line of sight, his gaze intense and knowing. Her stomach sank.

"Anything you want to tell me, sis?"

Lainey stared up at him. *Oh, no.* She swallowed hard. "No. Nothing."

He gave a little nod and stepped back. He looked as if he wanted to say something, then thought better of it and turned and walked away.

Ben made his way through the crowd to Lainey. Her gaze snapped to his and relief lit her big blue eyes just for a moment. Then it was gone.

"Sorry about that," Ben said, coming up next to her. She smelled so good. Like vanilla and something sinful. Sweet and sinful. That was Lainey, all wrapped up in one sexy package.

Sexy *pregnant* package, that was.

God, he was in trouble.

"It's okay." Her voice was a little remote. "Of course you know people here."

"Megan is an old friend, but not *that* kind of friend." Ben surprised himself by how important it was that she understand. "I was surprised to see her here."

She gave him a sideways look. "I get it."

He caught her hand and twined his fingers with hers. She looked down, clearly startled, then up to his face.

"Lainey. You are the only woman I can see." The words were rough in his throat, but true in every sense. There was no one but her. If things were different there would never be anyone but her. All he could give her was tonight. It had to be enough.

Her gaze stayed on his, her blue eyes wide and hopeful, fearful. He wanted to drown in them, in her. Instead he gave her fingers a squeeze and stepped back. "I take it we're supposed to sit down?"

A shadow passed over her face quickly, then she smiled. "Shall we?"

They made their way to the table. He noted she kept an eye on her parents, who were still mingling and mixing and chatting up the guests. The table was set for eight and Kevin was already there, his gaze firmly on Ben.

His words from the other night hit him hard. *No intentions.* Yeah, he was a liar. He wanted so much more than he could give her—wanted to give her what she deserved—and Kevin's hard stare said he knew it. Not only that, he knew Ben was going to walk. Ben met the other man's gaze squarely. They both knew she deserved better.

Dinner went fairly quickly. Prime rib, decadent desserts, rich sides all filled the plates. Ben hadn't eaten so well in ages. Lainey, he noted, only picked at her food.

"Not hungry?"

She looked up and flushed. "Not really. These things— it's not my cup of tea." She slid her plate toward him. "Here. Help yourself if you want."

He did fork up a couple of pieces of her prime rib, because it *was* prime rib and he was a guy. He caught Jacqui's fierce frown at her daughter as she got up and he wondered at it.

Jacqui walked to the microphone at the front of the room. After a little speech of welcome and thanks, she added, "Dancing will begin as soon as the last of the plates are cleared. Don't forget the silent auction—there's still time to place your bids."

"I'm going to hit the ladies' room," Lainey murmured to him. She stood and picked up her little silver purse. "Back in a few."

"So. Ben." Her father leaned forward across the table as soon as Lainey had left. "How do you know my daughter?"

Wow, was he sixteen again, or what? He kept his tone level. "Through my grandmother. Lainey's been helping her out at her place."

The man looked surprised. "Really?"

Ben nodded. "I think her visits are the highlight of Grandma's week." How could this guy not know the kind of person his daughter was?

"What do you do for a living?"

Ben tensed just slightly. This man could and would ferret out the truth, and Ben would bet he wanted to know. "I'm a firefighter."

Greg Keeler arched a brow. "Really? Where?"

"City of Grand Rapids." He hesitated for a beat as he met the other man's gaze. "I'm on medical leave right now." Better just to say it than have it found out and used against Lainey somehow.

The very fact he was even concerned was a problem.

The older man's gaze sharpened. It was no doubt only a matter of time before the man looked him up if he thought Ben was interested in his daughter. "I hope your recovery is going well."

Ben managed a smile. "Well enough." Actually, there was some truth to that. Being around Lainey had helped him. Better than any therapy.

Greg leaned across the table. "While being a firefighter is a very important job, you need to realize you're not what we have in mind for Lainey," he said, almost apologetically. "Her ex-husband is a partner in a very prestigious law firm. I understand they're considering reconciliation."

Ben's brow shot up, as did his pulse. He sure as hell hadn't seen any indication that Lainey was interested in her ex-husband. In fact, if memory served him, she was no fan of his. "Is that so? Then why isn't he here with her?"

"Because I didn't invite him." Lainey's voice was cold as she stood behind Ben and regarded her father with sharp eyes. "He's my ex-husband for a lot of very good reasons."

Her father sat back and shook his head. "Lainey—"

She shot him a hard look and turned to Ben as the band struck up. "Want to dance?"

"Of course." He pushed back from the table and inclined his head to Greg. The older man crossed his arms and frowned as he led Lainey away.

"How about a walk instead?" he asked. The band was playing, but it was too early to dance. They'd be the only ones on the floor, and possibly the center of attention. He doubted Lainey wanted that.

She nodded. "I'd like that."

He put his hand at the small of her back, because he couldn't not touch her, and they made their way to the glass doors at the other end of the room. They opened out to a sheltered patio that overlooked the water. It was chilly, but he figured he'd keep her warm.

As soon as they were outside she took an audible breath. Sympathy filled him. "Is that the first time you've breathed all evening?"

She gave him a rueful smile. "Seems like it. Old habits. I never wanted to do anything that might draw attention to myself. I always wanted to be anywhere but here."

"I can understand that." Seeing her interact with her family—except for her brother—was eye-opening.

"Can you?" She leaned on the railing and the position

allowed him a fantastic view of her breasts. He shifted position slightly so he could see better—if he chose to look—and so no one coming up next to them would get the same treat.

"You don't think I can?"

"I don't know. My childhood was so lonely. I didn't have a Rose. As you can see, I didn't even have normal parents." She didn't look at him. "What was yours like?"

He rested a hip on the railing. "Normal, I guess. Both parents—though they got divorced when I was twelve. My brother and sister. All of them live downstate, around Detroit. After the divorce things changed, but our parents took a lot of trouble to make sure we knew we were loved." Really, they'd been lucky. He could see that now, in Lainey's wistful expression.

She was quiet for a moment. "I'm sorry about my dad. I'm not sure what got into him."

"He wants what's best for you." The words caused an ache in his chest. It wasn't him. But part of him—a huge part—wished it was.

Her laugh was low and sad. "If that's true, they should know Daniel's not what's best. The man's a snake." She turned and looked up into his eyes. "There's no chance of reconciliation, by the way."

While he truly hadn't thought so, relief still trickled through him. "You definitely deserve better than a snake."

A smile tugged at the corners of her mouth. "Aw. That's so sweet."

He touched her chin. *You are the sweet one,* he wanted to say. Actually, he wanted to say much more than that, and it worried him. The band struck up a slower tune and he held out a hand. "Dance with me?"

She looked up, startled. "Out here?"

"We can go inside if you'd rather. But there are more eyes."

"Good point." She turned to face him and he pulled her into his arms, then steered her away from the railing into the deeper shadows caused by the overhang of the roof.

She felt so good in his arms. She fit so well. He tried not to think of the other night, when they'd moved together in perfect sync. He pulled her closer and felt her stiffen slightly. It shouldn't matter, but it did.

He lowered his head to her ear. "You can relax. I don't bite."

She gave a half-giggle, half-sigh, and he was pleased to feel her body relax a little. "I know. I'm sorry. Just trying to get through this..." Her voice trailed off as he tugged her a little closer, so her breasts touched his chest. Her breath hitched just a bit and she shivered.

"Cold?" His voice was low, and he pulled her in even closer. She'd be able to feel, now, just how affected he was by her. What he couldn't tell her was how right she felt in his arms, how much he felt as if he'd finally come home.

"Not at all," she breathed, and tipped her face up to his.

Unable to help himself, he pressed a kiss on her soft mouth. Two things crossed his mind.

He was in trouble.

And, after all she'd done for him, she deserved to know the truth.

CHAPTER ELEVEN

THE MOMENTS SPENT in Ben's arms were magical. Almost as magical as the other night. Lainey hadn't thought dancing could be so intimate, but somehow they were in their own little world of two. She didn't want it to end, and that was a first. But, since the band had taken a break for her mother to announce the winners of the silent auction, maybe it was time to take their own personal party elsewhere.

"Do you want to leave?"

Ben's arm was draped across the back of her chair and he brushed his fingers over her bare shoulder. "This is your shindig, Laine. You know the protocol better than I do."

She leaned forward to pick up her clutch from the table. "Then let's go. My feet are killing me."

His low chuckle warmed her. "Sacrifice over?"

"Something like that." She scanned the crowd. "I'll have to say goodnight to my mother. Give me a minute to track her down."

"I'll go with you." He unfolded himself from his chair and offered her his arm. She took it. All the vibes he gave off were those of a man who liked her, desired her—yet there was a layer underneath she couldn't quite get to…a place he kept away from her. It contrasted sharply with the intimacy of the evening. With how badly she wanted to open her heart to him.

How afraid she was, after tonight, that she already had.

Lainey found her mother near the auction exhibits. "We're heading out. It was a lovely party, Mother."

"You're leaving?" Jacqui's gaze darted from Lainey to Ben and back again. "So soon?"

Lainey kept her gaze steady on her mother's. "Yes. I'm tired and my feet hurt."

"Of course. I guess in your—" she lowered her voice "—condition that's to be expected." Someone called out to Jacqui then, and she offered her cheek to Lainey, who dropped the expected kiss. "Go straight home," she instructed, and hurried off.

Lainey sighed at the words and turned to Ben. "Shall we?"

"Absolutely." He put his hand on her back again—a gesture that Lainey was starting to love for its quiet possessiveness. It didn't take long for them to get the car and head toward home.

"Will you—will you come in?" she asked when he pulled in her driveway. The bold words startled her, especially in light of how their night together had ended before. Was she really willing to have him run away again?

He turned to her, and by the light of the dash she could see the pain in his eyes. "I'm not sure that's a good idea."

She sucked in a breath, the shininess of the evening tarnished. "Of course. Well. Thank you for everything." For the dances. For the kisses. For the feeling that this was actually going to be able to go somewhere when he must not feel the same. How could she have read it all so wrong?

He reached over the console and caught her hand as she fumbled for the door handle. "No. Lainey. Wait. I just don't want to hurt you."

She stared at him. They were in this far too deep for that. "We're adults. I know you're leaving, Ben. I know this isn't forever." But given the chance she'd take forever. The thought rocked her.

He rubbed his thumb over her lower lip and she closed her eyes.

"I can't stay the night."

The hesitation in his voice made her open them again. "All I was going to offer was coffee."

He laughed and rested his forehead on hers. "Lainey… God. I don't deserve you."

He got out of the car, and as he walked around to her door she whispered, "Yes, you do."

"Did you tell her yet?"

Ben put the leftover roast back in the fridge. For two people, they had enough to feed them for a week. Maybe two. "Tell who what?"

Rose wheeled around and he saw her frown. "Don't play games with me, Benjamin. When are you going to tell Lainey about Jason?"

He shut the fridge and stared at the sandwich he no longer had an appetite for. He was tired, he wanted to get out of the tux, and he had no idea why his grandmother had waited up for him. "I'm not, Grandma. She doesn't need to know." He didn't want her to think less of him.

Her gaze went to slits. "Oh, yes, she does. You are in love with that girl—"

Panic sliced through him. "She's hardly a girl—" *That* was what he protested? He'd meant to say no way was he in love with Lainey. Sure, she'd helped him open up in ways he hadn't thought were possible, but that didn't mean he was in love with her.

His grandma waved his words away impatiently. "Semantics. When you're my age a thirty-something woman is a girl. You love her—even if you aren't willing to admit it yet. She's got it equally bad for you. I would have thought going with her tonight would help you see that. You don't have forever, Ben. Ask Callie."

Her voice was quiet, and Ben sank down in a chair as if she'd taken an axe to his knees. "Geez, Grandma, how can you say that?"

She wheeled closer, her gaze intense. "Do you think Jason wasted one single minute when he first spotted that girl? No, he didn't. He had some good years with her, loved her fully. And he—he alone—was reckless and lost it all. How do you think Callie would feel, knowing you are throwing your own chance at love away because her husband is gone? Is that going to make her feel better? Bring Jason back?"

Her words pinged around in him, echoing in his head. "I— No, of course not."

She poked him in the chest. "Listen to me. I know a thing or two about love, having been married to your grandpa Harry for fifty-odd years. You've found a woman who'd give you everything. You're walking away because Jason isn't here. Ask yourself—would he divorce Callie if the roles were reversed?"

He shook his head and stood up. "Of course he wouldn't. But it's not that easy, Grandma. He went in that building after me. I shouldn't have been there to begin with. It was my job to keep him safe." *I failed him.*

"It was a miscommunication that was out of your control and not your personal responsibility," she said simply. "He made a choice. He knew the risks. You both did. It's part of the job. You weren't his babysitter. You need to go see Callie. But first you need to accept that it's time to move on."

He went cold. See Callie? See first hand the destruction he'd caused? He hadn't even been able to face returning her calls. He wasn't sure he'd be welcome, that she'd want to see him. He didn't want to make things worse for her, for her kids. For Jason's sake. For her own.

For his.

But this wasn't about him.

Rose laid a hand on his arm. "You need to accept that it's okay to move on," she said quietly. "You're a good man. You deserve Lainey, and Lord knows both of you deserve to be happy. Even beyond that, she needs you and you need her. Don't let it slip away."

Her words rang true. But he didn't know if he was capable of being the man Lainey and her baby deserved. The risk of failing them was far too great. He'd failed Jason, and by extension Callie.

When he closed his eyes all he saw was Lainey. All he heard was her laugh, her voice. He could still feel her in his arms. But he couldn't be in love with her. He'd shut that part of himself down for good.

Hadn't he?

It was time to sign the paperwork.

Lainey'd read over the pages from Jon and asked Beth's husband, who was a lawyer, to look over them as well. While technically she'd need to take him to court to finalize the custody transfer, it should be able to be handled with lawyers only. This was the necessary first step to being well and truly free of her baby's father. She signed them and put them away, both relieved and a little sad.

She went into the kitchen and had just started a pot of coffee—decaf, of course—when there was a knock on the front door. She padded over that way and took a look through the peephole.

Daniel stood on the front step.

Lainey inhaled sharply and leaned her head on the door.

She'd love to ignore him, but her car was in the driveway instead of the garage. And she knew he wouldn't go away.

She opened the door. "This is a bad time, Daniel. I'm really tired."

He looked her over, his gaze both hot and contemptuous, and she gripped the door tighter.

"I just want to talk."

He tried the old charming smile, but it did nothing but annoy her. She crossed her arms. "Try again. We've got nothing left to say to each other. Why are you really here, Daniel?"

He dropped all pretense. "You're pregnant." He nearly spat the words.

Her pulse picked up in warning. "Yes, I am."

"How are you going to raise it by yourself?" He stepped a little closer and she forced herself to hold her ground. "You'll be a single mother. Who's going to raise it with you?"

Ben. Oh, if only. "I'm going to be a single mother, yes. Did you need something? Because I've got things to do—"

He interrupted her. "You're making a mistake, Lainey. Your parents have opened their house to you. They're trying to help you. We all are. Don't you see? I can take care of the money problems you have. You won't have to do anything you don't want to do."

Anger spiked. "I won't have to do what? Work at a job I love? Something that has meaning to me? That I get up each morning and *want* to do? Why do you want to take that from me?"

He blinked at her. "No one's taking anything from you. We're offering solutions so you don't have to struggle anymore. Especially now that you are pregnant."

"What I need is to make my own solutions," she said simply. "Not have yours forced on me. And the fact you can't see that means you don't know me at all. You never did."

He frowned and put his hands in his pockets. "Of course I knew you. You were my wife for seven years."

And in all that time you never picked out one birthday gift. She shook her head. "I was a tool. I was the means to an end—which was my father." Funny how she couldn't muster up any fire. She truly didn't care. He was so far behind her now he'd never catch up.

His expression radiated sincerity, but she knew better than to believe it. "I'm sorry you felt that way, Lainey. I cleaned some things up before I came here. I've changed. I made a mistake or two. You of all people know what it's like to make mistakes."

The words hit home. Still. "Yes. I do. But my baby isn't one of them. Also, I never hurt anyone or deceived anyone like you did. You made a mockery of our marriage. Of me. And that's why, even if I'd ever loved you, I wouldn't get back with you. *That* would be the biggest mistake of my life." She stepped back. "Now, if you'll excuse me, my coffee is ready."

Daniel crowded closer and stepped inside the door. His tone was wheedling. "No, wait. It was good with us, Lainey. It's better for a baby to have a father. We can have some of our own."

"No." She'd never inflict a man like Daniel on a poor kid. No child deserved that. "You need to leave. Now."

Daniel grabbed her by the upper arms, and when she tried to pull away he dug in harder. She swallowed a yelp of pain. "Lainey. This is what works best for me. For both of us. You—"

The door banged open and Daniel let go of her in surprise. Ben stood there, and the smoldering anger on his face took Lainey's breath away.

"Get away from her." The words were a low growl.

Daniel reached for her again. "Lainey, listen—"

"Get out," she hissed. "Don't come back."

Ben took a menacing step toward Daniel and he took a step in the right direction. "She asked you to leave."

Daniel scowled, cursed, and slammed out the door.

She turned to Ben, willing her heart to return to normal, unsure if it was pumping so hard from the encounter with her idiot ex or Ben's very intoxicating nearness. "Why are you here?"

"I was in the neighborhood and saw him through the door." He shoved his hands in his pockets. "I thought you could use backup."

She pressed her hands to her face. "I wish everyone would stop trying to help me. I had it under control."

"Of course," he murmured. "I saw him handling you and jumped to conclusions."

She laid her hand on his arm as he turned to go. "No. Please. I'm sorry. I'm just so sick of my family interfering. You did me a favor by showing up here. It's not the first time he's handled me roughly."

His eyes went to slits. "He abused you?"

"No." She shook her head. "He'd grab me, like you saw tonight, but he almost never touched me. In any manner." Then she blushed as it hit her what she'd admitted.

Ben touched her face and the delicious roughness of his fingers on her skin caused a little shiver to run down her back. "Lainey. How could he be married to you and not see what he had?"

Her gaze pinged to his at his words and the rawness in his voice and she barely dared to breathe. The reverence she saw there made her want to cry. Daniel had never looked at her like that. Ever.

She clasped his wrist and turned into his touch. "I don't think he ever saw me, Ben. That's not what he wanted."

Ben didn't get that. He looked at her and wanted everything. Wanted the whole package. Wanted the baby, the chance to be a father. It was killing him. He didn't know how to reconcile things so he could have it. *Jason, dead. Lainey, pregnant. Baby, not his.* They all bothered him and worried him and he didn't know how to move forward. She looked at him with those big eyes and he wanted to take her in his arms, into his bed, and let her soothe away the pain. Only letting go of it all seemed like a betrayal to Jason. And dumping it on her was more than he could ask of her.

Would she think less of him? He couldn't deny it mattered, even though he wished it didn't.

"Ben?"

He looked into her worried face and couldn't help the question. He needed to know. "So he's not the father?"

Her head snapped up and she laughed—a sharp bark. "God, no." She stepped away and shut the door. "Can I get you something? A drink?"

He smelled coffee. "Coffee's fine."

He followed her to the kitchen, trying and failing to keep his gaze off her perfect ass in those clingy black pants. He leaned in the doorway while she opened cupboards and lifted slightly on her toes to get mugs. The movement pulled her shirt snug across her breasts and the slight swell of her belly. He wanted nothing more than to pull her against him, hold her tiny bump in his hands. The longing nearly brought him to his knees.

She poured the coffee with a slightly shaking hand, and he accepted his. She got out milk, sugar and spoons, and led him to the small table in the dining room. He sat opposite her and watched as she doctored her coffee.

"Let me tell you about my baby's father. This is not

a story I'm proud of," she said quietly, and took a deep breath. Then she poured out the whole thing, without meeting his gaze.

Ben cursed. "He didn't tell you he was married?"

She stirred her coffee without taking her eyes off the mug. "Nope. And I didn't figure it out. Pathetic, I know."

"He is. You're not." When her head came up and she opened her mouth he held up a hand. "Let me see if I've got this right. You were recovering from a marriage that was completely loveless and lacking in affection or respect of any kind. This guy showed up and took advantage of that. How is that *you* being pathetic?"

She stared into her mug. "I just should have known better."

"Oh, honey." The endearment startled him, but he meant it. "No. He took advantage of you. That's not on you."

"I could have said no." She shut her eyes. "It wasn't like I really wanted him. It was just the idea of someone actually wanting me."

"Yeah." He pulled her to her feet. "But if you had said no, you wouldn't have this." He laid his hand on her belly and her eyes went wide. She laid her hand on top of his. "Would you wish this away?"

"Never," she said quietly. She took a deep breath. "The only thing I'd wish for is a better father for him or her. Someone like you." The words were nearly a whisper, and her soft gaze caught his.

He froze as if ice had formed in his muscles. "No, Lainey, not like me. I'm no good for you, for a baby." He wasn't what she needed. Not anymore.

She saw the shields come down and all but heard the resounding clang as they locked into place. She forced herself to hold his gaze and pressed his trembling hand against her belly. He wanted this, wanted her. She knew it—could see it. Had been seeing it as they'd gone through the past couple weeks. She wanted him too, even knowing how impossible the situation was.

"Why not?"

He slid his hand out from under hers and stepped away. The coldness she felt was as much at the loss of contact as it was for his emotional shutdown. "I can't talk about it."

She gave a little laugh and fought against the burn of tears. "Oh? But it's okay for me to spill my shames to you? It's a one-way street?"

"It's not that simple." His voice was low.

She lifted her chin. "My problems aren't simple."

"No. No, they're not," he agreed. "I meant it's not—it's not something I can talk about."

That destroyed look was back, and her heart ached. She was falling in love with this man, and he would never let her close enough to help. To love him as he deserved. As he needed.

She thought of the nightmare but didn't bring it up. The fact he chose to shut her out hurt, but what claim did she have to him? They'd been physical, she was emotionally invested, but there was no actual commitment—nothing that would mean he should tell her what had happened.

Still. She had to try. "You don't have to carry this alone," she said quietly. "Whatever it is."

He stared at a spot on the wall, but she doubted he was seeing anything in the room. "Some things have to be," he said finally, and the pain in his voice burned in her heart. He shoved a hand through his hair. "I'm sorry, Lainey. It's just so damn hard to talk about."

She got out of her chair and moved to kneel next to him. He wouldn't look at her. "Why?" she asked, and held her breath.

His jaw worked. "I killed my best friend, okay?" At her

sharp whimper he looked her in the eye. "I made a stupid mistake and a great guy died. A family man. He left his wife and two little kids. Sons who will never know their daddy now because of a mistake *I* made."

Pain washed through her—for him, for the man's family. She wanted to climb in his lap and hold him, but settled for touching his face, feeling the roughness of stubble under her hand. "Oh, Ben. I'm so sorry."

His eyes glittered with unshed tears as he looked at her. "Not as sorry as I am. I'm not the man you want, Lainey."

"Don't you think I get to decide that?" she asked, and tugged him to his feet. He let her, and she slid her arms around him, rested her head on his chest and squeezed her eyes shut as she listened to the pounding of his heart beneath her cheek. The warmth of him seeped into her pores and pooled in her heart. He stood very still for a moment, then wrapped his arms around her, too. She hoped he would allow himself to take comfort from it, from her.

They stood that way for a few minutes, then Lainey heard her phone ring. Ben stepped back, the moment broken. "I'd better get going. You okay?"

She looked at him and saw the careful remoteness back in his gaze. Her heart ached as she nodded and followed him through the living room to the door. "Fine."

He turned around and lifted her chin, his fingers lingering. The look in his eyes was a strange mixture of regret and affection. He leaned down and planted a hard kiss on her mouth. "You're not any kind of damaged goods, Lainey. Don't let anyone make you feel otherwise. Ever. You're an incredible woman." Then he left.

Lainey pressed her fingertips to her tingling mouth, her heart heavy as the front door clicked shut behind him. The tears she'd been fighting finally broke loose, and as she sank back down at the table, head on her arms, she had another thought.

His parting words had sounded an awful lot like goodbye.

CHAPTER TWELVE

AT THE END of the next day Lainey went into the little office area in the back of the store and checked her books. The familiar feeling of dread pooled as she added up the numbers. Better, but not good enough. She could chart steady progress upward, though, so that was hopeful. But was it enough?

"What's the verdict?" Beth walked over.

Lainey leaned back so her friend could see the screen and rested her hands on her belly. "Better. Definitely better. But not there. Yet."

Beth hesitated. "Mark and I were talking. If you're interested, we can probably swing me buying in if you want a partner."

Stunned, Lainey stared at her friend. "I— Beth, I hadn't—"

Beth held up a hand. "I know you want to do this all on your own. But you can be a success even with a partner. It doesn't make it less because you have help." She smiled and touched Lainey's shoulder. "Think about it, okay?"

"I will," she promised.

After Beth left, she stared at the numbers on the screen. Beth buying in would mean a new cooler. Repairs on the van, which even today had given her fits about going into gear. Bigger payments to her parents and therefore being out from under their thumb earlier.

Excitement and hope flared.

It was tempting. But was it the right decision?

She stood and paced out into the shop. She took in the silk flowers, the cheery Halloween-themed window. Sure, the carpet was worn, and the cash register was old but completely reliable. The fresh scent of the flowers overlaid everything and made it feel almost homey. This place was more than just a business. She loved it—loved all of it. It suited her to a T. Because of that, she couldn't let it go under. What good was it to be determined to prove herself if ultimately it sank her? That would only prove her parents right and she'd be back where she started.

She'd gone too far to let it all go under now.

She took a deep breath and walked into the backroom. Beth was right. She just needed to make sure the numbers were stable enough for her friend to take the risk. And then she and Beth and Mark would look them over together. She wouldn't let them buy in if it turned out to be too risky. She wanted to succeed, but she was pragmatic enough to realize she wasn't out of the woods just yet.

A lightness she hadn't felt in a very long time crept into her heart. This was the right thing to do. Too bad she'd been so damn blind she hadn't been able to see it. Or maybe she hadn't been *ready* to see it. She owed Beth for putting it all into perspective.

After leaving work, Lainey pulled into Rose's driveway. She'd promised to take her friend to bingo. Ben's truck sat there, and she tried to quash the silly little spurt of anticipation. She'd stop in and say hello. Sort of face the elephant in the room head-on—see if his confession to her had done any good for him.

The light in the garage indicated he was in there, even though the big door was shut. She opened up the side door and stepped inside, almost holding her breath. How this went depended on how he looked at her when he saw her.

Her heart sank when he turned. His face was the polite mask he'd worn when she'd first met him. "Lainey."

"Hello, Ben." She kept her voice steady with effort. Two could play this game. He just looked at her and waited. "I just—wanted to see how you were. After last night." Darn it, she sounded tentative. But his impassive expression wasn't helping.

"How should I be?" He kept his gaze on her. Completely shuttered. "Nothing's changed, Lainey, if that's what you're asking."

Well, that was to the point. "Okay, then," she said stiffly. "See you around."

And she left the garage, slamming the door behind her. Not the most mature of moves, but the man frustrated her no end.

On the short walk to the house she took a couple of deep breaths, hoping Rose wouldn't notice her mood. She didn't want to be quizzed—just wanted to lick her wounds in peace.

No such luck. Rose took one look at her as soon as she entered the kitchen and frowned. "Okay. First Ben, now you. That boy's been in a serious funk all day. What happened? He won't tell me."

Lainey blanched but managed a small smile. "Nothing happened."

Rose shook her head. "Oh, no. I may be old, but I'm neither blind nor stupid. There's much more than that, isn't there?" She sat back and examined Lainey. "Did he tell you about Jason?"

She gave a little nod. "I don't know what to tell him, Rose."

Her friend gave a little sigh. "There's really not much to say. He's got a lot to work out. On top of that, nothing ties a man up in knots more than when a relationship that was supposed to be casual turns out not to be."

Lainey gave a little shrug that she hoped was casual, even though she felt anything but. "It's the wrong time."

Rose gave a decidedly unladylike snort. "It's always the wrong time. You don't get to pick when or who you'll fall in love with, child. I see how that boy looks at you. Does he know you're pregnant?"

Despite Rose's gentle tone, the words might as well have been a shout. Lainey winced. "Yes. How did *you* know?" Had Ben told Rose after she'd asked him not to?

"Not from him," Rose assured her. "I can just tell. You've changed physically. And the fact you told him should tell you something, honey."

Startled, Lainey met her friend's gaze. "Tell me what?"

"You told him before you told me," she said gently, and raised a hand when Lainey opened her mouth to protest. "No—no, wait. I'm not saying you should have told me first. But think about it. Why did you tell Ben?"

"I had to tell him why I couldn't go to the hospital for an X-ray," Lainey pointed out, but in retrospect she could see the holes in that theory. Why *had* she blurted it out?

Rose nodded. "But there were other reasons you could have given. Or, for that matter, no reason at all. He didn't need an explanation. A simple no thanks would have sufficed. He wouldn't have pushed. But you felt safe enough to tell him. Am I right?"

That was true. She hadn't needed to tell him. But feeling safe? With Ben? He made her feel anything *but* safe.

Well, that wasn't entirely true. He'd made her feel safe

and cherished the night they'd spent together. The danger from Ben wasn't that he'd take her for granted, or treat her like her ex had. It was that he made her want things she couldn't have, that he couldn't give. And she wasn't willing to open herself to any more emotional destruction.

"Lainey." Rose leaned forward. "I know you've been through an awful lot. You have very little reason to trust people. The fact you told him is significant. The fact he went to that party with you is significant. He hasn't done anything social in months."

"The timing is all wrong," Lainey said again, because it was true. "He's not in any place for a relationship, and I— Well, I really need to do this on my own." Actually, she was starting to rethink that statement. If Beth bought in to her shop what counted was making it a success. The same idea applied to her personal life. Having a partner in life would be wonderful—but only if it was the right man.

Was Ben that man?

Rose sat back. "I understand. I do. I just want to see both of you happy. And if the two of you could be happy together—well, that would do my heart good."

"I'll be fine," Lainey assured her. Fine wasn't the same as happy, of course, and she doubted very much the distinction would be wasted on Rose.

Rose studied her for a long moment, then nodded. "I'm glad to hear it," she said. "We should get going. Don't want to be late for bingo."

Grateful to be off the hook, Lainey stood up and gathered her purse and keys.

As she wheeled her friend down the ramp Ben came out of the garage. Her heart gave a little leap and she was glad she was behind Rose, so her sharp-eyed friend didn't read anything that might be on her face. He gave Lainey a nod and she managed to smile back. As he came closer she could see the stress lines bracketing his mouth. She wanted nothing more in that moment than to go to him and smooth them away, to hold him and be held.

She looked away instead.

Ben helped Rose into the car and took care of the chair while Lainey slid behind the wheel. As they backed out of the driveway Rose narrowed her gaze on Ben, who stood watching them, hands in pockets. She muttered something that sounded like, "Foolish boy."

No, Lainey wanted to tell her. He's smart enough to know his limits.

And so was she.

"So, we've got a Friday wedding this week," Lainey noted. The flowers were simple and seasonal, fitting for a second wedding for both the bride and groom. They were starting on the bouquets today. "And a big order for a baptism on Sunday."

"Isn't it great?" Beth asked as she cut open a flower box. "Word is getting out. We're doing good."

Lainey agreed. Part of her was a little sad, though, that her personal life seemed to be one-hundred-eighty degrees away from her growing professional life. But to dwell on it wouldn't do her any good.

"Speaking of weddings," Beth said casually, "how's Ben?"

Lainey sent her a warning look. "Beth—"

"What?" Her friend's innocent look didn't fool Lainey. She shook her head and Beth sighed. "Okay. I heard at the café that you and Ben were super cozy at the hospital gala." She plopped a box on the worktable and sent Lainey a mock glare. "Of course I didn't hear that from *you*. My supposed best friend and subject of such hot gossip."

Super-cozy. Well, she supposed they *had* been all

wrapped up in each other and the spell of the evening. Dancing and kissing in the shadows. His car in front of her house for hours.

"I— Well, yeah. I guess it would look that way." She winced. "Don't people have anything else to talk about? Surely there were more interesting couples than Ben and I?"

Beth gave her a pitying look. "Lainey, I think the interesting part was the chemistry the two of you have. I heard that you were so hot together people were concerned you'd combust. Or maybe get down right there," she added thoughtfully, earning a playful smack from Lainey.

"Well, it doesn't matter now," she said, thinking of last night and how he'd been completely shut down. Pain lanced through her. She'd give anything to have this work out, to make it so they could be a couple.

But that wasn't an option. It was silly even to think it was.

"How is that?" Beth asked. "The guy kissed you. At least that much. But from how red you just turned I'm guessing it's much more than that. He helped you move. He took you to a formal party on short notice. Guys don't just do that for women they aren't interested in."

"His grandma sent him to help me," Lainey muttered. Beth didn't know how far things had gone with them, but they must have been giving off some pretty serious vibes at the gala. "And that first kiss was a pity kiss."

"Pity kiss?" Beth raised her brow. "Oh, come on, Laine. Ben doesn't seem like that type. He's so reserved. He's not going to go around kissing women because he thinks it will make them feel better."

Beth had a point. Still… "I meant it was just the moment." They'd had a lot of wonderful moments that she held on to tightly. Privately.

"Moment or not—and I think you are withholding key information from me, but I'll let it go this time—there's clearly something between you. The question is, what are you going to do about it?"

A little shiver ran through Lainey. That was the question. What *was* she going to do? She knew what she wanted, but not what he wanted. She stuffed a 'mum in florist foam with a little more force than was necessary and nearly bent it. "I'm not going there, Beth."

Beth touched her arm. "All kidding aside, why not?"

She widened her eyes. "You know why, Beth. Look at my marriage. Look at how I got in this situation. I'm doing this alone. I'm barely hanging on. There's no way he and I could make it work, even if I wanted it to. I need to keep him at a distance." She wouldn't tell Beth about Jason. It wasn't her story to tell.

"So you'll shut him down?" Beth said quietly.

She winced. Actually, he'd shut *her* down. More or less.

Beth continued. "But you don't *have* to do this alone. That's the whole point. Okay, so maybe Ben's not the guy for you. I don't know one way or the other. Chemistry is wonderful, but definitely not the only thing to base a relationship on. But don't shut yourself off all the way. Single parenting is hard. You might want someone to share it with."

"I—" She'd love to share it with Ben. She didn't see another man coming into her life whom she'd want more. But it didn't look as if that was to be. Unable to finish her sentence, she cleared her throat and changed the subject. "Well, we've got a lot to do here. Let's get these done so the bride can relax."

Beth looked as if she wanted to say something, but simply shook her head instead.

Lainey knew she was a coward. But it seemed like the only way to protect herself.

That night, Lainey had just propped her feet on the coffee table and turned the TV on when a knock sounded at the door. She padded over and peeked through the peephole to see her parents standing there. It wasn't like them to drop by unannounced. She frowned as she opened the door.

"Is everything okay?"

"Of course. Do you have a minute?" Her father's voice was strangely formal. "We won't stay long."

"I—yes, I do." She stepped aside to let them in and tried to tamp down a little surge of nerves. There could be no good reason for this visit.

Jacqui looked around the room as she slipped off her shoes. Lainey looked too—she was proud of the home she had created. A fire crackled in the hearth, and the low light of the lamps cast a warm glow over the space. She took a seat on the slip-covered couch. Panda was draped across the back. The cat didn't even crack an eye open.

Her parents sat in the chairs while Lainey muted the TV. Frankly, *Survivor* was a great backdrop for her wranglings with her parents. She set the remote carefully on the end table, dismayed to note her hand shook slightly.

"Can I get you anything?" she asked, and they both shook their heads.

"This is certainly—cozy," Jacqui said carefully, and Lainey sighed. In this case, "cozy" wasn't a compliment.

"I think so," she said, choosing to ignore her mother's meaning. "I love it."

"Well." Always one to cut to the chase, her father leaned forward. "We've got some information you might find interesting."

Her heart kicked up a bit. "Information? About what?"

Her parents exchanged a look. "About Ben Lawless, dear," her mother said.

Lainey tensed. Oh, God. They'd dug into his past. She kept her voice level as she said, "Really?"

"Yes." Jacqui pulled some papers out of her monster bag and held them out. Lainey took them reluctantly. "I think you'll find it interesting reading."

Lainey laid the pages on the couch next to her. She couldn't bring herself to look too closely at them. *Local Firefighter Under Fire* was the heading on the first page. Poor Ben.

"Why are you doing this?" She tried to keep her voice steady but failed.

"So you can see once and for all why it's a bad idea to get mixed up with him. Lainey, he's directly responsible for the death of a fellow firefighter. Ben went in after being told not to. The other man went after him. As a result, a young family man is dead. Ben's been removed from the squad. He's had some mental health issues as well. He's not stable. It's in your best interests to stay away from him." She nodded at the papers. "It's all there."

Lainey sucked in a breath. "Oh, Mother. How could you? This is beneath you."

Jacqui recoiled and flushed slightly, and looked at her husband. Greg cleared his throat. "You don't want to get mixed up with an unstable man, honey. You deserve better."

Lainey stared. Surely they couldn't mean Daniel. "A lying, cheating man who threatens me is a better choice?"

Greg winced slightly. "No. Of course not. But if Ben isn't stable you could be hurt. And you've got a child to think about. You're going to be a mother. It's time you were responsible and made better choices."

Lainey's mouth fell open. She snapped it shut. "While

I appreciate you looking out for me, I'm perfectly capable of making decisions for myself. You don't know Ben. I do. He's a far better man than Daniel. Than most men. He's got honor, integrity and loyalty in spades. Not to mention he actually *listens* to what I say and doesn't make any attempt to manipulate me. He's a good man, and I never thought I'd find one like him. As for this—he's told me himself."

She stomped over to the fireplace and placed the papers on the flames. They went up with a *whoosh*. If only it were that easy to help Ben be free of his demons. When she spun back around she saw her parents staring at her and realized with a sinking feeling she'd said far, far too much.

"You're in love with him." Jacqui's tone was shocked. "What do you think he can possibly give you?"

Her mother's words stymied her. *In love with Ben?* She couldn't be. Could she? She'd been trying so hard not to be, teetering on the edge but holding her heart in reserve.

She swallowed and tried to focus. "He can't give me anything right now," she said, and heard the sorrow in her voice. "But then again he never said he could." *And I've never asked.* She'd been afraid of the answer. Just as she'd been afraid to admit she was flat-out in love with the man.

Jacqui simply stared at her, her throat working. Greg stood and pulled his wife to her feet. "Lainey, for your sake I hope this infatuation passes quickly. You've got a lot going on, trying to keep your shop going and getting ready for the baby. If you have a prayer of making this work you need to let Ben go. He's not the man for you."

"You're wrong," Lainey said, her voice quiet. She met her parents' gazes squarely. "He *is* the man for me." She knew it with all her heart. What she didn't know was how to make him understand it.

Greg herded a sputtering Jacqui out the door and Lainey sank back on the couch. In love with Ben.

She squeezed her eyes shut tightly. She'd been doing her best to ignore the truth, but there it was. She was in love with him—in all likelihood had been since they'd skipped stones at the lake. When he'd been so gentle with her. When he'd kissed her the first time.

Tears burned at the back of her throat. It was no good to love someone who had no idea how to accept it. Who was held up by the past, by something he couldn't let go.

She had to hope he loved her too, and would be willing to work through his past to give them a future. But what if he wasn't?

CHAPTER THIRTEEN

"Lainey." Her mother stood in the doorway of The Lily Pad, clearly agitated. "We need to talk. Can you take a break right now?"

Startled, Lainey took a few steps toward her mother. She hadn't thought she'd see her parents for a while after last night's little ambush had been thwarted. She'd never seen the older woman so distraught. "Mom? Are you all right?"

Jacqui shook her head. "I just—we really need to sit down and discuss this."

Beth hurried over to Lainey. "I can cover this right now. Why don't the two of you go ahead?"

Her eyes searched Lainey's face, and Lainey saw the concern there. If she disagreed, and opted to stay instead of talking to her mother, Beth would back her up. In light of last night's conversation with her parents, her mother's arrival this morning was a bit of a surprise.

She squeezed her friend's hand. To her mother she said, "Okay. How about Mel's?" It wasn't fully private, but this time of day—mid-morning—business at the café should be a little slower.

Jacqui nodded. "That's fine."

Surprised, Lainey grabbed her coat and followed her

mother out the door. She didn't think she'd ever seen Jacqui go to Mel's.

They walked in silence though the October chill. Halloween was only a couple days away, and November apparently had chosen to make an early appearance this year. Inside the warm café, Lainey led Jacqui to a corner table in the hopes they'd be undisturbed. They ordered hot drinks and sat in silence until the steaming mugs were delivered. Jacqui tapped her nails on the table relentlessly, a show of nerves Lainey didn't think she'd ever seen before.

Not wanting to wait any longer, Lainey reached over and touched her mother's hand. Jacqui looked more haggard, more tired, than Lainey could ever remember seeing her. "Mom, what's this about?"

Jacqui fussed with her coffee, then lifted her gaze to meet Lainey's. "I need you to explain how things got this way. How you could be so careless…" Her words trailed off.

"Careless as in getting pregnant? Or about Ben?" She hadn't been careless either way.

Jacqui nodded. "Either. Both. And you won't tell anyone who the father is!"

Lainey sat back. She had to choose her words carefully. "Mom, I wouldn't say I was careless. No, it wasn't planned. But it's not a mistake. As for the father…" She hesitated. She clearly had to say something, but what? She settled for an abridged version of the truth. "Well, he's not interested in being in our lives. He's got his reasons, and none of them are anything I want my child associated with." She hesitated just for a second before adding, "Why do you keep pushing Daniel on me?"

Jacqui looked her straight in the eye. "Because he can take care of you. And now the baby, too. It's going to be so hard for you to raise the child and run that shop. I'm sure he'd let you keep the store, and you can work when you want. But you wouldn't have to worry about money. Are you *sure* the baby's father is out of the picture?"

Lainey thought of the papers she'd signed with a little pang of sorrow mixed with relief. "Yes." She crossed her arms on the table and leaned forward. "Mom. I understand you want me to be taken care of. I do. And I appreciate your concern. But Daniel's not the way to do it. I'm managing—working things out. It won't be easy, but I'm going to make it work. You and Dad need to just let me do it."

Jacqui was silent for a long moment, fiddling with her untouched coffee mug. Then she said, "I just don't understand why you'd want to struggle when you don't have to. When there are people who can give you so much."

Lainey saw the puzzlement on her mother's face and knew she truly *didn't* understand. "It's not that I want to struggle. It's that I want to do something on my own. When you guys step in and try to take over you attach strings and conditions and you take the power away from me. It's not mine, then. Being a single mother isn't ideal. It will make everything a lot harder, to be sure. But that's how it's going to be, Mom. I can't change that." She took a deep breath and thought of Ben with a sharp pang. "If I ever get married it will be because I love the man, and because he loves and respects me for who I am—not who I come from or what I can do for him. Does that make sense?"

Jacqui clasped her hands tightly in front of her for a moment. Finally she lifted her chin. "Yes," she said quietly. "It does. Does Ben know how you feel?"

Lainey dropped her gaze to her mug of tea. Her heart squeezed. "I don't think so."

Her mother pushed her mug out of the way and leaned toward her. "Then you need to tell him. Sooner rather than later. Why would you let him walk away?"

Lainey's jaw actually dropped. "Mother…" she managed. "I— Whoa. I thought you were against Ben?"

Jacqui reached over and covered Lainey's hand with her own. "We don't want you to have to struggle when you have the opportunity to avoid it. But you need to be happy, too. It's been so long—" She stopped for a moment, then sighed. "I love your father, even with all his faults. When you talk about Ben you light up. The way you defended him last night—well, you should have the chance to see where that leads you. I'm sorry for making it so difficult for you."

It was quite possibly the first time her mother had ever really listened and actually heard what Lainey was saying. She got up and pulled her mother into an awkward hug, right there in Mel's. Her mother's quiet words were as good as Jacqui could do, and Lainey was willing to accept them as a start.

Her mother patted her awkwardly on the back. "Go get him," she said, and Lainey's eyes got damp. "And, please, if we can help let us know. I'll try not to shove myself where I've got no business being."

Lainey stepped back and laughed even as she swiped at her eyes. "Thank you." Jacqui wouldn't understand, but that was the nicest thing her mother had ever said to her.

"All right, then." Her mother gathered her bag and her coat. "I mean it. If we can help with the shop and the baby let us know."

"I will," Lainey murmured. She didn't want their help, if at all possible, but having it offered rather than rammed down her throat was a huge improvement. She tried and failed to picture her parents babysitting. The thought almost made her giggle. Maybe they'd come around.

She hurried back to work. Beth was ringing up a sale,

but by the time Lainey got her coat off and went back out front was already heading for her. "How did it go?"

Lainey reached for the watering can. "It was fine, actually. She made an effort to listen to me. I'm not sure she understands why I feel the way I do, but she seems willing to accept it. It's some small steps in the right direction." She'd take the olive branch and hope it held. To have her parents work with her rather than at cross-purposes would make everything so much easier.

That evening was pizza night with Rose. Lainey was half tempted to cancel. She was so tired, and the thought of seeing Ben and simply exchanging polite words, pretending there'd never been more between them, was just too hard.

But she picked up the usual pizza and headed out. She'd do her best to put on a happy face.

Ben was nowhere to be found when she pulled in, and relief tempered with a good dose of disappointment flooded through her. She tried to push it all away. She was here for Rose only, and had been long before he'd come back. She would be long after he'd left again.

"Come on in!" Rose called when Lainey knocked.

She pushed the door open and fixed a smile on her face which faltered when she spotted Ben's jacket draped over a chair. How far gone was she when the sight of a fleece could almost reduce her to tears? She busied herself putting the box on the counter and removing her own coat while making small talk. She thought she'd actually done pretty well until she sat across from Rose and looked at her sympathetic face.

"Oh, dear. You've got it that bad, huh?" Rose's question was gentle.

Lainey couldn't meet her friend's eyes so she looked down at the slice of pizza she had zero interest in eating.

Her answer stuck in her throat as if the words were glued there, and she was afraid if she tried to speak all her carefully rigged control would go right out the window.

The back door opened then, and Ben came in. Her gaze flew to his and Lainey would swear time stopped. Her breath caught at the pain and the longing she saw, which he quickly dropped behind the mask she was all-too familiar with. She looked away. She should have stayed home tonight. Rose would have understood.

"Pizza, Ben?" Rose's voice was overly bright, and it seemed to bounce off the tension that filled the room.

"No, thanks."

The deep rumble of his voice resonated deep in Lainey's soul. Oh, did she have it bad. Rose didn't know the half of it.

"I need this."

The jacket whooshed off the chair next to her and Lainey squeezed her eyes shut tight when she caught a bit of his scent mixed with the fresh air notes that came from spending a lot of time outside. She didn't dare look up until the door shut behind him.

Rose made a little noise of frustration in her throat. "Oh, my goodness, I'm not sure I've ever seen a couple so right for each other work so hard to avoid it! Talk to him, Lainey. Please. Don't let this get away. From either of you. You don't want to regret it later."

It wasn't quite that simple. "Rose—"

Her friend leveled her with a gentle look. "Do you love him?"

Lainey sucked in a breath. "Yes. Yes, I do." The answer was oh-so-easy, but not simple.

"He went back into the garage. Go to him. Please." Rose looked at her with shrewd eyes. "Don't waste anymore time. That little baby needs a daddy and Ben would

be a wonderful one. Plus, not only does he need you—
you need him."

He needs you. Lainey didn't know if that was true or
not. If he needed her, how could he shut her out and hold
her at arm's length? Still, she found her feet carrying her
out the door to the garage. Her heartbeat picked up the
closer she got to the building. Was she crazy to lay it all
on the line? She hadn't come here intending to do so. Even
though Rose was right. It *was* time. She couldn't go on in
this half-life. She had to know.

Ben looked up when she came in, and she caught the
longing in his eyes before he shuttered it. "Hi."

"Hey. How are you feeling?"

His voice was perfectly polite. She could almost see
the force fields around him, trying to keep her at a safe
distance. It hurt that after all they'd shared he could just
lock her out.

"Okay." It wasn't a lie. Pregnancy-wise, she was. Otherwise, not so much.

He nodded, then met her gaze. "What do you need,
Lainey?"

You. She took a deep breath and jumped in. "Can you
tell me the rest of the story, Ben? About Jason?" Since everything seemed to hinge on his friend's death, she needed
to know.

He set down the tool he'd been holding. His hands were
shaking slightly. "I told you the gist of it."

"Yes, you did. But I don't know what actually happened." She moved a little closer. Her hands shook so badly
she shoved them in the pockets of her coat. "I don't know
exactly why you blame yourself, because from what I've
seen you aren't so careless as to knowingly or intentionally lead another person into danger."

He winced, raked a hand through his hair. "Lainey—"

She kept her gaze on him steady. Kept her voice calm and didn't move any closer, so she wouldn't spook him. "Ben, please. Let me in. We've got the potential here for something wonderful, and I'd love the chance at a future with you. But with this between us we can't." She couldn't bring herself to ask if he wanted it, too. The very real chance of him saying no would destroy her.

"Don't make me a better man than I am." His words were harsh and he moved toward her, his gaze hard on hers.

She stood her ground as he stalked closer.

"I didn't get the order. Somehow there was a breakdown in the chain and I didn't get the order that the building was clear. As far as I knew there was one occupant left." He stopped, took a shuddering breath. "I went in. Jason came in after me because he recognized the signs that the situation was deteriorating rapidly. He'd gotten the order. He knew he wasn't supposed to go in." He shut his eyes. "He came in anyway. For me. When he had so much to lose. He had everything to lose. His wife—Callie. Those kids."

Lainey's eyes burned at the bleakness in his voice and she didn't even try to stop the tears. Now she got it. He blamed himself for living when his friend was dead. She came a little closer and rested her hand on his arm, feeling the tightness of the muscles beneath. He blinked at her, as if he'd forgotten she was there for a few moments, lost in his own private hell. "How can you blame yourself for Jason's choice? What does his wife say?"

He froze and then looked away, his jaw working.

Her heart sank. "Oh, no. Ben. How can she blame you?"

Misery was etched on his face. "I don't know if she does. I haven't seen her or talked to her since—since the funeral. She's called, but I haven't called her back."

Lainey inhaled sharply. "Ben, why not?"

He moved away from her, his movements agitated and

jerky. "I can't, okay? What if it's the wrong thing to do?" He paused and drew in a ragged breath. "You didn't see her at the funeral. She was so—lost. She's been through so much already. I can't make it worse for her. I can't take that chance."

She shook her head. "Okay, but who are you to decide what makes it worse for her? Ben, how can you possibly know? You're a living link to Jason for her, for her kids. That's so important. How can you leave them like that? Is that what he'd want?"

He turned around, propped his hands on his hips. "Lainey—"

She was too far in to back out now. "Go. Talk to her. See what she has to say so you can get some closure. If you can't do that we don't have a future. *You* don't have a future as a firefighter, much less as a husband. You can't punish yourself forever. You need to forgive yourself, and Jason as well. He didn't give up his life so you could spend yours all alone."

He opened his mouth, but snapped it shut when she steamrollered right over him.

"I love you. But if you can't choose me—choose a life with me over your past—then we've got nowhere to go."

She barely breathed as he stood in the middle of the garage and stared at her.

Finally he said in a low tone, "I can't risk it, Lainey."

Her heart shattered, the razor sharp edges of pain nearly bringing her to her knees. "Then you're not the man I thought you were."

It took everything she had to turn and walk away from the man she loved.

Ben stood frozen in the garage after Lainey had left. She had simply sailed out, her chin high, tear-tracks fresh on her beautiful face. He heard her car start, then the crunch of tires on the driveway.

The loss of her ripped through him. God, how could he be so damn stupid? He wanted nothing more than to go after her, tell her how much he loved her. But he couldn't.

Because he was an idiot. What kind of man let the woman he loved walk away?

One whose past held him firmly in its snare. He knew that. He'd allowed it because it meant he was able to hide, somehow thinking that would make up for the loss of his friend. Worse, he'd used it as an excuse to cement the belief he was better off alone. That was inexcusable. Even though over the past few weeks he'd been busy falling for Lainey. She'd burst right through his defenses, made him feel, made him want, and while he'd convinced himself those were the last things he wanted she'd gotten in his heart anyway.

But if you can't choose me—choose a life with me over your past—then we've got nowhere to go.

Her words echoed in his head. What kind of man chose to live in the past when the future hovered so brightly in front of him? Lainey wasn't wrong. It was past time he paid Callie a visit. Set some things right and got closure. Maybe Jason's widow needed it, too. And choosing to live his life and love Lainey seemed like a far better tribute to his friend's memory than staying in the shadows for the rest of his days.

Then he'd see if he could have a true future with Lainey. She deserved all of him—not some damaged shell. He'd prove he could move on. He pulled his phone out of his pocket, took a deep breath, and dialed a familiar number.

Beth came in and plunked down a small bakery bag. "Cheesecake muffin. Because I'm pretty sure you haven't eaten yet."

Lainey winced. "I'm trying, Beth. I'm just not very hungry."

Her friend nudged the bag closer. "I know, honey. But you've got to feed that baby."

Lainey managed a smile. "I know that. And I am." *Mostly.* Lainey opened the bag. Her appetite hadn't been stellar since her first conversation with Ben about Jason, and had virtually disappeared after their confrontation in the garage two days ago. He'd made his choice. It wasn't her.

So it was over before it really had a chance to begin.

The pain broke over her again. Every time the wave wore her down a little more. She took a shaky breath and took the bag from Beth.

"I know this is so hard for you. Can I do anything, Laine? I know I keep asking, but—" Beth broke off. "It's so awful to see you like this. Can you call him? See if you can work it out?"

Lainey managed a little smile. She knew she didn't need to pretend around Beth, but she was hoping to fool herself into thinking it wasn't as painful as she thought. "It didn't end in a way I can actually fix. He's got—he's got issues that only he can resolve. And he has to be ready to do that. I can't make him ready." And there was also the simple but excruciating fact she didn't actually know if he loved her.

Beth leaned forward. "I've seen him look at you, Laine. That man is in love with you."

"Maybe. But he never said the words, Beth." Her eyes burned with tears she did not want to shed in public. "I *think* he'd love me, if he could. But I don't really *know*. He knows how I feel." She took a shaky breath and tried to smile, even though it failed to actually form. "So I'm going to try to move on."

If only it was that easy.

"Oh, honey. I'm so sorry." Beth glanced back as the back doorbell buzzed. "Eat that. I'll get the delivery."

She left and Lainey opened the bag and removed the muffin, centering it on a napkin. She'd been through the whole thing over and over. No use going over it all for the umpteenth time. The story of a broken heart was as old as time. She'd manage to survive.

But it was a huge hole in her heart. She missed him. Missed what they'd never really had a chance to have. Missed what might have been.

That was almost as dangerous.

She broke off a small bite of muffin. Normally it was one of her favorite treats. It would take her all morning to eat it, because today she could probably eat the bag it came in and not notice any difference in taste. But Beth was right. She needed to feed the baby.

The front door chimed and Lainey's idiotically optimistic heart kicked, then crashed. It hadn't been Ben yet, and this time was no different. A smiling man approached the counter, wanting a dozen roses for his wife. Lainey put them together with a smile, but her heart ached.

"Thank you," he said as she handed him the roses wrapped in green and pink paper. "She's worth every rose you've got in your store. But I can only afford a dozen today."

Lainey gave a little laugh, but a little spear of sorrow pierced her heart. If things had been different would Ben have said the same about her? "She's a lucky woman."

He winked as he slid his wallet in his pocket. "Nah. I'm the lucky one."

Whistling, he walked out, and Lainey watched him go

with a heavy heart. People clearly could make love work. Some of them overcame crazy stuff to be together.

And some of them couldn't.

CHAPTER FOURTEEN

BEN STOOD IN front of the little white bungalow, with its cozy front porch and dormant rose bushes. A house not too different from the one Lainey lived in. Pumpkins on the front steps. Fake spiderweb on the porch. Like almost every other house on the block.

But this one belonged to Callie and Jason. Well, just Callie now. He swallowed hard at the thought.

He'd come to finally make amends—something he should have done months ago.

The front door flew open and Callie stood there, the baby—who wasn't really a baby anymore—on her hip. She looked at him steadily and his heart thumped in his chest as he started up the walk towards her.

"Callie." He swallowed, the words suddenly seeming inadequate. "I'm—"

"If you say you're sorry, Ben Lawless, you cannot take another step and come in this house." Eyes blazing, Callie stepped out on the porch.

Confusion stopped him in his tracks more than her threat. "What?"

"You heard me." She jerked her head toward the door and her coppery curls bounced on her shoulders. "Come in. We need to talk and it's cold out here."

He followed her into the house, the reminder of Jason

not as physical a punch as it would have been a few weeks ago. The oldest boy, Eli, who was three, looked at him out of his father's eyes and smiled his father's smile.

"Hey, buddy." Ben bent down and accepted the hug the little boy offered. His heart squeezed. He'd do better by Jason's kids if Callie would let him. He'd love to see them grow up—maybe play with Lainey's baby if she would forgive him.

"Have a seat." Callie nodded at the table which held a basket of crayons and a stack of coloring books. "Let me get them set up for a little while." To the kids she said, "How about *Bob the Builder*?" A chorus of yeses followed her words and soon cheery music wafted from the living room. She returned to stand across from him, her posture stiff.

"They'll be good for a bit now. Can I get you a drink?"

He shook his head. "Ah, no. Thanks. Callie—"

"No." She gave a sharp shake of her head, splayed her hands on the table and leaned forward. "You listen to me first—okay, Ben? I can't believe you stayed away for so long. It wasn't your fault. Jason did *not* die because of you."

Ben closed his eyes. While rationally he knew she was right that Jason had not died because of him—and a hard-won victory *that* was—being here, with Jason's young widow, he could still smell the smoke, hear the roar of the flames crackling in the back of his mind. It gave him a bad moment.

"I know that. It took me far too long to figure it out. I want to apologize for staying away so long. I never meant to. And I am terribly sorry for the loss of your husband and my friend."

"Thank you. That's an apology I will accept," Callie whispered. She threaded her fingers together. "While I know Jason for the most part followed the rules—he didn't want to be careless—he was at heart a risk-taker. Once he realized what had happened to you there was no stopping him." She took a shaky breath and Ben met her gaze, seeing the sadness in her green eyes. "He didn't think, Ben. That's the thing. He just acted. They told me—after—they told me they couldn't stop him. Nothing could have. He loved you like a brother."

"It was mutual." It was true. And he knew Callie was right about her husband. In a potential do-or-die situation there wasn't time to stand around and waffle about what action to take. He and Jason had both done the only thing they could do in the moment. If the situation had been reversed he would have done the same thing.

So many people said they'd walk through fire for their loved ones. Jason had actually done it.

The kids' laughter caused Callie to turn her head in their direction. She pulled out a chair and sank down into it. "I've been mad as hell," she said quietly. "But not at you. Or at least not about this. For staying away—that's something else entirely. Jason loved risk. I knew when I married him—well, I knew. I never thought it'd end like this, but it did." She tipped her head toward the living room. "And now they don't have a daddy. Jason didn't leave us on purpose. He wouldn't let you accept responsibility for his choices any more than you would have let him."

"I know that now," he said. "It took me a while to get there—longer than it should have. Callie—again, I am sorry. Sorrier than you know for your loss, for the boys' loss. Someone helped me see how blind I've been. It's been at your expense. I'm sorry." Lainey had been right when she'd said Jason hadn't given up his life so Ben could ignore his own.

Callie reached over and squeezed his hand, the sheen of tears in her green eyes. "Thank you for that. Please, don't be a stranger in our lives. You are such a valuable link to Jason, and I'd like the boys to know you. You can help them understand what their daddy was like as a fire-fighter."

"I will," he promised, relieved that the thought didn't fill him with the kind of pain he'd been accustomed to. The lightening of the load was an amazing thing, and while the apology he'd made had helped, it was Lainey who'd shown him the way.

He pulled Callie in for a hug. She hugged him back, then patted his chest.

"Who's the someone? She must be awfully special if you finally came to see me."

"Ah…" Uncomfortable, he looked into the living room, where the boys played with trucks and watched the movie. "She pointed out a few things to me that I'd been missing."

Callie gave a little laugh. "Well, I like her already. When can I meet her?"

He met her gaze. "Well, about that…"

Her eyes went to slits. "Oh, no. What did you do?"

Was he so transparent? He scrubbed his hand over his face, then gave her an abridged version of events and didn't cut himself any slack.

"Do you love her?"

"I do." There was no hesitation.

She gave him a small shove toward the door. "Then why are you still here? What you need to do is go back and see if she'll still have you." She gave him another little shove, her voice urgent. "Ben. You've got to go see if you can make it work. Don't waste any more time. You never know how much of it you have."

"I know. It's where I'm going next. Now I know—" He stopped, about to add, *what you and Jason had.* It seemed somehow cruel to bring it up.

But Callie nodded and smiled—a small smile, with tears in her eyes. "Yes. Now you know."

"I've got to go," he said. "I had to be sure you were okay."

"I'm hanging in there," she said softly. "It hasn't been easy, but I'm doing my best. I'll miss him every day for the rest of my life. But I knew my husband, Ben. I know how he was. I know *who* he was. And he's a hero."

"Yeah, he is." He drew her into another hug, rocked her back and forth. "Thanks, Callie."

She hugged him back tightly. "Go get her. Good luck."

"I will. And, God knows, I'll need it."

He left the house, with Callie standing on the porch, arms crossed against the cold, and drove away. He pointed the truck north, toward Holden's Crossing. Time to put the beginning of the rest of his life in motion. If Lainey would have him.

There was only one way to find out.

Lainey had shoved the last of the clothes in the dryer when she heard a knock on the kitchen door. It was seven-thirty on a rainy night. Who could possibly be stopping over this late? She trudged up the stairs and peeked out the peephole.

And gasped.

Ben stood there, rain glistening on his jacket. She blinked. Was it really him? Or was her mind playing tricks on her?

He knocked again and she jumped, her shaking hands making a fumbling hash of the lock and the knob. *Ben.* Why was he here? Could she take any more heartbreak? She was afraid the answer to that was no.

She swung the door open and simply drank him in. His intense gaze settled on her and she saw pain and longing there. Hope surged a little bit, but she tamped it down. He looked tired, and stress lines bracketed his mouth. Not for the first time she wanted to reach up and smooth them away.

"Lainey. Can I come in? I'll understand if you say no." His voice was a low rumble and she stepped to the side quickly, her heart hammering so hard she was afraid he'd hear it.

"Of course. I was just surprised." She shut the door behind him and turned to face him. As glad as she was to see him, a little anger flared. She welcomed it. She needed it to keep her distance from him until she knew why he was here. "Since you were pretty clear the other day that we weren't going to work out." She couldn't quite keep the bitterness out of her voice.

He let out a long exhale. The misery etched on his face echoed that in her heart. "I know. I'm sorry. I need to talk to you."

"I see. Well, come on in." Without waiting to see if he'd follow, she walked through the kitchen into the living room. She sat on a chair near the fireplace and wound her hands tightly together. The heat of the fire did nothing to soothe her nerves.

He didn't follow right away, but a thump from the kitchen area indicated he was probably removing his boots. A few seconds later he appeared and she had a hard time breathing. He seemed to fill the small space and absorb all the oxygen.

She gestured to the chair across from her. "Please sit."

He did, and she tried not to notice when he looked at her with a tenderness that nearly undid her. "Lainey. God, you're gorgeous."

She kept her gaze on his steady, even though she felt anything but steady inside. How could he say that? She'd barely slept and had no appetite. She was a mess, not to mention an emotional wreck. "Thank you." She didn't know what to say, what to ask. There was so much to say, really, she didn't know where to begin.

But, since he'd more or less rejected her, she'd let him talk first. He knew where she stood. She'd laid it out for him the other day in the garage. It was past time she could say the same about him.

He dropped his gaze, leaned forward and rested his forearms on his thighs. The awkwardness grew as he seemed to gather his thoughts. She watched the firelight dance on his dark hair. Finally, too tightly wound to wait, she gave in. She needed to know.

"Ben, why are you here?"

He looked up. "Should I be?"

The question threw her. "I don't know." Her voice dropped to a whisper. "You made it clear the other day you couldn't choose me." Despite her earlier flare of anger, she couldn't muster any heat in the words, only pain.

He took a deep breath and sat back. Her traitor cat came and wound around his ankles. She frowned at Panda, but of course the cat ignored her. Ben reached down to stroke his hand down Panda's back. "I was pretty screwed up, Lainey. In a lot of ways. I've still got work to do. I don't know when I'll be able to work again." He looked up and in his gaze she saw pain and something else. Her heart picked up. "You're going to be a mom. You need a guy who's stable. I can barely take care of myself. How could I take care of a family?"

"So you pushed me away," she said, unable to keep the hurt from her voice. She focused on the traitor cat at his feet.

He leaned forward and laid a hand on her arm, forcing her startled gaze to his. "I did. I thought it was better for you. I wanted to protect you," he admitted. "But you just kind of worked your way in and I started wanting more. A lot more. After you left the other day I realized how blind I'd been. I made an appointment with a counselor. And there was one last thing I needed to do."

"Callie?" she said softly.

He nodded. "I went and talked to Callie. Not for permission to move on, but because you were right. She was angry—but not for the reasons I thought. She was mad because she felt I'd abandoned her and the kids. She never blamed me. But even if I'd known that I'm not sure it would have made a difference."

His eyes were wet as he looked at Lainey and her heart broke for him.

"I blamed myself fully. But there were things that night that were out of my control, out of his control. I can't bring him back. But the way I've been living is no way to honor my best friend. Jason would kick my ass."

A surprised laugh bubbled out of her. "He sounds like a true friend."

Ben smiled. "He was. I wish you could have known him. He'd have liked you."

Tears stung her eyes. "I wish I could have, too. But—"

His smile turned sad. "But that's not how it is. I hope I can convince you to meet Callie, though. I think you'll like her. And the kids."

She circled back to the fact that had surprised her. "You saw a counselor?"

Ben nodded. "Well, not yet. The appointment is next week. Monday. One of the terms of coming off leave is I need to get a mental health exam, I guess you'd call it. I need to know—and my captain needs to know—I won't flashback and freeze the next time I go out on a call."

She swallowed hard. That didn't sound as if he was going to stay here. "Ah. Will it work?"

He gave her a crooked smile. "I don't know. I hope so. I'd like to be cleared in a month or so. I want to go back to work."

"That's great, Ben." She meant it. But, really, did the man have to drive all the way back here to tell her this? That he wouldn't be back, after all? A phone call would have given her a little more dignity. "Well, I'm sure they'll be thrilled to have you back."

Something in her tone must have given her away, because he looked at her quizzically. "They won't."

She stared at him for a moment, not comprehending. "But you just said—"

"I know," he interrupted her. "But you're jumping to conclusions. I won't be working in Grand Rapids. I'll be here. Or almost here. In Traverse City. Holden's Crossing is close enough I can live here. The job—it's time-consuming and there's always risk."

Her heart beat faster. Had he really just said what she thought she'd heard? "Oh," she said. "Here?"

Instead of answering right away, he came to his knees on the floor in front of her and cautiously laid his hand on her rounded belly. "I know it hasn't been that long," he murmured, "but I missed you. Both of you."

Lainey laid her hand on his and held her breath. She didn't trust herself to speak. She was afraid to ask the question, more afraid of the answer.

He slid a cold hand around the back of her neck and pulled her down toward him. "I love you," he whispered. "I love both of you. I missed you. So much." Then he kissed her, soft at first, then with more urgency.

"I love you, too," she whispered against his mouth. "Ben—"

He sat back and ran one hand down the side of her face. Her heart lifted at the reverence and love on his face. "So, to answer your question, yes. Here. In this house, if you want. I want to be your husband and a father to this baby. I know it's short notice, and I've been an idiot, and—damn it—I don't have a ring and you might not be ready—"

She laid her fingers on his lips, joy coursing through her. "I'm ready." Oh, was she ever? She'd been wrong about not needing a partner in her life—she needed Ben. She hadn't even known what she was missing until he'd come into her life. "There's no one I want to be with more than you."

His eyes widened and a slow smile spread across his face. "Are you sure?"

Her voice was strong and she was pretty sure she might burst with happiness. "Yes. I want forever. And I want it with you."

"Oh, thank God." He stood up and held out a hand, a wicked gleam in his eyes. "Then I say we go celebrate. Plus, I think we've got some making up to do." He gave her a little eyebrow-wiggle that made her laugh.

"Sounds good to me. We'd better get started." Lainey put her hand in his and smiled up at him, ready to embrace their future.

Ten months later

Lainey tugged at the bodice of her wedding dress for what had to be the fifteenth time in as many minutes. "Are you sure this looks secure?"

Beth, her matron of honor and business partner, laughed and pulled Lainey's hands down. "It looks great, Laine. No one can tell you've got nursing pads in the sexy bra under it. You are a gorgeous bride." She leaned over and plucked Lainey's bouquet from the box on the table, pressed it into Lainey's hands. "Here. Now, turn and look in the mirror."

Lainey did. The woman staring back at her barely resembled herself. Flushed cheeks, sparkling eyes, flowing off-white beaded simple strapless gown. The flowers, done by Lainey herself, were a perfect complement for a summer wedding in shades of pink and cream.

Beth touched the small veil that covered Lainey's head and shoulders. "See? Perfectly gorgeous. Are you ready?"

"Very." Lainey smiled at her friend. "I can't wait."

"Then let's go." Beth exited the small room, and with a deep breath Lainey followed.

As Beth took her place at the head of the aisle Lainey paused, out of sight of the guests in the sanctuary. A well of emotion threatened to break over her as her father and brother approached her. They were here to walk her down the aisle in this small church. Amazingly, her mother had exercised great restraint and hadn't interfered with the planning or the size of the wedding. Not too much, anyway. They'd made strides—especially after the birth of baby Lily.

Rose had her three-month-old great-granddaughter in the front pew. Lainey sincerely hoped she wouldn't have to take a break mid-ceremony and nurse her daughter.

Her heart was absolutely full.

"Honey, you look amazing," her father said, his voice rough with emotion, and Lainey blinked furiously.

"Don't make me cry," she managed on a laugh, and he squeezed her arm.

"No promises, there, my girl. It's your wedding. We may not have a choice."

She gave a little giggle as Kevin came to take his place at Lainey's side. He chucked her lightly under the chin. "Ready, little sis?"

She smiled up at him. Oh, was she ever? "Yes. Yes, I am."

The music swelled and Lainey moved to the head of the

aisle. She took the first few steps toward her future. Her gaze landed on Ben. Her steps nearly faltered as she took in how handsome he was in his tux and she couldn't take her eyes off him. He was hers.

Ben's gaze never left her, and she saw all the love, all the heat, all the joy in her own heart reflected on his face as she reached for his hands at the altar. Her heart swelled as she looked into his beautiful eyes.

"Hi," he whispered. "God, you're gorgeous."

She smiled back. "So are you."

Together they glanced at their daughter—the baby who was everything to Ben despite the fact she wasn't biologically his—then back at the minister, who now began the ceremony.

Somehow, despite everything, without even looking for it, they'd become a family.

Forever.

* * * * *

MILLS & BOON®
By Request

RELIVE THE ROMANCE WITH THE BEST OF THE BEST

A sneak peek at next month's titles...

In stores from 10th August 2017:

- **The Delicious De Campos** – Jennifer Hayward

- **Expecting His Child** – Paula Roe, Tessa Radley & Cat Schield

In stores from 24th August 2017:

- **Big Little Secrets** – Sophie Pembroke, Rebecca Winters & Soraya Lane

- **Forbidden Desires** – Dani Collins, Lindsay Armstrong, Marion Lennox

---

Just can't wait?
Buy our books online before they hit the shops!
www.millsandboon.co.uk

Also available as eBooks.

Join Britain's BIGGEST Romance Book Club

50% OFF your first parcel

- **EXCLUSIVE offers every month**
- **FREE delivery direct to your door**
- **NEVER MISS a title**
- **EARN Bonus Book points**

Call Customer Services
0844 844 1358 *

or visit
millsandboon.co.uk/subscriptions

* This call will cost you 7 pence per minute plus your phone company's price per minute access charge.

MILLS & BOON®

Why shop at millsandboon.co.uk?

Each year, thousands of romance readers find their perfect read at millsandboon.co.uk. That's because we're passionate about bringing you the very best romantic fiction. Here are some of the advantages of shopping at www.millsandboon.co.uk:

* **Get new books first**—you'll be able to buy your favourite books one month before they hit the shops

* **Get exclusive discounts**—you'll also be able to buy our specially created monthly collections, with up to 50% off the RRP

* **Find your favourite authors**—latest news, interviews and new releases for all your favourite authors and series on our website, plus ideas for what to try next

* **Join in**—once you've bought your favourite books, don't forget to register with us to rate, review and join in the discussions

Visit **www.millsandboon.co.uk**
for all this and more today!